THE YOGA
OF STRENGTH

A Fable

Krista,

Thank you so much
for the love and support!
I hope you enjoy the
adventure!

Much love,
Andrew

Cristo,

Thank you so much
for the love & support!
I hope you enjoy the
adventure!

Much love,
Andrew

THE YOGA
OF STRENGTH

A Fable

Book 1 of The Yoga Trilogy
by Andrew Marc Rowe

atmosphere press

For Ashley, the love of my life;
for Iris, my messenger from the gods;
and for Janet, my holy spirit.

A divine feminine trinity that showed me
what it really means to be a man.

"Yoga is the journey of the self, through the self, to the self."
-The Bhagavad Gita

"From sacrifice, bliss."
–Joseph Campbell

Chapter One
Separation

There is a page missing from the text of my life, though scraps of the words written thereon still come to me unbidden from time to time. I know that this page deals with dissolution, an unraveling of self from semi-formed tapestry of youth to a mess of filament lying disheveled on the tavern floor. More bruises were added to my collection, though I was not sure who the assailant - or, more likely, assailants - were. What I do know is that I awoke to a splash of water on my face that smelt of ancient piss on the morning of my birthday, with a pain in my head like I had been stabbed, groggily blinking my eyes awake to Rolf the Tavernkeeper's ugly face. He was holding a bucket in his hand and a furrow on his brow.

"You may be a Lord's son, but I'll be damned if I'm going to let you sleep on my floor any longer."

I rolled over, away from the prickly bastard, towards the front of the tavern. I settled in for a moment, hearing the Tavernkeeper make a displeased grunt and walk away on creaky floorboards. Once it could not be helped anymore, I opened my eyes. Shafts of sunlight were penetrating the front windows, catching motes of dust in the air and striking the worn wooden slats near the first row of tables.

"Fuck, what hour is it?" I said, turning back to the

unpleasant lowborn man. He had returned to his position behind the bar and was wiping the wood with a cloth that was fittingly maggoty for an establishment like his.

"I haven't been out to check the sundial since the cock crowed at about quarter after six, but I dare say three hours have run down since then." He let glee break out on his face, smiling a mouthful full of broken brown teeth. He waited for some reaction from me before pressing on. I gave him none.

"I heard you telling young Carla that you were to be inducted into your father's Order this morning." His smile grew wider.

"That is, before you puked ale up on yourself and collapsed from the bar. And before you woke up to tell the Miller brothers that their sister Theresa may as well trade in her shite singing voice and her poorly plucked harp for a harlot's tights so's she could sell her goods to the sailors down on the docks. 'Course, you were already black and blue before your face made mates of their boot heels." His grin looked as if it were going to stretch his face apart.

"Best check your trousers, lad," he continued. "There's a stink upon you that is better suited to a privy than the confines of this fine establishment." He laughed then, a hideous braying sound that reminded me of the donkeys the Serfs kept on the Estate.

"Even less so to the halls of the Blue Cathedral." He barely managed to choke the words out between guffaws.

I inhaled deeply, seeing red and willing it away. The trumped-up whoremaster was right. If I had not shite myself, someone must have shite upon me. I looked down and noticed the crust of vomit on the lapel of my jerkin. The last jerkin that my mother had made for me, still beautiful after years of hard use, soiled with filth. Disgust ran through me. I shifted to get to my knees, the vice of hangover's grip crushing my skull. A mucky feeling in the seat of my pants was matched by a cold wetness on the front. I staggered in a final effort to stand.

4

"Bugger the Christ-man, I've got to get to the Cathedral," I breathed to myself.

If you had told me that I, a lay-about Squire with no ambition beyond draining tankards and laying on the hay with paid tavern wench after paid tavern wench, was to be called into the nave of the Blue Cathedral on the morning of my twenty-fifth birthday for initiation into the King's elite Yellow Order, well... I probably would have believed you. After all, my father was Sir Peter Cardiff, one of the most respected generals in the whole of the Kingdom. And Sir Peter Cardiff commanded the Yellow Order.

On the night before I found myself lying in the Green Dragon, I recall stumbling home after a day of training with the rest of the Squires, bloodied and bruised and wondering whether or not a change to another vocational discipline was in order. I would say that Eric Wellan, the Squire with whom I was training that day, got it as good as he gave, but that would be a lie. I took a severe beating and barely managed to touch his shield with my training sword, let alone land a blow.

As I trudged along the muddy brown dirt of the path near the homestead, I contemplated talking to my father about laying down the sword and taking up the Priest's robe. Not that I had a great thirst for sermonizing and benedictions. But something - anything - would be better than this.

Ha! The thought of it! To ask the great Sir Peter Cardiff if he would allow his son to abandon his military training and deal in scrolls and censers instead. I would have been more likely to receive a series of lashes in the yard and weeks of thin gruel on the table than anything that even smacked in the slightest of support.

It was with these dark thoughts of defeat that I walked along the evening fields of the Cardiff Estate, ignoring the Serfs as I wound my way through the path that crisscrossed the waves of maturing grain stalks. They were no doubt smiling at me solely in light of my position as the Lord's son, not for any great love of the rake that ambled before them. After what seemed like ages of plodding, I crossed the threshold of my father's unremarkable cottage.

I could never understand how a man with my father's wealth, accumulated over decades of successful border campaigns on behalf of the King and indentured servitude from the peasants who tilled his fields, would choose to live in such a small and boring hovel. I heard my mother, when she was alive, henpeck my father to no end about building a bigger residence near some of the fallow land close to the forest. My father would just respond with a hostile silence or change the subject, usually to some mind-numbingly boring monologue about the ever-present threat from neighbouring Liseria. I had been bent over, unlacing my boots, when he started at me.

"I see you have had another lesson from the greatest teacher: pain."

I ignored him and finished the labour of undress. I winced from the stinging of the bruises, but I refused to cry out, to give the bastard any satisfaction. Unfortunately, that kind self-denial only generated pride in the twisted old man. Not that he ever had much call to be proud of me. I felt rage burn in my cheeks. After what seemed like an eternity of discomfort, both from the aftermath of the beating and from the piercing gaze of my father as he stood there, immobile in his judgment, I finished and rose to face the man.

"You received this missive from the Rectory this afternoon."

He handed me a piece of folded parchment. A relief of the Blue Cathedral of Isha had been pressed into the ultramarine glob of wax that formed the seal.

A seal that had been broken.

Rather than engage in useless indignation with my father, I bit my tongue, unfolded the paper, and read the words on the page. I was to ascend to Knighthood. Tomorrow, no less.

"You have been given a great honour, my son. I am proud

of you."

It was the most emotion I had seen out of the man for the entirety of my life. I would have reacted with some measure of surprise and wonder, if not for the wrath taking hold in me.

"Proud of me? Me? I just received a humiliating beating from the most useless of all the Squires in training on the grounds today. Most useless, of course, next to me. My sword did not once touch the man. And he's seven years my junior!"

I didn't pause for long enough for my father to interject. Instead, I began to pace.

"You want me, your cowardly son, the oldest Squire in training, the failure who gets passed over year after year, to finally come be with you on the fields of battle? To perhaps join you in a border skirmish against Liseria, so what? That I might make you proud? I will only disappoint you, and you know it! I hoped you had realized this and were preparing to give me a position as provisioner or to tend to the sheep or something more in line with my 'talents.'"

Burning needles had materialized upon my chest, stabbing me with hot fear, but I pressed on.

"But maybe that is not it. Maybe you know that I am a useless shite and you are counting on it. It would be perfect for you if I had my head caved in by a Liserian mace or my chest peppered with their poisoned arrows. With mother gone, and me to join her, you will be free to remain alone in this place, hoarding your gold and telling your terrible stories. Only whose ear will you bend, with me gone? Will you wear out your Serfs? Yes, perfect, that will give you opportunity to discipline them if they make the mistake of letting their boredom be known. Or maybe you will preach your drivel to the sheep and cattle. Beasts cannot demonstrate any dissatisfaction with the braying of a tired old widower."

When I came back to reality, I realized my left fist was clenched at my side and my right finger was pointing at the man who stood across from me on the wood of the cottage floor. Behind him, I noticed the eyes of my mother staring out from a portrait on the wall. The anger dissipated. I let my arm drop. Shame now crept in to burn my face.

My father, characteristically silent, stared at me. Where I expected my rage to be returned in kind, or at least a fuming passive aggression as answer to my display, there was only sadness in his eyes. After a short while, he spoke.

"I have always been proud of you, my son. It may be difficult for you to see that at times, but it is truth. I know that life has been... different, since your mother passed. It has been hard for me, too. I would give away all of my wealth and fortune to have her back again."

My skin was aflame again. I had decided that I would be needing some ale, and soon.

"If you truly feel this way, I will speak to the Bishop. We will cancel the ascension ceremony and I shall make you a member of the supply train. You are right: you have always have been a good hand at tending to the cattle. Perhaps you can find your peace there so doing in the rear guard."

There it was, a kindness offered up by my father. A mercy that I had neither expected nor for which I had hoped. I wanted so badly to agree to the proposition. And yet, now that escape from the Hell of military life was before me, I couldn't bring myself to welcome it.

"No, Father," I said, my head hanging in shame. "I will take the Knighthood. I will redouble my efforts in training so that I am prepared for combat, whatever may come."

I had pulled on my cloak and beat a hasty retreat from the cottage, down the path and into the city. The sun had been setting and I was hurrying to avoid having to deal with any of the lantern-lighters on the main road. I paused before pushing open the great oak door of the Green Dragon, long enough to make sure that the hot tears were off my cheeks and I had composed myself.

They would take my money and give me service, I had

reasoned, but the wenches were never happy to see sadness upon a man.

In fact, it had turned out that not a person had been happy to see sadness upon me on the eve of my entrance into the ranks of those who had seen twenty-five years on Clovir. I allowed myself to come back from my ruminations, back to the shameful reality of that morning. The ceremony was scheduled for ten o'clock. And I was a mess. I looked up at Rolf and sized the peasant up. He had the same dimensions as me, a fat bastard, though he looked a bit shorter. Still, I could not show up in the rotten clothes that clung to me. I would not be spared the whip this time.

"Go into your rooms and get me some trousers, a fresh shirt and a jerkin." I placed my hand on my hip. Mercifully, and inexplicably, given my state, my coin purse was still attached to my belt. It had yet some heft to it.

"You know that I will pay you handsomely for your rags, Rolf. Just get me some damn clothing."

★ ★ ★ ★ ★

I half-walked, half-ran down the road leading into the city. I did not want to sprint, which would have seen me arrive at the Cathedral quicker. I was, after all, still a pudgy oaf. I knew my limitations, not the least of all when it came to my physical abilities. Appearing a sweaty wreck in front of the mocking gaze of the citizenry as I took the Yellow would be bad enough, but moistening the flesh around my groin with overexertion would only bring the odour back. I had not had time for a bath and I was already late. Besides, Rolf's breeches bound the meat of my legs tight. I could no more run than I could land a decent blow with my sword.

As I passed through the main gate and the dirt of the outskirts turned to the cobblestones of Isha proper, I thought about my father. He would not be amused to see his second-born clad in the ill-fitting dress of a tavernkeep at this pomp-laden ceremony, even more furious to learn that it was because I had made a filthy mess of my own garb. I vowed to keep that detail hidden from the man, if I could. Thankfully, this was also a day of pride for him, something that might blind him further to the truth of his wastrel son. I would almost certainly escape his lashes, even though he was doubtless to have comments about my appearance. Rolf's shirt and jerkin did not fit down my torso, leaving a stretch of belly poking out like a thin roll of unbaked bread.

Thoughts of bread reminded me that my stomach was churning with bile. I needed to eat. Fortunately, a portly Baker had just set up his table along the cobbles of the eastern market, just minutes away from the Cathedral. Stopping a few feet short to retch into the gutter, I snatched up a couple of sizable brioches, flipped the man payment, and asked for some butter.

"Butter?" came the incredulous reply. "You knows we don't have that 'ere, sirrah. P'rhaps you can attend to Mr. Ivory's shop, just over there."

The Baker pointed down the street to the wood of the Dairy Farmer's market stall. I snorted, threw a couple of gold pieces to the Baker, and walked over to Ivory's.

"Butter," I said, slamming a coin onto the wood of the stall.

Moments later, I was slathering the brioches with the contents of a small crock. I mashed the bread into my face, the din of my heavy breaths echoing in my skull. I stopped just outside the heavy doors of the church and struggled to get the second loaf down my gullet. Damnation, I thought, I should have asked Ivory if he had any milk as well.

"Andrew?" asked a voice resonant with incredulity.

I turned to face my older brother, Gerard. He was, of course, immaculately dressed in his leathers and chain mail, with the tabard of the Yellow Order flowing down over his chest and groin.

Ah, the tabard. When I was younger, I would catch myself

constantly admiring the great yellow Dragon on white field, chest puffed up in profile and bearing monstrous open jaws. It was called the Dragon of Thrairn, and it was the symbol painted on all of the Coloured Orders' tabards. It was quite obvious on my father's chest and back as I watched him from the window in the living room of our cottage. He would alternately be coming home for much too short weeks or going off on campaigns that tended to last months at a time when this view of him presented itself, before the man had time to change into the fine but boring woolen garb of the nobility. I used to love to see him coming and hate to see him leave.

Now I wished I never had to see him again.

And here before me was Gerard, my brother. A golden boy in the truest sense of the word. The close-cropped blond hair, blue eyes, and beautiful aquiline face stood in stark contrast to my mess of mousy brown, matching chestnut eyes, and evident corpulence. He was father's first born, and to call him his favourite was among the least necessary statements in the small piece of the world we lived in. How could he not be? When he spoke, his voice never faltered. He was well loved by both the men of the Order and the women of the city. He never had to pay tavern wenches for sex - he got it for free from unmarried girls. And to top it all off, the bastard was a brown-noser, always pretending to one kindness or another.

"Are you alright?"

There was feigned concern in my brother's voice as we stood before the doors of the Blue Cathedral, with a matching expression on his face. Gods-damn him, I thought, searching for the lie. I decided that it might not be a feint. Was the great Gerard Cardiff actually concerned for his failure of a brother? Had I really fallen that far?

My mind recoiled as if it had been burned. Fuck him and his concern, true or false.

"I am fine," I snapped, placing my hand on the great ring of the Cathedral door. Before I had a chance to yank the blasted thing open, my brother placed his hand over mine.

"Please come with me," he said. "I will get you some clothes that fit. You cannot go in there looking like that."

There was no scorn in his voice, only sadness. How I wished for scorn. I recall thinking that disgust from him would have been preferable to the pity that this son of a bitch offered up to me, like table leavings for a crippled hound. Nonetheless, a change of clothing would reduce the risk of my father whipping me in spite of the auspiciousness of the occasion. I was never in the mood for corporal punishment. I followed my brother away from the doors of the Cathedral.

Thankfully, the barracks of the Order were only a short traipse through the streets of the Hightown district away. I tried to spend those few minutes in silence, but Gerard was not having it, even in light of my clipped responses to his questions.

"Rough night last night?" he asked, grinning at me.

"Eh, yeah, you could say that," I responded. I never liked interacting with my brother. This comrade routine was not new. In fact, it had become tiresome. When we were younger and training together, the bastard used to strike me with his practice sword when I was not looking and make light of my fatness with the Smith's sons. Not for long, though. He ascended to Knighthood within a year and left me rolling in the wind like the disappointing shite that I was. Soon after he became a Knight, though, he changed his attitude toward me entirely. The shift was seismic enough that I was not buying his wares. This was some put-on for the benefit of those watching our interactions. But I had to admit that did not explain his continued kindly demeanour in our private conversations.

"Today's the big day, brother!" Gerard said, slapping my back in an entirely unwelcome way.

It was at times like these that I thought of my mother. How I missed her! She always had a patient ear for me, ever since I was a little boy. I would return home to the hearth every night to tell her about my life, all the pleasant times out in the meadows alone, away from the insults delivered by my peers for the state of my physical body, a body which deteriorated further into rotundity as the years passed and I exited childhood. The pleasant times grew fewer and the storm clouds multiplied with the advance of time, and yet at the end of my day, my mother always had for me two things: a smile and a sweet pastry freshly baked in the stone of the hearth.

She had been my sanctuary, and she was gone! I had been left to pick up the pieces with a cold father and a brother whose mere existence rubbed my nose in the fact that I was a letdown.

"Big day for what?" I barked. "This is no honour, this grant of Knighthood. I did not earn it. I still have yet to pass any of the tests, yet here I am, being Knighted."

"Details! If you are really concerned about your combat abilities, I can help teach you. I want that distance that has grown between us to come to an end. So would Mother, were she here. Think about it." Still my brother smiled at me, his arm on my back. "What fun we will have together!"

"I do not want your fucking help, do you not understand that?" I fumed. "Ever since Mother died, I have been glad. Glad that Father has given up on me. Glad I do not have to hear him tell me every night that I should be spending less time shut up in my room or at the tavern and more time with you here at the Gods-damned barracks or practicing on the field. I am not a Knight, I have never been a Knight, and now our dear father has used no small measure of guilt to goad me into accepting this terrible joke of a position in the ranks."

"I will die out there, do you not understand that, brother?" I asked, the fire dimming in my voice as some long-standing defence within me inexplicably weakened. "I cannot fight. I am fat, useless, and a failure. I have spent seven horrendous years in training to your single one that saw you breeze through every test put before you. You were better than me in a month than I remain to this day. I just wish I was like you. Worthwhile, not worthless." A tear started to well up in the corner of my eye. I willed it back into my head.

"You have such worth already!" my brother said, his voice becoming grave. "Such worth. That said, of course I understand you, brother! Of course, of course I do! But let me tell you: it is not drinking and whoring and showing up a complete mess that will get you through this. You need to practice. The practice is rough, brutal stuff. I went through it - do you think it was easy for me? The hardest things always look easy from the outside. You have no idea what went on in here throughout the process," he said, pointing at the side of his skull. "The only difference between us is that I did not dally between childhood and becoming a man. The things I had to drop! To let go of the world... You do not know the price of what you seek. But the debt will be paid before you are through."

The last few words my brother uttered were choked with emotion. Was the chosen one about to cry about succeeding as a Knight? The stones on the bastard. I felt myself slip back into the embrace of my comfortable cynicism.

We arrived at the barracks, having each shut up during the last steps of our short journey. We crossed the red dirt of the sparring grounds, into the pavilion that housed the men. Mercifully, the place was deserted. Everyone must have been at the Cathedral.

"Now," he said, "You need a proper set of clothes. Come this way."

There was a warm expression on my brother's face again, and I hated him for it.

The living quarters were made with wood so dark it never failed to draw the eye. One morning when I was a child, my father had told me all about it, boring me to the point of tears in the toast that lay before me on the breakfast table. Apparently, the black-grained wood was called bear ash, imported from the far-off country of Kashya. It was incredibly strong. What is more, it could withstand the heat of a Dragon's breath. The barracks were made of it, our longbows were made of it, and the gates of Isha were made of it. I did not believe a word of it - neither the Dragon nor the idea that something that we use to keep our hearths warm could be invulnerable to flame.

Dragons. Imagine if were true!

I would be lying if I said the idea did not tug at some part of me. After all, I grew up reading stories of Knights and Dragons. But I felt certain it had just been my father lying to me for a reaction, a perverse action on his part to make me appear as a fool when the rug was pulled from beneath me, all in the name of building character. I had not taken his bait. Standing there that morning, I examined a wooden slat running across the wall. It did not look much different than the wood that father had chopped on our Estate to build our miserable little cottage, simply a bit darker. Maybe...

No! What rubbish his stories always were! A practiced liar was my father, nothing more.

"Here," said my brother, thrusting a stack of folded clothing into my arms. "These were supposed to be a gift for after you were inducted into the Order, but I guess you need them now. Matthew had your measurements in his file from the last time you were here."

I looked down. An ornate green leather jerkin sat atop a brown shirt and brown leather pants. The cloth of the jerkin was stitched with silver and brown thread, a sword pointing down and a Dragon encircling the blade and running all the way up to the top of the hilt. Matthew, the tailor, had not measured me for clothing for months. My gaze rested upon the belly that protruded. I was drinking freely of the ale. But I had also been training. Had I become fatter since then?

"Thank you," I said, looking up at my brother. "This is a kindness I was not expecting."

"Ah, do not get all weepy on me," Gerard said, his brow

crinkled with a smile. "Go get changed. I will be waiting out in the yard."

I walked into one of the rooms of the barracks. It was as spartan as you would expect for a Knight's quarters. There was a small bed with one of the thinnest mattresses I had ever seen, covered with a white sheet tucked under a yellow blanket. Next to the head was a small night table. Under the bed, a chest built from the same wood as the rest of the structure was only partly hidden from view. The Knights could not have what meagre bits of wealth they accrued from years of wage slavery in service to the King destroyed by Dragon fire, I mused wanly. I realized that I was to sleep in one of these bunks, this very night. With the other warriors.

A warrior? Me? The pounding in my head returned and I thought I was going to retch. Why was I doing this? It was suicide!

Thankfully, the moment passed. I slipped on the clothing. I was surprised to find that there was no struggle. It slid over my bulk without any effort at all. I had assumed I had gained weight since last the tailor had measured me. My tits certainly looked bigger than they had been. Yet here I was, dressed in what can only be described as finely fitted new clothing, nothing stretching to accept me. I exited the room to find my brother waiting for me out in the yard again.

"From tavern wretch to Squire on the threshold of greatness, I bow to you," Gerard grinned and made a mockery of the gesture.

That arse! Every time, when I let myself get carried away and think some form of kindness of spirit has attached itself to his being, he proved the lie of it. I shot him a glare and spit out words of thanks for the clothing.

We passed the sundial on the way to the Cathedral. The morning's service would soon be finished. Picking up the pace, Gerard shot out ahead of me, breaking into a half run. My headache pounded in the morning sun. Sighing, I kept up the pace and felt the sweat start to form on my skin and my breath leave me.

"Damn it all, Gerard, slow down!"

He turned around to smile at me, then picked up the pace. He started to trot, then broke into a run. I tried to follow, wheezing my way on for a while. I stopped, screamed, and gave him a vulgar gesture meant to signify a wanton tart's sex.

"Go then, you son of a bitch," I said to him. "You are no brother of mine. You think you can buy me off with gifts of new clothing? That you can give me a few scraps and then kick me like a dog when I am down?"

"Andrew, you live life too seriously," he said, laughing. "I was only trying to make sure that you get to your own ceremony on time."

"Yes, I will arrive a sweaty mess, eliciting pity and scorn from the congregation. Meanwhile, you, my brother who runs miles every day, will shine as brightly as the morning sun. All the women there will want to fuck you as you stride up to the pews reserved for members of the Order. What few dutiful ladies will be in attendance for my consecration, anyway." My words grew vicious again. "Too bad for them that you will cast them aside for buggery at the barracks with your brothers-in-arms."

Gerard began to laugh again.

"Stop laughing!"

"Why would I not laugh when what you say is funny?" Still, my brother smiled at me.

We walked the rest of the way in silence to the Cathedral. Mercifully, I had remembered despite the hangover haze to give my arse a proper wiping while I was at the barracks and no stink wafted up as I felt the sweat slide down my legs.

I gazed at the Blue Cathedral as we approached. It was on the corner of two streets in the core of Hightown, that part of the City reserved for the wealth and nobility. The building seemed to emanate out of the cobbles, the steeple stretching far above the large noble mansions that were erected next to it. The face of the building was made with a light blue marble, blue marble that housed stained glass images in the windows. Stained glass that depicted images of brutality: Knights running swords through Demons, blood spurting out onto their mail, men savaging each other in a similar fashion, a man nailed to a cross and bleeding to death. Above the glass, I could just barely make out a crow taking flight from the cross at the top of the spire.

Why did a place holding itself out as a house of peace project such vicious images onto the city? The Church of the Christ-man, my parents' Faith, seemed horrible, especially compared to what little I knew of the other holy traditions with adherents in Isha. But I had passed through their places of worship from time to time and had sometimes listened to them speak or watched them in prayer. Some men from the east, who paid homage to a fat and jolly god, seemed content to just burn incense and sit down with eyes closed. Others imbibed potions to give them visions of Demons, a practice that sounded completely horrific and without any merit at all. Still others simply sat in huts with crackling fires until they reached the point of passing out. And they all proclaimed to know the truth of existence, claiming the superiority of one god or another, some idol with salvation up its sleeve. It was all shite, of that I was certain. The only world that was real was right in front of me, even if that world heaped insult after insult upon me.

Grinning his perfect grin, my brother pushed open the doors of the Cathedral, and ushered me in to the darkness.

Chapter Two
Downward Motion

Truth be told, it was not all that dark in the Cathedral. Morning light entered through the stained glass. There were candles burning in sconces on the walls and on the ten enormous blue pillars that stretched the gap between the curved ceiling and the huge slabs of similarly-hued marble that made up the floors. Most of the floor was covered with a criss-cross of gold-edged crimson runners and three separate rows of pews that stretched back to the dais, pews that could sit around fifty men each.

Pews that were mercifully nearly bare.

Thor's Day morning services were not exactly the most well-attended of the week, a fact that had not been lost on me. My father may have been "proud" that his second-born was to enter the Order, but that did not mean he meant to publicly rejoice in the fact. My very existence was an embarrassment for the man, no matter what lies he might tell me to coax me into doing his will. A terrible Knight certainly sounded better than a terrible Squire.

Seated in the first two rows of pews were maybe a few dozen or so Knights and Squires, a smattering of my brothers-in-arms who enjoyed the habit of laughing every time I whiffed a blow or landed on my ass when I tried to mount a horse.

These were the people that refused to sit with me during meals and would make "jokes," like leaving a box of beetles under the sheets at the foot of my bed or pissing in my mug before handing me ale. I had not broken bread with these sons-of-bitches for four years, having long since given over to taking my meals in darkened corners of the training grounds rather than in the din of the mess hall.

Then I spotted her. Marissa Rice. The romantic obsession of my short and unremarkable life. Her father, Captain William Rice, was one of my father's lieutenants. He was a cruel taskmaster, much detested by me and every other man under his command. In this, at least, I had some support. The other Squires all whispered his name with curses on their breath. His daughter, though, she was unlike him in every way. She was a vision of beauty. Her nose stood out from her face in perfect harmony with her cheeks, and her small mouth seemed to resonate with unexpressed secrets. Her hair was a shock of golden-brown, tresses of pulled taffy that wove together into a flowing tapestry that cascaded down her neck and shoulders.

Marissa's beauty was not just physical. She had grace and poise that made me believe she may have better been suited to life in the Heavens than here on Clovir. Kind to me, she was a rare flame in the damp misery of this world. When I unfailingly reddened as I spoke to her, she never once smiled in mockery. When I lost my words, which happened often in her presence, she patiently waited for me to find them. She asked me questions and seemed interested in my answers.

When I looked at her, the hairs on my back stood on end.

Thank the Christ-man for my brother's kindness! I had not the slightest whiff of an inkling of a notion that this woman would be in attendance for the utter joke that was about to take place. I thought back in horror at how I was prepared to show up in ill-fitting clothes and stinking of shite. It was less out of clear filth-soaked necessity and more out of hatred for my fellows. If I had really wanted to, I could have found the proper clothing on my own, before my brother's intervention. But I had wanted to play the part, to be the complete fuck-up of a son and a Squire. My father deserved it, the withering cold bastard. My brother, the infallible cock, he deserved it. The slack-jawed Squires and cruel Knights that were to witness the spectacle: they deserved it, too.

But, Marissa. She did not deserve it.

I didn't really desire to jeopardize my relationship with that creature out of spite for my family and comrades-in-arms. If I am honest with myself about my intentions back then, I was less worried about Marissa's true feelings than what it might have done to my chances of getting her into the marriage bed. She was incomprehensibly beautiful. My eyes and loins dripped with lust at the mere thought of picking that sweet fruit.

Ha! It was an idea that was as insane as the like of which that rattled around in the skulls of the wretches clinging to a half-life up in Meadow Hill Sanitarium! She would never agree to marry me, much less fuck me. Marissa was as devout as any of my female counterparts, the failures at life of the fairer sex who took the nun's habit out of desperation when no man found her fit for marriage or for bedding. At least the former type could find work at establishments like the Green Dragon.

I have already listed my faults with varying degrees of repetition, but here they are again: gluttonous, bad at fighting, cowardly, deceptive, lazy, lustful. Nearly every single activity that crucified bastard up on the wall at the head of the Church preached for or against, I dutifully avoided or gleefully gave my full participation.

And why not? It was all rot, anyway. The Christ-man telling me to love my fellow man... I would not do that if my fellow man did not love me first. And it was abundantly clear that he did not. So I would do my drinking and whoring and lying, to Hell with the Christ-man. He was only a superstition kept alive by lascivious old Priests with a taste for boy flesh and the ignorant idiots that chose to believe in pleasant lies, rather than the harsh truths of the reality that surrounded them.

It was in this state of dark meditation that I approached the dais. My brother took his leave from my side and sat down with my father, who was glaring at me. I fought back the smile that rose to my lips. I could hear his admonishment now: smiling would be a step 'too far.' This was a 'serious occasion.' I could not bring myself to look at Marissa. Even now, decently dressed, I felt a burning in my cheeks and chest at the idea of even meeting her gaze. Instead, I chose to keep my eyes fixed ahead. Next to the ornate wooden pulpit, Bishop Charles Mountpence was staring daggers at me as well. I stopped in the middle of the aisle, as though I were frozen.

"Squire Cardiff, how good of you to join us."

Despite his words, it was clear that the Bishop did not think that my presence was a good thing. I knew he did not like the way that I hung around at the Cathedral during breaks in training from time to time, trying to feign reasons for being there that did not involve ogling at or stammering out a hello to young Mistress Rice.

The piercing ring from the belfry that sounded next shocked me so much that I nearly exited my flesh through my skull. With the remnants of last night's drink upon me, I staggered. I heard laughs from all around me. Apparently, the people in the pews were amused by my surprise. My chest tightened and my face reddened. Those fucks.

"Ah, there is the 11 o'clock bell now." Disgust seethed in the Bishop's voice. Again, I fought back a smile.

"Sir Peter, if we may?"

I heard a yawning of wood from the pew and the shuffle of boots as my father came up to join us on the dais. He took his place next to the Bishop. The two of them looked quite the pair, my father in his full Knightly dress, adorned as befit the Commander of one of the King's most elite units of shock troops, and the Bishop in his own opulent black and silver spiritual regalia. In a story book read to children, an image like this might be found on a page next to words describing how the cleric blessed the veteran Knight as he set off to defeat a Dragon.

Too bad this was not make-believe. All I saw was two tired and miserable old men whose cocks were about as likely to function as the holy water in the basin next to the Bishop had the power to save a baby from a lifetime of Hell. Or to bless one such as me with the good fortune of being a halfway decent Knight.

I admit now with no reluctance to praying as I stood there, listening to the liturgy read by the Priest and repeated by the congregation. At the time, if you had accused me of it, I would have denied it to the ends of the earth. I would have called into question your own beliefs, your prowess, your sexual preferences. I would have bubbled over with hate, but I would not have admitted to having said a few words of prayer as I stood in the magnificence of that Cathedral. I prayed for ability with the sword, I prayed for success with Marissa, I prayed for worldly fortune. Most of all, though, I prayed for protection from poisoned Liserian quarrel.

I was a coward first, after all.

"Now," barked the Priest, having finished droning on about the Christ-man and bread and fish, "Squire Cardiff, are you prepared to swear fealty to your King and to Holy Mother Church?"

I looked at the Bishop's face, at the contempt that lurked therein. The holy man's hatred had not abated during the reading of the liturgy. I briefly thought to offer him a choice epithet from my repertoire, the ones I reserved for the foolish faithful. Then I looked over at my father. He was watching me intently, but there was no malice there. His brow was relaxed, his pupils were deep pools. At the time, I couldn't put my finger on what it was that gave me pause, but I recognize it for what it was now: pure love. I saw love in my father's face and it stopped me from descending into the muck.

I was shamed.

"Yes," I responded, lowering my eyes. "Yes, Bishop Mountpence. I swear fealty to my King and to Holy Mother Church."

Chapter Three
Freefall

I wish I could say that ostentation followed the ceremony, that we all sauntered on an appropriately languid retreat to some banquet hall with tables packed to the rafters with roasts and breads and sweets, with me at the head of the column, the rest of my fellows raining down open handed smacks upon my back and whooping merrily as we made our way across the cobbles. That was the way it was after Gerard's ceremony. Instead, once the Bishop finished the consecration, the solemn gathering stood up in silence and walked out of the building. I knew that they were all at the ceremony out of respect for my father. Active celebration lay beyond the limits of that respect.

I expected nothing less, and yet the slight stung all the same. One more insult to add to the ever-lengthening list of indignities that I had received at the hands of my peers.

Instead of to a party thrown at one of the more respectable public houses that I avoided like a plague for their patrons with sticks wedged firmly up their arses, my brother, father, and I broke from the group and walked in silence back to the family homestead. We sat down in the cottage to bowls of stew prepared by Mrs. Tarrant, one of father's leaseholds, some small ale cooperatively brewed by the women of the Estate, and some bread baked by Mrs. Richardson, yet another indentured

Serf.

Oh, the bounties bestowed on the Lord of Cardiff Estate.

"Andrew," said my father, breaking the quiet as he sopped up some broth with a hunk of bread, "you are Knighted at long last. Are you prepared to serve your King and country?"

Ugh, Christ-man preserve me, did we have to have this conversation again? Did we not just go through the motions with the Gods-damned Bishop? And not a single word about my birthday, but of course I had not expected a whit. We had not celebrated a birthday under the roof of my father's cottage since mother had died.

"Yes, Father," I mumbled into the steam rising from the bowl in front of me. 'Please shut up,' I did not add, though it was a struggle to refrain from doing so.

"Good," he continued, pausing for a moment to bite into some of his soaked bread. "You need to understand that as a Knight of the Yellow Order, you will be given no special treatment as my son. You will be dealt with the same as any other fighting man. And you will be put to work."

If I had been receiving special treatment up until this point, I quaked in my boots at the thought of a loss of my privilege.

"Now," Father said, dropping an octave to the hushed tone of conspiracy, "I have news for both of you. This will be announced by the criers tomorrow at the eleven o'clock Hear Ye, and remains a state secret until then, so do not discuss it with another soul until after the news has been released officially. The Yellow Order is to voyage south, to the Kingdom of Erifracia. As you know, King Revanti is an ally of our own King Janus. The Erifracians are having issues with marauding pirates in the port off of the capital, Tunuska. We are to lend our aid until the problems is resolved."

"Why cannot the Erifracians deal with the problem themselves?" Gerard asked, dropping his spoon onto the table and staring at my father intently.

"Oh, I am sure they could, if they wished. Erifracia is one

of our closest allies, and I believe the two Kings have decided that we should bleed together that we might grow closer as nations. The pirates are just a convenient excuse. The entire Yellow Order will be sent down to the coast for this military and diplomatic action."

"What of the other Orders?"

My brother played the perfect dutiful, interested son. For my part, I folded my arms over my belly and watched the exchange with a cold detachment.

"The Red and Blue Orders will deal with defence of the Kingdom in our absence. Liserian spies in the City are sure to inform the Empress that we are operating with reduced numbers, so it will be even more important to keep our borders well-tended."

My father turned to me.

"Andrew, I am placing you in Butterfly Company, under the command of Captain Rice."

My heart sank. Love his daughter Marissa though I may, Captain Rice was infamous for his brutality. My infatuation with his daughter had only made the Captain grow even more surly towards me, and I had not even been a subordinate by this point. My brother, who had shown me kindness earlier that day and with whom I would have preferred to have been placed, was an officer in Dragonfly, another Company. But I could not show my father any weakness, any outward sign that his dictates had affected me in any real way.

"Why must the names of these units be so womanly?" I said with a put-on chuckle. "Butterfly, Dragonfly, Mosquito, Beetle - these are creatures to be squashed beneath the heel of an enemy's boot. At least the Blue Order has ferocious sounding names: Bear, Lion, Tiger, Hawk."

"Damn it all, Andrew, have you learned nothing at all during your training?" My father punctuated his roar with an open-handed slap on the wood of the table. "You will show some respect!"

"You know that I have not learned a God damned thing! Respect what? You? This fucking Yellow Order, bane of my short and sad existence here on this Earth? The King? You can all go fuck yourselves, for all I care. It is clear to me now: the only reason for my induction today was that you did not want to leave your home tended to by the likes of me. You would prefer to have me in your little army of serial buggers, where you can keep an eye on me and make sure that I do nothing embarrassing to your precious honour."

"Yes, Andrew, as per usual, the world is filled with dishonourable buggers and you stand on the outside looking in at the Sodomic mess we find ourselves in, sole male member of humanity without cock in arse." My brother looked acidly at me as he spoke. "You are a joke, little brother."

"Enough, both of you!" my father yelled, picking up the reins. "I am sick and tired of the shite that you have been peddling, Andrew, this doom and gloom and abject cowardice! You are a Cardiff! Yes, you will come to Tunuska and you will fight pirates. And yes, you may die with a corsair's blade in your belly. But Christ-man damn it all to Hell, you will fucking try!"

My father turned his attention to my brother. "And you, Gerard, you think yourself impervious to the flight of an arrow or the slash of a sword? You may be good, but you are not *that* good. Your arrogance is clear to me, the way you speak to your peers and the way you hold yourself, the way you have spent your days dishonouring your own brother with word and action. It is a folly of youth, but follies will get you killed at any age."

Father turned to address us both. "You are not fucking men! You are fucking boys! And you will grow up, or I will disown the both of you!"

At that, both my brother and I clamped shut, though part of me screamed to laugh at the way the words had come out of my father's mouth. I could count on one hand the number of times that my father had sworn an oath, even fewer the number of times he had done it when he had known that we were present to hear him do so. My father did not speak again until the flush of red in his cheeks had abated.

"Finish your meals and get the fuck out of my cottage. Back to the barracks, both of you. I do not want to see you until tomorrow morning. We leave at the first sounding of the cock's crow." My father paused. "Andrew, I am not an idiot. I know what occurred this morning. Understand me: if you get so drunk that you stagger out to the docks just as the final ship is leaving, my first act as your Commander will be to put you in the stocks on the ship for a full week. If I need to send some of my men to come and fetch you off the filth of a bawdy house floor, you will spend the entire journey locked in oak. I warn you: the Erifracian sun is without mercy." He stopped and looked at us one more time. "Christ-man!"

My father launched his bowl at the wall. The crock smashed to bits, sending ceramic shards and mushy root vegetables out in a spray onto the surrounding wood.

Taking this as our cue to leave, my brother and I stood and quickly filed out of the place. After we exited, we looked intently at each other for a moment. I opened my mouth to speak, but no words made their escape. Gerard looked as though he wished to speak as well, but found himself equally incapable. Feeling the awkwardness mount, we each silently set off on the path, splitting from one another at the first fork we could find. My brother's path would take him down the road to the city, the one onto which I was funneled led into the forest. My father might have told me to go back to the barracks, but I thought it high time for my first act of disobedience as a Yellow Knight.

It was still mid-afternoon by the time I entered the wood. I did not know where I was going. All I knew was that I was between a rock and a hard place. My father's outburst proved to me one thing yet another time: I could not rely on anyone in this world. Ever since my mother died I had been alone, and that was not likely to change any time soon. I walked and walked and walked, taking a meandering route through the paths that ran along the forest floor.

I looked up at the canopy. Although there was some sunlight filtering through the gaps in the foliage, I could not make out how far up the branches stretched. I recalled then that we had freshly entered the Septembus Month. The leaves had yet to change colour, to begin that long slow procession from green to yellow to red and finally to brown, slipping from the cradle of life to die on the forest floor. That summer was ending, there was presently only one sign: the chill in the air that had started to creep in at night.

At least by going south we would avoid the crush of cold that robbed my homeland of comfort every winter.

If I am being honest with myself, beneath the bleak cynicism that had worked its claws deep into mind in those days, part of me was excited at the prospect of heading to unknown southern lands with my father and brother. It was a feeling that I had not felt in years, not since the time that my mother was alive.

I smiled then. It was the first time I had looked on what was about to occur with something that approached excitement. I know now that what I felt was a yearning buried deep inside. A desire for something worthwhile in this life, a light to shine upon the dim lens through which I viewed the world. The anticipation spread from my chest out into my fingers. The sensation was welcome.

Maybe, I mused to myself, there was a way I would not fail in my travels.

This voice of aspiration was small in my head, and one that I completely dismissed out of habit. Hope was for fools, ones that found their ends at tip of an enemy spear or behind the bars of debtor's prison when the business venture failed. Just as quickly as it had appeared, hope drifted into the ether, replaced with a sudden return to the senses. Senses that were reminding me that I was nursing a monstrosity of a hangover and running on a couple of hours of sleep.

I sat down to rest against the base of one of the enormous trees just off the dirt of the path, enjoying the soft embrace of the grass that stretched up to accept me. Slumber followed.

✳ ✳ ✳ ✳ ✳

I awoke to screeching cicadas. The light had fled. The late summer night's chill had descended. My hand was invisible in the gloom, no matter how close I brought it to my face. Looking up, I noticed that there was some dimness barely filtering down through the canopy. I never paid attention to the procession of the moon and its phases, but my mind was called back to a drink-addled conversation I had with one of the harlots at the Green Dragon the previous night, a verbal intercourse between stinking drunks that bore all of the usefulness that such speech has a tendency to bear. She was of the more mature stock, a seasoned old prostitute named Tara. Old was relative, though, at least as far as the whores of the City were concerned. She could not have seen more than thirty-five summers.

"Da moon, me ducky," she cooed, "Da moon's full tomorrow night. My girl in da Purple Run, one a dem red-robes wit' da fancy jewelry on her wrists, she rolled da bones for me last week. I'm ta find me way out of this shite hole on the day da moon is full."

I had raised a glass to Tara's good fortune. I was so deep in my cups that I would have raised a glass to a man with the dexterity not to piss on himself when he was out for a slash, and there had been precious few of those left at the Green Dragon at that advanced hour.

Full moon. If I could get out from the cover of the forest, I would have little problem navigating my way home, assuming there were no clouds in the sky. Buried as I was in darkness, I was as likely to find my way back home before dawn as the pigs that roamed the Estate were liable to sprout wings and fly off into the great blue yonder.

I stumbled about for a time, arms outstretched, scrabbling on the rocks and twigs. My mind was racing. I had felt hope earlier that day, and here I was having it snatched out from under me again. Just my Gods-damned luck. I fell down twice, when my foot got caught in what felt like gnarled roots. After an eternity of desperate scrabbling, I sat back on hard packed dirt, exhausted. Defeated.

I remember the sound that came next very well. It was a loud and abrupt noise. It reminded me of the claps and crashes of the fireworks that old Roger up on the hill used to launch every summer at the Midsummer Festival, before he took a stroke down at the Green Dragon, getting tugged under the table by one of the young maidens fresh into the business.

It was the sound of a thick branch snapping under the weight of something heavy as it pounced.

I did not have time to react to what I heard. I was suddenly struck by a furry warm bulk and knocked from my sitting position onto my back. What air was left in my lungs made a hasty retreat and a weight pressed so heavily onto my chest that I could not draw any more back in. I felt a crushing sensation in my right forearm, like it was caught in a vice. It was pinned against me. If I had the air to do it, I would have screamed. I reached out with my free hand to try to push off the beast that had attacked me.

When I had regained a small measure of my senses, I assumed a wolf was my assailant. Packs roamed these woods and played marauders to the dirt-poor forest-dwellers, hunters and foragers who ended up at the taverns on the outskirts of Isha, usually the Green Dragon, soon besotted and eager to loudly tell stories of chicken coop raids and children torn apart when they wandered out of the cabin at night. Then my fingers found warm fur, but there was something unexpected about it. It much too short to be that of a wolf. And whatever it the creature was, it was larger than a wolf, nearly as big as me.

An enormous paw was crushing my sternum. Beneath the beast's skin, I could feel hard tense muscles. Pushing the animal was about as useful as my sword arm in combat. Pain blossomed in my arm and my chest burned.

This was it, then.

Thoughts of death and defeat swirled in my head. I was to be suffocated by some unknown beast, never to know the touch of a woman who had not first been paid in cold hard metal, never to have slain an enemy in battle, never to have even tried and failed at being a Yellow Knight.

At that moment, the spiteful cynicism that usually dominated my skull let off. And let off completely. I had a flash of some insane insight, something that was so completely incredible as to be a complete hallucination, but paradoxically impossible not to believe. In my mind's eye, I saw myself crushed beneath the unseen black beast, my forearm in its jaw. From where it was biting me, an iridescence of incalculable beauty was flowing out and into me. It spiderwebbed up my arm until it reached my torso. Then it exploded up into my mind, petals of every colour in the rainbow filling up my head.

With that image, the voice of hope was back and unopposed. And it was strong. It commanded me to try. I was to attempt to live by whatever means necessary. I pulled my left hand from the fur and reached out on the ground beside me, searching for something, anything that might help me survive. A frantic scrabbling of my nails on cold hard dirt was all that my efforts delivered. Red spots began to appear in my vision. I felt consciousness slip.

Just before I tumbled beneath the waves, my hand found purchase on a rock. It was not a large rock, barely bigger than my palm. I did not think, I simply struck out. It must be said that I prefer my right arm in all things. My left arm is fairly useless. It is one of the reasons I was such a terrible fighter, though there are many. This time, though, my left arm did not fail me. I am certain I hit the beast in the head, for it broke its lock on my arm and hissed. It reminded me of the sound the house cats that roamed the Estate made when I hurled stones at them in youthful and unfocused anger, albeit several octaves lower. The beast shifted and I was able to draw a great breath. I struck out again as I heaved in great gulps of survival.

The rock once more found its mark. This time there was a great roar from the creature. I screamed as I readied myself for a third blow. The creature must have regained its bearings, because I felt another smash and the vice tightened again, this time around my left shoulder.

Who was I kidding? I asked myself. I was a failure. I was simply to die ignominiously, here in a cold dark forest of my homeland to some beast rather than the bright hot sands of a foreign territory beneath the point of a barbarous sword. Despair did not quell my curiosity, though: what was this creature that was attacking me? I could not see, but what I felt and heard did not match any experience or description with which I was familiar.

My right arm throbbed. I felt hot fluid run down from my wounded forearm onto my hand. The beast began shaking its head, sharpening the pain in my shoulder with a white-hot crescendo. I cried out again.

I heard a shout, then, from some distance away. A man's voice. I could not make out what was said; the speech was strange. It was a foreign tongue, though not entirely unfamiliar. It sounded a bit like the language the Priests at the Cathedral liked to use when they read from their great and yellowing tomes, dead words from the long dead Heraclytan Empire. Then again, it was completely different. Too many harsh consonants and strange clicks to be Heraclytan. All I do know is that there was a crackling noise like the sound that precedes the boom of a thunderclap. Bright green light followed. The beast released my arm and its bulk slumped over me again. I did not make a move. I was tired, so tired.

I let darkness take me.

Chapter Four
Terminal Velocity

My next memory is that of a smell.

A sharp and acrid odour, a little like the reek of burning hair. Unlike that particular stench, there was a sweetness to it. It reminded me of the citrus fruits that are ubiquitous in the lands of Kashya far to the southwest during the winter months and which make their way across the continent, avoiding hated Liseria packed into the holds of merchant vessels that brave the winter Frost Channel, arriving in Thrairn in semi-rotten dribs and drabs as gifts exchanged by the nobility during the Feast of the Christ-man, our solstice celebration at the end of the Yule Month. But this foetor was an order of magnitude more offensive than decayed fruit. My closed eyes watered and burned when I tried to open them, so I squeezed them as tightly shut as I could.

I moaned and shifted. I was on my back, lying on a hard lumpy mattress and covered by the thinnest and roughest sheet and blanket that had ever touched my skin. Sometimes I forgot that, despite the bastard's utter cheapness in most things, my father spared no expense when it came to comparatively small comforts like soft blankets. Every time I took a tavern wench abed in a room in the Green Dragon, I was reminded of this quirk of my father's regular penny-pinchery. But the bed coverings in which I found myself wrapped in this new and unknown place were even worse than the flea-bitten rags that coarse pimp Rolf deigned to offer the clientele of his house of ill-repute, something I had not thought possible.

Strangely, the only agony I felt was related to the noxious fumes that enveloped me. My left shoulder and right arm, which I recalled shortly after awakening to have been savaged by the beast, felt completely fine. I tried to rub the right with my left, to feel the injury. My saviour must have dressed the wound extremely well for me to be so pain-free and I was curious about his efforts. I found that I could not lift my arm. Something bound my wrist to the bed.

"Do not move," boomed a heavily-accented loud male voice somewhere off to my right. "You have been gravely injured. I am helping you to heal, but if you move, you will interfere with the magic."

Vowels rolled off the man's tongue in a way that was contrasted against the sharpness of the consonants, which were dropped or reshaped according to the imprint of his mother speech. The accent was wholly unfamiliar to me.

"Magic," I repeated. I laughed in a shrill manner that made me cringe as it was occurring. "'Interfere with the magic,' he says. I suppose that you'll tell me next that you keep a Dragon as a pet."

I sometimes made jokes when I was scared. Brought to death's door by an unfamiliar beast and saved by a man who claimed that magic was real, I found myself to be completely terrified. Magic, that easy explanation for all sorts of impossible things, was found in the story books reserved for children and that is where any sensible person left it. Which is why I despaired for the sensibility of my unknown host. By about ten years old, most children in the Kingdom ceased believing in fairies and Dragons and got on with miserably toiling in the muck with the rest of humanity for the few coins that would see them through to their deathbed.

Every once in a while, though, something would give me a taste of the older, more innocent days. As I said before, my own father had told me and my brother in a manner that was purely serious that the wood of the barracks could withstand Dragon fire. With gravitas that equaled my father's when he told us about the barracks, my mother once confided in me that she could not explain it, but she believed in a force beneath the surface, something that was guiding the direction of humanity. Something that could be directed into conjuring the elements out of thin air. She said that she believed that it had not always been such a ludicrous proposition, that at some point in our history, men and women, regardless of who they were, could tap into this source and do great feats of magic. Neither had evidence of their claims, and so I scoffed at it all, thinking my father lying and my mother superstitious. And now here I was, bound to a cot by some madman who told me my bonds were to prevent interference with the stuff of make-believe.

"What kind of arsehole keeps a Dragon as a pet?" my captor asked with a chuckle.

Who was this person? Gritting my teeth, I decided to open my eyes in spite of the burn. Thankfully, it had subsided by that point and I could look around with little discomfort. But I was still bound by my wrists and could only move my head a few inches in any direction.

I found myself in what appeared to be a small shack. There were shelves on all the walls, shelves which were lined with a variety of vials and small crockery. The edges of the shelves were covered in little rectangles of paper, labels for what lay above them, no doubt, written in an unfamiliar script. Bundles of dried herbs hung from the rafters, rafters which started from the walls barely a half dozen feet from the ground. Steam was rising from the small cauldron that bubbled on the hearth. In front of the cauldron stood the man whom I assumed had saved me from the beast.

He was smiling at me a smile that was completely without

malice, which I took to be a good sign. His skin was very dark, darker still than the Erifracians that I saw holding court at the castle from time to time. He was wearing a black sleeveless vest with strange designs stitched in extremely colourful thread - pinks, oranges, greens, and blues. I recognized Snakes and flowers, but there were other shapes and patterns which were more abstract, with soft cheerful edges. The vest was atop a plain white shirt that stretched from his shoulders down to his hands, hands that were covered by black leather gloves. His pants appeared to be made of leather that had been dyed an extremely bright shade of purple.

Frankly, the man looked every bit the lunatic that I had suspected when I discovered I was in bonds for fear of interfering with 'magic.'

I opened my mouth to speak, when all of a sudden my attention was drawn to my own body. I could see that the man had removed my shirt left my pants on, quelling the creeping fear in the background of my mind that I had been buggered in my unconscious state. I noticed that the finery my brother had given me before the initiation yesterday had been unceremoniously dumped in a pile next to the bed. These details, if unnerving, were and remain comparatively of little interest to me. The sight that completely robbed the words from my mouth was floating above the wounds I bore.

A cloud of coruscating green mist was swirling in the air just atop my arms. Through it, I could see the flesh that had been torn in my left shoulder and right forearm. In the new valley in my forearm, the white of my arm bone glowed brightly. No blood flowed. In amazement, I watched as strips of muscle and sinew formed out of the void within the mist, materializing an inch or two from my arm and finding their way down into the wound where they became part of my body. It was then that I noticed that the mist was sparkling in a shaft of sunlight streaming in from the window next to the hearth.

Practical matters trumped even the impossibility that I was

witnessing.

"Fuck! What time is it?"

Awe was displaced by fear of what I knew my father would do to me when he found me... if he and the men did not shove off without me. If that happened, I felt sure to be disowned. My father blew a lot of hot air, but he was acting strangely these past days. First, his completely uncharacteristic mercy when I shared my doubts with him, then his outburst with the swearing and the smashing of his own precious property. Normally the man was made of indifferent stone, disinterested and immovable. Horrendously boring, but safe in his predictability. This new caprice that had caught fire within the old man might very well yet render unto the world a human being with a full emotional range, but I felt those flames might consume me in the process.

"I have to go!"

"I cannot recommend that you go anywhere," said the man, "not for five days. Otherwise, that could be bad." He pointed at my right arm, the one with the exposed bone.

"Five days? In five days the Order will be almost halfway to Erifracia. And I will be dishonourably discharged from His Majesty's Yellow Order for desertion." I peered down at the wound. "That looks like it is stitching back together fairly nicely. It should not take more than a half an hour! Why five days?"

"This magic will soon heal you completely of your physical wounds. But your soul is tainted. We have to follow the moon cycle, my friend. We are just beginning to pass through it. The creature that attacked you was cursed. If I do not speak the words of an incantation at the end of the cycle, you will be cursed yourself."

Skepticism flared in my brain. I saw the green magic this man was working on my arm, and I had to accept what I saw. Magic was somehow real. Here it was, bounded in reality in a way that I could understand. But this was just some new - or old, if Mother was to be believed - form of healing technology. Talk of souls and taints and curses found a less sympathetic place in my heart. I heard this kind of thing from the beggars in Isha, throwing chicken bones in darkened alleys, making proclamations about the future, and, most tellingly, reaching out with open palms to the passersby. It always infuriated me to see those charlatans take advantage of scared strangers the way that they did.

"What is your name, peasant?" I had always felt a surge of pleasure when I pulled rank on my social inferiors. I found it to be strangely absent.

"My name is Ernesto. Ernesto Libélula."

"And where are you from, Mr. Libélula?"

"Atika."

Atika. I had only heard the name once. It was a land far to the south, farther still than Erifracia. The tale I had heard of the place gave the impression that the Atikans were savages, living in small bands in pockets of backwards civilization that dotted the steaming jungles whence they came. If I were to correctly understand the scribe who had related to me his knowledge of the place over several tankards of Rolf's finest, the people of Atika lived the short violent lives of the uncivilized. Atikan ends usually came about in one of the hundred instances of inter-tribal wars that raged at any given time. That, or they would succumb to the bite of one poisonous creature or another. There was some other rot about talking monkeys and tree-men, but such embellishments were normal for these types of ale-loosened stories. My storyteller had heard this account of the place from one of the mission Priests who foolishly risked life and limb to spread the story of the Christman, much to the delight of the tithing pederasts of the Church.

If ever a man knew how to perform magic, I was not surprised that the one I encountered came from Atika.

"Mr. Libélula. You appear to be a man who likes his privacy. In fact, I would wager that you thrive on it. I doubt anyone knows you even have this little cottage hidden away so close to the capital. Your magic: it is quite wondrous. And very useful. I suppose that you keep yourself and your magic hidden to avoid being coming in to opposition with His Majesty?"

Libélula did not react to my words. So I pressed on.

"You will complete this healing magic, whatever it is, close up my wound, and unbind me from this table. If you do not, as soon as you do release me, whether that is five hours hence or five days hence, I will go straight to the Commander of my Order. I will inform him that an alien from Atika kidnapped his second-born son and prevented him from doing his duty to the King. At best, you and your green mist will be pressed into service in the court of the castle or on some shitehole battlefield on the Liserian border. At worst, you will be publicly flogged, hanged, and gibbeted. Hopefully, for your sake, one after the other."

I surprised myself at how forthright I was in my dealings with the man. Usually when interacting with strangers, I did a lot of mumbling and looking down. I had my eyes locked on the strangely-clad magician.

Libélula approached me, coming to stand at the foot of the cot upon which I was strapped.

"Very astute of you, Sir..."

"Cardiff. Andrew Cardiff, Knight of the Yellow Order, at your service." I had heard that authority-laden introduction used by my brother on the few occasions I had been out in society with him since he had been inducted. The maidens whom he addressed that way always seemed to swoon a little, and their fingers seemed invariably to crawl up to meet the tresses of their hair. I remember looking forward to the day when I would be able to use it as a weapon in my battle against the fairer sex for access to that which lay beyond the knickers. Little did I know that my first time uttering the words would be in such ignominious circumstances, with so unappealing an audience.

"Sir Cardiff, it appears that you have me at a bit of a disadvantage. I was going to ask you to keep this matter, as well as the matter of my existence here, between us. That beast—"

"What was that beast?" I said, interrupting the man. Yet another first for my cowardly self. Fear usually prevented me from exercising my will in conversation. "It was no wolf. Tell me everything you know, or I will report you."

"It was a beast from my homeland, Sir Cardiff. A Jaguar, it is called. A cat that prowls the jungle, killing humans and smaller beasts with little discernment between the two. My own cousin, Guillermo, met his end at the claws of such an animal. How it made its way up here, I have no idea. I am investigating that very thing. I would not think such a creature would survive its journey, cold as it is here in Thrairn. I suspect black magic, with a blacker purpose to match. There is a chance that my suspicions about the creature are incorrect and it merely found its way up here on an Atikan merchant bark. In fact, if the moon were not full last night, I would have never suspected evil magic. The black sorcerers of my homeland: their strongest spells are always cast in the bright of the full moon. I have many enemies, enemies who would prefer to see me dead than doing my work here. My suspicion is that the Jaguar was sent to kill me. I would like to bless you after the moon's power wanes, to ensure that you have not been affected in any way."

"So," I said, silently scoffing at the superstition of the savage before me, "it is not exactly the emergency you described earlier. You are telling me that you want to keep me here on the off chance, that what? I am cursed by black magic?"

"Yes, Sir Cardiff. But please, do not think this matter is not of grave importance!"

I looked down at my arms. Through the mist, I could see that the muscle had knit back together and the first layers of skin were forming.

"What exactly is it that you do here, Mr. Libélula? And why are people trying to kill you?"

The man shifted on his feet. We had been sharing eye contact throughout our exchange, something that I had not often had the Courage to do since the days my mother walked Clovir, and usually only with her. He broke from my eyes and looked out the window.

"I cannot divulge that."

"'Cannot divulge that?'" I fumed. "I hold your very Fate in my hands. Whether or not you find yourself at the end of an executioner's knot could very well be determined by my actions, and you deny me what I want?"

I marveled at my words. I had never yelled at a man, let alone a man as clearly powerful as the one before me, in such a way before. In spite of what I said, it was he who held my Fate in his hands, and not the other way around, but I had threatened him regardless. Such was hardly the act of a coward.

"You will have to be satisfied with what I have told you, Andrew."

He used my given name, taking on a level of familiarity that would normally prickle under my skin when used by a commoner. But I felt no hollow rage at the man for the liberty he took. Perhaps it was because he saved my life, both with some unknown magic against the creature that assaulted me and the healing spell which was returning my Strength to me as we spoke.

"Very well, Ernesto," I said, returning the gesture. I was beginning to like him. "Perhaps we can come to some sort of agreement. I am going off on a campaign. I need to be at the docks. I was supposed to be there about two hours ago, based on the angle the sunlight is coming in through that window there. If I leave now, I will be placed in the stocks for the entirety voyage. My father threatened to do that to me and I honestly believe he will follow through with it. If I do not go, I will be stripped of my Knighthood. I cannot stay the five days that you require. But I would like to visit you again when I return. Perhaps I can come and see you once we have completed our work?"

The words came out of my mouth in a stream of perfect order. I might speak with this kind of eloquence with my brother or father, but a stranger? Unless I was in my cups, I was more likely to find myself staring down, stammering out broken phrases with a burn in my cheeks.

"I do not like this, Andrew," Libélula said. "I do not like this at all. But I understand that you are compelled to leave and I am honour-bound to not hold you against your will. I do not let you go because of the threat that you will bring this Kingdom down on my head. I do it because I respect your wishes. I hope that you understand that."

The man unbuckled the leather thongs that held me to the table.

"Thank you, Ernesto," I said. "I will tell no one of your existence here."

"That is all well and good, Andrew." Ernesto chuckled. "Besides, if you did, most others would think you insane. Your threats were empty. At least, I knew them to be. You would not be able to find my cabin again. My magic keeps me invisible to the outside world. There is a reason you have never seen or heard of me before."

"So why did you help me? You could have left me to die in the jaws of that... what did you call it? Jagwire?"

"Jaguar, Andrew. Jag-waar. And I could not do that. Just as you are compelled to return to your Order this morning, so too am I compelled to help those in need. But I cannot force help on them. That would be doing them violence."

I looked down at my arms. The green had dissipated. The flesh looked as though nothing had ever happened. I pulled on my clothes as quickly as I ever had and burst from the cabin.

Chapter Five
Drag Force

I ran the entire way to the docks. By the time I made it to the outskirts, my lungs burned so badly that I thought I might drop from a heart attack. Part of me hoped for one. It would have brought an end to the whole damn mess of my cowardly life. Seeing an opportunity to cease the torture that was physical activity, I thrust a bag at a farmer leading a donkey towards the heart of Isha. There was enough coin in the pouch to buy a beast of burden like the one I sweatily clambered up onto at the livery four times over. To sweeten the honeyed pot even further, I told the man that I would leave the creature with the harbourmaster for him to pick up later. He grinned as he unloaded a brace of saddlebags, threw them around his own shoulders, and spat at the ground as I urged the donkey on.

My breath returned to me as I rode at a mind-numbingly slow pace along the cobbles into town. Some of the commoners I passed giggled at the sight of my perspiration-soaked figure on the donkey. I tried to ignore them as well as the corresponding burn of embarrassment in my chest and cheeks. I knew I looked a disheveled mess, yet again. Libélula had graciously stitched back together my clothing, and I had not realized to thank him for it before I was well on my way. But my hair was unkempt and my repaired shirt and jerkin were well stained with sweat in lieu of the sour ale of yesterday. My father, if he was still in port, was going to kill me. On top of putting me in the stocks for the late hour at which I arrived.

I dismounted just as I reached the enormous gate that lead into the harbour proper. When I crossed the threshold, I paused for a moment to look around. The port was shaped like a U, surrounded by the tall cream stone and mortar that made up the walls of the city. Several long wooden quays reached out into the icy blue water. Citizens and sailors milled about the place, thronging around the fishmongers' stalls and onto the boats, creating a din that could compete with the market in the poorer west end of Isha on the busiest Saturn's Day of the year. On the ramparts above, a dozen or more unloaded ballistae were angled down towards the boats that sat bobbing in the harbour. I could just barely make out the sunny glint of metal bracers worn by the City Guards standing next to the massive siege weapons. A silent word of thanks to no one in particular emerged in my mind when my eyes finally set upon four massive yellow sails flying high above the little fishing skiffs that made up the bulk of the vessels stationed in the water.

They had not left yet.

The harbourmaster was none too keen to take the donkey. In fact, he looked like he was puffing himself up to tell me to make myself scarce, probably on the assumption that I was some dirt farmer from beyond the outskirts. I considered letting him turn me out, so that I could take joy in watching him squirm as I haughtily informed him that he had just told a Knight of the Yellow Order to fuck off. Unfortunately for my arrogant young self, I didn't have time to toy with the man. Once I identified myself, he straightened up, saluted me, and took the beast's reins. I returned the gesture stiffly, feeling an impostor throughout.

"The King came to port not half an hour ago, sir," the man said thickly through his beard. I felt his eyes run down over my sweaty body and rumpled jerkin, judging me. "I believe he is addressing the lot of you Yellow Knights. You may wish to make yourself over to Pier Four immediately, sir."

I muttered a word of thanks, tied the donkey onto the lantern pole next to the harbourmaster's office, and marched into the crowd of bodies near Pier Four. Within a couple of minutes, I found myself behind a mass of yellow cloaks. I caught the gaze of my brother, who was near the back of the crowd. When he looked at me, his bloodshot eyes looked like they were going to bulge out of his skull, if not for the crease of the furrow on his brow. He the returned his stare to the King, who was standing on the deck of one of the Order's enormous ships. I did the same.

"... duty to the people of the Kingdom of Erifracia, our brothers and sisters that dwell in the sandy lands to the south. These people deserve our love and respect, as the Erifracians have naught but the same for the people of the Kingdom of Thrairn. We will help them eject the scourge of corsairs from Tunuska, and our nations shall grow together in the result..."

King Janus droned on about his plan, a plan that my father had already divulged to us. Surprisingly, the King was not dressed in his usual courtly regalia of purple and white. Instead of finery, he was wearing a suit of leather. The boiled grain was clearly immaculate, even from my distance several dozen feet away, and it was embossed with a white-painted Dragon of Thrairn on the chest. It certainly did not look like it had ever been dragged along the floor of a tavern or trampled in the muck of a training ground, unlike most of the ones in the crowd on the pier. His crown sat atop his head, a simple band of gold that rose up in five ornate white-gemmed points to surround the salt and pepper of his close-cropped hair. On his belt, the King carried a longsword. On his feet, he wore simple black boots.

"... and so I will be joining you on your voyage. King Revanti and I have much to discuss, and it would do well for the people of Erifracia to see that King Janus of Thrairn does not simply sit idle on his throne while his men are in their lands on campaign. We will sail together, and I will keep court with the Erifracian ruler while you undertake your duties on the sands of the beach and waters of the bay.

"One final note," the King continued, his voice becoming serious. "I ask all of you men to keep the honour of Thrairn in your hearts and minds when you conduct yourselves. While making use of prostitution is a grave crime in our fair Kingdom, an offence against the state and a sin against our Holy Mother Church, I do understand that, ahem, virile men of your ages, good breeding or not, have certain requirements during periods of rest and relaxation. Especially when blood is shed or yet to flow. There may be such quiet moments while we are in Erifracia. King Revanti has graciously offered up a list of brothels and public houses that you will be permitted to frequent." King Janus held up a piece of paper.

"I command you, as your liege, to honour the list. You may find yourselves offered better rates or other incentives to go spend your gold at locales not found upon this parchment. Do not give in to temptation. It is not just a matter of reputation. Thrairn has many enemies in Tunuska. Enemies that would see you dying with some venereal fever or fatally slashed with a poisoned blade. King Revanti has given me his word that these establishments are safe, a word that he has given me no cause to doubt.

"Now," the King said, his eyes scanning the crowd, "I understand that we have a new member of the Order. Called into service yesterday, if I am not mistaken. Sir Andrew Cardiff, will you please come forward?"

Beyond the King, I had noticed that my father had been standing quietly, surrounded by his four Captains, including the bastard William Rice. Both my father and he nearly jumped out of their skins when the King uttered his words, then they looked at each other warily. For my part, I felt a bizarre mixture

49

of emotions. First, of course, there was glee at the thought of embarrassing my father and my new Captain. There was shame, as well, to be found so unkempt when I first met the King as his newest subject-in-service. But there was also a faint note of pride, a feeling of respect for the King and for myself to have found my way into the ranks of the Order and to be addressed publicly in this manner.

It was a rather foreign feeling.

My cheeks burned as I slipped through the mass of yellow-hued bodies on my way up to the boat. The four members of the King's personal body guard, heavily armored Knights with white cloaks on their backs and visors covering their faces, moved out of the way to allow me passage up the gangplank. I made it to the deck, where more white cloaked men stood watch next to the King, each with a hand on the pommel of his sword and expressionless metal covering his face. I took a knee before my monarch.

"Sir Cardiff, please rise," the King said, smiling at me. "I understand that you have been a Squire for a long time."

"Seven years, sir. I mean, Your Grace," I barely managed to croak the words out through a wave of timidity as I got to my feet, the same wave that always crashed over me when I found myself in a large group of unfamiliar people.

"Seven years! That is a long time to spend in purgatory! But now you stand before me, having come to the end of your journey. How do you feel?"

"Fine, Your Grace. I feel fine, indeed."

Curiously, I actually did feel fine. These were not the pretty yet meaningless words normally spouted from one's mouth in a social interaction as contrived as this one. I felt something strange happening in my body, the same thing that occurred when I had been bitten by the Jaguar, and when I spoke to Libélula without shying away. Where normally I would be beset terror at the prospect of interacting with a man as great as the King in front of all of my peers, the burning in my chest was beginning to subside. I noticed that I was hunching over as I stood on the deck of the ship. I consciously straightened out my shoulders and drew myself up.

"I must thank you, Your Grace," I added, bowing. "Pardon the language," I dared, "but I know not whether the promotion was deserved based on merit or just because Terence was getting tired of striking me in the arse with his big wooden sword."

I pointed at the quartermaster for the Yellow Order, who doubled as trainer for the Squires. I was as shocked as any present that I was jesting in this situation. What is more: jests that cut myself down instead of a fellow Squire of a lower station, perhaps the bastard son of a lesser Baron. Who was this graceful person who was standing in my boots? The King chuckled, and the men on the pier laughed, too. A warm feeling blossomed in my breast.

"Regardless of how I got here, Your Grace," I continued, buoyed, "I am now a full member of the Yellow Order. I vow to serve you and Thrairn to the best of my ability."

The King smiled at me. "I thank you for your vow, Sir Cardiff."

"Your Commander," King Janus continued, gesturing to my father behind him, "informs me that your talents lie less with the blade and more in your skull. 'A man of great intellect,' I believe you said, Peter?"

I looked to my father, shocked and awed that my father kept me in such high regard. Could I have gotten the man wrong? Was he more than the boring old curmudgeon I had judged him to be?

"I believe I may have said something of that nature, my liege," my father said curtly, staring at me with an intensity that threatened to bore a hole in my forehead. "Most likely I was deep in my cups."

The crowd erupted in laughter again. The King laughed, too. This time rage flared in my chest. Here I stood before King

Janus, being congratulated on my ascension, and still my father found time for insults. That arrogant son of a bitch.

"Perhaps you do your son too little credit, Peter. He is *your* son, after all." The King turned to me again.

"Andrew, if you will permit me to address you with this level of familiarity, would you consider joining me for dinner this evening? It has always been my philosophy that men should be relied upon for their Strengths. I have many trusted advisors, but perhaps it is time to see whether the vigor of youth could shed the light of a new perspective on the many concerns of the Kingdom."

You could have knocked me over with a feather. After a pregnant moment where I gathered my thoughts, intently aware of the eyes upon me, I found my voice again.

"Please excuse me if I do not drop my own formality when I address you, Your Grace. I would be honoured to do so."

"Good," said the King, smiling broadly. "Now, please go rejoin your fellows, Andrew. I believe Commander Cardiff has a few words to say to you all."

I walked back down the gangplank into the sea of yellow. Unlike the smiling face of the King as he addressed me, I saw nary a kind expression among the mob. I cannot imagine that they were happy that the slovenly son of their Commander was asked to sup with the King. I was happy with the offer, but the whole thing reeked of nepotism, even to me. Despite the seemingly unveiled hostility, the men grudgingly moved to allow me passage. My respite came when I nearly walked into my brother, who was beaming like the great amber orb burning in the firmament. I took my place next to him and he playfully whacked me in the arm with a gloved fist.

"Men of the Yellow Order," shouted my father over the noise of the harbour, having taken the King's place front and center on the deck, "we go now on a campaign. Unlike any of the previous campaigns we have set off on together, we do not fight to defend our homeland. We fight to defend the people of an alien land from an alien force. We do not do this because Thrairn is the weak vassal of Erifracia, despite what you might hear from red-robed traitors sneaking around in the taverns and whispering rebellion. We do this because we have an ancient ally in that great nation, and alliances need to be maintained through great sacrifice from time to time."

My father began pacing back and forth.

"I will not play mother to you and sweeten reality: the blood of your comrades-in-arms will soak the sand of foreign beaches, and a number of you will never see a dawn in Isha ever again. You may come to question everything: your orders, your Commander, your King. I need not remind you that you would be best served if you kept such questions to yourself. They are normal. These are the weapons of fear, needles which will try to worm their way into your hearts and consume you. The only antidote to such devastation is Faith, both in yourself and in your brothers. You are not here by way of accident, by base circumstance. You are here because you are Knights of the Yellow Order, tested in the crucible of your training and, for some of you, previous campaigns. I ask you to remember that you have been found worthy of the cloaks that rest upon your back. Do not dishonour the Order or your King.

"Most importantly... and forgive me for placing this before you, my liege," my father turned to bow curtly to the King.

"Most importantly, do not dishonour yourselves."

Unlike a certain horrendously sweaty and late man who arrived unarmed on a donkey, my fellow Knights had stopped by the armoury before making their way to the ships and were fully equipped with sword and shield. The longswords issued by the Order were appropriately utilitarian. Forged of steel with a simple guard, they each bore a black leather grip and a steel pommel which had been painted bright yellow. Beneath the cloaks on their backs and resting above the cloth of their tabards hung the kite shields of the Yellow Order.

One time, after several mugs of ale, I had heard my father

describe the shields to be in the shaped of a tear drop falling toward the Heavens. Hanging from a leather strap on the back of a Knight, a yellow Dragon of Thrairn snaked its way up to roar in profile towards the left of the man wearing it. The rest of the shield gleamed brightly with polished steel. Besotted with drink or not, I understood why father had waxed poetic about the beauty of the shield.

The men pulled their swords from their belts and the shields from their backs. They began clanging the flat of their blades off the shields in perfect unison. I looked at my brother, who had joined the fray. He returned my gaze, with a smile that looked like it threatened to split his face in two. The men added shouts to the pleasant metallic cacophony.

I was swept up into the frenzy and surprised myself when I whooped out my respect for the man on the deck of the ship.

Chapter Six
The Sudden Stop

After his speech had sufficiently blooded up the men, our Commander informed us that we were all to go to our respective ships. I had always assumed that, if I was ever inducted into the Knighthood, I would be fighting alongside my brother. Now that moment had arrived and he was a Dragonfly and I was a Butterfly. We were under the same banner but Fated to spill blood in two different companies. When my father informed me of my Fate, my initial reaction to the news was one of rage at the thought of boot-licking for William Rice. Now, under the morning sun in Isha Harbour, I was faced with a stark reality I had not before contemplated: I was to spend ten days at sea without seeing the face of my brother. My father was to sail on the Butterfly vessel with me, but his presence would provide as much comfort as a splinter from the wood of the deck. My brother, for all his insults and jokes, was... important to me.

I asked Gerard if he would accompany me to see Terence the quartermaster before we boarded. I did not share with him my feelings about his role in my life. There was no need. Gerard simply nodded in agreement and followed me over to a place on the dock near the pile of rigging where Terence stood, flanked by two donkeys loaded with saddlebags and a smattering of wooden crates with the tops pried off.

"Terence," I said, "I would like my equipment."

"Yes, my Lord," came his non-plussed reply.

My eyebrows shot up of their own volition. I had forgotten that I now outranked the man before me. I looked him over in my quickly assumed new light of superiority. He was old, older than most of the men in the Order. The majority of soldiers of his vintage were either feeding the worms on the Liserian border or retired to a quiet life in the countryside. Not Terence, though. He was a lifer.

He had white hair and skin that looked like it might cave in on itself before bearing another wrinkle. Dressed plainly, in old worn leather, a black patch was strapped around his head, covering his left eye with cowhide so weathered that it looked grey in the sunlight. It was rumoured that he had lost it at the training grounds as a Squire. He was never permitted to fasten a yellow cloak and raise a sword in war because of that handicap. A nobleman forever relegated to the role of quartermaster, subservient to each and every Knight, from the grizzled veterans to the jumped-up incompetents with Commanders for fathers. Not that Terence was any slouch in simulated combat. I had healed from a countless number of bruises delivered by him with the business end of a wooden sword.

I felt a small twinge of respect for the elder man then. A small twinge that I soon buried in a heap of impatience.

"Hurry up, Terence." I chewed the words as I spit them out, relishing that I could now say such things to a man who had humiliated me at the training grounds so many times before, even if my losses of face were always transmitted in the spirit of lessons from teacher to student.

A full suit of leather armour and a chain shirt were my Destiny in terms of attire for the foreseeable future. Once the Commander gave his first speech of the campaign, it was well-known Order dogma that all Knights were to be combat ready until he gave the other speech, the one at the end, the one that would bring about an end to our bloody duties. The beautiful jerkin my brother had given me would have to be retired for a while. Terence mutely handed me a leather satchel into which I could load the relics of my civilian life. I wondered aloud to Gerard at the necessity of having us sweltering in the armour while we were on the waves.

"We are going to fight pirates, are we not, little brother?" Gerard winked at me. He dropped his voice to a loud whisper. "Do not bellyache like that in front of Captain Rice. It appears you may have escaped the stocks for the voyage - Father could scarcely lock you in wood when the King himself invited you to dinner. If you cross Captain Rice, though, that bastard will have no problem dumping you in the drink and dragging you by rope from here to Erifracia."

I glanced away and uttered a word of unconvinced disgust.

"I will say it again, Andrew, for fear my words do not cross into that thick skull of yours: for the love of the Christ-man, mind your Ps and Qs. I would hate to hear that you found yourself lashed for that sharp tongue of yours... or worse." Gerard's eyes flashed with crazed intensity as he said those final words. Then he barked at me to pull on my armour.

I smiled at Gerard. Here he was, surprising me with kindness yet again. He proceeded to show me how to strap the leather of my breastplate together. Leather pants were sewn for me by a pair of seamstresses kept on retainer by the Order after the ceremony the day before, according to measurements that were taken at one of the monthly physicals that the Squires were subjected to by the Royal Chirurgeons. At least something worthwhile had come from those periodic invasions of my privacy.

My very own tabard billowing, shield on my back and sword on my belt, Gerard placed an object in the palm of my hand. My fingers wrapped around the wood of a handle. It was my mother's mirror, the one she used to use when she was getting ready to go out into public, whether it was to visit the market stalls or to a state dinner at the palace with my father. The grain of the wood that surrounded the piece of polished metal was very dark, almost black. On the back, a rose set in a circle had been etched into the wood and painted white, green and red.

"Gerard-"

"Take a look, brother," Gerard said, cutting me off and moving my arm such that the mirror was positioned directly in front of me. Getting the man to talk about Mother was pretty much a jest that meandered with us through our lives since her death. He would always interrupt me, change the subject or otherwise put a roadblock in place. I decided to play along, rather than kick up rancour. He was both my brother and my brother-in-arms, now. I had to respect him or lose respect for myself.

Or so it was said.

There I was, clad in the armour of the Yellow Order, staring back at myself. I did look sharp, like a man who actually knew how to swing the blade at his side. Still, I could see the fat little boy eating too many sweets beneath the grey, brown, and yellow. The fold of skin under my chin might have been much smaller than it ever had been, but it was especially disgusting to me then. I nearly threw the mirror onto the dock. Instead, I slammed it on a little table Terence had set up with armaments.

"Easy with that!"

"Take it back," I said, thrusting the mirror at my brother. "You were always her favourite. Take the damn trinket."

I felt hatred swell again. At the reading of my mother's Last Will, when Father's solicitor informed us that my brother was to receive the mirror, I seethed with rage. Out of all of the effects that the woman had, the mirror was the one that was always with her. It was the item that was most hers. And she had left it to Gerard. Yet another treasure for the boy who had it all. Now the man who had it all.

I stalked away from the quartermaster and my brother. My brother called out to me, asking me to wait. I could not exchange any further words with him. I knew that if I turned to face him, I would feel the hot sting of tears on my cheeks. I could not allow it. Not here. Not in front of Gerard, my brother whom I could not admit to myself that I loved. Not in front of Terence, the man who was more father than trainer to me. Not in front of my brothers-in-arms, who would further think me womanly than they did already.

Not anywhere.

Chapter Seven
Survival

The rest of the day passed in a blur. Walking up the gangplank with my stomach in a knot, I encountered a squat unfamiliar man nearing middle age. He was wearing an felt tricorner hat and leather vest. On his vest had been stitched a patch: a pickaxe crossed with a shovel in front of the field of a green kite shield, the badge given to the many civilians that worked in supporting roles for the Knights of the Coloured Orders. With a pleasant manner and a thick commoner accent, he introduced himself as Jason and asked for my name. I grunted it out, clutching against my belly the leather satchel into which I had stuffed my non-combat attire.

I was directed to a small cabin below deck, smaller even than the cramped broom closets that the men were given at the barracks. Four hammocks hung from the walls. A cupboard near the entrance opened to reveal a storage area that was divided into four sections by a brace of wide planks in a cross configuration. I could barely squash my satchel into one of the quarter-sized compartments. The ship builders certainly expected a spartan approach to life from the vessel's prospective sailors. What need does a Knight have for crass niceties like personal effects, I mused to myself.

"The King sweet on you, Andy? Sounds like he's buttering

you up for a slobbery knobbing up in the Royal Cabin."

The voice came from a man that had been lying on one of the hammocks out of view from my vantage near the door to the cabin. I nearly jumped out of my skin, awash in a fright that was quickly replaced with joy.

"Simon, you sneaky bastard! I nearly had a Gods-damned stroke!"

Simon Tomley was a few years my junior, one of my former fellow Squires. He had been at the training grounds with me for three years before he was called up to the ranks. His induction had not been more than six months before that morning we set off for Erifracia. A kindred spirit, he was another fat lazy slob of somewhat lesser noble birth who shirked his duties the way most men breathe. Much fatter than me, as it happened.

He was the closest thing to a best friend I had ever had.

Simon was lying on the hammock, hands clasped behind his skull. Still fully attired in his combat gear, his sword was standing in its scabbard against the wall next to him. A red beard grew thick on his face, running into close cropped hair of the same shade. He wore a pair of pince-nez spectacles that I knew were less out of necessity than an odd vanity that supposed they looked good atop his nose. He would never have been inducted into the Order if he really needed them, Baron's son or not. And he was thin, now.

"What the fuck happened to the rest of you?"

"A few months of the shite rations and labour from dusk to dawn... I guess that's the prescription for the portly among us."

Simon always used euphemisms when referring to the fact that we were, or had been, fat arses, a kindness that I never offered myself nor him. I had always maintained that he was deluding himself.

"Christ-man, Simon, you look like the rest of them now! A regular skinny James, you are. Good for you, brother. I, on the other hand, will be as 'portly' as one of the hogs loaded in the decks below until the day I die."

"Andrew! Christ-man damn it all, you'd best not start with your depressing rot already! Besides, your head is fucked. You would do well by a visit to the Psychoprobist. You've barely a fucking belly. Save your grey drivel for tomorrow, or the next day, when you're puking your guts up into the waves."

Simon made a bubbling noise with his mouth and cheeks, then sat up and mock retched over the side of the bed. I laughed.

"Regardless, with William Rice as your commanding officer," Simon continued, "you will get so badly shat upon with duties that there is no way you will be able to keep the extra weight on." As if processing what was coming out of his mouth at the same time that I was, Simon's tone changed and his face became suffused with something I had never seen there before. It resembled sadness. Or was it anger? He stared off at the blanket on the hammock across from him.

"Come now, Si, cunt that he is, there is no way he is that bad. What did he do to you, jam a stick up your arse?"

Simon's head swiveled towards me with great speed, his eyes open and his mouth slightly ajar. He seemed again to consciously recall something, at which point he closed his mouth and a smile unmatched by the expression on his eyes forced its way onto his lips.

"You wish! You filthy bugger. I bet the very thought of that is making you randy right now."

Simon grabbed at my crotch. I pulled away from him. It always annoyed me when he got on with these types of jests. Maybe it was growing up with a brother who had deemed the height of wit to be striking me in the cock when my head was turned, laughing like a hyena with his friends as I lay crumpled in a heap on the grass, sick and praying for the pain to pass. Maybe it was the ease with which the other Squires called each other "faggot" and "queer," as if it were the worst insult in the world. Maybe it was related to the time I was lasciviously

62

groped by another man at the Green Dragon whilst I had been drunkenly explaining to him the idiocy of the temples to the Christ-man and belief in God. I had run out of the establishment, right back to my father's house, and gone directly to bed.

Simon laid back on the hammock, hands folding and finding their way behind his head again. His face had taken on the colour of his hair, a flush that subsided within a few moments, as if it had never been there at all.

"So, a dinner with the King, then? What will you talk about? Great matters of state? Or will it be more your area of expertise?" Simon put on a formal accent that mimicked the posh my mother had drilled into me in my youth. "Perhaps your Majesty would like to know which taverns to skip for the sourness of their ale? I can also edify my Liege as to which whorehouses he might avoid because of the rashes their lovely ladies render unto one's cock."

"He probably wants my advice on how to rid the Yellow Order of the Knights whose sword arms are better suited to rubbing their knobs in the fields behind the training grounds than running their enemies through with cold steel," I retorted with a laugh.

✳ ✳ ✳ ✳ ✳

Simon and I spent the rest of the morning catching up. I had barely seen the man for more than a moment here or there since he was called into the Order. I understood from him that Captain Rice had been making him work extra duties because of a burning hatred the man had for the weaker amongst us. Rice bordered on obsequious with Knights whom he had deemed very much worthy of the yellow cloak, but for the less able amongst us he had naught but scorn. As a few hours slipped away and no one else joined us, it became clear that Simon and I would be alone in this cabin together. I was surprised, given how many men were sailing on the ship. It was a behemoth, but even the biggest ships in the King's navy have their limits. I shrugged it off. However it had occurred, I was happy for the respite from other people.

Around noon, I could feel the swaying of the boat deepen. Simon surmised that we were leaving port, and I agreed. My father had explained during his speech that we would be expected to pitch in with the sailing of the boat, but our duties would not begin until our second day at sea. We were to have a feast on the boat the night we departed, before the hard work began in earnest.

Well, those of us who did not become sick from the swells.

I watched as Simon went from smiling and cracking jokes to staring off into space with eyes of glass, his mouth puffed out and urging, to finally retching all over the floor of the room. Normally, the foul appearance or acidic stench of vomit would send me off into a fit of retching myself. I always found the expulsion of waste through one's mouth to be the most heinous of offenders when it came to the human body's less delightful functions. This time, though, I watched and breathed in the filth without even the slightest crinkling of my brow. I could tell that it stank, and stank bad. I simply observed it with a detachment that was novel to me.

"Christ-man, Si, what did you have for breakfast?"

I thought about following it up with a quip about the fact that he predicted this ignominious Fate for *me*, but I laid off. Simon could barely string together a response. I took another look at the mess. During our conversation before his descent into sickness, I had explored our cramped living space. Hidden beneath one of the bottom hammocks I had found a long-handled mop and a weathered old wooden bucket, sealed with grey pitch. I fetched the items and showed them to my friend, hoping he would find the wherewithal to clean his own vile excretion up. He took the broom and used it to prop himself up. His fingers let go of the pail just as soon as I handed it to him. Thankfully, the bucket did not land in the vomit. I stooped to pick it up. The grey pallor on my friend's face had intensified.

"I will be back in a moment."

I snaked my way through the extremely narrow hallway, up to the sunshine on top of the deck again. I breathed deeply of the salt air and smiled.

"Andrew Cardiff," I heard a voice snarl behind me. "Good to see you aboard." The voice dropped to a hoarse whisper. "Just you wait till the work starts tomorrow. I don't know what you did to find yourself wedged up the King's arsehole in this way, but you are my charge now, and I aim to make those soft fingers of yours bleed. Your 'friend' will not interfere with my rights as your Captain."

I spun to face the man.

Standing on the top deck behind me and leaning out over the railing, William Rice was wearing his battle gear, same as the rest of us, though with a considerable paunch that made my own fatness look like a bit of extra skin. Like me, he was not wearing a helmet. He was mostly bald, with only a short semicircle of black hair speckled with white around the circumference of his skull that looked a bit like the style of the monks of the Cistern Monastery, albeit suffered in a much less intentional manner. I am sure that William Rice would have ransomed his own mother for enough hairs for a half-way decent comb-over. Instead, he had just a handful of wisps that blew like a rat's mangy fur in the wind. The bone white pate beneath shone moon-like in the sunshine. A leathery mess of deep gouges and crow's feet, his face had the appearance of a raisin that had been left out in the sun for a decade. Watery grey-blue eyes blazed with hatred, and his scowl seemed like it more belonged on a dark-humoured caricaturist's canvas than reality.

"Captain Rice," I snapped my left arm by my side and my right one up into a salute, just as I has practiced a million times during my years as a Squire. "I look forward to serving under you."

Rice grunted and looked out to the sea. I suspect he was hoping for more of a rise out of me. I was glad to have denied him whatever base satisfaction the trumped-up cretin desired.

I turned around again. Whatever dark emotions bubbled up from my interaction with my Captain, I had my nauseated friend in the cabin below to consider. As I moved away from Rice, I knew that he was staring holes in my back. Where to find some water? I could not simply turn and ask such a simple question of that miserable cunt. He would no doubt take some ludicrous offense at the idea that I would debase a man of his rank with such a triviality.

There were others milling about the deck, but they all seemed to be sailors busy with the task of making sure the ship was doing the appropriate shiply things. I did not want to interrupt them in their duties. Perhaps another Knight could help me, I mused. I scanned around for yellow cloaks, making sure to avoid eye contact with the good Captain again. The only yellow I could see belonged to two men bent over the side of the vessel, no doubt suffering the same rotten infirmity as Simon below. Next to them, a grey-haired man wearing a striped shirt and blue breeches stood idly smoking a pipe. His face was even more wrinkled than Captain Rice's, with a grey beard covering up most of the creases. He had an enormous black patch over his right eye that made Terence's similar accessory seem that of a posing quibbler and there was something hanging around his neck, an unseen piece of jewelry below his shirt and attached by a length of twine. Intimidating barely covers it. I approached, faintly noticing the bucket smack off the side of my thigh as I marched.

"Excuse me, sirrah-" I began.

"I ain't no sirrah, me b'y."

"Alright. Well, then-"

"You can call me Willis. Nar, Willie. Most of the other lads on the ship call me Willie, dat dey does."

"Willie, then. Willie, do you know where I could fill up this bucket with some water? A friend of mine has gotten sick below deck."

The dry parchment of Willie's voice croaked out an abrupt laugh. "We're surrounded by da stuff, b'y."

I raised an eyebrow and looked out over the side of the deck. We were several dozen feet from the top of the surf.

"Sure enough we are, Willie. But I doubt I can dip this in that," I said, gesturing with the bucket to the side of the ship. "My arms aren't quite long enough."

"Christ-man somersaultin' in the garden, lad, did dey not teach you anything at your fancy academy for rich b'ys? Or were you too busy with all your swordfightin' for a bitta common sense?" Willie gestured to a coil of hempen rope piled on the deck between us.

"Tie that to that," Willie said, mimicking my voice as Simon had done.

"My accent is as posh as all that, eh?" I asked, picking up one of the coil and tying it around the metal of the bucket handle.

"You speaks as proper as the King he's self. Ya don't sound like you was raised in the Run, lad, that's for damn sure."

The Run was the Purple Run, the only slum of Isha. It was an ironic name. Purple is the colour of regents and that place was as squalid and hopeless and abjectly unroyal as any shitehole in the known universe. My own known universe, anyway. The City Guard barely had any presence there. My understanding was that they just made sure that none of the horrors, criminality, and poverty within escaped into the rest of the city. I had heard it was something to do with the Thieves' Guild, some trumped up gang Lord named Mad Derrick scaring the Guard into an arrangement that put an end to wanton bloodshed.

My mother, while she was very alive and I was very young, would tell me scary stories in the light of the dying hearthfire before I went off to bed. These stories mostly concerned cutpurses and beggars of the Run who would steal everything from a Lord's son and leave him naked in the street. Or the butchers that would cut up highborn little girls and spread pieces of their corpses throughout Isha. Just for being a member of the nobility.

When I asked Mother how they would know, she always replied, 'They would be able to tell who you are from the way you dress and the way that you speak.'

"I guess they would indeed be able to tell," I murmured.

"Whazzat?"

"Nothing. Nothing, Willie. Thank you for your help." I dropped the bucket into the drink and spent the rest of my labour in silence while smoke from the man's pipe invaded my space. If I did not blindly assume any better of the commoner, I would have wondered that the man was intentionally blowing it in my direction.

Simon's mess cleaned and him helped into bed, he turned over and away from me, breathing heavily with eyes closed in concentration. I returned to the hammock on the other side of the room, where I removed my equipment and decided to have a little nap myself.

★ ★ ★ ★ ★

I cannot remember the content of my dreams that afternoon, but I do know that I awoke in a cold sweat to the dinner bell. My body felt like it had been through a wringer. This was a different soreness than the bruises I had received at the end of Eric Wellan's practice sword, bruises which ached still. It was almost as if I had not slept a wink, though I had snored away the bulk of the afternoon. Was it a side-effect of Libélula's healing magic? Or, less pleasantly, perhaps the man was right about the curse?

That experience in the forest seemed to me like it had occurred years ago, even though it had just done so the night before. I rubbed my shoulder, where a gouge should have been, and marveled.

Simon groaned and turned over. He looked like he had not slept a moment, either.

"I do not think I will be eating today, Andrew," he said, groaned, then turned back to face the cabin wall. "Enjoy your courtship with the King."

The King! I had nearly forgotten about my supper meeting. And I had none of my personal items with me.

"Simon, do you have a mirror?"

I procured the necessaries of grooming from my unwell friend and prettied my appearance as best I could. I took solace in the reality that I did not have an option for dress - I was to wear battle gear. Even taking off my chain shirt and tabard the way I did for my nap was considered improper, a transgression for which I could have received a lash or two if Captain Rice had caught me.

Back on the main deck, the sun was bisected perfectly by the horizon as it made its way down and out of the sky, forming a semicircle and accompanying dusk. I scanned the deck, an enormous platform bustling with bodies summoned by the ringing bell. After a moment, I found what I was looking for. The white cloak of a member of the King's bodyguard. He was standing on the upper deck, beside a door on the port side. As I approached, the man must have caught a view of me through the narrow horizontal gap in his visor.

"Through here, Sir Cardiff," came a grave though helmet-muffled voice as the soldier pushed open the door. "Be very aware: we will be watching you closely."

The door opened into a large cabin. Inside, there were several sconces on the walls with candles burning, the wax below the flames at different stages of melt. Enough light was pouring in through the half dozen port holes on two sides of the room to make the candles unnecessary, though that was changing quickly. Wooden girders jutted from the ceiling and connected with the ribs on the walls, wooden supports that bore ornate designs etched into the grain. In the center of the room was a rectangular table with eight chairs perfectly arranged around it. The tablecloth was dyed a rich purple and upon it were placed carefully arranged white plates, shining silverware, and golden-yellow napkins. A large silver serving platter with a polished dome sat in the middle of the table, flanked by yet more candles. A couple of servants were standing at attention in the shadows near the back. Across from them, bunched in a corner, stood a trio of white cloaks. A low din emanated from the mouths of the people on the chairs, all swept up in quiet conversation.

At the head of the table sat the King. To his right, perched on a ninth chair that did not match the other eight, sat my father. The rest of the seats were filled with exceptionally well-dressed men I did not know, clad in robes and jerkins and other finery that I thought we had left behind in Isha. All the seats were filled, except the one immediately to the King's left. The King smiled at me and gestured to the chair.

A vice gripped my heart. I was to sit next to the King? Perspiration broke through the flesh of my forehead as I made my way to the chair and sat down. All of the voices ceased as if on command.

"Good evening, Andrew," said our regent.

"Uh, good evening, Your Grace. Father." I nodded at my Commander, who grunted and returned the nod.

"You must be wondering what you are doing here," continued the King, pouring out some wine from a decanter I had not noticed into an equally hidden glass and placing the filled crystal in front of my plate. "I certainly would be, were I in your shoes."

"That is a very accurate assessment, Your Grace," I said, with the best smile I could muster.

The King laughed.

"I was not jesting earlier, when I said that I would seek your input on matters of state. The men here at the table, they are those closest to me, members of my Inner Council. Your father is not technically a member of the Council, but I always find myself seeking his counsel nonetheless." The King laughed at his own joke. I remained mute, my tongue tied.

"Right to it, then." The King said, gesturing with open palm as he began to speak. "It was decreed centuries ago, when the Kingdom was founded, that the King of Thrairn must maintain an Inner Council, and that Council must be kept unknown from the citizens of the realm. Further, it was to consist of seven men, no more, no less. Every King in the intervening years has maintained an Inner Council with seven members. Seven - an odd number so that there can never be a deadlock. The King cannot make decisions of import, such as the institution of a new tax, a declaration of war, or the formation of an alliance, without the consent of a majority of the Inner Council. Fetters on the power of the King: one of the better kept secrets about the Kingdom." Again, the King laughed at himself, though this was less mirthful.

"One of the members of my Council, a Knight of your Yellow Order, died recently. Lord Reginald Quigley, bless his soul, perished not three days ago. One of the other rules: any time a Council-member dies, he must be replaced within seven days time. And so you sit before us, prospective new member of my Council. And a Yellow Knight, to boot."

The King stopped and stared at me for a few moments, long enough to make my skin crawl.

"Why me, Your Grace? Why not some other Lord? Why not my father?" I managed to croak weakly.

"You assume I have a choice in the matter. That any of us here have a choice in the matter. Aside from you, of course." The King laughed yet again, and it was definitely hollow this time.

I noticed then that the sun had fully set. Through one of the portholes behind the King, I could see the bright white light of the moon beginning to creep up on the horizon. In spite of how bizarre this evening was turning out to be, I felt a calm descend upon me, scattering the knot of fear that had bound up my chest.

"You can come in now," said the King.

A door in the back of the cabin flew open and a woman emerged from the dim light beyond. She was slight and small, and she wore a long flowing red robe that covered most of her body. A matching hood was pulled up around black hair, black hair that threatened to spill out over the alabaster skin of her face. Her features were delicate, yet simultaneously sharp and aquiline. Piercing emerald eyes stared out from the folds of scarlet cloth. There was something about her, some intangible quality that screamed power.

"This is Kathryn the Silent."

"Uh, Your Grace," I began, looking back at my host. The woman was beautiful, achingly so. But it was what she was wearing that gave me pause. I vaguely recognized the red robe as the garb of an unlawful sect within the city.

"Not all members of the Red Tradition are disloyal creatures, Andrew," the King responded to the unasked question. "We have to denounce those that wear the red robe and foment dissent and revolution against the Crown in the streets of Isha as rebels, impotent as those calls for insurrection may be. But there are many, like Kathryn, that do not take a political position. These are people that wear the red solely in private, so that they might do their work without drawing attention. And the work that they do is very important. In fact, you might even say that the Red Tradition is the glue that holds the Kingdom together. It is for that reason that I will only denounce the rebels, those cowardly wretches that take up residence in secret places within the so-called Purple Run, and not imprison or ban the cult altogether."

I looked back at Kathryn. She was gorgeous in a way that I had not before seen in the scores of women I had come across throughout my life on the soil of the Kingdom. The woman was staring at me with an intensity that made me uncomfortable. I felt cold fingers dance along my back, raising the hairs as I forced myself to keep from shying away from her.

"What is the Red Tradition?" I asked, returning to the King again.

I did not know very much about these 'rebels', as the King had called them, though I had seen them before. Once, when I was still a teenager, I had encountered an old grey-bearded man wearing a red robe in the street while I was walking with my mother. He had flipped a washtub and used it as a platform, or perhaps a dais, from which to shout. We did not stop to listen, but it was hard not to hear him as we walked. He sounded like a demented prophet, gesturing wildly as bracelets jangled on his wrists, screaming that the King was a liar and stole everything from the people of the Kingdom of Thrairn. The King was no better than a slavemaster and the people of the realm would be better off if he were deposed. The common people should be the ones in power, not the King and his nobles!

When pressed for details by the crowd, the man looked pained and could not respond with anything beyond platitudes, which angered some of those gathered.

Mother told me to ignore him and to keep walking. Still, some people were listening people of obviously lower social class than us. These were the throngs attracted to men like the red-robed crier, since what he offered was the promise of some form of equality. An equality that even I, young in my privileged position, knew not to exist in Thrairn. I remember well as the hateful stares that these people leveled at me and my mother. Fear gripped my heart and I asked Mother to pick up the pace. She simply looked down at me and smiled. Then she pointed to the dozen men with downward pointing crimson equilateral triangles on their chests, the symbol of the Ishan City Guard, standing at attention behind the rebel, right hands firmly gripping the hilts of their clubs.

"The Red Tradition is an ancient order of magicians, Andrew. Plain and simple. The Mages carry a power the likes of which the rest of us can only dream." The King gestured to Kathryn.

The woman raised her hands, placed them together in front of her chest as if she were preparing to pray, murmured something, then drew them apart. Flame licked at her palms, illuminating the room with a ghostly glow. Conjured flame would have been one thing, but the flame itself was an ethereal shade of blue that seemed not of this world. From where I sat, a half dozen feet away, I could feel cold emanating, sucking heat and pricking at the flesh of my exposed face. Then, as quickly as she had created the icy fire, she slammed her palms together and it was gone.

I had already been exposed to a miraculous healing magic at the hands of Ernesto Libélula, but I was nonetheless awed by the raw display of power that this woman possessed. Awe that was written on my face like ink on a scroll.

The King laughed, this time more happily. "Have we completely upended your world yet, Andrew?"

"This is incredible, Your Grace," I managed, forcing myself to turn my attention from the green-eyed sorceress back to the King. "But I am still not certain what it has to do with me."

"Everything," Kathryn said. Her baritone voice was like a deep silk that wound pleasingly into my ear. I looked up at her, but she had returned to a state of mute attention and was now staring straight ahead, apparently consumed by some point above the head of a rapt nobleman.

The King's habit of laughing at everything, which I found annoying at first, was quickly growing on me. He did it again and spoke.

"Kathryn is a woman of few words. Few, mysterious words. Allow me to illuminate them for you. You might be thinking: who even made the decrees about the formation of the Inner Council? The alliance between the Crown of Thrairn and the

Red Tradition is as old as the Kingdom itself. You might even say that the Red Tradition started the Kingdom. The Mages have influenced the major decisions of the realm since the beginning, including the makeup of noble families and the royal dynasty. None of the Aquester line had any say in who they were to marry. Even I myself, I was told by the Council that I was to marry Sylvia Redonius, whom you know as Queen Sylvia and mother of my two daughters. I make very few decisions myself. It seems the Council would even tell me to wipe my arse if I did not already do so on my own."

Another somber laugh.

"It is important to realize that the Inner Council rarely makes a decision for me that is not the decision I want to make myself," he said, his voice stilted. "And so I happily comply. I do admit there have been some moments where I felt like throwing the whole seven of you lot into a dungeon and taking control myself, fuck the Council." The King's voice became heavy as he spoke those last words. You could have heard a pin drop.

Then the King guffawed and all of the people at the table laughed along with him. It was the laughter of nervous men.

"But, the feeling always passes. Perhaps the Red Tradition has cast some spell of obedience on me, but I have long since abandoned caring about those matters. Those of the Tradition would tell you that the Kingdom of Thrairn has persevered as long as it has because every single one of my forebears has followed the dictates of the Inner Council without fail. You look at the other Kingdoms in our part of the world - Liseria, Erifracia - these are infant realms. Their predecessors collapsed under conflagrations of their own making, or in wars with Thrairn, or through some poisoned blade treachery that pitched them into revolution."

"Thrairn," said Kathryn, interrupting the King, "rose from the ashes of the Heraclytan Empire centuries ago. It has been foretold that so long as the Red Tradition and the Crown are unified, it will never fall."

"Alright," I said, feeling uncomfortable but somehow pushing forward nonetheless, "so you have a council, chosen by the Red Tradition, that tells you what to do. I understand that. At least, I do as well as can be expected. But, you still have not answered my question. Why me?"

"I honestly have no idea why you were chosen. I doubt even Kathryn could tell you."

We both looked at the witch. She shook her head.

"This is the power of Prophecy, Andrew," Kathryn said. "The elder Red Mages retreat into seclusion regularly in a cave at the top of the highest mountain in the Crooked Spears. There is no way to even reach the cave without the magic of levitation that the ancients of the Red Tradition alone enjoy. They spend twenty-four hours within the icy cavern. After they complete their divination rituals, they return down the mountain. Since I finished my apprenticeship, I was told to watch you, that great change would arrive soon you would have an important role to play in that which is to come. I spent over a year observing you. When Lord Quigley died, I let the King know that you were to take your place with the Yellow Order and with the Council."

"But I am an utter shite with a sword!" I replied, ignoring my skepticism about the Prophecy and horror that I had been watched by Kathryn for a year. "And on a horse. Rubbish with combat tactics, too. Just speak with Terence Indigo! I am one of the worst fighters to ever befoul the sands of the training grounds. Pardon the language, my liege, but now I find out that I am made a Knight solely because some old bastards in red robes pulled my name out of each other's arseholes? I have spent seven years in a state of failure as a Squire."

"And you might spend another seven years failing as a Knight." The King's tone had become very harsh. "Truth be told, I do not care whether you do well. You may very well take an arrow in the eye from a corsair on the way to Erifracia. If that happens, the Mages of the Red Tradition will just complete their divinations again and a new member of my council will be selected. But you are now offered a position on my Inner Council. And it is indeed an offer. You are permitted to say no."

With that, the King waved. A servant approached and pulled the dome from the enormous platter, momentarily fogging the room with a cloud of aromatic steam.

Kathryn nodded to the King, then turned to me.

"I know that none of this makes sense," she said. "I was where you are once. It is hard to suddenly accept the existence of that which you have been convinced was unreal your entire life." She bent to place her lips to my ear. Heat rose in my cheeks. "Do not let the Prophecy go to your head," Kathryn whispered. "It is no doubt true, but there is no telling what any of it means, even for someone who has studied at the Red Keep. I, too, was told I had a role to play. But I do not think myself any better than anyone else for it."

With that, Kathryn stood and placed her hand on my shoulder. She murmured something I could not make out and I felt a coolness descend from her fingertips, through my armour, and into my flesh.

I would say yes, I decided.

Chapter Eight
Devastation

"Knight Cardiff, get a mop."

Swab duty. It had already been five days at sea and every single one since the first had been spent mopping non-existent filth from the deck of the ship for the chimera of red face and spittle that was Captain William Rice. At least the first day I had an actual mess to clean up.

Good old Captain Rice thrived on spreading misery to the Knights beneath his command. I hated him so much that I had reached a bizarre intermittent state of serenity about the matter. I would not get angry with a wolf for his desire to consume flesh. It was his nature. How could I hate William Rice for being a stiff cock of a commanding officer?

Very easily, it turned out, as these brief bouts of serenity retreated quickly into hatred. But his pettiness did not bother me beyond a passing loathing anymore. I saw him for the sad old bastard that he was.

I walked to the small door just below the raised deck where the ship's wheel was located and retrieved the broom and bucket from within, listening all the while to Rice call off the roster of my fellow Knights in Butterfly Company. He took a while. We were 75 in Butterfly, and the whole of the Yellow Order numbered 300. Knighthood was indeed elite: at 300 each, the Primary Colours of Thrairn totaled 900 men across the realm.

In order for a new Knight to be inducted, a current one has to either die or retire. In my case, putting aside all of the bizarre discussion of a Prophecy, a middle-aged Knight named Reginald had perished of dysentery a week ago, puking and shitting himself to the point of expiration in a tavern bed while enterprising whores scoured his effects for coin. Now here I was, scrubbing the weather-beaten planks of the Holy Yellow Sailing Ship in his place.

The Knighthood system was completely fucked, of course. What would happen if a significant number of Knights suddenly died in battle? Would the Priests call into service a bunch of Serfs armed with pitchforks and crude breeding? What if the ships we all traveled upon were overrun with corsairs and the remnants of the Yellow Order were sold into slavery or executed on the bobbing waves? Where would the King and his Bishop get another of their holy 300?

And what of the Squires? Those poor bastards like my former self. The unlucky ones waited in the wings for years before one of the Knights died or retired and they newcomer could take his place. This cold reality was reflected in a tale that had wound itself through the training grounds during my years of failure. There had been a Squire, Walter Greenfield, who had thwacked his wooden sword off practice shields for nearly two decades before he was called into service. He was greying and almost into his fortieth summer when he entered the nave of the Blue Cathedral. The story went that, prior to his bittersweet redemption, he suffered nearly twenty summers of dashed hopes mixed with anemic and gradually more unconvincing explanations to fellow tavern regulars as to why he was not yet wearing a coloured cloak.

There were, of course, other options. First was the City Guard, those trumped up ruffians with a reputation for sadism. They enforced the laws of the Kingdom within the City of Isha, when they were not laying unnecessary beatings upon or taking bribes for protection from the citizenry they were sworn to protect. The pittance of a salary paid to them and active participation from their supervisors did not do much to dissuade such behaviour. Base commoners, the lot of them.

The other option was donning the White. There was no White Order, but there were plenty of men with white cloaks and fully visored helms in service to the King. They were called the White Guard. A step up from the City Guard, these were men who had dedicated themselves to serving the King at home in Isha as bodyguards and overseers of the King's Justice. They also were assigned to keep the law in the Thrain lands beyond Isha, where the City Guard did not roam. It was also not elite - members of the lower classes were permitted to join. All that was required was six months of training and an oath to the King. The pay was abysmal - only slightly better than what was paid to the City Guard - but the culture within the force was different. Perhaps it was that the white cloak did command a level of respect from the populace unknown to the brutes with the inverted red triangles on their chest. Not like that reserved for the Coloured Knights of Thrairn, but it was something.

Both were beneath me, as far as I was concerned. The City Guard for obvious reasons. Even wearing a white cloak meant taking a turn as a wholly uninteresting creature. Members of the White Guard were mostly illiterate and uneducated, the chaff to the wheat of the Coloured Orders. Peacekeepers, playing eternal guardians to a well-protected King or dealing in petty squabbles between lowly provincial subjects of the realm, white cloaks would never travel to strange lands on campaigns, unless they were called to accompany their liege in his travels. Present voyage excluded, the King traveled quite seldom.

The King. The man to whom I now owe my allegiance as a Knight. And as advisor. It was jarring, to say the least, this whole Red Tradition business. A puppet king led by a bunch of random citizens chosen by a smattering of old bastards with conjured fire between their fingers. I honestly thought it was some kind of practical joke for the majority of the time the King was telling me the tale, a kind of hazing or initiation ritual my father had put him up to. I stopped clinging to that theory when it became clear how elaborate the whole thing was. And that was without even discussing Kathryn's demonstration. The King told me I had a choice whether to join or not, but that choice was a choice in name only.

I was not prepared to turn down a shot at power. Real power.

After I accepted, the rules came out. There were only three. One: I was only to discuss the Inner Council at Inner Council meetings. I was never to talk about it with anyone else on my own, including my father, who had been watching me silently throughout the entire exchange. Two: I was never to acknowledge other council members if I met them in the street or in social settings. If formally introduced, I was to act naturally. But I was never to become publicly or privately close with the people. They were to remain strangers, preferably. Acquaintances, at most. Three: I was never to suggest to anyone that magic was real. As far as I was concerned, magic was make-believe.

The *real* kind of magic, anyway. Idle talk of sorcery was commonplace in Thrairn. The populace were quick to point their finger at neighbours with allegations of witchcraft, especially if it was a bad year for potatoes and the accused was a layabout. That kind of notion of magic was where the Church came in, declaring pogroms and slaughtering unlucky citizens and foreigners with abandon unfettered by the King. No matter how barbaric its actions, the Church of the Christ-man was seemingly given *carte blanche*. It was permitted to write all the laws that were to save our souls: against Witchcraft, Buggery, Apostasy, to name a few. According to Kathryn, the latitude given the Church was part of the deal between the Crown and the Tradition.

That said, anyone who ever dared to speak about the Inner Council or real magic was to be executed by the Mages of the Red Tradition, no questions asked. It is why the heretical members of their sect, those defrocked and exiled ones on their washtubs spouting dissent, only danced around the truth of what they were. The King and Kathryn were very clear: any literal suggestion of the reality of magic would be met with deadly force.

What if the heretics were to band together and challenge the rest of the Red Tradition, I had asked. It was Kathryn who responded then. Because they are kept in check, she had said. The look in her eyes told me all I needed to know about what "in check" meant.

It was around this time that I began to wonder whether "Kathryn the Silent" was an appropriate nickname for the verbose Mage.

In any event, that had been it. There was no council business at dinner, no poll to be taken. We had simply eaten our meal in silence. Before I left, I asked the King how I would know when the next meeting was. I would know, came his cryptic reply. And then it was back to my cabin that smelled of sick and rumbled with the snores of my old friend.

If it were not for the blue flame I had seen between Kathryn's palms, I would have simply chalked the entire night up to lunacy on the part of the King, perhaps a man falling victim to the scourge of syphilitic fever. But the power of magic was compelling. Truth be told, I would have appreciated an opportunity to further bend Kathryn's ear. And not simply because I felt myself drawn to the woman in a way that transcended a simple desire for discussion. Libélula had made me believe that I would be dismissed as a madman if I ever spoke about magic, and a day later I was inundated with talk of it. And so I wanted to hear what Kathryn thought about my encounter with the enchanted beast and the Atikan's healing magic. But talking about that felt... wrong, for some reason. In any event, the Mage did not stay for dinner. After she heard my affirmative response to the King's grand question and our discussion of the rules, she simply turned on her heel and left through the back door of the cabin.

"Knight Cardiff, get your fucking arse in gear. Right. Now."

My nemesis stared at me from across the deck. I was still standing in front of the mop closet door. The rest of Butterfly Company had scattered to the four winds, off to complete their menial jobs in service of the Holy Yellow Sailing Ship. I saluted the bastard and got to work.

✶ ✶ ✶ ✶ ✶

We were about a day's voyage from the Tunuskan port when disaster struck.

Our route took us along the coast, one that would see us avoid the squalls and storms of deeper waters. The trade-off, of course, was that we left ourselves open to the shoals and massive rocks that jutted up to threaten the hulls of vessels on their way to and from Tunuska. In order to make the trip successfully, the Order had hired an expert navigator, a seasoned old greybeard sea cat by the name of Willis Coulter.

Willie.

He had spent the majority of the days before the catastrophe in the crow's nest, sporadically shouting orders into the wind, orders which were picked up and repeated by a string of sailors on the mast and deck, all the way down to the ear of the man on the wheel. I was swabbing in the hot sun under the watchful glare of Captain Rice when one such order made its way down the line. From the corner of my eye, I saw the sailor on the wheel spin the thing to the right until it banged and stopped. A few moments later, a loud crash sounded and a good three quarters of the men on the deck were sent flying onto their arses, myself included.

From my new seated vantage, I watched as Willie dove from the top of the mast, arcing his body down with his hands outstretched above him. When he disappeared from view, I could not hear whether there was a splash by fault of the building din. Sailors and soldiers were shouting and running every which way: over to the side of the boat, down through the doors leading below deck, up the mast to get a better view. After a few moments, it became clear in spite of the chaos that the boat was listing.

Badly.

"We've struck a rock and are taking on water! Abandon ship! Abandon ship!"

The call came from one of my fellow Knights, another member of Butterfly Company promoted into the ranks not two months before I was. He had appeared from below decks, sopping wet and wild-eyed. Adam Canter, I think his name was. Like most of the other men, I had painstakingly avoided his company, though he seemed like a decent sort. He only spent a couple of years at the training grounds. Whilst there, he did not give me grief for existing: we simply did not know each other very well. The man was only a few feet away from me as he shouted his fearful refrain.

"Shut your fucking hole and get below deck!"

Captain Rice was nearly on top of Canter, shifting his stance to maintain his balance on the skewed planks beneath him. The officer's hand found its way to the hilt of his sword. Canter's eyes bugged out of his skull and he tried to move past his crimson-faced antagonist. He shouted again for everyone to abandon ship.

"You do that one more time, Knight Canter, and I will run you through." Captain Rice spat the words through clenched teeth. He was glaring at the novice, jaw set with eyes that matched Canter's in intensity, though they bore a boiling ferocity where the young man's face demonstrated only panic.

The ship heaved and the angle of the surface beneath us

became even more pronounced. We had all squat down into a crouch to avoid losing balance. The shouts from the other men on the ship became more frantic.

"Abandon shi-"

In one fluid motion, Captain Rice removed his sword from its scabbard, inched his squat legs closer to Canter, and buried the blade in the psychologically disintegrating man's belly. I could scarcely believe my eyes. If I were not so terrified by the implications of an officer killing a man for insubordination and the greater mess in which we found ourselves, I would have been frozen with shock. Instead, as if I were in the eye of a tempest, I watched the slaying with a measure of serenity, knowing I might be next but scarcely bothered by the notion in the slightest.

Captain Rice pulled the bloodstained blade from the man. Canter slumped to the ground. He looked like he was trying to speak. Blood started to dribble out the corner of his mouth.

"Knight Cardiff, are you going to get below deck, or do you need to be told a second time?"

I started towards the door, thankful that Captain Rice was going over to another pair of yellow cloaks instead of following me to the door below the upper deck. I was at the door when the ship shuddered again. The ship was turning on its long axis, threatening to spill us over the port side into the drink. I was nearly crawling to avoid falling. None I had seen had actually dropped over, but it was only a matter of time. The door to the decks below stood askew before me. Was I really prepared to head down into that death trap? I turned my attention to the water over the port side.

The sun was shining down from its zenith in a pure sapphire sky. The water was greenish blue, a much more inviting hue than the cold azure of the waters around Isha. We were in the shallows. I could see white sand through the water. Further away, dozens of sharp, black, angular rocks poked up through the seascape. I might have thought it the counterpoint beautiful, had I not been on the verge of shiteing my leathers.

That was when I noticed him. A man in a red robe was standing on a skiff about two hundred feet from our vessel. He had his hood pulled up over his head. Over the midday breeze, I could hear strange words emanating from the man. It sounded like the Heraclytan used by the Priests of the Christman when reading from their dusty old tomes. Then my eye was drawn to motion near the gunnels as Willie scrambled aboard.

My mind made the link and I recognized then that it was our former navigator's direction to the helmsman that had seen us founder upon whatever rock had smashed through our hull.

"Treachery! We are betrayed!" I pointed towards Willie's new ship.

After I shouted my warning, I met Captain Rice's gaze. His eyes were full of hatred, a hatred that I thought might see me run through for my own refusal to follow orders, a hatred that dissolved into wide-eyed surprise as they followed my outstretched arm towards the boat in the shallows.

"To arms!" Captain Rice shouted.

He drew his blade and moved towards the side of the deck. It was at this point that the sky grew dark. I looked up to see that a great black cloud had formed above our ship, blotting out the sun in its enormity and seething menace. Within crackled blood-red lightning.

To add one more element to the disarray, I then heard the doors to the cabins above me blow open. I looked up to see white cloaks crouch-shuffle out onto the deck, followed by the King. His embossed leather chest piece looked like it had been hastily applied. The sword swung at an angle from his hip. The hair below the crown was a mess. He must have been sleeping. Sleeping in a world where afternoon naps were permitted, a world where rules prohibiting the removal of battle gear during slumber did not apply.

"Captain Rice! Where is Commander Cardiff?" the King bellowed.

My father! I had completely forgotten about the man. And now that his life was most definitely in danger, all prior thoughts of my own certain death fled. In fact, I did not think. I just rushed towards the door to the decks below, unable and unwilling to do anything but try to get to him, no matter the risk.

"He is below deck, Your Grace!" Captain Rice replied, before shouting at me to hold fast and prepare to defend the ship from whatever witchcraft this red-robed interloper had prepared for us.

As if on cue, there was an unearthly tearing sound and Captain Rice's words were cut off. Bright red light exploded in my field of vision as lightning from the cloud arced down the mast, igniting sail and wood as it descended. Distracted, I lost my footing and tumbled toward the railing on the side of the ship. I feel certain that I struck my head on the way down, because there is a black hole at this point, a void where memory should be.

Chapter Nine
Amongst the Wreckage

An ungentle plunking noise woke me from my slumber. I soon recognized it as the sound of water dripping. I opened my eyes and sat up.

I found myself in what appeared to be a cavern, made of dark rock that was glistening with moisture and dimly lit by a half-dozen torches jammed into cracks in the walls. Large stalactites were clustered in the corner in front of me. There seemed to be a large pool to my left, though I was having a hard time seeing that far away from the torchlight. Seated on a piece of dry land that stretched out into darkness behind me, the appearance of my surroundings was of much less concern than the fact that my view was obstructed by metal bars running parallel and perpendicular to the ground beneath me.

I was a prisoner! And I was not alone. The cage was big enough for at least the other four yellow cloaked men that were lying in the gloom next to me. It was too dark to see their faces. Looking out through my confines, I saw more cages with more prisoners stretching back into the shadows behind me. I tried pushing the bars, in some vain hope that the cage would not be attached to the ground. A complete lack of give exposed the fantasy of that thought. I grabbed at my hip, at the place where my blade should have been. I laughed mirthlessly at my moment of naivete. Of course, my weapon had been taken from me.

Christ-man, what a fucking mess. I knew I should have accepted my father's offer to serve in the rear guard, feeding horses and slaughtering cattle. I might have found myself without the respect of my peers a cloak on my back guaranteed, but at least I would be at one of the barges at the back of the fleet. I perhaps would not have been picked off by a red-robed man on a strange tide. Now I was to be killed or buggered. Or both. My addled mind screamed that I would be subject to both. I felt hot tears sting my eyes.

"Whazzat? Cryin'?"

I recognized the voice, but wished I did not. The traitorous dog Willie. He was on the outside of the cage.

"Knight Cardiff. Ha! You know what? Maybe I don't give a flyin' fuck about titles anymore, Andrew. Andrew fuckin' Cardiff, the King's pet nobleman, cryin' like a babe. This is as rich as the King he's own self."

Willie was no longer dressed in his sailor's stripes. He had traded it in for his own suit of leather, albeit one that was much more worn and weathered than the ones that had been distributed to the Knights by Terence. In fact, it looked like the armour worn by the White Guard, quite a bit older than any I had seen. No chain lay atop the boiled hide, but a small sword, more of a dagger than a combat blade, hung from a scabbard strapped across his chest. He was still chewing on his fucking pipe. And wearing his big black eye patch.

"Why are you doing this?" I looked down at the fellow Knights in my cage. They were still unmoving.

"Why are you doing this?" Willie mimicked me, as he had on the deck of the ship days before. This time his voice boomed with the full nakedness of his derision. "Ye'll find out soon enough, me b'y.

As if on cue, another voice broke through from the darkness.

"Ah, first one of the lot on his feet. Has it said anything intelligible?"

"Actually, me Lard, I t'ink dis one survived. I found 'im cryin'. I doubt he'd be cryin' if he was raised up by them magics 'a yours."

"Perfect. I was hoping that a few of the drowned ones were not actually dead. They will serve as a little display for you, to show you what this sorcery can do in a combat situation. The issue should resolve itself within the next few hours."

I could not get a good look at the person speaking to Willie, but his accent told me all I needed to know about his high birth. He was yet another of the Ishan nobility, with a voice like one of the pretty boys from whom I spent my youth taking steaming mounds of shite. He even sounded my age. I saw the shape of him turn and move away, through a man-sized hole in the rock face, punctuated by a clomp of boots echoing through the cavern.

"Willie, please let me out of here," I whispered, my hoarse voice laced with abject fear. "My father will pay you anything you want. The man has been hoarding gold his entire life! Just name your price! I am sure it is much more than what that man is paying you."

Willie spat. "Just like ya fuckin' rich noble cocksuckers. Try to money your way out of it. What if the problem wadn't money, me b'y? How would you get out of the shite of life then?"

"What do you want, then? What can I do? What can I get you?" I felt tears running down my cheeks again.

"H'ain't fuck all you can do, me b'y. What he's offerin'," Willie pointed to the portal out of the cave, "you h'ain't got. So shut the fuck up, sit yer arse down, and wait for da fun to begin."

With that, Willie walked off into the darkness himself, past the portal. Straining my eyes, I kept thinking I could make out his figure standing up against a wall. I searched the rest of the darkness, trying to find other human beings to reason with. There were none. Spirit sagging, I collapsed down to sit against the bars.

Christ-man, I mused, returning to my narrative of self-pity. Here I was, a brand-new member of the King's Inner Council, about to become privy to all the secrets of magic of the realm. My opinion would count for something. I would help to shape the history of Thrairn, Hell, of the whole world! And Kathryn. I had been thinking about that woman non-stop, thoughts of her physical beauty and about the magic she might teach me. Certainly, the Red Tradition would permit the transmission of a few twiddly spells and charms to a member of the nobility in service as member of the Inner Council. I had already promised to keep the secret.

I had also been thinking about what this all meant for my station with Marissa Rice. I knew that I could not talk about the Inner Council, but if I could succeed with this shadowy seat of power, maybe, just maybe, I could succeed as a Knight. If I could do that, bedding Marissa was all but assured.

And now it was all fucked, thanks to a foul-tongued turncoat navigator with hatred for the nobility and his Red Mage master. I slammed a fist on the cage.

I heard a groan from one of the cells next to me, followed by the clinking of chainmail.

"Hello, is anyone there?" I whispered, praying Willie did not hear.

"Cardiff, is that you?" he boomed in response.

Rex Volstead. One of the biggest whoresons I had ever met during my time at the training grounds. Hell, he had been a torment to me even before that, when we were schoolboys. Rex was a couple of years older and took great delight in beating the living shite out of me every chance he got. I had tears of joy in my eyes the day I heard he was called up to be a Yellow Knight a few years before. Butterfly Company, of course. Through careful ministrations and excessive precautions, I had managed to avoid speaking with him since the day I myself had been inducted. That luck had come to an end.

Still, 'the enemy of my enemy' and all that.

"Yes, it is me," I said, whispering desperately. "Listen, Rex, there is something really fiendish going on here. I think there is more witchcraft to come. We need to find our way out..."

"What the fuck are you talking about, Cardiff? Where is Captain Rice?"

"Shh, keep it down. We are being watched. Now, have a look around your cage. See if there's anyth-"

"Ah, another one up," Willie said, approaching our cages and sliding his dagger from its scabbard. "And talkin' of escape already. Now, now, lads, ye will shut yer fuckin' holes or I will gut ya like the couple of rotten fish ye is. This is yer only warnin'."

Volstead did as commanded. He knew the language that Willie was speaking. He had been speaking the same tongue since he was a little boy. It was the miserable dialect of the bully. Part of me wanted Rex to keep talking, the little boy bearing all the bruises of his youth on his sleeve suddenly faced with an unexpected shot at revenge. The other part of me, with a mercifully louder voice, called for cooler heads to prevail. My own neck was on the chopping block, too, and, glancing around at the unmoving yellows cloaks that surrounded us, I noted that allies seemed to be in short supply.

Willie walked away, though he stopped closer to the cages this time, in view of the dim torch light. He would not be out of earshot for even a faint whisper.

Time passed. I cannot say how much, but it felt paradoxically like both an eternity and an instant. I am certain of what came next, though. It was a moan. A moan unlike anything I had ever heard before. It sounded like thick wet paper soaked in mucus tearing, opening a hole in reality and pouring skittering insects from the abyssal depths beyond. Given what happened next, that sound was as appropriate as it could have been.

Through the dim light, I could just make out another man on the floor of Volstead's cell stagger to his feet, yellow cloak wrapped around his torso. His movements were wholly unnatural, as though he was a marionette operated by a stinking drunk festival clown. He moaned his hideous moan yet again. I had already guessed at what was coming, based on the conversation between Willie and his master, as well as my blossoming acceptance of the reality of magic, but to actually see the dead man rise sent waves of revulsion crash down through every fiber of my being.

The creature began an inhuman shuffle towards Rex. There was no question as to its intentions.

"What the fuck!" Volstead screamed, a shrill womanish sound full of fear that would have given me great joy had we not found ourselves in such a Hellish reality. Instead, all I felt was a terrible fear for the hideous end he was surely about to meet. A black despair washed over me, as I knew my turn was next. I contemplated a desire to quit and lay down all hope threatened to engulf me whole.

Then, just as it had happened when the Jaguar in the forest was about to finish me off, a flash of incalculable iridescence, rainbow bright, exploded in my mind. It ignited a spark of hope - of rebellion - in the shadow of my mind.

"Fight him, Rex!" I screamed, grasping the bars between us and squeezing.

"I don't have my fucking blade, you fucking arse! And it's Kris! Kris, snap out of it, buddy!"

"You think that thing is your friend? Look at him, listen to him! He is a thing and that thing going to hurt you! Use your goddamn fists! I know you are good enough with them!"

The undead creature made its way over to my former nemesis and reached out with stuttering arms. Volstead shouted when it found purchase on the armour on his chest. It tried to pull him down onto the ground. In response, Volstead dug his heels in and tried to push the creature off. Undead jaws made to lock onto his forearm, but Volstead deftly avoided the bite. The bastard had always proved himself to be a picture of dexterity at the training grounds.

This was a little different than wooden swords and shouts from Terrence, I mused between my shouts of encouragement.

The enchanted creature kept its hold on Rex, trying to bite the man while Rex pulled and twisted, trying to get free. This happened several times over. The problem with the undead thing was not that it was quick, it was that it was erratic. I was having an incredibly hard time predicting what it was going to do next, an uncertainty that Volstead seemed to be suffering from as well. Nonetheless, the bully was proving to be worthy of the yellow cloak on his back.

He eventually got free of the creature, managed to wind up a punch, and connected with its face. The thing staggered, then kept coming. Volstead got another blow in, and another one. The thing was knocked to the floor of the cage by the force of the onslaught. Either fully in the throes of a blood lust, or not willing to give up his advantage, Volstead picked something up beside him and then began beating the creature's face in with it. Dark red blood sprayed up from the eye socket of the Knight formerly known as Kristopher Warren.

I was cheering him on throughout the battle. Curiously, I noticed from the corner of my eye that Willie had approached. He had not said a word. The Mage emerged from the portal and made his way over next to our betrayer, also unnervingly mute. He was so dimly lit I could not make out any details of his appearance. When I turned my attention back to the fight, I noticed something that made my heart sink.

"Rex! Watch out! Anoth-"

The words caught in my throat. One of the other dead men in the cage with Volstead had grabbed his ankle. It broke his attention from the fight with the shambling corpse, which took the opportunity to grab his left arm, pull, and bite down into the flesh above his collar bone. Blood spurted over the dead Knight's face, and continued to spray out in regular pulses.

When I was at the training grounds, one of the things that Terence instructed us on every week was the anatomy of the human body and basic Thrain medicine, that specialty usually reserved for the Chirurgeons of the realm. By way of justification, he told us that we needed to know the facts about our own weaknesses and those of our enemies, as well as basic methods of dressing wounds in the field. Given that I had listened to the boring old bastard drone on weekly for seven years about bones and blood vessels and splints and poultices, I could have written a test on everything the man taught us backwards and blindfolded.

The creature had punctured a primary artery, that was certain. Rex would be dead in a couple of minutes or less. I slumped down in my cage as my former tormentor's life eked out onto the stone beneath us, him screeching bubbling terror as the dead things began feasting on his flesh. Despair returned.

Then I heard a moaning in my own cage.

Chapter Ten
The Storm

The first one upon me used to be one of the older Knights in the company, a slender man with grey-speckled hair and dark, unnerving eyes. That is, they used to be unnerving. Now they were dull, vacant, and accompanied by a face equally absent intelligence. Knight Dalton had been his name. I had hardly known him, not even a first name. He was rumoured to be quite the lech, though, with appalling sexual appetites that kept him relegated to only the most adventuresome whorehouses in Isha. I wondered if the Red Mage's dark magic had left him any memory of who he had been in life.

He crawled toward me.

I shut my eyes. I was prepared to let the thing tear me apart. This whole life I had been leading - what a joke. No one had taken me seriously for twenty-five years, and now that someone - and not just someone, but the King himself - had done so, I was to be slaughtered by a dead pervert.

I thought of my mother, that beautiful creature who was taken from my life much too soon. I thought of my brother, a better man than me in every way. I hoped that the ship carrying Dragonfly Company had managed to avoid hiring a seedy navigator ready to toss those men to this evil sorcerer. I thought of my father, the man who seemed to think me worthy, despite all of my failures. I surprised myself in hoping my father was not subjected to the horrendous Fate of actually becoming one of these undead things, or worse, having to spend his last moments vainly trying to fight them off. I thought again of Kathryn and Marissa, how I would never be able to prove my worth to either of them.

How I would never be able to prove my worth to myself.

I felt a dead hand through the leather of my booted foot. Its fell touch brought me back to reality. The situation upended on itself again and I saw a rainbow flash in my mind as purpose blossomed in my chest like righteous heat. I could not wallow in despair and perish: I had to fight. So what if Rex Volstead had bled out ignominiously in his cage like a rat? I would not let myself go down the same way.

Rebellion burned strong in me for the third time in my life. This time, though, there was something different about it. For one, the familiar iridescence in my mind's eye did not dissipate. And the feeling was more urgent, more insistent, and accompanied by noise this time.

The sound was a buzzing that reminded me of a bee in flight, a bee that kept getting closer and then moving away in time with an unheard rhythm. Its oscillations served only to add fuel to the fire that raged within the core of my being. Each time it approached, I felt my body tense up, readying for combat. When it moved away, the intensity did not lessen, it simply set a new bar for my own ferocity. A ferocity that was as new to me as the sun upon a newly born babe's face.

I opened my eyes. The former debauched fiend had its right hand on my left boot and was pulling himself along the floor of the cave with his free paw. I do not think the necromantic magic worked as well on the thing as it had Kris Warren. Its arms seemed to be as effective as soaked bread. It flopped inconsequentially, though it did not release my foot.

I smiled. I could kill this creature.

I tried to stand, but it was proving difficult without full use of my left leg. Eventually, through sheer force of will, I was able to get to my feet. By the time I made it up, the thing had both of its hands on the one boot and was trying to pull himself in to bite my foot. I raised my right heel and brought it down as hard as I could.

The sole of my foot struck an ear and then glanced off down onto the ground. I tried again. And again. And again. My strikes were doing nothing, aside from threatening to throw me off balance and to the ground, where the creature would be able to crawl onto me. His teeth were about to close onto the toes of my boots. The frustration stoked rage.

My heart was on fire. The invisible bee buzzed close but rather than move away again, it continued towards the center of my skull. I closed my eyes and every colour I had ever seen, including ones unknown and which seemed impossible, showered my mind in a dazzling splendour that carried me off into a state of bliss that defies any attempt to reduce the experience to human language.

I wish I had a better memory of what happened next. I was told what happened, of course. But as for an account how it felt from my perspective, I could not tell you the slightest detail. The only thing that I do recall was that a sound emitted from my mouth, a sound that was not of my own volition nor conscious creation. Something else had taken control of my throat. It was a deep and powerful noise. One that I had heard before.

It was the growl of the Jaguar.

Chapter Eleven
Respite

"Andrew? Andrew Cardiff?"

The words echoed faintly in my head, as if the speaker were miles away, yet still they reached me. I tried to shift closer to their source. My eyes burned at a bright light beyond the lids and tears escaped through the corners. I was not about to open them.

"It's you! The King'll be pleased! 'e asked me to find ya!"

The voice was louder now, and familiar. I felt cold wet rock beneath my hands. I tried to push myself up from my position lying on my back. I managed to get up a couple of inches before I fell back.

"Yer injured! I'll get one a da Physikers."

The bright light, the man's torch, I realized, began to fade as it moved away.

I recognized the voice, then. It was Jason, the civilian who had welcomed me onto the Holy Yellow Sailing Ship nine days before. Well, perhaps nine. It might have been twenty. I had lost consciousness twice. All I did know was that it felt like an eternity since I had found myself on Thrain soil. I tried again to push myself up. My arms betrayed an exquisite soreness and were completely without Strength. It felt like I had been at the training grounds for a week straight with no rest. I allowed myself to slip back onto the stone.

My mind's eye started to rock back and forth in my head, as though I were back on the ship and we were experiencing particularly rough seas. It was a disorienting metronome, one that was picking up speed as the moments passed. The rhythm robbed me of consciousness yet again.

When next I woke, my body was surrounded by something soft. I felt around with my fingers. I was in a bed! Had my experience in the cave been nothing but a Hellish nightmare? Something brought on by head trauma when I fell from the ship?

Suddenly and without warning, a memory flashed into my mind with blinding intensity and perfect chronology.

I was at home in my own bed, on one of the pleasant midsummer mornings during the yearly month-long break from school. It was a mercy, being away from the bullies and concerns that would be waiting for me when the headmaster called us back into that boxy little schoolhouse to swelter for weeks as the rest of the hot days of the year slipped away.

During this period I was allowed to spend my days with my nose buried in books of my own choosing, instead of the boring old tomes that were force-fed to the noble children of the city by mostly unsmiling authoritarians as their pupils approached their teenage years. My own mother, bless her heart, never said a single critical word to me when I chose to spend sunny day after sunny day curled up on the fauteuil near the hearth, reading old tales about heroes and Dragons or modern stories of a future where horses had been replaced by steam-driven behemoths of metal and fire. My father always had sharp words for she and I when he discovered, whether through subtlety or express interrogation, that I had been at home reading while he toiled away at his military duties. I was thankful that my mother never gave in to his demands that I be forced to go outside and "socialize" with the dismal creatures that formed my peer group. When my father went off to the barracks in the morning, she would smile at me and ask me if I wanted to go to the library.

This particular morning was doubly exciting for me as it was my birthday, a day that was fortunate enough to arrive during the break every year. Unfortunately, my birthday that particular year fell on the weekly rest day, the Sun's Day. Some Sun's Day I would be lucky enough that Senior Knight Cardiff, as he was ranked then, would be out in some foreign outskirt of the Kingdom on campaign, but this was not one of those mornings.

"Andrew," he called from the threshold of the room. "Mother has your porridge ready. Come on down and eat. Daylight is burning. We need to get on our way to the pond."

Christ-man, I had thought. I had forgotten that my father had cooked up a plan weeks before that we go on a fishing trip together on my birthday. 'A formative male bonding experience for our troubled son,' or some such bollocks, was how he had explained it to my mother, unaware that myself and Gerard had been listening to their conversation from one of the doorways to the hearth chamber.

When my mother responded with the notion that it was my birthday and I might want to spend it the way I liked, perhaps reading, my father had become cross. I was not to be wasting any more time with 'that fucking claptrap,' he said. It hurt, hearing that. For my own father to dismiss what I loved in three harsh words. It might have pained me, but it also infuriated me. I was angry that he was such an uncultured boob with no appreciation for art or its purpose in a life well lived. I carried that simmering black emotion with me as the weeks passed and my special day finally arrived. There was no reasoning with Father, no matter how much I impressed upon him the joyous reality: Mother had gone to the library and borrowed the newest book written by Percival Spence in his long-running series about General Klarity's war with the goblins of Purth.

When I descended to get my porridge on the morning of my birthday, my father was all smiles. He was sitting before his own steaming bowl, having waited for me to join him before he broke his fast. I sullenly joined him and partook in the charade.

"You are going to love this, Andrew," he said, over loud smacking mouthfuls of the gruel. "There is nothing more relaxing than spending a few hours out in the quiet of the forest, listening to the birds chirping, waiting for a gentle tug on the line. Did you know your grandfather used to take me fishing, every Sun's Day? We walked the Verdant Glen, down to the Pond of Sacrifice - the same place we are going. The best fish are found there, you know..."

Pierce my fucking eye with an arrow, I had thought. The whole endeavour sounded as boring as the arithmetic lessons that Mistress Zona tried to drill into our heads at school for hours every Tiw's Day and Thor's Day. That is, when school was in session. It was decidedly not, and to have my short window of liberty impinged upon in this manner... how could my father insist upon ruining my twelfth birthday with this rubbish? I could not bring myself to say anything to him, though. He was my father, and it felt wrong to piss on his fervour. It probably would have sent him into a downward spiral of alternating snapping interjections and periods of quiet pregnant with dissatisfaction unexpressed. Not to mention that the mere thought of saying something dismissive to my father scared me worse than the thought of the goblins of Purth suddenly materializing outside our door, lusting for my blood.

And serious thoughts of imagined monsters danced through my head quite a bit in those days.

"What about Gerard?" I offered, vainly dreaming that my older brother could act as surrogate in my stead for whatever wholesome fiction Father expected out of the morning's activities.

My father glanced up with his eyebrows raised. "He left at

the crack of dawn. I am not sure where he went, but I think he told your mother that he was going to meet with Mitchell and Otis for the day. It will just be me and you."

Of course, he had. Ever the dutiful son, out playing with his friends as was 'normal.' What he wanted. What Mother and Father wanted.

After we had finished our breakfast, Father thrust a bundle into my hands. It was a pair of breeches that stopped just above the knee. "For wading in," he had said. After I struggled to get them on (the measurements that my father's tailor had for me were a bit stale and my sedentary life was just beginning to make itself known about my waistline), we walked outside, to one of the many outbuildings found along the outskirts of the Estate. Father came to a stop and hailed one of the Serfs who was standing with his shoulder up against the shed, absorbing some of the warm morning light through the bald pate on the crown of his head.

"Cyril," my father called, "good morning to you. Do you have those fishing rods we spoke about?"

The man grunted out something unintelligible, followed by a "miLord" that was only slightly easier to comprehend. He walked into the open doorway and returned momentarily with two long brown sticks with some sort of contraption near the handle. From an opening in the device, a thread ran up along the shaft through a lengthwise trio of eyehooks, out through one final smaller eyehook near the tip, to dangle a mean looking barbed fishing hook that glinted in the sun.

I know now, of course, that these were simply fishing rods. They were not especially fine works, but in my later years, I would come across much lesser exemplars peddled by merchants of questionable scruples in the alleys of Isha near the Purple Run. These rods were simple, strong, and utilitarian: fitting for the humble craftsman who had created them. To my newly twelve-year-old eyes, innocent of much beyond hatred for the man who gave me life and bearing a mind keen with imagination, they appeared to be some sort of magical device crafted by elves.

"Thank you, Cyril." My father handed the Serf a small leather bag with a drawstring around the top that clinked with coin as it was passed. Cyril poked his fingers into the top, spread them, looked inside, then looked up at my father with eyes wide. He muttered something again and shook his head.

"I insist, my friend. You do fine work for your family and for mine and you deserve to be properly compensated. Now," my father continued, turning to me, "Andrew and I are off to put your handiwork to good use. Enjoy the rest of your day, Cyril."

And just like that, we were off.

During our walk to the pond, Father never said another word to me. I had resented him that, I realized during this recollection, awake in that alien bed. He was a man of so few words, and I was a boy of so many. He could have said something, anything, and perhaps that would have deflated the ire that was building in my young and flabby chest. I spoke to my Mother frequently, and when I did, she hung on every word and even exchanged a few of her own when she could get one in edgewise. I was, of course, quiet around my peers. Whenever I thought to speak up in class at school or make friends with some of the other Lord's sons, I lost command of my tongue and felt an insurmountable burning in my cheeks. The same thing happened when I even thought of approaching Marissa to talk to her.

Marissa. I could not hate her for the way she made me feel, but I had blamed those other boys for my cowardice, for the reminders that they bore simply by their presence. I realized then that self-loathing was wrapped up in the feelings I had for my peers, that perhaps my hatred for many of the strangers in my life was less about them and more about me. It was easier to despise than to face the notion that I was weak.

My father, too, he would not let me forget. Every easy step

he took, every kind word he uttered, every time he took charge of a situation completely unbounded by any second-guessing or compromised confidence. Even that morning, paying the Serf much more than he was owed. The out-of-character largesse. The bastard was tight, except when it came to giving people money so that they would like him.

At least, that was the way I felt about him as a boy.

By the time we made it to the pond, a storm cloud had settled over our heads, out of place in the bright sunshine of the Julian Month.

"Now, Andrew," Father began, handing me my rod, "there are several things you need to know about fishing. The first is bait..."

I stood there, silently fuming, listening to my Father drone on about the niceties of getting a fish to bite the hook at the end of the stick. I was young enough that I had not yet developed the craven assertiveness I later used to bar the way for the man, wretched Courage that might have seen me declare unequivocally that I was bored of the whole endeavour and was going to retreat to the house to read my new book. So, I stayed. But I certainly did not make any efforts to convince him that I was enjoying myself. My father refused to take the bait that I offered him, standing with two hands on his rod and beaming with a smile while I hunched over, scowling, and lazily flicked the line into the pond.

"There will come a day, Andrew," Father said after a few interminable hours of this torture, "when you will wish you had taken the time to enjoy the fruits of life more. It is all well and good to enjoy what you love, and it is clear to me that you love those books of yours, but you have your own story to write. It will be a sad tale indeed if you stay forever friendless and shut into the house."

At the time, I had silently raged at him for his patronizing tones at my twelve-year-old self. As I lay in the strange bed in a strange land those thirteen years hence, I reflected upon the

Wisdom of his words. I was on an adventure. Though I had come to the brink of death on two separate occasions, the past two weeks had been days of living: true living. Even if it was under the command of a terrible cunt of a man and sharing a room with a seasick best friend. I wondered how I had muddled along before then.

I opened my eyes.

Chapter Twelve
Whetstone

I found myself in a large room made of rough, off-white stone, on a simple bed that looked big enough that four people might be able to share it comfortably. On the walls, sconces with unlit candles jutted at even intervals near the ceiling, except where they were interrupted by a large open window to my right. From my vantage point on the bed, all I could see through the opening was the blue of the sky, which was cloudless and bright enough to indicate that the sun was shining at its apex, or very nearly so. On the wall opposite the foot of my bed, the portrait of some unknown dark-skinned fop dressed in a ridiculous doublet stared intently at me from its location above a small fireplace. To my left was a large wooden door, with ornate patterning like that upon the paisley cloaks in fashion with the nobility back in Isha carved deep into the ebony grain. The leather and chainmail that had been glued to my flesh for the entirety of the journey thus far was sitting neatly on a green upholstered chair with a matching footstool.

I drew the single thin sheet that had been draped across me off and stood up. The limited bed clothing came as no surprise when I felt a warm breeze blow in through the window and kiss my naked flesh. I looked down.

Shock, then. Where once there had been soft pudginess,

only hard muscle and sinew was showing beneath the skin of my abdomen. I knew I had been losing weight at a steady rate when I was on the ship, with its manual labour and bland food. I had been looking forward to a day when I would be as skinny as Simon had become. I did not expect things to happen so soon!

I realized then that I had no idea how much time had passed since the shipwreck. How I had escaped the Mage's prison was a question whose answer was equally unknown to me. As gratifying as the disappearance of the fat on my body that had dogged me since the days of my misspent youth was, I had more pressing concerns. First, to determine my location. I dropped my feet over the side of the bed and approached the window, noticing as I did that whoever had undressed me had enough of a sense of shame to apply an unfamiliar pair of linen skivvies.

The building I was in was perched high up on a hill overlooking a cove surrounded by high cliffs which jutted out into emerald water. My room was even higher still from the base, maybe five or six stories up. Little houses made of what looked to be the same off-white stone of the chamber and topped with roofs of thatch and dark lumber dotted the landscape that angled down as it approached the water. The houses higher up on the hill had large swathes of land that looked to be tilled and planted. The closer they got to the water, the more densely homes were packed together, coming together ultimately into what looked like a bustling port city with a large harbour and docks at the cove's edge. Based on the size of the bed, the size of the room, the fop on the wall, and how dizzyingly high up I was, I deduced that I was in the city's associated castle.

It had to be Tunuska! By the grace of whatever God or Gods alternately offered boons and fucked mortals with a capricious glint in their watchful eyes, the mission had not been utterly ruined by Willie's betrayal. I looked back down at the docks. It was filled with barks and skiffs and bigger ships, with sails obscuring a great deal of it. That said, it was easy to spot three grand sets of yellow sails and I felt some further measure of relief – it had only been Butterfly Company's ship that had been destroyed!

I picked up my armour and dressed myself, heartened. The clothing was loose, but not as loose as I had expected. Had I less weight to lose than I had dreaded? Or had I simply not appreciated how much seven years of training had done for me, drinking and whoring be damned? Perhaps Simon was right: perhaps my view of my own body was somehow warped when compared with reality. I noticed then that my sword was not amongst my effects. I hooked an empty scabbard onto my belt and felt as naked as I had when I woke up. It felt good to drape the yellow from my back again, but I knew it would not be long before I started to swelter as I had on the ship in the hot sun.

I went to the door, grabbed the large ring that formed the handle, and pulled. It did not budge. I tried again, digging the heels of my shoes into the stone and giving it a good haul. There was not even the slightest creak. I tried pushing then, though I could see the way the hinges to my left were set up and knew that the door simply did not open that way. I then put a fist up to the door, preparing to call out to whoever was beyond.

"Stand clear!" came a voice from behind the threshold, accompanied by the metallic clang of a key in a lock. It was my father's voice. I did as he commanded, just barely avoiding the several inches thick wood that swung open to reveal my Commander flanked by two men in white cloaks. The door banged against the stone with a smash.

"Sit down." My father said, pointing to the chair. His voice was tight and hoarse, as though he had been yelling all night. The look in his eyes told me all I needed to know about the Wisdom of trying to protest. I complied.

He just stood there, several feet away from me, watching me intently. I noticed then that the white cloaks had their hands on the grips of their swords and were eyeing me with the same look my father had on his face.

"What are you?"

I looked at my father, my mouth agape. After a few moments, I found my words.

"Your son?" I proffered, more question than statement.

"My son. My son, the boy with so much squandered potential, the one who finally appeared to be making something of himself? Or some foul beast in sheep's clothing?"

"Father," I said, suddenly feeling very alone. Tears began to make their way into my eye sockets, "what are you talking about? I am your son!"

"I watched you. From one of the prisons. I watched you scream encouragement to your comrade before he fell dead to some necromantic monstrosity. I felt great pride at your spirit, even though I knew that the young man's death meant that all of us that survived him were doomed to be eaten alive by dead things. Then, when you found yourself in combat with a corpse of your own, you shapeshifted into a terrible black beast of unspeakable ferocity to tear rotting flesh from bone. That was not sufficient, however: your witchcraft-stained heart was compelled to rend each and every one of the other men in your cell to bits.

"Not all of them were dead," my father said, his tone dropping in volume, "but you already knew that. Did you care when one of your comrades-in-arms lifted their arms and screamed for mercy? It mattered to you not one whit, that was as clear to me as was the spray of blood onto the stone of that cave. All you cared for was a lust for carnage of the type reserved for Demons. A black furred Demon from the pits of Hell."

My father crossed himself then. It was the gesture used by the Priests of the Christ-man. I took it to be a bad sign. He was anything but devout.

"You are no son of mine." My father's words echoed in the

chamber with some finality.

"Father," I said, "I did not know-"

"How long have you been hiding your true nature? Who is paying you? Are you in league with those that took us? What is your goal? Is it the King's throat?"

My father had pulled his blade from his scabbard. In a moment it was less than an inch from my throat. My father's hot stinking breath caressed my forehead.

"You may be my son," he whispered, "but I will do my duty to the Crown."

"Please, Father, I am as confused as you are!"

Something must have reached him, deep as he was in his pit of fear. To this day, I am not sure what did it. It may have been the desperation in my voice or the truth in my eyes. His threat may very well have been a bluff all along. Whatever the cause, the man withdrew his blade and placed it back in its scabbard. He reached out and tore the yellow cloak from my back. Then he ripped off my tabard at the shoulders and gathered the garments up into a ball.

"You are no longer a Knight of the Order. You will not be meeting the King again. Not now, not ever. Your work with the Inner Council is done. You are to be quarantined, until one of the King's red-robed pets gets here and decides your Fate. You are lucky that you are not on your way to the gallows this morning. If it were up to me, I would see you exiled from Thrairn forever."

My father turned to leave. The white cloaks filed out ahead of him. I somehow managed to find the Courage to speak, amidst all the darkness.

"How did we escape?"

He did not turn to face me.

"We did not escape," he said, after an interminable moment. "Your brother and Dragonfly Company found the shipwreck and managed to track us to the Mage's lair. He escaped, but true Yellow Knights put the dead men to the sword."

"And what of the red-robed man? Did you find out who he was?"

My father whipped around.

"No. Do you know? Are you in league with him?"

"No, Father, I have never seen him before. He tried to kill me, along with the others. I met another Mage, before we left Isha-"

"Bah, magic, I have no fucking interest in it. It is a coward's vocation," my father said, taking on the same cold and dismissive countenance I knew for so many days of my youth. He turned again. "If there is any truth to what you are saying, the Red Tradition will get to the bottom of it. By whatever means it must."

"Wait, Father, would you just listen-"

The door slammed in my face just as abruptly as it was thrown open. I smacked the wood a few times with an open palm, then walked to the foot of the bed and jumped on.

The passage of time slowed and I found myself swimming in a black abyss.

$$\bigstar \ \bigstar \ \bigstar \ \bigstar \ \bigstar$$

"Andrew?"

The question came from a voice beyond the door as the sun was going down. It was preceded by a series of knocks. It opened and Simon appeared at the threshold, wearing his Knight's armour and unnecessary spectacles. Before he could step in, visored white cloaks entered before him and took their places next to the door.

"You can leave us now," Simon said, turning to the men.

"Our apologies, Sir Tomley," said one of the men with hidden faces. "Commander Cardiff's orders."

"Fine, stay then," Simon said, sitting on the chair as I sat up in bed. "How are you doing, Andrew? You alright?"

I stood and crossed to the man. I embraced him where he

sat. He laughed and gave me a couple of pats on the back before pushing me off of him.

"A fucking cat, Andrew?" he said, laughing as I took my place at the side of the bed. "First this magician turns the sky black with red lightning, then we are imprisoned, then dead Knights rise from their eternal slumber to attack us, and then you turn into a cat? Our lives went from dreadfully boring to incomprehensible in a series of hours. I thought I knew you well!"

I laughed myself. It was indeed absurd, and it would be even funnier if it were not true. But the memory of my recent interaction with my father poked in and sobered me again.

"I have no idea, Simon. I was attacked by something similar myself, on the night before we left Isha. Another magician, one from Atika, saved me from the beast and healed my wounds with magic."

"And you didn't think to say, 'hey, Simon, listen to this? Magic is real!'"

"I could not," I said, turning my eyes to the floor. "I made a promise."

"A promise," he said, incredulous. "To who?"

"'To whom,'" I replied, unable to stop myself in spite of the gravity of the situation.

"What?"

"Never mind. Look," I said, returning my gaze to my friend. "I cannot talk about it now. Given what occurred, I think that all secrecy around magic is coming to an end. But I cannot talk to you about it until I confirm something with someone. I can tell you that none of it was intentional, that I did not even know I whatever that transformation was in me until my father told me about it just now."

"This cloak and dagger shite doesn't become you, Andrew," Simon said, frowning and waiting a moment before continuing. "Alright, have it your way." Simon paused again. "Your father: was he pissed?"

"You are Gods-damned right he was," I replied. "Do I look like I have a yellow cloak? Look at my tabard!" I pointed to the remaining piece of torn material on my chest. I paused for a moment. "Who did I kill?"

"You mean he didn't tell you?"

We were interrupted then. A knock came and the door flew open. The white cloak standing on the wrong side of the doorframe barely got his hands up in time to catch it. A red-robed head with black hair spilling from the opening at the bottom of the hood poked past to look at me. There was no fear in her eyes, only curiosity.

"Andrew?"

"Kathryn," I said, sitting back on the edge of the bed. I was too exhausted from grief to put on a show of manners for the woman. "I suppose you would like to examine the freak. Please, come in."

Kathryn came in, bearing a burning candlestick and accompanied by another pair of men in white cloaks. She turned to them and pointed to the door. "Out." Then she pointed to the men who accompanied Simon. "You too," she said.

"But, Mistress-"

Kathryn looked at the visored men in a way that I hoped she would never look at me. They glanced at each other, shrugged, and exited, letting Kathryn know they would be just outside the door. Kathryn then turned to Simon.

"Excuse me, sirrah," she said. "You will have to leave."

"Whatever you have to say to me, you can say to him." I said.

"You know that is not true, Andrew," Kathryn replied. "Or have you forgotten your vow already?"

"You think that still stands? After all of the examples of magic-"

"You are treading dangerous ground, Andrew," Kathryn said tersely. "Though I might be a Novice, I am still a Red Mage as well, and I am well-positioned to execute standing orders to maintain the secrecy of what we do. This may change, given what has occurred, but as of right now, your friend cannot be present for this."

"Simon," I said, "it is alright. When I am freed of this place, I will come and find you."

Simon rose and brushed his lengthening red hair from his face. "What the fuck happened to the world? I won't shite you, Andrew. I'll probably be at one of the brothels on that list the King gave us." he muttered, giving Kathryn a wide berth as he exited.

Kathryn made sure the door was shut, sat down on the chair, placed the candlestick on the floor between us, folded her hands over a crossed pair of legs, and looked at me expectantly. Her eyes pierced me to the core, just as they had the night I met her on the ship.

"If you want an account of what happened down in that cave," I said, feeling compelled to speak by the silence. "I cannot give one. Not one that makes any sense, anyway."

"Do not worry. The Red Tradition is not ignorant of this kind of magic. We have some knowledge of men that transform into beasts. I myself have personal experience. The scourge of lycanthropy is nothing new."

I waited for her to continue. She did not.

"That is it? 'The scourge of lycanthropy is nothing new'? That is really all you are going to say? I have no memory of what happened, but I am told I killed a man. My father just stripped me of everything that I am and disowned me. Perhaps you might offer more?"

"What else would you have me say? I informed your father that this was a type of magic that renders the victim unconscious while transformed, that you could not be truly held accountable for what you did because it was involuntary, that we should try to understand how you were infected, rather than kill you or exile you."

Kathryn sighed and shifted back in the chair. "He is as stubborn as he is resolute. Unlike the King, who celebrates the secret of magic, your father views what I do as a necessary evil. Necessary only because the King deems it so and he is a loyal countryman. If it were up to him, every single member of the Red Tradition would be dangling from a hangman's knot. He saw you tear out the throat of his friend and lap blood from the wound. Your father knows you hated the man and he is certain that there is more motive there than truly exists."

"His friend?"

"Captain Rice. He was in the prison cage with you."

My heart sank. William Rice... I did hate him. I wanted to take joy in the news of his passing. But he was indeed my father's friend and, more importantly, he was the father of the woman I lusted after. Marissa. Once she heard the news, any chance that I had with her would evaporate into the ether. My unrequited desire for her flesh would never be satisfied. She would undoubtedly come to despise me the way that I did another man...

The one who slew my mother.

I stood and walked to the window. The last of the sun had disappeared behind the water. Lantern lighters were making their ways through the streets of the city and up the dirt paths to the farmhouses, dodging the strange beasts of burden and carriages that were no doubt taking the younger crowd into the public houses for their first pints of the evening. I was reminded then of Isha, of the childhood that I had left behind.

"What now?" I asked, keeping my back to her.

"Now," Kathryn said, "now you will tell me how you came to be possessed by this curse."

And so I did. I told her about my encounter with the Jaguar, with Libélula, his healing magic, how he had asked me to stay until the full moon had completed its cycle and say his incantation.

As I told my tale, Kathryn's brow receded into a furrow.

"This is bad," she said, when I finally finished.

"That is it?" I shot her a scathing look. "I know 'Kathryn the Silent' is a nickname, but you could give me more than that!"

Kathryn sighed. "I am not overly familiar with Atikan magic, but I have studied it to some extent. Our magic, the magic of the Red Tradition, the magic of Thrairn - it is a magic separated from Faith. Yet nonetheless dependent upon it. This might make little sense, but I will try to explain the nature of magic to you.

"There is a reason that the Priests of the Christ-man are given such a wide berth in our country, despite the abuses of power and position that are as clear to all with half a working brain. Their work sustains us Mages of the Red Tradition. That is not to say that many of us in the Red Tradition are as bound by the dogma and ritual with which those Priests are enamoured. The Christ-man is a symbol, nothing more, but it is the Faith of the people that worship him that matters. Think of the dead god as a lightning rod, one that gives power to our magic. We are forever bound to what the people believe and our magic is a reflection of that. For all their idle talk of witchcraft and superstition, our people believe in what is plain to see in the physical world: raw elemental power - fire, lightning, ice. And so the Red Mages have mastered the power of the elements.

"This all stretches back to the Heraclytan Empire, to the actions of a man named Emperor Traximus. He did something to the fabric of reality. He opened a Rift, and this allowed Chaos to seep in. Everyone was able to wield magic in the result, which meant pandemonium. The Red Tradition closed this Rift through rituals of Order, and that is why dogma and ritual are necessary. The further away from the sealed Rift one stands, the easier that one might learn how wield magic absent these rituals and dogma. Erifracia is too close to the Rift, and so the rules of the Red Tradition apply here. There are tales of great magic learned by simple self-reflection in the far off lands of Atika and Kashya... but perhaps this is too much detail. Suffice it to say that the Red Tradition's magic is of a practical, ordered, elemental sort and it is fixed."

"This is the law of magic in our universe," Kathryn continued, unclasping her hands and letting them come to rest upon the arms of the chair. "It blooms where it is planted. But Atika - this is a wild country. It is a place of villages and rivers and jungles and terrible beasts and plagues. It is a place where survival is much less guaranteed that it is in Thrairn. In Atika, they have their own Priests. Ones that they call Seers. Men or women, as shocking as that might be to one raised in the tradition of the Christ-man. These Seers do not worship the Christ-man. Most of them have never even heard of him. Instead, they worship the jungle itself, as well as the creatures inside. These Seers believe that everything - from a palm tree to a frog on its leaf to the dirt it grows out of - has a spirit. And they call upon these spirits to weave their magic.

"Unlike in Thrairn," Kathryn said as she stared unerringly into my eyes, "there is no split in duties in Atikan magic, no Priesthood coupled to an order of Mages. Instead, the Seers play both roles: cleric and magician. The spells that they cast reflect this. There is an element of divinity woven within the magic of the Atikan Seer, an element that is absent our own magic. Like the power to heal. Our magic is very secular, utilitarian. It can be used to perform great feats of elemental destruction, but it must be hidden because knowledge of its existence would clash terribly with the dogma of the Christ-man's church, which it paradoxically needs to survive." Kathryn paused. "Does any of this make sense to you?"

"In a manner of speaking," I lied, having lost the thread of understanding some minutes before. I was certain now that 'Kathryn the Silent' was an ironic joke. "So what are you trying to say to me about this curse?"

"Well, for one thing, I cannot help you get rid of it. My

magic is Thrain. And it is somewhat limited. Each of us has a specialty from which we cannot easily stray. I am a novice and can only conjure the frostfire that I showed you the other night on the ship. I could put together a draught from the herbs of Thrairn that would stop your blood from poisoning from a rotten wound. If you were bitten by a lycanthrope from Thrairn, a wolf or a badger man, I might be able to help you remove the curse. But this wound is deeper. It cuts to the quick of who you are.

"You need to find this Ernesto Libélula again," Kathryn decided. "That is, if you wish to rid yourself of this magic. The magic of Thrairn - we may be able to help you learn to control it. Indeed, Thrain magic is rooted in control, so extreme is the influence of Order near the Rift. You could become a very powerful man, if you were in control of this thing."

As if on time with the end of Kathryn's words, the door flew open again. This time it was the King, rushing in. Instead of his battle dress from our time on the ship, he was clad in a traditional purple jerkin and green hose. Soft white felt shoes were on his feet. One of his crowns was perched on his head. Like all my visitors, he was flanked by two men in white cloaks. My father was trailing behind him.

"Your Grace, if you would just-"

"Silence, Peter," he said, looking at me with inquisitive eyes. "Kathryn, can you please give me a risk assessment?"

Kathryn got to her feet, gave a quick curtsy, and began her report.

"There is no risk, not right now, anyway. The magic seems to be triggered when Andrew is in a moment of great distress. It has only happened one time. He was bitten by the lycanthrope while back in Thrairn, just outside the city the night before we left. The magic has some relationship to the moon cycle, as all lycanthropy does. I would consider him low-risk unless he is put in a battle situation. Or when the moon is full. It is Atikan magic, and beyond my ken."

"The man who rescued him, this Libélula," continued the Mage, "he told Andrew he would be able to remove the curse. However, we in the Tradition may be able to enchant him so that he might master the power. No guarantees. But, that is also beyond my skills. That would require that he come with me to the Red Keep in the Crooked Spears, where we could consult with one of the Viziers."

"This is all just a little bit much -" began my father.

"Peter. Out."

The King glared at the man who gave me life. My father in turn shot me a withering look and stormed out of the room.

"Andrew," said the King, sitting down in the chair that Kathryn had vacated, "you have caused me no shortage of problems. No shortage of problems, that is, on top of the splinter and destruction of Butterfly Company at the hands of a necromancer. What am I to do with you? As Commander, your father is free to oversee the Yellow Order as he sees fit. On top of your expulsion, he wishes for you to be exiled. It is only because you are his blood that he does not call for the noose."

"I am less certain of your evil, however," said the King, smiling sadly at me. "Kathryn tells me that this is an involuntary curse, and I believe her. But I also do not wish for my armies to risk being subject to the destructive dark magics of foreign lands. So, it appears we have two options: remove the curse or tame it. The safe option would be to simply remove it. But if we tame it, we may have a very strong weapon indeed. The story your father tells of your Strength and ferocity is quite the tale."

"I have decided that I prefer to tame it," the King said after a pause, "to have you serve me with your power. But this is too grave a decision to come to on my own. I will have to convene the Inner Council for guidance. It is very evident that your bias in this matter is without question. Nonetheless, you are a member of the Council. You will be called upon to give your vote, Andrew."

"Very well," I said. "And what of the Mage? The man who raised all of our dead countrymen?"

The King and Kathryn exchanged a strange glance. Something heavy and unsaid hung stagnant between them. Then Kathryn turned and spoke.

"He is a member of my Order, based on reports of the red robe that he wears. He escaped through some network of tunnels in that cavern when Dragonfly Company arrived, along with Mr. Coulter."

"Do you know him?" I asked. "Certainly your Red Tradition is not so large that you would not know who he is."

"Andrew," said the King, "perhaps it would be better if we let you rest. We can discuss all of this later."

Chapter Thirteen
Shedding Skin

After my 'guests' left, I went directly to bed. The interplay of the emotional fallout of my dealings with them and the soreness from my experience in the cave had conspired to drain all of the good from me. The sleep that claimed me was black and dreamless. When I woke, it was to another bright Erifracian sun streaming shafts of light into my chamber.

I had been too distracted to notice the day before, but a crust of white salt had developed throughout the leather and the chainmail was beginning to turn red with rust. The boiled hide was not nearly as stiff as it once was. My foray into seawater had fucked my armour, well and proper. I dressed in it regardless.

Convening the Inner Council would take three days, the King had said during our previous day's discussion. In the meantime, he was not going to quarantine me, but, given the threat I posed, I would not be given free rein to wander on my own. I was to be escorted everywhere by a pair of white cloaks. Kyle and Reed were their names, brothers from Thrairn. Given the heat, they were permitted to remove the thickly visored helms that were part of the White Guard standard issue. The morning they were assigned to me, I took full advantage of my newly granted freedom, even if it was freedom with a caveat. I was not sure where I would take us, but I had to get out into the sunshine and rub shoulders with people who were not royals or military.

When we got outside, I had a chance to take in Tunuska from a different vantage point. The castle was every bit as as magnificent as I had expected, based on my previous vantage up in one of the four towers that jutted out from each corner of the square building. In one of the many books I had devoured in my short years on Clovir, I had seen an illustration of this type of tower. Minarets, they were called. In the center of the castle, a large bulbous dome extended out into the hot sky. The whole building was made of the same off-white stone that was featured in every structure the eye could see. It gleamed like stripped bone in the morning sun.

The path down to the village was bustling with activity, seeing enough traffic that a thin layer of dust kicked up from the dry earth hovered interminably a foot or so above the ground. The people of Erifracia themselves had brown skin and hair as black as cinder. I had seen traveling merchants in Isha that looked like the people we encountered on horse-like beast, cart, and foot that morning. But those meetings were a rarity and this throng a new experience. They all murmured to each other in the alien tongue of Erifracia as we passed. We received curious glances from some of the people, mostly children. The majority of the faces were redolent of suspicion. We did our best to ignore all of them.

Camels, these strange beasts of burden were called. At least, that is what Kyle and Reed informed me when I exclaimed my awe to them.

I got to know my guards a little bit, trading stories about growing up in Isha and the taverns and brothels back home as we made our way down the winding trail. Both of them were unmarried and in their twenties, like me. The only real difference between us seemed to be that I was of noble birth and they were the sons of a cobbler in the poorer western district of the city. Their uncle Chris had been a white cloak, which is how they became interested in their chosen manner of service to the Crown. By the time the noon sun rose, the men had stopped gripping their swords and stiffening their backs and had adopted an altogether easy attitude towards me. They were told I was dangerous, but appeared to have simply forgotten about the threat I posed.

If this had been two weeks ago, I had mused at the time, I would have simply shut up and remained sullen, too self-conscious and resenting my sobriety to engage with the brothers. Especially with commoners like these. That was before the world had begun to change. Magic was somehow real. I had stared both death and exile in the face and survived to tell the tale. My Knighthood might be in question, but I was still a member of the Inner Council. I was happy to be alive and genuinely interested in the stories of other men, nobility be fucked. As her father's assassin, I did have to accept that the place in Marissa's heart that I coveted was most likely closed forever to me. I was pleased to find that some new serenity accompanied the thought.

Reflecting as we walked, I acknowledged to myself that I barely knew anything about Marissa, aside from a stirring in my loins whenever I looked upon her or caught her scent. We would exchange pleasantries those times when I had enough Courage to say anything to her, nothing deeper than surface level. She was some ideal I was chasing, a human being for which my body demanded fornication. I had thought that I loved her. I wondered whether I really knew what that word meant.

I came down from my reverie as we entered into the splendor of the market. I had heard stories about the place when I was a boy growing up in Isha. Erifracia was a marine country, a peninsula that found itself surrounded on all sides by the ocean. Though there was a large desert in its north, arable land made up the lion's share of its geography. Arable land that was tilled by Serfs beholden to the nobility, just like in Isha. But unlike my home country, Erifracia thrived on exports, and spent a large chunk of its resultant wealth on imports from the merchantmen vessels that teemed into its ports along the coast. Consequently, Tunuska was a renowned trading hub. The market stretched out countless city blocks in every direction and it was rumoured to contain every herb, salve, sword, fermented drink - you name it. If it existed anywhere on the four corners of Clovir, it could be purchased at the Tunuskan open air market.

And here I was without a coin purse.

"Say," I said, "do either of you have any Erifracian coin?"

"You think we'd be hanging around this place for days and not've changed our gold and tin into the local stuff?" asked Reed, pulling out a small leather bag and emptying its contents onto his palms. "We'd have gone mad or buggers without at least one cunny bought and paid betwixt us." A dozen or so golden coins, much wider but flatter than the coins of Thrairn shone in the noonday sun. On their faces was an embossed image of a stern fellow bearing a bushy mustache. Revanti or one of his forebears, no doubt.

"Erifracian dinari. They buy dark-skinned whores as easily as they do the local honeyed wine. Sickly stuff. The wine, not the talent."

I laughed, though my heart was not in it. My skin crawled at the man's words, but more so at the reptile that flashed briefly on his face. At the moment, I was about as interested in drinking and whoring as I was in repeating any of the arithmetic lessons Mistress Zona drilled into my head in my youth. I wanted to see the market. So we set off.

The sights and sounds of the place were without equal to my twenty-five-year-old mind, but the smells were something else entirely. To this day, I have not forgotten the odours. Near the butcher stalls a rancid stench of meat in the first stages of putrefaction hit us like a foul wall. Well before we arrived at the rows of perfumeries, I nearly choked to death on the florid aromas that wafted on the air. A reek of shite announced that we were getting close to the livestock vendors. A completely alien symphony of strange and beautiful scents told us that we were upon the spice merchants.

Of all of them, it was the smell of roasting goat that brought our little company to a halt.

"I have not eaten anything today," I announced to my guards. "Is there any way you fine gentlemen would loan me the coin to buy some of this meat?"

"Fuck loans," said Kyle. "This one is on us, Andrew."

The white cloak raised three fingers, a single gold coin changed hands, and a quarter piece of a chopped dinar went back into his open palm. We were each given a plate filled to the brim with food - chunks of spiced goat, rice that looked as if it had been painted yellow, and pieces of some sour purple vegetable that tasted pleasantly of salt and earth. We took our first bites, looked at each other, glanced at the merchant, who winked back at us, and wolfed down the entire works within a couple of minutes.

"That was incredible," I declared to the man who did not speak a lick of Thrain. Recognizing his lack of understanding, I bowed to him to get the message across. He just laughed good-naturedly and smiled.

"Where next?"

"I need new clothing," I admitted, looking down at my armour. "I am not a Yellow Knight anymore, so I am not beholden to their stupid fucking rules about battle dress."

My new friends chuckled and we wandered aimlessly through the stalls. There was no one to ask for directions. At least no one who looked like they spoke Thrain. So we simply drifted with me in the lead. I felt pulled through the sea of people. This was accompanied by a strange sensation. It was as if some vice were tightening in the back of my skull. After what must have been a half hour or so of wandering, we found ourselves at an Armourcrafter's stall.

The vendor was a portly fellow with a thick black moustache, a yellow robe with curving white patterns stitched into the borders, and enough gold rattling around on his wrists and fingers that I am surprised he had enough Strength to even lift his arms. On a huge wooden board behind him, leggings, pauldrons, wristguards, chestpieces, and all manner of other bits armour hung from pegs. The make was much different than what was on sale in Thrairn. It was browner, certainly: less metal, more leather. What metal there was appeared to be only decorative, with the silver and black cast of pewter inlaid against the boiled grain of the hide. But the leather did look different, some quality that I could not place...

As I stared, I eventually noticed two bodyguards standing mutely in the shadows under a cloth overhang off to the side, with expressionless faces and curved swords on their hips.

"Welcome, welcome, my young friends," said the man in a heavily accented Thrain. "I am Rufil. You are with the King who has just arrived, yes? No need to say, no need to say, I can tell by the white cloaks." The man bowed with a flourish, as deeply as his considerable bulk would allow. "We of Tunuska welcome you to our humble city."

"Uh, thank you," I said. Rufil had an unshifting smile and hands that did not cease moving. It did not take a Mage of the Red Tradition to divine that this man was as slippery as a greased eel.

"I am just looking for an update," I said, pointing to my ruined armour. The rust on the chains appeared to have grown fuller and deeper throughout our morning's travels.

"Ah, yes, yes. You wish to replace your northern steel junk for the famed Erifracian *cuir d'arbalest*? You will see, nothing like it in all of the world."

I recalled then some mention of Erifracian armour in one of the history books I had read in the early days of my training to be a Yellow Knight, a tome handed to me by a gruff Terence

Indigo. He admonished me to study it well. The book was as dry as a cow pat left to roast in the heat of a Julian Month sun, but I had retained some of the descriptions within, it seemed. The creation of *cuir d'arbalest* is a secret that Erifracian tanners have kept for centuries. It was said to be so strong that it could stop most crossbow bolts in full flight, much like Thrain steel. Only the enormous arbalest had a chance of getting through, but there were never any guarantees. By the time a man could reload that missile-launching behemoth, the bearer of the extremely light armour was usually upon the arbalest wielder. The Erifracian army could run for hours with it hanging from their bodies. These southern men had spawned a terrible reputation for blitz campaigns against their enemies. It was not until Thrairn developed a massive longbow made of bear ash that could pierce unfailingly this *cuir d'arbalest*, a weapon which required so little skill that it could be wielded by hunting Serfs pressed into service, that the Erifracian advantage had been tempered.

The countries became allies, then.

It turned out that I could buy any suit of armour for nearly a song, given that we were members of the visiting army. In clipped Thrain, the armour merchant told us the whole story of our privileges. King Revanti was giving merchants rebates so that we could buy necessary supplies at a discounted rate. Whorehouses and ale were full price, except the ones designated by King Revanti. The seedier spots were undercutting the legitimate ones, whose rates were reduced, but not quite as generously as the sanctioned ones, as King Janus had warned us. The merchant told us in hushed tones about a brothel, the Black Mamba, that was offering full service to Knights of the Order for a quarter dinar. The price of the meal we just ate, I acknowledged to my companions. My member burned with imagined disease at the mere mention of what could consequently only be a den of crushed dreams and despair.

Satisfied that we were well aware of the niceties of the economic climate of Tunuska, Rufil returned to the matter at hand. Next, he said, came the choosing. Kyle and Reed kept pointing out to each other a chestpiece, one with an interesting pattern on the front. There was something about it, something that I could not put my finger on...

"One of my finest pieces," Rufil said, after I asked to look at it more closely. "It comes as part of a set. I will not break it up. If you are to be taking this one you will need to take it all."

I dared not tell the merchant that I had been defrocked and most likely not eligible for the rebate. Thankfully, neither did Kyle or Reed. Reed loaned me (and I made sure it was a loan this time) the five dinari necessary to buy a full suit of Erifracian *cuir d'arbalest*, including gloves and boots.

Coin in hand, I nodded, handed Rufil the dinari, and watched the merchant struggle with his bulk as he pulled items down from the wall. Then he whistled at one of the silent guards and the armed man pulled a few other necessaries from a heretofore unknown storage location off to one side of the tent.

The armour was as stiff as steel. I rapped a wristguard with a knuckle, half expecting to hear it ring. The many inch sized pieces on the chest were woven together like scales, overlapping and able to bend and warp with my body as I moved. The pants, boots, gloves - all were the same. The only pieces that were made of a single unbroken covering were the wristguards and the greaves. On the chest was painted a large red Snake that spiraled in on itself to eat its own tail. Its eyes were made of steel. Given the armour's functional similarity to that beast's skin, I thought the image apt. I asked the merchant about the design.

"Ah, yes, Snake is the mark of the crafter. It is terrifying, is it not? Good to scare your enemies before you defeat them. The crafter is not an Erifracian himself, he is Atikan. My peers told me I was crazy to take on a savage from that wild land as apprentice. But he has learned our ways well, would you not say?"

Atikan.

"This armour crafter - did he make any of the rest of these?" I asked, pointing to the armour on the wall behind the merchant.

"No, young sirrah. The only pieces I have for sale from this man - they are in your hands."

Atika. I had barely heard of the place until my encounter with Libélula. That I should be cursed by some magic generated in that place, find my way to this stall, then buy the one suit of Erifracian armour made by a crafter from Atika... a shiver wended its way down my spine.

"Thank you," I said, turning to go. Something between panic and wonder beat a crescendo in my chest.

"If you want somewhere to change, my friend, please go and see Ali at the Black Mamba! It is on Gingari Close. Just ask a city guard to direct you - most of them speak Thrain. And tell Ali that Rufil sent you!"

The merchant's words slithered around in my head as if a pitcher full of oil had been poured in through my ears. I knew I should not trust the man, but something compelled me forward in spite of my misgivings, just as it had brought me to Rufil's stall. I shrugged off the wariness building in my breast. After all, I did need a place to change.

And to catch my breath.

Chapter Fourteen
Every Soldier's Due

It was an age before we found the Black Mamba. Having received directions from a half dozen guards, words of advice that we could barely parse through nearly unintelligible Erifracian accents and the thick mustaches that seem to be highly in fashion amongst the men of the city, we eventually reached our destination. A black Snake slithering down an inverted pentagram painted beside the doorframe was the only indication that we had stumbled upon the right place. Instead of the hastily set up fornication tent with questionable sanitation that quarter dinar sex suggested, we instead found ourselves before a palace made of black and white marble.

The front doorway, 'shut' with a curtain made of beads suspended from the top of the frame, opened onto a foyer with a host of couches and chaises longue. Small tables cluttered with crystal bottles bearing dark spirits and dirty glasses clogged the pathway through. Men who seemed to be of every ethnicity under the Clovir sun were splayed out on the soft furniture, some smoking the long pipes of the poppy worshippers, others gripping snifters of drink, all of them completely disinterested in the newly-entered trio of soldiers. A large desk sat directly opposite the door, behind which stood a madam. A madam whose light skin marked her as out of place in that city as the three of us.

"Welcome to da Black Mamba," she said as we approached. It was no great feat to detect an accent from the heart of the Purple Run. "B'ys from T'rairn, is ya? You t'ree looks like yis could use a little rest and relaxation. Well dat's exactly what's on offer here, me honeys."

She was older than us, much older, that much was clear. She wore a wig to give herself a full head of flaming red hair. Naught but grey and white underneath, I suspected. Deep creases on her face and a beat-up smoking pipe were enough to give the elderly former prostitute a distinguished look. She used a wrinkled hand to gesture incessantly as she spoke. Willie's betrayal had made me very suspect of the people of the Run. Couple that with the unctuous friendliness, I decided that this woman was too earnest by half.

In the unconscious days of my youth, I would have jumped at the madam's suggestion. Hell, if it had been two weeks prior, I would already have picked out my whore and would be following her to a room in the back. The cheap service, the splendid surroundings, the madam foreign to this place... I knew long before we even stepped inside that something did not feel right. Still, I had found myself compelled to enter. Now I wanted out as quickly as possible. I glanced down at the stack of armour in my hands.

"Actually," I said, "We are supposed to tell Ali that Rufil sent us. I am just looking to rent a room so that I can change." I waved my load to punctuate my point.

"Oh," the woman said, feigning sadness. "Let me 'ave a look fer 'im. Yis can 'ave a seat wherever yis likes. Feel free ta take some of the booze or the pipes if yer offered. No charge fer dat."

I looked at Kyle and Reed. They were staring wild-eyed at a large-breasted and beautiful woman dressed only in a pair of gold lace briefs holding a tray of glasses of brightly coloured liquids as she entered from some dark corner in the back of the brothel.

"I trust this place as much as I would one of the venomous creatures after which it is named," I said, glancing around to make sure no other plainly obvious speakers of Thrain were about and gesturing with my pile of armour toward a tapestry on one of the walls. It had been woven with the image of a black serpent, wrapped around a tree in a verdant forest. "Fucking vile animals."

"Come now, Andrew, no need to look a gift horse in the mouth," replied Kyle, feigning respectfulness and deftly swiping what looked to be a glass of whiskey as the woman passed. He put it to his lips and drained it in one go.

"Are you not on duty?"

Both of the men shot me stormy looks.

"I thought you was an alright sort, Andrew, not one to go tattling to the King about a few lads having a bit of fun while we are stuck in a foreign port," accused Reed.

"No, no," I said, backpedaling. Dread descended on me in a thick black cloud. My chest burned as I considered the possibility of betrayal by my guards, whom I realized I was counting on for protection. "That is not what I meant. We need to keep our wits about us. This was a mistake. I think we should leave."

I turned to again attempt the maze through which we had entered. I noticed then four men armed with curved swords and clad in *cuir d'arbalest* were standing in the two corners near the exit.

"Soldiers from the north," boomed a voice behind me in perfect Thrain. "My favourite customers! I must thank Rufil for sending you our humble way when next we meet. Welcome to the Black Mamba. I am Ali. How may we please you? I know! You would like every soldier's due!"

Ali was a thin man where Rufil had been fat. He was dressed in a papery robe similar to Rufil's, except that his robe was orange and the ornate patterns threaded on the edges were black. On his head was a hat that seemed to be less a hat and more a hat-shaped ball made of silks of every colour on the face of Clovir. Incredibly, he seemed to be wearing even more jewelry than Rufil. On his hip, I coldly noticed a jeweled hilt jutting out from a long curved scabbard.

His face was smiling. But I could not help but notice that his eyes were not.

"Ali," I said, trying to respond before my eager guards had a chance to ruin our chance at escape, "we must apologize. We were just leaving. It is my fault. A moment ago, I realized that I must be back to the castle before sundown." I gestured to the fading afternoon light that was pouring in through a series of small windows on the side walls. "I do not think we would make it back in time unless we leave now." I paused momentarily. "King Janus's orders." I added, praying that my tone did not betray the fear that was galloping through my body.

Kyle and Reed shot me withering looks, in such unison that it looked as though they had been rehearsing the act.

"Just arrived and preparing to leave! I must protest, young masters," said Ali, not breaking his false smile. "Allow us to fulfill our guest-host obligations. We will be subject to the wrath of Xenia if we do not. She is a capricious god, and we cannot allow the Mamba to fall into her disfavour.

"Besides," our insistent host went on, "we are grateful for Erifracia's alliance with Thrairn, a peace that has lasted many years and resulted in much commerce between our great nations. We would like to show you our gratitude, beyond simple words. Will you not stay, perhaps to come to know some of the Black Mamba's beauty?"

With that, the madam gestured at an unseen doorway behind the desk, obscured by a long curtain. Unlike the serving women that moved mutely back and forth between the foyer and the back halls, the women that entered at the madam's command did not even have a pair of briefs to cover themselves. There were eight of them, mostly Erifracians, though there was a woman who looked to be Thrain and one darker still than the locals. Her skin was as black as a moonless night, her breasts were perfectly proportioned to her body, and her features were sharp yet smoothly angled. Her face was empty of emotion and her large eyes were inscrutable pools, but she was without a doubt beautiful. I had only seen people like her at a distance once or twice in my life in Isha...

"Ali," said Reed, looking over at me with a triumphant smile, having taken advantage of my silent moment of wonder, "perhaps we are not required to be back at the castle so soon. We can stay for a little while, before we will be missed."

Kyle nodded vigorously at his brother's words. I looked back at the Mamba's guardsmen. They were staring at us, faces set and gripping the hilts of their swords. Most of the customers in the foyer were drunk or had dissolved into a poppy torpor, but those that seemed still to have some sense about them were looking back and forth between us, evidently terrified of the bloody potential that hung heavy in the air.

Sighing, I turned back to Ali.

"Perhaps we can stay an hour, sirrah, no longer."

✶ ✶ ✶ ✶ ✶

Ali must have noticed my interest in the woman black of skin as readily as my compatriots. I gather that is why within moments of my acceptance of his offer of hospitality, we had each been whisked into the back with the prostitutes we had chosen. Kyle and Reed took no time in selecting two of the Erifracian women. I was not even asked. I was simply informed that the beauty was named Nimba, she was Atikan, then she grabbed my hand to lead me down the white and black marble of the corridor.

My surprise at the woman's provenance was muted. It was almost as if I were expecting to learn she was from Atika.

The room we eventually found ourselves in was just as ostentatious as the rest of the Black Mamba. Warm air floated in from a large window with a gold curtain, one that rippled in the evening breeze. A large bed in the middle of the room was lined with what looked to be black silk sheets and was flanked by two tables. On one rested a decanter half filled with wine and two glasses. On the other table lay a number of leather implements and chains, the tools of the bizarre sexual fantasies that frequently came to life in brothels, the ones that involved beating the shite out of a woman. Or having her do the same to you.

I had never understood these bondage practices, as I had heard the acts called in a tavern a few years prior. At a brothel, I might have been fucking whores, but I liked my fucking to be tender. This tying up and striking - it seemed to me as though some trauma from the youth of those interested was echoing into adulthood. Perhaps the enthusiasts of the practice had been struck one too many times by their mothers when they stole blueberry pies off the windowsill. Or were not struck enough.

I understood even less those that preferred to take the beating than give it.

Regardless, I was not obligated to use the materials provided. Nor was I even obligated to have sex with the naked beauty sitting on the bed, a creature whose face seemed to tell a sad tale, a yarn of pure misery. Given her expression, I would not have been surprised to learn her entire family save her perished in a fire earlier that day. More likely her story was some dark mosaic of slavery and murder, the other thing for which Tunuska was famous. Regardless of what had happened, it was evident that her spirit was crushed. Now that Ali was no longer in the room, the woman seemed to have little use for pretending at being happy.

In years past, a hired whore's sadness would give me as much pause as a wolf might hesitate before pouncing on a disabled rabbit. But I had had a taste of the horrors of captivity and knew this woman was as much a prisoner as I had been in that cave with Willie and his master. Any interest I had in taking advantage of my host's hospitality evaporated as I considered the true circumstances of this 'transaction.'

Hairs rose and rippled into a wave along my back as I made a decision.

"Nimba," I said, hoping against all reason that the woman spoke Thrain, "I am not going to fuck you. I came through here to change, and that is all that I will do."

She stared at me mutely. It had been worth a shot.

I began to take off my old armour, piling it up on the ground next to the bed. After I had gotten down to my skivvies, the woman got on her knees on the bed and turned around, presenting and waiting for me to mount her, as if she were a sad cat in heat, resigned to her Fate.

"No, no," I said, gesturing wildly with my hands and eyes, "no fuck, no fuck."

She turned to look at me, raised an eyebrow, then sat back down. I returned to the task at hand.

Wonder built in my heart as I pulled each piece of leather over my flesh. Armour like that does not need a tailor, Rufil had explained to me. Unless I was a man of unnatural dimensions, very big or very short, the straps that hooked the armour to my body could be adjusted to fill any gaps. I had tried on the gloves and boots before I had left. In fact, I had kept the footwear on since I had left the man's market stall. But now, donning each individual piece... it was as though the suit had been tailored perfectly for me. The straps were pulled all the way, leaving no flesh uncovered. My body was the key to its lock.

Sensations of awe danced along my spine again as I looked up. Nimba, satisfied that she was not going to be asked to complete her vocational duties, had fetched a mirror from some nook or cranny in the bedroom. The mirror was no doubt used by the women to ensure that they looked as fresh as the morning's dew after each client took what he wanted and left her to pick up the pieces. Instead of aiding in the rejuvenation of a prostitute's looks, this time the device was called upon to show me how I looked in my new Atikan-crafted *cuir d'arbalest*.

I was shocked. I barely recognized myself. Gone was the unruly mess who barely made it to his own consecration into the Yellow Order in one piece. In his stead stood someone who would cause would-be interlopers to think twice... no, three times, before attempting to engage in a fight. For the first time in my life I looked competent. Threatening, even. The polished steel eye of the red Snake on my chestpiece caught the sun through the window and glinted.

I smiled. The only think missing was a sword. A deficit that I promised myself to rectify, and soon. The danger crawling through the Black Mamba was all the convincing I needed that being without a sword in this foreign land was extremely ill-advised. Unfortunately, the two white cloaked men getting "their due" in the other rooms were under strict orders that I was not to be armed.

I thought back to my conversation with my King the previous day. He had explained that, while he was not concerned about the contents of my mind and heart, his most loyal general and friend, Peter Cardiff, was convinced that I was a traitor to the Crown. If he had permitted me a sword, Commander Cardiff might interpret such an action as an outright dismissal of his opinion and his judgment. The King did not want to do that to his friend. "A political decision," King Janus had called it, smiling a smile that reminded me of the one worn by Ali when he spoke. The King finished by telling me that the white cloaks assigned to my detail would protect me just as well as they would protect the army and people of Erifracia from me.

I gestured for the woman to put the mirror away. She dropped her arm and mounted the bed again, sitting down with a sigh. She muttered something in her alien language. I put my hand to a phantom coin purse on the side of my hip.

Fuck, I thought, I would have tipped her for no other reason than to allay some of her unhappiness. I dealt with my own guilt for giving the woman nothing by telling myself that gratuities were almost certainly all collected with force by the seemingly vicious bastard known as Ali.

Nonetheless, I did not want to be in the room with the Atikan woman anymore. We did not understand each other and the whole thing was utterly contrived. It would be an awkward way to spend a further half hour, which is what I surmised had elapsed while I dressed and preened. I recalled my experience with whores back in Isha, during those black times when the frantic thrusting was over and I was left to contemplate the company of a stranger and the void of faded sexual attraction, my downward spiral usually hastened along by receding drunkenness. At those moments I questioned whether giving in to my lustful appetites was worth it, though my misgivings always seemed to evaporate along with the hangover.

"I am going to return to the foyer," I said, knowing that the only thing the woman would understand was that I was leaving the room. Her downcast face was burned into my mind as I made my way through the halls back to the main area. Perhaps she would pay in her own way for failing to keep me in the room for the full hour, I mused as I walked, saddened by the thought. And then I heard it. Something familiar and terrible. Something that sent a dagger into my heart and my shoulders up into a hunch.

It was the voice of the Mage from the cave. Willie's master. He was speaking in one of the rooms off the hallway to my right. Like all the doors in the Black Mamba, the only thing between me and him was several strings of multicoloured beads hanging from the lintel.

My hand went to my bare hip, where my sword should have been. Despite my armour, I may as well have been naked. If he found me, I would have no way of fighting back.

139

Remembered images of black clouds and red lightning came unbidden into my brain. I considered walking past, getting out of there and running back to the castle as quickly as possible, white cloaks be damned. I could always beg forgiveness of the King, lie to him and say that we were separated in the crowds in the market. I would beg forgiveness of Kyle and Reed as well, informing them that I must have fallen ill from heat-rotted goat flesh in our meal earlier that day and had to return to the castle. It was a near-perfect plan, one that would get me back to safety.

How easy it would have been. To run, to lie. I took my first step to continue down the path back to the foyer.

Then it happened again. Shades of the rainbow lit up at the edges of my vision, casting beautiful colours into view. The little voice inside of me, the one that had told me to fight against the Jaguar and my enemies in the cave, returned. It roared up inside of me as the colours deepened, much stronger than it had been before. It commanded me to stand next to the frame and listen to the Mage so that I could relay his words back to the King.

'Take the risk!' said the voice inside my head. 'You know where that other path leads. You have walked it so many times before.'

The voice of Courage, I realized, was speaking more sense than the voice of fear.

Chapter Fifteen
The Covenant

"... the Red Tradition is splintered, broken," said the voice of my former captor. "You cannot be cowed by the infallibility of King Janus anymore. His Mages have turned against each other, spitting venom and shedding Red Tradition blood."

"And how have you come to know this?" asked someone with a very distinct Erifracian accent but impeccable grammar. "How can I trust you? You yourself are a Mage of the Red Tradition, perhaps legitimate, but you may yet be just another heretic. A madman Hell-bent on fomenting war between two Kingdoms at peace. One of those scorned and broken creatures that screams terror at crowds in Isha, one who has escaped the King and the Tradition and secured passage down here to my country."

"Well, therein lies the rub, does it not?" My former captor replied. His voice was very posh and refined. Every word was carefully chosen for pronunciation. "See, no anti-magic bangles. They are impossible to remove without the aid of one who binds the fallen Mages, a Red Praetorian.

"King Janus has committed a sin," he continued, "one so grave that the Red Tradition is having trouble deciding what to do with him. They have sent their Viziers to the Crooked Spears in order to read the winds and divine the path, but they have yet to return. That has not sufficed for all. Not for most, even. And those most can be swayed. Most of the Mages believe the King needs to die for his transgression, or at least replaced."

"What did he do?" asked the Erifracian voice. "Tell me. All of it."

"He defied the Council. In a very serious manner. It was several years ago. The fact of his betrayal only became known to the Mages of the Tradition within the past few weeks. By some barometers, what he did was not of much importance. The murder of one of his subjects. That does not mean that those more... fervent among my number are prepared to forgive and forget. He was expressly prohibited from killing this person and did so regardless. The King must do what the Council says, and through those puppets he is fed the dictates of the Red Tradition. He is to pay homage to the infallibility of the word of the elders without question, without wavering. That is the bedrock of what keeps us alive. It has been prophesied that the rebellion of the King would signal the crumbling of the Red Tradition. Many scoff at the Prophecy, but others do not. Some of our number believe in the rest of the Prophecy, that when the King of a southern realm sets foot in Isha, the slate will be wiped clean and Balance will return to the realm."

My former captor cleared his throat and paused. Silence hung heavy for a time.

"The Red Tradition has not encountered this situation before this Aquester King," the Thrain man said finally. "It has sown confusion and fear as surely as might a sudden failure of the Tradition's magic. Some fear that this is what happened, given how well everything has been prepared.

"That is, of course, not the case. The magic remains intact and the Red Tradition a threat. And so this endeavour is not without some danger should our gambit fall flat. But what is life without risk? I represent those that would see you fulfill the Prophecy. The Kingdom of Thrairn is ripe for the plucking, if only you would take what is rightfully yours. All of the longbows in the world cannot stop your army if there is no one to draw them. No one with the Strength of the Red Tradition behind him, at any rate.

"And so," the Erifracian said, his tone having softened somewhat. "What would you have me do?"

"I would not presume tell you what to do, King Revanti," the Mage continued. "But, I do know that this peace is a lie. You hate King Janus, hate that he is a guest at your castle, hate that the glory of his Kingdom makes your own look like a little desert-licked backwater. How he mocks you with every step, every decree, every voyage to your Kingdom to help his poor, weak ally to fight a few ship-bound pirates.

"It does not have to be that way. It is true: the Red Tradition has long served Thrairn, keeping loyalty to the Aquester line, all the way back to Karl Aquester, first King of Thrairn. The covenant has survived the creep of centuries. Now, that covenant has been broken. There are some who think it may be salvaged, but the wise among us know that there is no coming back from this. King Janus is finished."

"You are a fool," said King Revanti with a scoff. "You think me one, at least. The Red Tradition has always served the Thrain crown. This is some sort of trap."

"The Red Tradition has served royalty other than those that have sat on the throne of Thrairn, Your Majesty. Before the Kingdom of Thrairn even existed, our forebears were in league with the Heraclytans, that Empire lost to time that was brought down by its own hubris. In a way much like King Janus's own folly. The Red Tradition does not serve just anyone, King Revanti. We serve Kings and Queens, Emperors and Empresses, ones who have proven themselves worthy of our blessing. Our loyalty is utter, once a covenant is made. All we ask is the same in return."

"What is in it for you?" The King replied.

If I were discovered now, I realized, there would be no

formality. I had heard too much. I would just be run through by one of King Revanti's guards. Guards who were no doubt standing at attention in some corner of the room. I felt perspiration bead on my forehead and my chest tighten.

"A return to Order for the Red Tradition, of course," my former captor said. "'An Order untainted by betrayal.' That is my stock answer, anyway. A pretty reason that I will give to the members of the Tradition when they ask for a reason to follow me. Those fools think that Order is what will save them. That can be their reason. They do not understand that clinging to Order is what got them into this mess in the first place. I will be perfectly honest with you, King Revanti, as what I seek from you is a partnership of equals. What I would really like is freedom.

"There are those in the Red Tradition, a select few in positions of power, too many for me to deal with on my own, who have refused to allow any Red Mage to research a certain school of magic, one that holds great power and promise. I would like your support in removing these people. They are old. Ancient, really, and well-past their time. You may not be a Red Mage, but your soldiers can kill men just as easily with a sword as we might with a lick of conjured flame."

"What is the school of magic?" asked the King.

"Necromancy."

There was a long pause then, a time for King Revanti to digest the man's words. I knew the bastard's proclivity for death magic all too well. Who was he? I had learned that he was a Mage of the Red Tradition, but I did not have a name to bring back to King Janus. I could tell him of a plot to depose him, but that was all. I leaned closer, willing the man to reveal himself to me.

"I accept. When will you have an answer for me about whether or not you can convince the other Mages-"

I became aware of the footsteps coming down the hall much too late.

"You there! What are you doing?"

Chapter Sixteen
Skimming the Depths

The guard who had spotted me eavesdropping was between me and the foyer. Between me and escape. I did not stick around to see if I could talk my way out of formal Erifracian spying charges or, more likely, a quick blade to the guts. Instead, I turned on my heels and ran down the corridor in the opposite direction, to the end of one hallway, and another, and another, deeper into the belly of the Black Mamba. Through beaded doorways to my left and right I could hear screams of sex and pain, a terrible cacophony that was pierced intermittently by the sound of the guard behind me shouting in Erifracian.

The hallway was exhausted in about five turns. When I rounded the final one, rather than more corridor stretching out ahead of me, a white marble wall with a black coiled Snake painted in the center brought me to a halt. I turned to face my pursuer.

Gone was the guard. In his place was a man wearing a red robe cinched around the waist with a simple golden rope. He had long blond hair that had been pulled back into a perfect knot at the back of his head. His eyes were a blue as cold and deep as the frozen ocean of my homeland. A long bright pink scar ran from the forehead over his left eye down to wrap around a shorn chin. His arms were folded across his chest. He was smiling the kind of smile a viper might have for a mouse it cornered.

"The venerable Andrew Cardiff," the man said, taking a mockingly deep bow, "it has been a while. Welcome to the Black Mamba. Please, will you not join me for a mug of ale?"

The man pointed back the way we came. Every part of me was afire with the needles of fear. He recognized me. And I had run from him. I sensed that he was not stupid - just the opposite. There was no doubt in my mind that the next thing for me was a doom written in arcs of red lightning.

I felt like disobeying the man, to simply refuse to move and take whatever Hellish end he thrust upon me. Instead, he waved a hand at me and I felt that strange sensation of a vice tightening in the back of my head. Then the compulsion began. I felt my legs move of their own volition. I walked past him, fear seeping into my bones with every step.

"I must say, what a performance you put off the other day in the cave," the man said, proceeding alongside me in a manner as casual as if we had been friends since the days of suckling at our mothers' bosoms. He draped his arm over my shoulder.

"Very well done indeed," he continued. "I do not believe I have ever seen a cat as large as that before. And to have struck down that fat old Captain as he begged for his life. It gave me quite a chuckle. I would have liked to have spoken with you then, before the 'great heroes' of Dragonfly Company saved the day."

"Who are you?"

"Ah, it must be very frustrating indeed, to be at such a disadvantage," the Mage said with a shrill laugh. "I know you well, Andrew, very well. I did my research on you when the masters of the Red Tradition plucked your name from the ether. Research that took me deep into the past. A past within which was buried a treasure. Quite a treasure, indeed."

"Ah, here we are," the man said, gesturing with his free arm to a beaded doorway on our left. "After you."

I split the beads and walked into a large room, much larger than the one where I left the unhappy prostitute. As I entered, I noticed a triangular table with three upholstered chairs to my right. The upholstery was dyed black with white lines that exploded from the center of each in a pattern that was as intricate as the stained glass in the Blue Cathedral. To my left, a small bed, neatly made, was pushed all the way into the corner. In the middle of the room was a large circular rug with two cushions on opposite ends. The cushions seemed to be in a competition with each other for which could be the most brightly coloured in all shades of the rainbow. The sole window was as triangular as the table and located high up on the wall near the ceiling.

It was a very odd place.

"Please, please, have a seat," the man said, having entered behind me and gesturing to the cushions. My jaw unconsciously dropped as he pulled two mugs out of thin air with a flourish of his wrist. He let them go. They did not fall. A bottle appeared from nowhere behind the man and floated over, turning down to pour out a ruby coloured liquid that I immediately recognized as frothy ale into the waiting mugs.

I gaped at him.

He smiled. Then he grasped the body of one of the mugs, turning the handle towards me and thrusting the vessel in my direction. It left his hands and floated across the gap between us. I took the mug when it arrived, filled with mistrust at the fluid inside. The man shrugged and took a long draught out of his own vessel.

"Where is King Revanti?"

"My, my, my, did they not teach you manners where you come from? Please, sit."

I again wished to deny obeisance, but felt myself nonetheless do as he commanded, getting down onto one of the cushions and crossing my legs. Momentarily awed by the sensation, I noticed that the leather of my pants did not constrict me in any way as they stretched. I glanced down to admire the armour, placing my mug on the floor next to me.

"A fine suit, is it not?" asked he red-robed man. "I made sure that we had your measurements perfectly."

I looked sharply up from my distraction.

"My measurem-"

"You are new at this, are you not, Andrew?"

"What are you talking about? To whom did you give my measurements? I chose this armour at the market today, bought it from one of a dozen such merchants in the market. And I chose it randomly, no one suggested that I take it."

"Random chance," he said with an incredulous laugh. "It was your heart's desire, was it not?"

I gaped. I did not know what to say to the man. Red lightning and the lifting up of dead men were within the Mage's repertoire. He could conjure ale and mugs from the air. But this...

"You can control minds, then," I said, putting the unexplained compulsions of my day together. "If you can do that, why do you not simply force King Revanti to invade the Kingdom of Thrairn and fulfill your Prophecy?"

The man brayed like a hyena, as if I had said the funniest thing he had ever heard. Tears streamed down his face. The spectacle made me feel very odd, as if I had made a terrible mistake in front of my peers and was paying the humiliating price.

"Mind control is nothing of interest," he replied, wiping his cheek with the back of his hand. "It works only on those who wish to be controlled. If someone hands you their Destiny, why not force them to do as you command? More captivating to anyone interested in magic is the ability to control one's own Destiny. To read the signs. It is a path open to all. I was able to, once," the man trailed off, some measure of sadness evident in his voice.

"Divination is a fool's errand," he continued, snapping back to his confident and polished tones, "as far as magical ability goes. It is one of the easiest of the magical feats, and also one of the least reliable. And it takes a fool to believe in divination. Some of those who wear the red robe believe in it utterly. Fools, the lot of them. But those fools are the also the most powerful of the whole Red Tradition."

"So, you merely guess the future? And your leaders think this makes you powerful?" I said, sitting back into the soft cushion. "And I thought you represented those that believed in the Prophecy!"

"An old Mage," he said, "long dead now, once said that there is a difference between knowing the path, and walking the path. Those who seek to know the path at the expense of walking it set themselves up for destruction. But sometimes the truth of the prophecies cannot be denied. It is a matter of discernment." The Mage took a sip from his mug before he continued. "And there are other errors, ones of details. Sometimes the divination is right, but the timing is incorrect. I have a perfect example, and it concerns you. Just one month ago, I was at my home in Thrairn, eating breakfast at my kitchen table. For absolutely no reason at all, a mug fell off my shelf. Intuiting a grand change coming to the land, I slew a crow and read its entrails. In the gore, I saw the death of a member of the Inner Council. Nothing specific, of course, but a general sign that someone was about to die. The omens that followed: there was a certainty to them! I had never seen such a clear demonstration of prescience. This foretold death was to occur that very night. It was grand news, as I had been waiting for my opportunity to undermine the King for years. The sun dropped down behind the horizon and crept back up the next morning. I spoke with my colleagues in the Red Tradition. No news of a member of the Council dying. I was maddened - I had put so much stock in the prediction! I paced around my laboratory, wondering if I had lost my abilities, if my entire existence had been one big delusion. Doubt tried to worm its way into my mind and destroy forever my ability to do magic. We learn from the beginning that magic takes utter Faith, you see. And I was losing mine."

"I spent days in this state," he continued, "utterly defeated. Days that stretched into a week. And then, much to my delight, a hawk from the Crooked Spears delivered the news: Lord Reginald Quigley had shite his life out in a tavern bed. He needed replacing. And so, I went to work."

"As I said," the blond-haired Mage stated, sitting back on his cushion, "the timing is sometimes wrong."

"How does this explain the armour?"

"I have no idea," he responded matter-of-factly. "I was given an order from one of my partners in this matter. I am not the only one in the Red Tradition who wishes to see a paradigm shift in how we manage our affairs on this planet. We would have a lessening of Order's grip on Thrairn. And I am certainly not the man best suited to divination. But this partner of mine is quite..." the man trailed off as he had before.

"While you were unconscious," he said, picking up the thread again, "I had one of my men take your measurements. When I arrived in Tunuska after your escape, I gave those measurements to an Atikan Armourcrafter. I asked him to put a rush on it, and to adorn it in any way he saw fit. He worked through the night and produced that. I told him to sell it to a merchant named Ali. Then I waited for you in the market, enchanted you to buy it, and that was the end of my involvement. Like I said, I was told to do so. I know better than to ask why. You cannot walk the path without submitting to it."

"Who gave you the order?" I said, confused. "You knew I was going to escape?"

"Like I said, it was one of my partners. You may meet this person eventually. Or you may not. The mystery is comforting, is it not?" The Mage sipped his beer again. "I barely escaped that cave with my skin intact. My partner knew I would see the other side. An envelope was waiting for me when I returned to the Black Mamba, filled with instructions. She seems to have plans for you. I have been doing this long enough to understand that if I had killed you or otherwise interfered with the orders... well, I would have paid in ways I do not want to imagine."

I gaped. I was dealing with a madman. The existence of the Red Tradition I could deal with. Magic was not easy to swallow, but the fantastical books I had read as a child prepared me for it. Even lycanthropy - I hated the idea of losing control and becoming a monster, but I did not think that I had been driven insane in accepting that I had been cursed in this manner. This man, though... he had abdicated his will to his belief in Prophecy and harboured a degenerate obsession with necromancy. He was planning murder and I had witnessed him commit grand treason. Not to mention his reason for all of it was so that he would be left alone to raise the dead.

"The Red Tradition is full of lies," the Mage continued. "Listen now to this one. It is taught to every prospective Mage in his or her quest to become a wielder of the elements. Magic lives and dies on the caster's ability to put himself aside entirely and follow the little voice inside that makes quiet suggestions about how to act. To follow the omens. The best magicians, the ones who progress beautifully in the Red Tradition, are the ones who live their lives entirely in this manner. They are given power in exchange for their service. The bad ones, the ones who fail utterly, think that they are the ones in control, that universe is subject to their will, rather than the other way around.'

"That is what they say, in any event," he said with a shrug. "My own 'little voice,' the one that has guiding me since I started with the Red Tradition - it has gone silent. Ever since I divined the death of Lord Quigley. 'We all have to work with the universe if we have any hope of realizing our dreams.' That is what we are all told in the Red Tradition at our first day at the academy in the Crooked Spears. 'We must never put ourselves ahead of our work. A head bowed low will soar.' What rot!

"All I have now is myself, my *own* voice, not some little voice that quietly demands my obedience," he said, looking beyond me at some point on the wall behind where I sat. "And my magic, which has not failed," he continued, conjuring a little ball of red electricity that arced back and forth between the fingers of his open palm. "And my dreams."

"Your dreams?" I said, raising an eyebrow. Fear for the consequences of speaking my mind gave way to a wave of righteousness from the depth of my being. "Your dream is that everyone would leave you be so that you might desecrate corpses into creatures that will... I do not know, fight your battles for you? You are completely insane."

The man threw his head back and laughed his shrill laugh again.

"Perhaps I am! But mad or not, I am still a man. Of course, I have dreams, Andrew. And my desire for the freedom to practice necromancy is not so cheap and trite as that. Indeed, raising the dead sometimes does create a monster that seeks to feed on the flesh of the living. But that is less an intended result than side effect. Those renegade Mages that have gone before me in the Red Tradition, the ones who sought out this power, their records are clear: there is much Wisdom within the skulls of dead men. That they attack us when they return from the dead does not change that. The knowledge within - it expands after a man crosses the threshold into the next world. There is information there, information that holds the key to immortality! The key to godhood!"

"But it cannot be just any old dead man," the Mage said after his pause for effect became overwrought. "There is magic in the blood of the nobility. Before my own inner voice died, the Prophecy was clear: I will eventually extract knowledge of immortality from the head of a dead nobleman. The timing of that extraction is up to the vicissitudes of Fate. The vision was unmistakable: there I was, surrounded by the corpses of noblemen and a group of men Hell-bent on the destruction of the Kingdom of Thrairn when I passed through the final threshold. And no little voice to tell me yes or no. Just orders from my partner. So, I follow the orders without question and know that I will eventually arrive at my destination. You are lucky – if it were up to me, I would have slain you long ago."

He smiled a black grin that caused my eyes to go wide with terror.

"King Janus does not realize how precarious his position has become," he continued. "The Red Tradition turns against him. Erifracia will go to war with Thrairn, just as certainly as you sit there before me. Do you even know what he did?"

A loud crash sounded in the hall, followed by shouts and the clanging of metal. I stood up. My malefactor did so, too, eying me with great intensity. He had drawn a dagger and was twirling it by its pommel on the tip of his index finger. I would have been impressed if I were not so worried for my survival.

"You said you would not kill me!" I shouted as I backed away from the man, towards the chaos beyond the door. "You said that there is more to my Fate!"

"I merely said you would survive the cave. And I am getting tired of waiting for my dead nobleman. The time is right because I say it is."

The hilt of the dagger dropped into the palm of the man's hand.

"Fate has her plan. I have my own."

Chapter Seventeen
Nox

The man in the red robe rushed at me... and continued on past, cackling at the unwarranted fear upon my face.

"You still confuse Fate with Destiny!" he said, turning before he disappeared. "One is chosen, the other is heaped upon you. Guess which is which!"

I thought for certain that he had meant to open my throat. He was toying with me, trying to get some reaction from me. On that piece, he had succeeded - the man was completely insane. And insanity breeds unpredictability as surely as night banishes day. I looked up.

Stars twinkled through the triangle of the window. Those at the castle would be looking for us soon, if they had not commenced the search already.

My chest pounded shards of unease as I poked my head through the beads and looked to the source of the clanging and shouting. In the torchlight beneath the sconces, Reed was locked in combat with a man dressed in *cuir d'arbalest* and wielding a curved blade. I recognized him as one of the brothel guards.

Reed was losing. The guard was bearing down on him with a series of blows that had pushed him up against the ivory marble of the hallway wall. I felt certain that it would be only a moment or two before Reed missed a parry and found his head removed from his shoulders. I looked down to my hand.

For some reason, I had picked back up the beer mug during my conversation with the lunatic Mage, despite having had no intention of drinking whatever substance was inside. It was still full. I cocked my arm back, praying that the years spent practicing my aim with wooden javelins at the training grounds in Isha had not been in vain.

Both Reed and I were pleased to learn that they had not.

The mug connected with the guard's exposed ear, sending a spray of beer and bits of fired clay all through his jet black hair. The man swore in Erifracian and turned to look at me. It was all the distraction that Reed needed. He must have learned through the previous moments of the fight that the *cuir d'arbalest* was not going to surrender to his blade, so he found the gap between the man's pants and chestpiece at the level of his lower belly and applied pressure.

The brutality of a disembowelment can be overwhelming, especially if you are not used to such horrors. I retched involuntarily, sending out bits of half-digested goat onto the black marble of the floor. Reed got clear of the dying man and gave me a few soft open slaps on my hunched over back.

"Thanks for the help! I owe you one, Andrew."

I stood to face my bodyguard.

"What the Hell is going on?"

"She tried to murder me! The whore. It was after we finished. I was layin' down, eatin' a few of the grapes they'd set out. I only just noticed the tiny stiletto in her hand in time."

He held up his own hand. It was wrapped in a bit of torn cloth. A dark red stain had formed on the area around the palm. I noticed then that he had taken the swatch of 'bandage' from the end of his white cloak.

"I actually had to grab the blade," Reed continued. "Better that then get the shiv in my guts, I figured. Christ-man, does it sting." The white cloak punctuated his words by flapping his bandaged hand for a moment. "After I turned it around on her and put an end to the schemin' bitch, I got dressed and came out into the halls. I must've been wandering for ten minutes before I ran into him," he finished, pointing to the dead man. "He did not want to talk. I wonder whether Kyle- Kyle! we need to find Kyle!"

"The man in the red robe," I said, grabbing Reed's arm, "the one who left before me, did you see which way he went?"

Reed shook his head.

"I was busy." The white cloak gestured to the corpse again.

"Fair enough."

I walked over to the dead Erifracian and stooped to pick up the curved sword that was still in his hand. A hand that was stiffening with "the mortis," as Terence had called the tendency of dead men to harden into their final shapes. After a few tense moments I managed to bend the fingers gripping the hilt and extract my new weapon.

"Scimitar," Reed said, nodding to me.

"Yes," I replied, inclining my own head to him. "Scimitar."

Chapter Eighteen
Pressure

I spent seven years training with a sword. Seven long years of listening to Terence drone repeatedly on to me and the other Squires about proper positioning, how to keep yours trained on the eyes of your enemy, that trusting our instincts and making sure to follow through on each blow with our bodies would see us through. Seven long years of psyching myself up ahead of spar after spar, telling myself that this day would be the day that I won, that I was Peter fucking Cardiff's son, for the Christ-man's sake, of course I could win. Seven long years of missing blocks on easy to spot attacks, being too scared to press whatever small advantages I gained, and whiffing blows against my training partners.

Seven long years of failure.

Every time that I was defeated, I told myself that it was simply because I was not meant to be a Knight. For some reason, Fate had decided that I was to be tortured with desire for a vocation at which I was simply rubbish. There *was* desire there, as loath as I was to admit it at times. I wanted to be a Knight more than anything. But the shoe fit like a ballet slipper on a donkey.

When I picked up the Erifracian sword in that brothel, thoughts of my previous disappointments played through my mind like a marching band dancing down the cobbles of Hightown during the Midsummer Festival. The thing now, of course, was that this was not practice. Failure here meant Erifracian steel splitting my abdomen the way that Reed's blade had done in my sword's previous owner.

As the white cloak and I stalked the halls, Reed first and me following, the vice of fear gripped my heart. I was going to be killed, I decided. Even if we made it out of the Black Mamba, war was coming. King Revanti was going to try to kill King Janus before he left port, if the overheard conversation was to be believed. Not to mention the Prophecy of the collapse of Thrairn in the wake of Janus' defiance of the Inner Council. Even if Janus escaped this place, I would be called into service to defend the realm. I needed to get better with a blade and there was no time left to learn.

That was not even taking into account the utter terror about the lycanthropy diagnosis and what it meant for me.

As we passed the multicoloured portals, Reed stuck his Thrain blade, straight and familiar to the alien curvature of the scimitar in my hand, into the beads and pushed them aside so that we could peek in. The first six doors passed in this way revealed whores and clients deep in contractual performance. Not a one of them noticed the two armed men creeping around in the corridor.

The seventh door, however...

"No," said Reed, his voice barely audible against the sound of the beads clacking together. "No, no, no, no..."

Kyle's naked body was slumped in a corner against white marble, scarlet running down onto his chest from a slice in his throat. The murder weapon lay on the black stone near his knees. Kyle's right hand and forearm were covered in bright red blood. He must have tried in vain to stem the flow during his last moments.

Reed kneeled before his brother and reached out to grab him. I looked around, terrified that the guilty prostitute might be lying in wait with her stiletto blade to do us in, too. But we were alone.

"Reed, I... I am sorry." I could not think of anything else to say, feeble though it was.

The man in the torn white cloak heaved his loss silently from his crouch next to his brother. I was thankful for his forbearance - a wail of grief would have no doubt generated some unwanted attention from the other denizens of the Black Mamba.

I realized then that I had erected a wall between myself and others throughout the frustrated years of my youth. My parents had been right in their admonishments - I did not have many friends and I could not say that I felt much, if any, empathy for others. I was too absorbed in self-pity, bellyaching to my mother for my own lot. Any overt concern for others that I did display was usually a show, something that I did because it was the thing to do to prevent further alienation. Now, though, seeing this man, having lost his brother...

It reminded me too much of my own grief when I learned that my mother's life had been ended by a thief's knife.

I knelt down next to Reed and put my arm around him. He responded by putting his arms around me and squeezing. The sound of sobs were muffled by the hard pack of my *cuir d'arbalest*. I cradled his head in my hands, looking over him at the corpse of his brother.

Kyle. The man who had been alive and breathing mere moments before, with whom I had traded stories about growing up in Isha in the sunny hours of that very morning. He was two years younger than I. Twenty-three, innocent of most things that did not involve putting his cock into a woman for money. A mere babe, murdered for some irrational Prophecy and a scheme to raise the dead.

"Reed," I said, pulling away from him and allowing red emotion to ignite in my chest. "I am very sorry for Kyle. But we need to get out of here and must not tarry. An assassination plot against King Janus is in motion."

"Assassination plot?" Reed asked, drying his eyes with a towel he found on a table.

"King Revanti. He means to slay him and seize the power of Thrairn. There is a Prophecy-"

"The power of Thrairn?" Reed asked, having finished for the moment with his grief. "Do you mean an invasion?"

I had forgotten what it meant to be uninitiated into the mysteries of the magic that lay beneath the surface of the world. How much longer such secrets could be kept before the seams exploded and spilled truth into the public consciousness was unknown to me. Best to control the tide, then. It meant breaking my oath as a member of the Inner Council, but according to the blond-haired Mage, the Red Tradition appeared to be about to betray my country in any event.

"It is a long story. One that I will tell you on the way."

"But, what about -"

Reed's words wilted in his throat and he simply pointed to the corpse of his brother.

"We cannot do anything for him," I replied. "We will certainly join him if we do not leave now."

"I will come back for you, brother, I swear it," Reed said, cradling his dead brother's head.

Standing from my crouch, I picked up the scimitar I had laid next to me. After a long hug of Kyle's body, Reed stood and grabbed his own blade.

"Let's go," the white cloak said, wiping his face once more.

✶ ✶ ✶ ✶ ✶

Reed led the way again. I made up a story about how I had injured my sword arm during my time with my captors, a small lie to keep him from asking the question that I knew was rattling around in his head: should not the Yellow Knight be the one leading the charge? After all, I was a Primary Colour of the Kingdom of Thrairn. The cream of the crop.

Hah.

In the flicker of torchlight in the hallways of the Black Mamba, shadows crept and bent into shapes that threatened to jump off the stone of the walls and throttle us. To alleviate the pressure, I gave Reed an accounting, as far as I dared. I told him that magic was real, but not the full extent of it. I did not get into the details of what the red-robed man had told me, only that I had found my captor from the sea cave in the horrific den of sin in which we found and that he plotted to raise the dead again. I thought better of telling the white cloak about the irrational divination story and the source of the armour I was wearing. Reed responded by informing me that he had heard rumours about the horrors that Dragonfly Company endured during their rescue of the remnants of Butterfly and did not need much convincing about the truth of what I was saying.

After my briefing, I shut up. Reed did the same.

We took our time, sneaking forward into the maze. Both of us had forgotten the sequence of right and left turns that had brought us from the entrance to our position deep in the brothel. On the way in, of course, we had assumed that our respective hostesses would lead us back into the foyer of the building when we had finished. I realized then that throughout my life, my mind, nearly without exception, had a tendency to wander to thoughts of the past or the future. The only times where that did not occur was during a spar, or when I was reading a book, or otherwise gathered up by excitement into a state of presence. What was it about the mundane that made it so easy to ignore in service to a desire to be elsewhere than wherever I had been at that given moment? I had not realized the importance of slowing my mind down, of paying attention to each moment on the path, as I was doing now, with my life hanging in the balance.

If I survived this, I vowed that I would never make that mistake again.

We passed scores of rooms wherein prostitutes and clients making their lustful exchanges. As luck would have it, in spite of what was occurring within the rooms, we encountered not a single soul in the hallways. It did not make the entrance any easier to find. And so I practiced my new revelation, of holding on to the present moment through an intentional returning of focus to my senses. I scanned the walls as we walked, concentrated on the sensation of the boots on my feet, on the heft of the sword in my hand, the air entering my lungs.

Thoughts of doom and fear of what was to come did try to intrude, but I simply did not follow them down the corridors in my mind that they urged me to go. I kept bringing my mind back to what my senses were telling it of the world at that exact moment.

After a while, all sense of myself seemed to evaporate. Memory of my identity seemed irrelevant, and all thoughts of the potential of what might occur in the future simply ceased to encroach upon the spotlessness of the experience. Time itself lost all of its meaning and I felt at home. It was a taste of eternity, and it was accompanied by kaleidoscopic images at the edge of my vision and a hair-raising awe that moved in waves down my back.

And then the never-ending hallways ended and we were at our destination. There were two ways of approaching the atrium: a pair of doorways that would bring us past the front desk, portals that were separated by yet another large wall of white marble. The light was much brighter through these doorways. Reed approached the one on our left. He stuck his head out to take a peek. After a moment, he stepped through.

Needles ran up my arms and into my chest. I bargained with myself for a moment about the virtues of staying hidden in the halls of the Black Mamba forever. Then I forced myself to do the same.

The quiet was eerie. When last I was there, a dull roar of conversation between the other guests, the ones who had not yet succumbed to smoke or drink, had threatened to drown out the fearful thoughts in my head. Now the place was bare of people and vice. There was not even a single pipe or a drinking glass on the tables. The only detectable motion came from the dance of the torch flame in the sconces on the walls. Stars twinkled and a sliver of moon shone through the open-air above. That is when I noticed her.

The aged madam was still in her position behind the bar. Gone was her red wig. I had been wrong in my estimation earlier, that she would have been white or grey underneath. Jet black hair that seemed to be plastered to her scalp shone brightly in the torchlight. It was as if she had applied half a crock of shoe polish to her skull. She was sipping from a little white china tea cup. Next to the saucer was an uncorked bottle with a clear liquid inside.

"Ah, da b'ys from T'rairn. I trust yis was taken care of." She looked over at us and drained whatever was left in her cup. She placed it in the saucer and poured another to the brim. "I ain't even gonna ask where yis got one a dem Erifrayshy scim-ee-tars. I hope yis ain't aimin' ta gut me wit it."

After perfunctorily winking at me, the madam resumed an entirely disinterested expression. It was disarming, given what she had just said. I unconsciously gripped the handle of my sword tighter.

"Uh, greetings," I said. "No, no. You are safe. As long as you are not aiming to open our necks with a stillett- Wait, Reed!"

In a flash, the white cloak closed the gap between us and the woman. He had brought his sword down to rest inches away from her neck.

"Your fuckin' whore killed my brother," he said through gritted teeth. "The one you gave me tried to kill me, too." Reed glanced momentarily down at the bandage on his right hand before returning his stare to here. "Tell me why I shouldn't put an end to ya right here."

The woman did not even flinch.

"Dey ain't me whores, lad. Dey's Ali's. And he don't tell me squat. I just does what dat cross ol' fucker tells me."

"Reed," I said. "Please. She might know where King Revanti went. Or that red-robed lunatic."

After a moment, Reed backed away. He did not return the blade to its scabbard, preferring to eye the woman with an intensity that screamed bloody violence.

"Where is everyone?"

"Gone or whorin'. Once dey's done whorin, dey's gone. Which reminds me: get da fuck outta here."

I could hear Reed's breathing increase its cadence. I looked at him and shook my head.

"I do not think that you appreciate the position you find yourself in..." I said, willing her to co-operate. "What was your name, again?"

"I never told ya. Ruby." The retired prostitute did a mock curtsy before skulling the entire contents of the tea cup.

"Ruby. Did you see King Revanti leave? What about a red-robed man with blond hair?"

"Ya 'tinks I got dis old at da game by being ready ta give up whatever secrets I has whenever some young buck t'reatens me wit' a big knife?"

Reed approached her, ready to swing.

"Yes, yes, course I did!" Ruby shrieked, her facade finally shredded as she dropped the tea cup and threw up her hands. "But I don't know nothing, 'onest. Ali just popped out about a half hour or so ago and told me to shut 'er down. So I told da b'ys ta get da fuck out and cleaned da place up wit' a few 'a da whores. Dassit! 'Onest."

She spread two knobby hands ravaged by arthritis.

I did not trust the woman for a moment, but we needed to get to King Janus. I considered, for a moment, killing her. How easy it would have been, just to slice her open and leave her to feed the maggots. There would be no worry about her telling her master about our escape. Revenge was sure to feel good.

But a little voice, deep inside my mind, the iridescence-heralded conscience that had told me thrice to fight to survive, now commanded me to leave her. It simply was not right to murder in cold blood.

I placed a gloved hand on the blade of Reed's readied sword and drew it down.

"Let us go, Reed. There is nothing more for us here."

✱ ✱ ✱ ✱ ✱

A palpable tension was on the air in the darkened streets of Tunuska, though that feeling might have been a projection of my unquiet mind. Torchlight led us along the hard-packed dirt, past closed market stalls, drunk Tunuskans and wary Erifracian guards glowering from their posts. They mercifully did not recognize us as foreign interlopers with secret knowledge of their King's bloody plot against our own. I had no scabbard, but I hid the scimitar from them on the side of my thigh nonetheless. They looked to be on high alert, but it was clear from their inaction that their orders did not include apprehending Thrain soldiers.

Yet.

The terror I felt was related to a threat of a more immediate nature. The notion of getting as lost as we had in the corridors of the Black Mamba dogged me. Thankfully, Reed had already spent a few nights navigating his way back to the castle from the brothels and quickly deflated my worry when I voiced it to him.

"We just have to head towards the light on the hill," he said, pointing his blade to the castle windows burning brightly against the starry sky with a curved slice of moon above the horizon. I imagined that Reed must have recalled then that during previous evenings he had his dead brother as a traveling companion, as he became quiet and his movements then took on a nearly imperceptible stiffness.

We were nearly back to the start of the incline that would

lead us up the hill past the farms and to our final destination when we ran into trouble.

"Andrew! Andrew fuckin' Cardiff, izzat you? They let ya out of the castle?"

Simon had stumbled out of a small building, his armour crooked on his torso and his pants looking as though they were about to fall off. The pince-nez spectacles on his nose were completely askew. The scabbarded sword on his belt flailed wildly as he closed the distance between us.

"Simon," I replied, hugging the man and noticing that he reeked of ale.

"Out whorin' are ya?" Simon said, drawing away from me and smiling broadly. He did not wait for my reply. "Some good, ain't it? Better than the Green Dragon. These Erifracian girls can suck the shine off a pommel, I shite ya not." He stopped and looked from me to Reed. "You headed back to the castle? I'ma come with ya."

"Siiiimon! You not going to run off without paying, arrre you?"

A dark-skinned man with a heavy Erifracian accent was at the door of the building that Simon had just left. In the light from the torch over the portal, he was clearly visible. He had no shirt or shoes on and was wearing what looked to be green velour pants cinched with a black rope. He had one hand cocked out in front of him expectantly and wore a coquettish smile on his face. It appeared that he had the black soot used by the local women as makeup around his eyes.

A look of terror passed over Simon's face.

"I don't know what youse talking about, mate."

"You suck cock, you pay," the man said, frustration blossoming on his face.

"I never sucked no fuckin' cock, you fuckin' fairy creep," Simon said, his eyes darting to me. "I fucked an Erifracian girl."

"Simon, you want me get Altaïr? He make you pay. You no like that." The man thrust his hand out insistently once more.

167

"One dinar."

"One dinar, eh? For the girl."

The Erifracian man shrugged. "If you like. For the girl." He winked at Simon.

Simon walked over towards the man. He placed a hand onto the little leather pouch on his belt, pretending to pull it off. As he got closer to the man, his hand moved to the hilt of his sword.

"I ain't no fuckin' sissy, mate! Tell 'em!"

"You – you fuck girl, like you say. No cock." Now it was the Erifracian man's turn to become scared.

Simon returned his hand to his coin purse and pulled it off. He withdrew a coin from the purse with his left hand and put the purse back on his belt. Backing up slightly, he held out the coin in the palm of his left hand. The Erifracian man could not reach the coin from where he was standing, and had to lean over towards Simon to get it.

I figured out what Simon was doing right at the moment that he did it. As the man leaned in, Simon drew back his free arm back. He slammed his fist forward into the man's jaw. There was a sickening crunch and the man's head twisted in an unnatural way. He fell forward and his body began to shudder and flail and bounce on the sand of the street.

"I ain't no fuckin' sissy!" Simon screamed the words at the man's seizing face.

"Simon," I shouted, feeling sickness suffuse my gut. "What the fuck are you doing?"

Simon looked at me. There was something in his eyes, a rage of incalculable black immensity that obscured any familiarity I might have otherwise sensed in the man. And then it fled and my friend was back. A pained look blossomed as he turned his eyes towards the man flopping around on the ground beneath him. Then the Erifracian stopped moving and lay still.

"I – I never meant to-" Simon began. "It's just that..." Simon dropped to his knees. "Hey, hey, Aziz! Are you OK, mate? I'm sorry! Andrew, come and help me!"

I started to move towards the pair, glancing at Reed as I did. He seemed to be completely disengaged from the scene, scanning around for danger. I crouched down next to Simon to look at the man. There were no visible signs of breathing. I thought back to Terence's medical training then grabbed the man's wrist and put my finger over the artery, looking for the telltale pulse that would let me know he was alive.

I could not find it.

Our problems multiplied when an enormous hirsute man dressed in a strap shirt and bearing a proportionately large club stepped from the threshold of the brothel into the torchlight. He shouted something in Erifracian back through the door of the whorehouse, then turned to face us.

"Simon, form up next to Reed," I said, moving into position and bringing the curved sword up into the ready position, another automatic heirloom from our training with Terence. Simon complied. Three more armed men, these ones smaller and bearing exotic swords like the one I had in my hand, swarmed out of the doorway to the brothel.

"Fucking Christ-man," I muttered.

I am both ashamed and proud of what happened next. I am ashamed because these men, as seedy as they must have been for choosing to work security at a brothel, were simply defending themselves from an attack on the place they worked. Not to mention avenging the life of one of their charges. To be fair to the muscle, fighting off threats to the brothel was their raison d'être. The intimidation that a giant with a club must convey to the patrons of such a place could only go so far. Sometimes you had to actually bash a fucker's head to pieces. It was part of the deal.

But what set this off, the insult: it was a horrific turn on Simon's part. I saw that he was clearly was battling a Demon. And he was losing that battle. He had just murdered a man for nothing. Fear of what his peers would think of him for enjoying the company of a man. My own idiotic jokes about being buggered aside, I could not have cared less what Simon chose to do with his mouth. Especially not then. This was an unnecessary waste of time, given what was at stake in the castle up on the hill. And these men we were about to put to the sword - they were only doing their jobs.

The pride, then. For a time afterward, I could not explain to myself what had happened next. I assumed that it was because I was the bearer of the Jaguar's curse. Some Atikan magic must have been guiding my feet and sword arm as they danced their bloody dance. But I know now that this was base self-doubt. I could not have spent seven years at the training grounds without some of the Wisdom hard won from those drills and spars having worked itself into my mind and body.

The difference between this fight and the innumerable failures at the training grounds, as far as I could tell, was that I had purpose now. If I did not win, the Kingdom of Thrairn was doomed to fall to treachery. Maybe it had already fallen, but I did not know that for sure. To boot, and perhaps the most disconcerting: the red-robed lunatic might discover the secret of immortality and set himself up as a living god.

Not to mention the fact that it was a matter of kill these men or have our corpses feed the fishes of Tunuska Harbour.

The first man on me was not the big one, and I thanked the stars burning bright above us for that mercy. He was dressed in *cuir d'arbalest*, same as me. Like mine, there were scant few gaps in his armour.

He made the first move, a quick jab with the end of the blade. I easily pushed it aside. He came at me again, this time with a series of quick chops in succession. I deflected them all.

'Patience is one of the surest ways to win a battle,' Terence had told us during one of his many lectures under the cold grey Ishan morning sun. 'If you can, learn your enemy's movements so that you might use them against him.'

A calm had descended on me as I kept up a defensive wall against the Erifracian man's sword. It was not like the spars at the training grounds, when I was painfully aware that all of my peers were watching. As it had in the Black Mamba, past and future disappeared. There was just me, the guard, and the deadly danger of the moment. I paid perfect attention to each swing and the resultant clang of metal on metal.

It was clear that the Erifracian was slipping into the throes of rage. His face, which had been set at the beginning of the battle, had degenerated into a furrowed mask. In his world, I assumed, I was supposed to do more than simply block his attacks. He shouted something unintelligible at me, though I understood perfectly well that it was something not too kindly. He was getting tired of my implacability.

'Your enemy's frustration is one of your greatest Strengths,' echoed Terrence's words in my head. 'A frustrated enemy is one that makes mistakes.'

I kept up my defensive wall, taking a moment here and there to glance over at my compatriots. They were holding their own, though the big man and one of the others had ganged up on Simon. I would need to finish my fight in order to help him.

And quick.

I heard the little voice in my head, then. The faint sound of Courage. Only it was not as faint now. It was growing in volume. And it was telling me to stand and fight, but to concentrate on my own battle. I could not split my attention between myself and my friend, as concerned as I was for him. And I could not fail to heed Terence's words. I had to be patient and take my time. I could not insert myself when the time was not right. The hideous corollary of this realization was that if Simon died, such was his Fate.

Que sera, sera.

It was a phrase in the dead language of the Heraclytan Empire. One that my mother used to repeat to me on those long evenings when I came back from the training grounds, stinking of sweat and failure, swearing up and down that I would never succeed as a Knight. She had told me that those unfamiliar words meant that I could not change the outcome of things in this world. I had to let go of control, of trying to force things. My mind was getting in the way of my success. She intended it as a comfort. I always took it to be the height of pretentiousness and idiocy, a cold black mark on a woman who was otherwise replete with warmth and light. To my young self, giving over to Fate was the coward's way to escape responsibility for his actions.

I finally understood what she meant on that night, under the light of the Tunuskan crescent moon.

The Erifracian was on me again, raining blows in perfect time, like the even ticking of the metronome that Marissa Rice had shown me one sunny afternoon during a respite from training as I watched her play the organ in the Cathedral. I saw my opportunity and went for it. I raised my left forearm, knowing that the *cuir d'arbalest* would absorb the blow, and that it would cause me great pain. There was a chance that my arm would break. But I had to risk it.

The Erifracian's sword connected, ringing out on the hard leather. My arm exploded in pain, pain that threatened to break my concentration. But the arm did not break and my focused sharpened, instead. The man had over extended himself, creating a gap between his chestpiece and pants.

Taking my lesson from the technique I saw Reed employ at the Black Mamba, I jabbed my sword into the gap and pushed with all my might.

I was not awake when I had previously taken a life, when I had become the Jaguar and killed Captain Rice. I do not recall him pleading for his life, nor do I recall snuffing out the light in the man's eyes. As far as my conscious mind was concerned, my soul had no bloody tally, no deaths to its name.

The look in the Erifracian's face in the torchlight chills my bones as I think back on it, even to this day. It is not an enjoyable thing, taking a life. It is the most horrible action I have ever encountered.

And the first time you do it is the worst.

Chapter Nineteen
Three Things

"Andrew!"

Reed's cry broke the spell that had come over me as I watched my Erifracian foe's life slip away. I turned.

The white cloak had dealt with the guard who had formed up on him with a perfectly aimed slice of his sword, leaving his assailant to noisily expire from a near-decapitation. Simon, on the other hand, had shifted quite a distance away from the two of us and appeared to be bleeding from a pair of flesh wounds on his arms, inflicted from the sword wielded by the smaller of the guards that attacked him. The large man with the club kept winding up and missing Simon as he dodged farther and farther away.

I was thankful that Simon still retained some measure of dexterity in spite of the alcohol he had aboard him. But his luck could not last forever. It was two against one, and one was a behemoth. Reed and I closed the distance as fast as we could.

It quickly became clear that the smaller of the two guards that attacked Simon was not wearing any gloves. As we approached, Simon struck the man's wrist, taking the whole hand off. He screamed in pain and dropped to his knees. Simon had knocked himself off balance when he threw his weight into the blow and he hesitated as he tried to get control of his weapon again. The giant took this opportunity to kick him in the chest, sending him to the ground. He raised his club for an overhand blow. Simon saw this and rolled out of the way.

Well, almost out of the way.

The sound of the hard wood connecting with the sinew and bone of Simon's right forearm sent shivers down my spine. He screamed in pain and rolled around on the ground. The giant was winding up for another smash just as Reed and I finally closed the gap. The white cloak cocked his sword back low, like he was holding at bat in a game of rounders, the stick and ball game other children used to play in the sun-soaked fields outside of Isha while I quietly kept to my books under the shade of the trees.

Thankfully, the hulking man was not wearing *cuir d'arbalest*. Reed's sword struck him in the meat of his calf, going through and stopping at the back of his shinbone. The man shouted a curse and dropped onto his arse. I took the opportunity to bury the scimitar to the hilt down through the narrow space between the bones in his shoulders that Terence had taught us would allow access to a man's internal organs. He groaned and fell over.

Reed picked up Simon's sword and finished off the handless guard before dropping it back to the ground.

I rushed over to Simon, who was cursing and rolling on the ground, cradling his arm. The flesh had turned black in a circle on his forearm. The bone inside was almost certainly splintered. It would be a stroke of luck indeed If Simon survived this without losing the arm. He had not yet noticed me and Reed. I put a hand on the wounded man's shoulder.

"Simon... Simon! We need to get out of here. Now. Can you walk?"

He cursed as he pushed himself up with his good arm. I told Reed to turn around and tore some more of the tattered white cloak off from the bottom. Trying my damnedest to recall what Terence had taught us about making a sling in the field, I tied it off around his neck. Simon whimpered in response to my ministrations.

"There, that is one thing for which you are in my debt," I said with a smile.

With some effort, Reed removed his sword from the giant's leg. I tried pulling the curved sword out of the big man once, but it was impossibly stuck in the mess of tissue in which it had been buried. Sighing, I stepped back. Noticing a wineskin on the dead Erifracian's hip, I picked it up, opened the top, took a whiff, and smiled. I walked over to Simon, placed the wine skin in his left hand, and unclasped his sword belt in spite of a weak protest.

"I am borrowing this. You are in no condition to fight. There, that wine: that is the second thing."

Simon greedily suckled at the opening, as if he were a fresh babe and the skin held his mother's milk. I attached the sword belt around my own waist, bending to pick up Simon's sword. There was some crimson staining on the blade. I used a little strip of the cloth I had torn from Reed's cloak to remove the blood, then slammed the sword into its scabbard.

"Let us go."

We did not encounter any more trouble during our trek up the hill to the castle, though Simon did his damnedest to make sure that there was no quiet, mumbling pain and pleading forgiveness. Reed remained mute.

"Listen, Andrew," he said, "I don't like men, I want ye to know that."

"Simon," I replied, "I do not care about your proclivities one way or another. The only bastards that would are back in the churches of Thrairn, diddling little altar boys and choir girls in the shadows while they call men like you an abomination."

"I'm serious!" Simon insisted. "I love women. I love Kelsa more than anythin' in the world. That thing with Aziz was – it was... It was that cock fiend Captain Rice that began all of this!"

Kelsa Upshall. Simon's betrothed. I was invited to the

wedding, which was supposed to happen in a matter of weeks but had been shifted to the Yule Month because of this Erifracian campaign on which we found ourselves.

"What?" I asked, perking up at the sound of our former Captain's name.

"When I first came on to Butterfly Company, they hazed me. The way they always does. You're lucky you came in when ye did and missed it. The other lads beat the shite out of me with few rollin' pins, made me eat a slice of bread onto which they all spilled they's seed, made me walk through the barracks naked while they all cat-called me. Then Rice called me into his bunk, the one he has away from the rest of the lads in Butterfly.

"He pulled his pecker out and made me suck 'is cock while he had a knife in his hand, threatenin' ta gut me if I telt anyone," Simon said, sobbing through the wine haze. "It was terrible, disgustin', and the noises 'e made... I 'ated him, 'is red face, 'is fat belly, 'is little tiny cock. The bastard." Simon went quiet for a moment. "I was so happy when I heard you 'ad kill't him." There was another pause. "I found myself looking for it again, after he had done it. I can't explain it, but there was something about it that made me want to do it again."

"Christ-man, Simon," I said, "I am sorry that you had to go through all of that."

Simon guzzled more wine from the skin before continuing.

"It's only when I'm deep in me cups that I gets the urge. I went to the brothels in Isha, found men who was willing to let me suck them off. But I could never bring myself to kiss them or do anything else with 'em. I feel nothin' towards these men, not really. They were just creatures that could fill me urges. And I gets the urges every time I drinks. I can't help meself. I don't know what I'm gonna do. It's a fuckin' crime in Thrairn, you knows that, right? Men swing from the gibbet every week in Isha for Buggery and Indecency charges. And 'sides that, who the fuck would understand it? There's no room fer it. As far as most people are concerned, yer either a real man or a bugger. If Kelsa finds out, I'm sure we're finished. And it was all because of that fucker Rice. Thank ye again for tearin' 'im apart."

Simon took another long swig and prodded tentatively at his injured arm with the skin. He winced at the pain.

"And now I've kill't a man because of it. Christ-man, what a fuckin' mess."

"I am indeed sorry, Simon," I said, unsure of what else I could offer the tortured man. I felt a tingle down my back as I felt compassion for the man. Rainbows edged into my vision. "Whatever happens, we will get through it."

Simon smiled grimly at me in the dim light and grunted.

The castle gate was set into a circular wall that surrounded a large courtyard. At the opposite end of the gate, the wall joined the tall tower of the castle proper, a wall that was under constant patrol by a dozen or so guards in the ramparts. We were hailed in Erifracian as we approached. A response in Thrain resulted in a bit of shuffling and hushed speech between the men. I imagined then that we were fucked, that King Revanti had completed his betrayal, and we were about to die from a volley of Erifracian arrows.

I recalled with some hope that King Revanti was waiting on our red-robed malefactor to confirm that he could convince the other Mages to abandon King Janus. Perhaps there was yet time, I prayed.

"Yes," came a heavily accented voice from the wall above, "yes, you come in."

After we all sighed our relief, the Erifracian guards on the walls did not interfere with us any further. As we approached the door to the castle, two visored white cloaks as well as the helpful creature named Jason flew out of the portal at a gallop and nearly bowled us over. Jason's tricorner hat fell off his head.

"Malley?" asked Jason after he collected his hat from the ground. "Reed Malley? What happened to you? Where is Kyle? Is that an injured Knight? May I help in any way? Perhaps fetch a Chirurgeon?"

"Please," Reed said wearily. "Take us to the King."

I was disarmed again, as soon as the white cloaks understood who I was. Nevertheless, they grudgingly took us up to King Janus after promises from us all that it was an emergency and that we were prepared to face whatever Justice our ruler was prepared to dish out if we were found to be wasting his time. Simon stumbled a few times on the seemingly endless stairs, nearly smashing his head open in the process. I grabbed and held him by the good arm. Maybe more wine for the man had been a bad idea after all.

When we arrived at the door to the King's room, another pair of white cloaks came to stand on either side of us, hands on the hilts of their swords. The man next to me was close enough that I could feel his breath on my neck and smell the food from his supper off his clothes.

"Andrew," said King Janus, "what is the meaning of this? Do you know what time it is? Am I to regret my decision to not place you in bonds?"

He was standing in night clothes of purple cloth, with slippers and a matching hat with a peak that fell lazily to one side. Outside the window behind him, the stars were still burning bright.

"Where is Kathryn? We need her."

"What is happening?" the King said, ignoring my question.

I told the King the story, as best I could. I omitted certain details about our encounter with Simon and how he ended up with us out of a desire to protect the man from the King's Justice, which would indeed see him executed. And it would not have been for the accidental slaying of the prostitute.

"Your Grace," I said, "the Red Tradition and King Revanti both are plotting to betray you. We need to get you out of here.

I do not know whose murder they believe you have committed without sanction. What I do know is that my former captor believes in this Prophecy beyond a shadow of a doubt.

King Janus looked at me without responding. He had a furrow in his brow. He was staring at me, almost through me. It was an uncomfortable feeling. A memory returned to me, then. It was the red-robed man, asking me if I knew what King Janus had done before we were interrupted by the sound of Reed and the guard locked in combat in the hallway without. The questioning tone of his voice, the look of curiosity in his eyes... Was the King hiding something from me?

"Good," King Janus said with a laugh that broke the tension. "Thank you for bringing this to my attention. I am aware of the problems with the Red Tradition, and fortunately things are not so rosy for those that oppose me as that Mage would have you believe. The Prophecy is not given much Faith within the Red Tradition. But, Revanti's treachery is news to me. You are correct. We need to get out of here."

"As for the rest of it," Kind Janus continued. "I have been beholden to the Red Tradition for forty years. What you say about the source of your armour: it is not the strangest thing that I have heard through my dealings with them. Not by a long shot. But the necromancy is a grave problem. And the Mage's partner: it sounds to me like there may be more than just the two of them. I fear that this cabal that they belong to may be the greatest threat of all to peace in Thrairn. You are right, I need to speak to Kathryn."

"Richard," he said, looking at the white cloak next to me. "Go fetch Commander Cardiff. We will need to co-ordinate our exit carefully.

"Reed, I am sorry about your brother," the King said, switching his attention to the exhausted soldier next to me. "His death will not have been in vain. You will find your revenge before this is all over." The King looked to my other fellow. "Simon, I will send for one of our Royal Chirurgeons to look at your arm." The King then turned again to me. "Andrew, there is a room across the hall that is empty. There are several beds within. Please, go and rest for a few hours. Take Simon and Reed with you."

We were ushered out by the white cloaks and brought to the room which the King meant. There were five beds arranged in a mish mash in the center of the room. In one corner, there were mops and buckets and flasks and bottles piled up next to them. A tiny sliver of window cut into the bare walls allowed some draft in to air the place out.

After we had gotten inside, we all took a bed for ourselves, hauling off our armour and groaning with the cuts and bruises of battle. Simon's groans were accompanied with sharp intakes of air every time he shifted.

"Andrew, thank ye for not tellin' the King the truth of me story."

I rolled over onto my side, yawning.

"Whatever your crime in killing that man, I cannot agree that the gallows should hold your Fate. There, saving you from certain death: that is the third thing," I mumbled, letting sleep take me.

Chapter Twenty
Freedom

"Get up."

Father. How many times had I heard those words from that man on a cold foggy morning in Isha before training? I opened my eyes. Simon and Reed had disappeared from the cots next to me. He was standing at the threshold of the room. I sat up and stretched.

"I understand you have told the King a story. One that has him second-guessing his ally, King Revanti. A story that has led him to give the order to evacuate this city." He dropped his voice to something barely audible. "You are playing a dangerous game."

"Please, father," I said, "Dad. Enough of this suspicion. I am your son. I am not your enemy. I love you."

Three little words. Ones that I might have said to him twice in my life, when I was very much younger.

My father looked at me, his face inscrutable.

"William was my friend, Andrew," he said finally. "He had his faults, but he was a good man. I looked to him for counsel. To not have him around... this has not been easy for me."

"I am sorry for your loss, Father. I am. And I did not mean to kill him, you must believe me. I do not remember any of it."

I paused, considering my words. I began getting dressed.

"I had to kill two men yesterday, and I was certainly conscious for that. I would be more than happy if I was never forced to take a life again. And those deaths... I suppose those deaths could be described as the legacy of your friend."

"What? What do you mean by that?"

"Nothing. Nothing, never mind."

"No, you are not getting off as easy as that! What did you mean?"

"This does not leave this room. Do I have your word?"

"What?"

I paused then, gathering my Courage. Anxiety pulsed fire from chest to toe as I approached the threshold. To speak to my father in this manner was completely against all of my conditioning. But I could not risk my father telling anyone who might see Simon hang for his alleged crimes.

"You heard me," I said finally.

My father just stood there for a moment, before nodding his assent. He crossed and closed the door behind him.

"You have it," he said turning once more to face me.

I was standing now, dressed in my pants and my undershirt. I stopped in my labour to get my armour on so that I might look at the man who gave me life.

"Had you never heard the rumours?" I began. "About what he did with the men under his command? The furtive, grasping shame that would have seen him swinging from a hangman's knot if the Judges and Priests had their proof? Hell, forget the law and the clergy - he forced himself on those men. That is wrong, Father. By placing me under his command you almost sentenced me to the same Fate. Had we not been on our way here the very day after I was, I probably would have had to choke on the man's shame the same as the other Knights of Butterfly Company.

"I suppose it would have been difficult to rape me with the thin walls on the ship," I said with solemnity. "Or perhaps I was to be spared his attentions since I am your son. Not all men are graced with that manner of protection."

My father was silent, then. His eyes were cast down to the bare cream stone on the floor of the storage closet.

"Ah, so you have heard the rumours about him," I said, noticing the accusation in my tone and consciously releasing it. "I am sad that I killed Captain Rice, father. It certainly was not my place to do that. But do not stand there and tell me he was a good man."

My father looked up at me, tears in his eyes.

"And what of his connection to the Erifracians you killed yesterday?" he asked. "I understand you killed the guards of a brothel? How is that connected to William's activities?"

"'Activities?'" I scoffed. "You do the arithmetic on that one, Father."

I turned from my father then. I gathered my thoughts. As I did, I notice that the hairs on my back were starting to stand on end. Colours at the edge of my vision returned.

"I have reflected long on it since last night. It would seem that lust born of dark compulsions and violence begets more of the same. And the shame attached to it means that a man just might do anything he can to prevent his peers from discovering that shame. Something born of violence in turn. Something that might bring the guards of such a place down on him and his friends. I will speak no more of it."

I spun to look at my father again.

"Remember your vow of discretion."

The conversation dried up for a time. I pulled on the rest of my armour as my father stood quietly and watched me.

"That is fine armour," my father said. "I prefer the heavy chain of Thrain Armourcrafters, but I certainly appreciate grand craftsmanship when I see it."

I realized with a happy surprise that I had not shied away from this confrontation with my father. In years past, I would have avoided such an encounter by retiring to my room or running off to a tavern. I had just spoken my mind to him and he had listened.

My father looked at me in a way that I had never seen him look at me. Was that sheepishness on his face?

"I forgive you for what happened with William, my son," he said. "Fucking magic – what I would not do for a return to my youth, when I was ignorant of its existence." He paused again. "I owe you my apologies as well. I-I am sorry. For finding yourself forced to kill. And for your friend. I hope that there is some hope for him."

I crossed the distance and took my father in my arms and squeezed him hard. He was not used to such displays of emotion. He patted feebly at my back. I was happy for it, for I knew it to be the limit of his capabilities. And he did push it to that limit. My tears stained the leather beneath his chain mail.

"I forgive you, too," I said, feeling waves of bliss cascade down my back as the hairs stood on end once more. Closing my eyes, the kaleidoscope had returned.

Chapter Twenty-One
Crossroads

"So, the men of Thrairn are leaving," Kathryn said, disapproval evident in her voice. She had arrived several minutes before, just after myself and my father were called into King Janus' chamber. She stood by the window, arms folded and staring at the King, who was dressed again in immaculate combat leathers and watching her languidly from his seat on a bench at the foot of the bed. Kathryn's hood was pulled back. Jet black hair lay amongst the red folds of her robe in tresses. Green eyes burned bright against ivory skin. Ghostly fingers ran over the flesh of my back as I gazed upon her.

From where I was standing by the door I could barely see a bright dawn poking up over the horizon. In the moments before Kathryn had spoken, the King had done a decent job of explaining what had occurred. She had considered his words for a long moment before speaking.

"Why was the Inner Council not convened before that decision was made?"

"Emergency situations are an exception to the hand wringing of the Council. And I would say that this is an emergency situation." The King glanced over at me. "Besides, based on what Knight Cardiff had to say, those elements of the Red Tradition that would see me ousted are gaining in power."

"Christ-man, Janus, so to solve that issue you just took another unilateral action? This will just feed the fires of the dissenters. We are not ready to take on the Red Tradition yet! This was not part of the plan. Did you speak to-" Kathryn looked at me sharply for a moment before ceasing to speak. Was that a look of worry that had descended on her face as her eyes met mine?

"And what would you have me do?" King Janus asked, picking up the thread where it had died in Kathryn's throat. "Stay here and wait for Revanti to come with his bleeders? To be gutted like one of his pets while the Council crawls together to tell me 'yes, yes, you should run back to Isha'? Twile and Respero are on a skiff somewhere between here and Thrairn. They are supposed to be here tomorrow in time for the evening's vote, but it might be days before they arrive. If they do at all, given the corsairs that we came down here to help deal with in the first place. And you know that I need a quorum!"

"Forty years," Kathryn said coolly. "Forty years of service to the Red Tradition. You might have your differences with the Council, but have you not learned patience and discipline? Have you not learned the price of letting those virtues fall by the wayside? You were told by the Council to come down here and work with Revanti! That was the decree, and you are breaking it. It has not changed, not until the Council convenes and votes on the matter. If you do this now, no one will be able to deny the evidence of this breach." Kathryn sighed and her tone became conciliatory. "I am not saying that I distrust what Andrew has said, not at all. I would have you use the proper channels, yes."

Kathryn turned to look out the window, placing her hands on the sill as she did.

"You know where my loyalty lies, Janus," she continued. "It goes much deeper than what I owe the Red Tradition. And you have it until the end, however that comes. But you are playing an incredibly dangerous game." Kathryn swiveled her attention to me. "Speaking of dangerous, are you planning on taking him with you?"

"Kathryn the Silent, my arse," King Janus said with a harsh laugh. "You speak more than the Queen Mum did before she passed, bless her heart. Knight Cardiff is a loyal Knight, one to whom I owe my thanks, perhaps my skin. And you already deemed him safe. Are you retracting that diagnosis?"

"I had expected him to be out of here one way or another after the Council convened tomorrow night!" Kathryn said. "I did not think he would be by your side for any longer than that. If he is cursed like the lycanthrope that I studied during my formative years at the Red Keep, then the danger he poses increases as the moon grows large in the sky. But that man was doomed to shapeshift into a badger. Andrew's affliction appears to be... different, somehow. And he will be traveling with you for some time." Kathryn crossed her arms. "He cannot stay with you."

"'Cannot'? You are giving me orders?" King Janus watched Kathryn, who had retreated into muteness. "So you are volunteering to take him, are you? Back to the Spears?"

"Perhaps. Such a decision requires a vote, as you know."

"Fuck the vote. Will you take him?"

"This path you are taking: you know it is rebellion, do you not? This is an act of war. The Red Tradition will be all but forced to abandon you."

"And so what if it is?" the King asked with one of his laughs. "You know I love you like a daughter, Kathryn, but I see the writing on the wall. There is a change coming, I can feel it in my bones. And you magical types always tell me to trust my intuition. What am I even doing as ruler, if only to act as puppet to red voices from the shadows? Am I not a King? Can I not be trusted to make my own decisions without interference?"

"It is making your own decisions that has landed you in this place! The Red Tradition has given you plenty of chances,

Janus. Chances out of respect to your forebears. But its patience has come to an end. You will always have allies, you know that. But I would not try to make more enemies! Not right now."

"I agree that it is dangerous," said the King softly. "But freedom always bears a heavy price."

"Janus," Kathryn said, smirking without humour at the King, "those are pretty words. I listened to the grand speech that you gave to Andrew just a couple of weeks ago when he was inducted to the Council. All your proclamations about how you did what the Council told you and enjoyed the same. Did you mean any of what you said? Do you mean it now?"

"The whole Council was there with me!" King Janus slammed his hand on the bench next to him and rose to his feet. "You think I had any choice but to say those words? I am tired of the Red Tradition, tired of following orders. Tired of every little Gods-damned rule. You know this! You expected this!"

"And the secrecy!" King Janus continued, beginning to pace back and forth. "Andrew told his friends about the existence of magic. He felt compelled to do so by circumstance. By the Red Tradition's rules, I should have him turned over for execution. For being honest. And what of the men of Dragonfly Company who witnessed the dead men rise? They bore witness to magic. What Fate does the Red Tradition intend for them?"

"No, Kathryn, the time of the Red Tradition's stranglehold on Thrairn is at an end," the King said, gesticulating madly now. "I will not submit one more decision, one more life to its bloody crucible. I know that there are those that wish to bring about an end to the tyranny. They shout from the streets of Thrairn, bound with the anti-magic jewelry that your precious Red Tradition gave them as a gift to go along with their exile. Those men and women are like muzzled dogs. They cannot speak of magic because of the perverse retribution the Tradition has laid upon them. They see in me a pawn of their masters, a political enemy that they *can* fight. They hate me only because I serve the Red Tradition. If they instead saw in me an ally, a man who sought an end to their captors, perhaps that would change. And you have the power to release them. The Tradition thinks that it is invulnerable. Since the days of the fall of the Heraclytan Empire, when the closing of the Rift meant the raising up of Order at the expense of Balance, the Red Tradition crowned itself the ruler of the land, secret though that rule might be. The Mages think that exclusive access to magic gives them licence to do as they wish with whom they wish. It is time to teach them that such arrogance will see them finished. The people will know that magic exists, for better or worse."

"We have spoken about this countless times before," the King said, dropping his arse back on the bench with finality. "The question is simply one of timing. What is that saying I heard in the dungeons back last Harvest Month? Ah, yes: it is shite or get off the pot time, Kathryn. Will you join me?"

Kathryn looked at me, fingers having moved up to the side of her head to run along one of her tresses.

"Yet more pretty words, Janus," Kathryn said, maintaining her gaze in my direction. "Pretty words full of the out-of-touch idealism to be expected from the nobility. I know better than to believe a word of it." Kathryn paused. "You know that such action will put your throne at risk."

King Janus nodded.

"I have already told you that you have my loyalty," Kathryn sighed, looking at him. "And you are right - it is what we have planned. Our allies will be overjoyed that the time has come. It will mean that I can no longer return to the Red Tradition. They will know what has occurred here, that the Inner Council has been rejected. And that I was a part of it.

Kathryn turned again to stare at me. "What is your plan for Queegan?"

"Your bro- that blond-haired madman?" The King said, looking at me as well. "My plan is to find him and have one of my men run him through."

"That simple, eh? And what of his heart's desire? The man seeks immortality. He is not the first. And he will not be the last. But unlike those others, it appears he is getting dangerously close to what he is compelled to seek out. From Andrew's description of his encounter with Queegan, it sounds as though he has already decided to kill members of the nobility. There is power in blood and in Prophecy. You know that better than anyone, Janus."

Kathryn turned her gaze back to face the King of Thrairn. "If there is one thing that the Red Tradition's texts warn all Mages about, it is the perils of necromancy. There is nothing concrete about the consequences of such magic, but there are whispers of something great and terrible. It is universally regarded as a bad idea."

"Then we will simply have to find him before he completes his quest," King Janus replied, having returned to his position on the bench at the foot of the bed.

Kathryn looked at me. It appeared as though the faint hint of a smile attempting to break through found itself onto her face. "What about his partners? Do you have a plan for these others? We do not even know who they are!"

"Kathryn, what are you-" Brow furrowed, the words caught in the King's throat. He looked over at me with a strange look in his eye, then back at Kathryn, and smiled. I felt odd, like there was something going on that to which I simply was not privy.

"This is where you come in, Kathryn" he said, his tone having suddenly become unctuous. "I need you to find both Queegan and his cabal, to ferret them out so that we can bring an end to their threat. But not immediately. We have more pressing concerns."

Kathryn laughed a shrill, insincere sounding laugh and turned to the King. I cocked an eyebrow.

"Janus, you cannot be serious!" she said unconvincingly. "I

am barely out of my apprenticeship. Queegan has many years of experience on me. And his partner - this person would be even more powerful."

"Well, what would you have me do? Hope that Revanti does not slay me before the next Council meeting? Should he not, submit to the Council?" King Janus said, raising his voice. "A Council for the Red Tradition, allies that appear to be on the doorstep of betrayal? Does none of what is asked of us seem wrong at all to you?"

"You know my doubts, Janus!" Kathryn said, returning the shout as sincerity flowed into her speech again. "You know very well that I am as finished with the Tradition as you are. But what chance do we have of changing any of it? You do not even have a plan."

"My plan, my dear," said the King, "is to get back to Isha. After that, we will have to deal with the Red Tradition. And with Erifracia. And with this Queegan. And his master.

"One step at a time."

King Janus looked at me.

"What about him?"

"He will not be traveling by boat, that is for certain," Kathryn replied. "It is much too risky. He might decimate a whole ship if he transforms at sea."

"The overland route then?"

"It will have to be." Kathryn said, staring at me.

"Do I have any say in this?" I asked, knowing the answer before I did.

"Not a whit," said the King, laughing hard. "Best get used to it. Call it Fate, if it makes it any easier."

Chapter Twenty-Two
Fate

"Gather up your things. We leave in one hour."

Kathryn's words were the final piece of the whole mess to which I had just bore witness. I could not disagree with the position that King Janus was taking - I might have taken it myself, were I in his position. But the idea that we were going into open rebellion against the Red Tradition *and* fighting King Revanti *and* hoping to find Queegan before he discovered the secret of immortality *and* hoping the wild card that was Queegan's cabal proved itself to be a problem that was solvable, all without a plan... the word 'hopeless' came to mind.

Not that I would be involved in figuring it out. For now, at least. Something bothered me about the exchange between the King and Kathryn. There were too many words caught before they were said, too many furtive glances pregnant with suggestion. I felt certain that some of what was discussed was somehow a falsehood for my benefit. Or, more likely, my detriment. I was equally confident that, given that our moment of escape from Tunuska was at hand, now was not the time to deal with it, so I returned to the task of getting ready.

My 'things' consisted of the *cuir d'arbalest* on my body and the thin cloth garments I wore beneath to keep the rough material from chafing my skin. I had already abandoned my old ruined armour at the Black Mamba. I thought with some measure of wistfulness of the beautiful jerkin that my brother had given me, the one that was inside the satchel crammed into my cabin on the Holy Yellow Sailing Ship, the vessel that lay at the bottom of a rocky tide up the coast from Tunuska.

Thoughts of my brother made me keenly aware that I had not yet thanked him for his help in escaping the clutches of Queegan in the sea cave. So I told Kathryn that I would meet her in the courtyard once the hour was up.

As I descended the stairs, passing Erifracian guard after Erifracian guard stationed on each floor, I was reminded of one of the King's admonishments before our meeting broke up: "Do not let on to the Erifracians that we are planning on leaving." It was a smart idea, to take into account the possibility that King Revanti might have given his men standing orders to keep us in Tunuska, to restrain us if necessary. Our plan relied heavily on the element of surprise, although I was curious about how much surprise a full complement of Knights on the move to the harbour could muster.

I had a bad feeling about it, one that I could not shake.

I tried to push thoughts of doom from my mind as I reached the bottom floor, proceeding across the huge hall, through the open doors and into the sun of the early Erifracian morning. The men of the Yellow Order were in a makeshift barracks, a collection of large tents clustered together in one of the corners of the courtyard.

As I approached, I could hear a din of conversation emanating from the canvas walls, punctuated every few moments by laughter. I poked my head in one of the tents. Within, some of the faces I recognized as being those of Beetle Company. A couple of the men looked up at me from their seats at the foot of their cots. I smiled, closed the flap, and walked over to the next tent.

Only to be greeted by the unknown faces of Mosquito Company.

I again made my exit before any of those inside could raise a word of protest or try to engage me in conversation. In order to get to the next tent from where I was standing, I had to cross a little gap, in the center of which a campfire was burning. There were a couple of men wearing yellow cloaks seated on benches close by. One of them was using his sword as a skewer for a slab of meat that was being licked by orange flames, flames barely visible in the morning light.

"Andrew fucking Cardiff, as I live and breathe."

The man with sword still in scabbard seated on the bench next to the 'cook,' slight and black-haired where the other was enormous and bald, rose to meet me. I vaguely recognized these men as being my fellows in Butterfly Company. They were several years older than me and I would not have met them at the training grounds. The man on his feet was smiling.

"I think we owe you our thanks."

"Uh," I began to reply.

"For ridding us of Captain Rice, of course. We barely saw any of it - we were a little preoccupied with trying to keep a dead Frank Miles from biting us until one of the boys from Dragonfly showed up, smashed open the padlock to our cage, and beheaded the bastard. But still, what a service you did us all, taking care of that black-hearted bugger Rice."

I paused for a long moment. "You are welcome..."

I stared for a moment, trying to place names with faces. I never really paid any attention during the cursory introductions after I was inducted into the Order. And I had not exactly made friends since my induction.

"Vale," the standing man pointed to himself. "Roger Vale. And this is Iggy Corcoran."

The man roasting the meat paused and looked up at me.

"You ain't gonna turn into that big fuckin' cat again, is you?" he said gruffly.

I shook my head.

"Fair 'nough," he said with a shrug. "Want some

breakfast?"

Roger laughed. "In spite of his splendid manners, I can assure you that Ignatius Corcoran is in fact a noble. The Corcorans have a small Barony inland in Hume Province. The King's Thrain does not make it unscathed quite that far from the capital, I warrant."

The bald man snorted and returned his attention to the task at hand.

I beamed with pride. I had spent nine long days on a Holy Yellow Sailing Ship, swabbing the decks and eating meals in my bunk alone or with Simon. In my view, the other Knights of Butterfly Company clearly regarded me as a pimple on the ass of the company, an up jumped imbecile whose appointment into the ranks was nepotism at its most foul. It was not as though they tortured me with malicious pranks. They had simply ignored me, as I had them. Now, it seemed, the wall of silence had been torn down.

All I had to do was shred my commanding officer to pieces.

"I am sorry, gentlemen," I said. "There is nothing I would rather do than join you for your meal. Unfortunately, I have to head off in less than an hour. And I need to see my brother." I glanced around quickly to see if there were any prying Erifracian ears. I decided to trust these men.

"They cannot risk me being on the boat with you, so I have to take the overland route home," I whispered.

"Overland!" cried Roger. "You will be three weeks - at least - before you step foot on Ishan soil. And Christ-man - the border mountains will be no small task. Tell me you will be accompanied."

"Indeed I will be," I said, not wanting to continue this sensitive conversation with a shouting man. "Listen, I need to find my brother. In which tent might I find Dragonfly Company?"

Iggy pointed, grease from the roasted meat running down the fuller on the side of his blade. "That one."

"Thank you, gents."

✶ ✶ ✶ ✶ ✶

My brother was not inside the tent. Met with a host of sullen faces lying on bunks in the growing heat of the morning, I asked a member of the throng where I might find Gerard Cardiff.

"Training yard."

I followed a man's thumb cocked lazily towards the back flap of the long rectangle of the tent. The others returned to their conversations and daydreams. As I approached the exit, I noticed the growing sound of metal clanging on metal. A knot tightened in my chest. I had become nervous at the thought of seeing my brother. What would he think of me, of the strange turns of Fate that had brought us to this moment. Would he be happy? Angry? Feel betrayed? Would he still be my brother?

'Fuck him.'

I came to a stop before I even made it to the flap. The voice that said the words seemed like it was right next to me. I jerked around to look at the men in the bunks nearby. One was reading a pamphlet, another was picking the filth from underneath his toe nails with a dagger. A third had his eyes shut and lay on his side.

Nobody was paying attention to me.

I understood then that the voice had emanated from within. But this was not the same voice of hope and rebellion, the voice of light that had told me to fight in my terrible moments when defeat seemed all but certain. At the edges of my vision, colours threatened to spill over into what I could see. But instead of the joyful iridescence that had accompanied that previously-heard voice of hope, it was all sickly greens and yellows, foetid hues from some unseen malignancy. This was something different than before: something darker, something malevolent. A thin bead of sweat sprouted on my skin. Sweat that was unrelated to the rising temperature in the tent as the

197

sun made its daily climb. I waited a moment, taking deep breaths to combat the pulse that I could feel pounding through my body and increasing in frequency.

It was crazy: there was nothing there. It was just a trick of my mind, a spirit addled with worry about the journey ahead and all of the uncertainty that it promised. Yes, that was certainly it.

Finally satisfied that I had composed myself, I stepped out into the sunshine.

Gerard was locked in combat with one of the other Knights of Dragonfly.

Dressed in the standard issue chains and leathers, they were using the training swords that Knights used, tools made of blunted metal and paintless pommels. The swords were much heavier and more dangerous than the wooden ones wielded by the Squires, though still less than lethal. You might break skin with a good smack of the business end of one of those things, leave a hefty bruise, break a bone, or accidentally put out an eye, but that was about the extent of the damage possible. Strapped onto their free forearms the men wore the teardrop Dragon shields of the Yellow Order. A large white circle was painted on the dirt around them, crossing beyond which meant forfeiting the battle.

The men seemed to dance with each other, a beautiful synchronized play of parries and blocks and feints. It could not last long, of course. Combat with a sword and shield is one of the most tiring things a man can attempt. After a few minutes of pitched battle it feels like you are holding up a bag of lead in each hand. Your breath tears sharply at your chest until you would like nothing more to drop onto your back to heave and pant until the red stars in your vision pass. No matter how much a man trained, there was a limit to how much that he could handle.

Gerard, of course, was one of the outliers. A chirurgical man with a blade who seemed like he would never run out of steam.

Before long, the result I viewed as inevitable became reality. Gerard feinted to the right and his opponent went for it with his sword, an attempt to parry a blow that never came. With a vicious swipe, my brother's sword landed on the man's open flank with the flat side, sending him stumbling. Gerard took the opportunity to kick the man in the arse. He fell to the ground and landed with a smack on his chin.

"Good show, Kevin," Gerard said, reaching to help the man up. The Knight named Kevin stuck an index finger up to Gerard, asking him for another moment of respite on the sand as he heaved, spitting blood from what could only be a tongue bitten on impact. Gerard asked if there was anything he could do, then looked up at his audience when Kevin shook his head. He smiled at a couple of the other Yellow Knights that had clustered around, before finally setting his eyes on me.

"Andrew!"

He ran over and gave me a big hug. Completely unprepared for the show of emotion, I gave him a few smacks on the back with my open palms before reluctantly returning the embrace he would not release.

"It is heartening to see you in good health, brother," Gerard said, finally letting go and pulling away to face me. "I thought you might have been... well, let us not dwell on what might have been."

"No, let us not," I said, feeling some of the familiar discomfort I felt when interacting with my brother. "I am leaving on a caravan back to Isha in less than an hour. I wanted to thank you for your rescue."

Gerard looked me over again. "Caravan? It is because of this jungle cat business, is it not? What happened? Were you really cursed by an Atikan magician?"

"I still cannot believe this is reality," I laughed mirthlessly.

"I was attacked by a beast, the magician saved me. The beast was magical, and yes, I may be cursed."

We took a few moments to catch up. Gerard told me about a peaceful sea voyage until the flaming mast of Butterfly's ship was spotted bobbing among the shoals of the coast. Dragonfly tracked us to the cave. He acknowledged that he had never been more scared as he had been when he encountered the dead men risen in that sea cave. By the time he had made it to my cage, I was unconscious, lying naked in the cage in a mess of gore. He had not seen me in full transformation.

In turn, I told my brother more about Libélula, my time on the ship, the horrors of the sea cave, the hole in my memory where the slaughter of Captain Rice should have been, my misadventures in the Tunuskan market, the perils of the Black Mamba, and my first sword battle. I left out a detailed explanation of how the sword battle came to be out of respect for Simon.

"So," Gerard said after considering a moment, "your blade arm has been whetted with Erifracian blood. Do you think you can beat me now?" Gerard had retrieved the other practice sword from a recovered Kevin and threw it to my feet.

My older brother had taken me out on the training grounds in Isha on many a Saturn's Day for years during my time as a Squire. He would drill sword discipline into me for some of the time we were together, but the lion's share was reserved for sparring. Spars that would find me face down in me muddy dirt, usually accompanied by a smack on the arse with the flat of his blade. I would turn red and fume. This would just encourage him in his laughter.

'He is arrogant. You should teach him a lesson.'

I nearly spun around again, before I recognized the voice. It was coming from within, the same darkness that had called to me as I was walking to find my brother. Memories of years gone by spilled into the river of my consciousness as the sickly green and yellow materialized at the edges of my sight again.

I recalled the days of our childhoods, when my brother would gang up on me with our cousin Kurt, playing tricks or laying abject beatings on me. I recalled the pride with which Father had announced Gerard's ascension to Knighthood and the accompanied pomp and circumstance at his initiation. I recalled the way that Marissa Rice had looked at him one afternoon when he came into the Church while I was shirking my duties and spending time quietly basking in her presence. I recalled the poise and grace with which he delivered his speech at my mother's funeral. I recalled each and every humiliation that I suffered at the hands of Gerard Cardiff, whether intentional on his part or simply by virtue of the contrast that I offered as irredeemable failure to his unending string of victories.

"Let us see," I replied through gritted teeth, picking up the practice sword and letting anger flow through me. I heard something that resembled a growl, seemingly far off in the distance as my sight sprung a leak and the miasma of yellow and green hues invaded all that I could see. I got into place on the sand.

My eyes were locked on Gerard, who sauntered over to his position opposite me. I saw in the periphery of my vision that a few more men had gathered around the edges of the training circle. One of the older Knights asked us each if we were ready. Gerard nodded his assent.

As did I.

Chapter Twenty-Three
Regret

A sharp cry from the older Knight in Dragonfly Company started the match. I flew at my brother and came down hard with a cross-swing that nearly caught him off guard. He got his shield up just in time to feel the metal ring out with the savage blow. He staggered for a moment, looked up at me wide-eyed, then narrowed his expression and returned the assault.

I blocked each of his blows and ignored his feints. I knew the way he fought - I had spent the early days of my youth watching him with envy. I thought again of our Saturn's Day spars. They were my father's idea, given Gerard's proficiency and my uselessness. He thought that I could learn something from my brother. At the end of every afternoon, after making me taste the dirt of the training grounds several times over, my brother or I would throw our hands up at the futility of the exercise and quit, much to our father's dismay.

Now, though, things had changed. Flames of rage, born from years of unfulfilled dreams and failures, ignited in the center of my chest. The fire spread through my limbs and into my head. The hateful voice had gone silent but the green-yellow haze at the edge of my vision had crept in to bathe the entire world in the sickly hue. All thought was replaced by a burning serenity that threatened to consume me.

And my brother.

I rained down the blows and kicks as quickly and with as much precision as the moment afforded. And there was a great deal that arrived when I let go into my baser desire to hurt the man. Gerard did all that he could to avoid or block my attacks. I could tell that he was not expecting this: he had most likely wished for a gentle spar between brothers seasoned by combat, something sedate and as unevenly matched as the spars of our younger years, a symbol of a loving reunion after we had both stepped through the threshold of manhood. He would still win easily, of course. He would smile lovingly at me from his perch, and I would thank him for the opportunity to have my arse handed to me.

Instead of this fiction, Gerard found a vicious opponent fighting for the transgressions a past life, one full of hatred and regret. And nothing was certain. If I had been him, I would have been sorry to have unleashed what I did.

The inevitable happened before too long. One of my strikes connected. Gerard screamed and fell to his knees. His left wrist had broken and the flesh had separated a few inches, but there was a still enough fascia and sinew left to hold it together. His cries snapped me out of my crimson fugue. I recalled my chirugical lessons from Terrence and noted with thanks that no blood was spurting from the wound. The artery was still intact.

Dropping my blade, I rushed over to help my brother.

"Get a Chirurgeon!" I screamed at the slack-jawed crowd. "Now!"

"I am sorry," I said to my brother, who was holding his left forearm in his right hand, panting and grunting with pain.

"Get the fuck away from me, you lunatic!" Gerard shrugged off the hand I had placed on his shoulder and screamed.

'He is weak. You are strong. This is the way of the world.'

I silently told the dark voice to fuck off and backed away from my brother. The green-yellow cast that had overtaken my sight began to separate in the center of my vision and fade out to the edges, eventually disappearing altogether.

The Dragonfly Chirurgeon and his apprentice arrived moments later, pulling a flask from his belt and pouring the contents into my brother's throat. After waiting a few moments for the Blessing of Morpheus to take effect, the Chirurgeon grabbed his hand and set the wound. Gerard screamed agony into the Erifracian morning sunshine. I said a silent prayer to whatever Gods or God that I had always denied that my brother would not be crippled by this.

"Remind me to never cross you."

I turned to face Roger Vale. He was not smiling. I did not answer. I simply hurried past him and on to the rendezvous with Kathryn.

Chapter Twenty-Four
The Trail

Kathryn was near the gate of the castle, mounted on a camel. Gone was the red robe in which she had been clad since I had first met her. In its place, she was in riding leathers and a big hooded woolen orange cloak, embroidered with intricate whorls and patterns called paisley that reminded me of the arabesques painted on the walls of some of the buildings in the city. The cloak had seen better days, the edges fraying and tattered, but it was nonetheless beautiful. Around her neck was a black kerchief with gold thread along the edges, knotted at the back. Her black hair was whipping up with intermittent gusts of the wind and flowing out behind her head and to the side.

I took stock of her beauty again, then, realizing after a moment that my lower jaw had drooped a bit before chomping it closed again.

Kathryn's camel and the one next to it were fitted with bridles and ropes and saddlebags, great leather things that I hoped were filled with food and drink. Between us and the southern reaches of Thrairn lay a vast desert that had a reputation for swallowing men whole. Kathryn's camel spit at me as I approached.

"What is all that commotion?" Kathryn demanded.

"I just beat my brother at a spar, is all." I had a hard time looking up at her.

Kathryn gave me a hard look with those searching green eyes of hers, her body framed by the sun progressing ever upwards in the sky. I tried to ignore her gaze her and walked up to the beast meant for me. The stirrups had a different shape than those of the Thrain horses I had learned to ride in my years of training for Knighthood, but the principle was the same.

My cheeks burning as I thought back to what had just happened with Gerard, I had a hard time concentrating. I hopped up, slipped, and stumbled back to my feet. I tried again and failed in a similar fashion. The third time was the charm. I mounted bearing a face red with embarrassment. Kathryn graciously paid my efforts no heed. She continued to stare at me until I felt compelled to speak, keeping my voice low in case the guards near the gate knew Thrain.

"I suppose you removed the red robe so that you would not be flayed in the streets."

"Queegan is fomenting betrayal against Janus with Revanti's aid. He has a reputation for brutality that goes far beyond the mountains we are to cross. I am sure he would pay dearly to prevent any interference with his plans. As a member of the Tradition in this land, my capture would probably warrant a bit of torture or flaying before having my head lopped off by an Erifracian axe."

My jaw dropped again, this time at the coolness with which she had described the precariousness of her position in this desert Kingdom.

"In any event, I am finished with the Red Tradition."

"Just like that?" I asked, feeling boldness rise in my chest. "King Janus - or, 'Janus', - says the word, and you are finished." I paused. "He is a bit old for you, is he not?"

Kathryn snorted. "Christ-man, you have no imagination, Andrew. I am not shagging him. And the decision was mine. I do owe him my loyalty, but that is the extent of our entanglement."

"Why? What has he ever done for you?"

"I will not speak of this with you," Kathryn said, finality in her tone. "Now, are you ready to go?"

I thought back to my night at Libélula's cottage and then again to my brother, who I had hastily left broken back at the sparring circle. What had I been thinking, hurting and leaving him like that? I was disgusted with my callousness. A dark laugh echoed in my head as I looked up at Kathryn.

"You do not know any healing magic, do you?" I whispered, glancing at the guards. "Like what the Atikan magician used on my shoulder after the attack?"

Kathryn narrowed her eyes at me. "No," she whispered back to me. "As I told you - Atikan magic is *different* than ours. It was born in the jungle, far away from the influence of the sealed Rift in Thrairn. It is kissed with the Chaos of life and death. Healing magic, poison magic, spirit walking, shapeshifting: these are all the possible with the discipline of Atikan magic. There are even records, unreliable though they may be, of Atikan sorcerors communing with divinity, whatever that means.

"The Gods, or God, are all questions, the answers to which hold no interest for me," Kathryn continued haughtily. "Red Tradition magic is the stuff of the real world. We can conjure fire, water, lightning, air, and some simple physical items. Influencing unquiet minds is a perennial favourite. Most exotically, some members of the Tradition can divine the future. Badly and with little reproducibility, but it does happen. That is enough for me. But to answer your question, the healing of wounds is something I decidedly cannot do. Why do you ask?" Kathryn looked me over for injury and found none. She looked at me again with suspicion. "What did you do?"

"It is my brother," I admitted, feeling the red rise in my cheeks again. "I hurt him. Badly. At the sparring grounds. I nearly cut his hand off."

"Did you fetch a Chirurgeon?"

"Yes."

"Then that is all that is to be done," Kathryn said, clicking her teeth and grasping the reins, bringing her camel up to a loping walk towards the gate. I did the same.

"Besides," she continued in hushed tones, "even without the Red Tradition's rules to bind us, it would be better if it were not generally known that magic was a power that can be wielded by human beings. At least, not human beings ostensibly allied with their rulers. People fear magicians, for we possess abilities that make them feel weak. It does not matter that the reality is that, even with the strong influence of Order in the realm, magic is a skill that can be learned by anyone. The problem is the price: it requires long study and the engagement of all of a person's faculties. You have to force yourself to believe in the impossible. It requires a tremendous development of will. Most people would rather live out their lives in ignorance. And if the history of Thrain Justice for charges of Witchcraft has taught us anything," she said quietly, "it is that the masses will purchase in blood the privilege of not knowing."

"How can you be so sure?" I asked. It seemed elitist and wrong to me to keep such secrets relegated to a select few, especially now that we had chosen not to be bound by the rules of the Red Tradition.

Kathryn shut her mouth entirely as we passed the Erifracian guards, who looked at us and the camels with suspicion. I was happy then that I had been stripped of my yellow cloak, feeling a moment of terror that our plan had been discovered. I was sure they would not let us out through the gate, then exhaled a great gulp of breath when we found ourselves on the other side, unmolested. Kathryn did not answer my question when we were safe once more, preferring to give me a withering look when I brought it up again.

Before us, the path down to the village snaked its way through the black earth of sparsely vegetated fields that appeared to be lying fallow this season. A handful of Erifracians were out on their morning errands, ignorant of the looming spectre of war and devastation. The way ahead forked: one path I knew, it led back into Tunuska. The unknown trail would take us off into natural desolation. I looked to the amber mountains far off in the distance. The sparsely distributed small bushes and spiny green plants that dotted the landscape closer to the city seemed to be even less common that way. We were not quite in the desert, but it was clear that Tunuska was teetering on the edge.

"Wait, Andrew! Wait!"

I turned. Simon, wearing his yellow cloak and tabard, approached at full speed, arm in sling, his loose sword belt sending his scabbard banging off his thigh. He looked as if he had aged several years, haggard and loping along as he kicked up dust from the path. Next to him, Reed, face set ahead of his flapping white cloak, was keeping up easily.

"What are you doing? Should you not be preparing to leave?"

"We are coming with you," said Simon. "King Janus' orders."

"When did the King tell you this?" Kathryn gave the man her death stare.

"This morning. When I was in the Chirurgeon's tent," Simon said, holding up a forearm that had been set with plaster. I nearly fell off my camel with the stench when the wind picked up his scent and brought it in my direction. The man reeked of a terrible hangover.

"He told us that we were leavin', takin' our ships back to Isha," Simon said, visibly gulping back a retch. "He said that you weren't comin' with us, that you had to take the overland route because of fear of Andrew's curse takin' him over on one of the ships. He said that it would be better if you had someone you know with you for the journey. You know, for protection. My left sword arm is just as good as my right. Well, almost. Here, this is for you."

Simon passed Kathryn a note, sealed with purple wax and bearing the seal of House Aquester. Kathryn popped it open and began reading.

"It is as he says," Kathryn said, folding up the parchment and putting it into one of her saddlebags. "We are to have company on our trek across the mountains, Andrew. Janus is concerned for our welfare, it would seem."

"I still do not understand why we are taking the overland route," I said. "Could I not have simply been locked in the brig for the voyage? Do not misunderstand – I am happy to maintain my freedom, but taking the overland route seems unnecessary."

Kathryn looked at me strangely, as if I had tread onto ground she had not expected me to notice, before saying, "The risk is too great. And besides, if the entirety of the Yellow Order is slaughtered in Tunuska, someone will need to return and warn Isha of what is to come."

"Christ-man," Simon said, interrupting after loudly passing an enormous bolus of gas, "do you have some ale?"

I shook my head impatiently and looked again to Kathryn.

"We only have two dromedaries," said Kathryn, changing the subject and leaving me thinking yet again that there was something that she was not telling me. "We cannot waste any more time fetching another two-"

Before Kathryn could finish, Simon had scrambled up onto the space behind my camel's hump. In spite of the residual effects from the previous night's debauched events, he seemed to retain some of his nimbleness.

"Plenty of room," he said, breathing stale beer into the back of my head.

'Another weakling,' said the black voice in my head as the familiar pestilential colours edged into my vision briefly, 'and a bugger. Best watch your arse when you bed down.'

I made a conscious effort to ignore the poison this strange new voice spoke. Simon may have killed a man, but I knew it to have been an accident. And I knew him to be remorseful. I would have liked for him to have faced Justice for his actions, for one should not be permitted to simply strike out at his fears with impunity. But I could not hate him. His revelations had pushed me to the limit of my own understanding of human sexuality.

Sighing, Kathryn looked at Reed and pointed to the rear portion of her own camel. Reed forced a thin smile and mounted.

"We are going to need more food and drink."

✶ ✶ ✶ ✶ ✶

I had assumed that Kathryn was going to find someone to take us across the desert. I was sure that somewhere between that fork and the place where the scraggly little plants disappeared completely a grizzled local was going to take up the mantle of guide. Instead, we proceeded for hours directly towards the mountains, which had to be to the north. They still jutted out into the blue of the sky in the horizon, only very slightly bigger than they had been earlier that morning. The path we were on became less clearly worn the closer we got to the desert, having disappeared entirely about a quarter of an hour before.

The sun was past its zenith, beating down on our sides from the west. We were well into the afternoon and the heat was oppressive.

"Kathryn," I said, "do you have any idea where you are going?"

"Somewhat," she intoned lazily.

I felt a knife twist in my chest.

"Are you fuckin' cracked?" Simon asked, beating me to my own instinctual response. "We're heading into the biggest

211

known desert on Clovir! And you 'somewhat' know where we're goin'?"

Kathryn pointed to the east. "Just over that way, there is water. Lots of it. The ocean we came in on. We follow the coast up to the mountains. The trail through will be marked."

"And what of food and drink?" I said. "I am sure we could have returned to the market in Tunuska to get some more provisions for our expanded party."

"We have been over this," responded Kathryn. "The timeline would have been too tight. I was not about to risk our capture if we failed to escape the city before the Yellow Order made its escape through the harbour."

"This is madness!" I said, exasperated. "What are you proposing?"

"Take a breath, Andrew," Kathryn said. "All is well. I have a plan."

She pointed to the east again and turned her camel towards the way her hand pointed. There was no path in that direction, only white sand.

After a few minutes of riding, the horizon seemed to split in two, with both top and bottom slices made up of the same azure blue of the sky. I noticed then the sweat dripping down my forearm to bead and drop of the cuff of my armour onto the rough hair of the camel. I had visions of being cooked alive in the leather if we continued on in this manner.

"Where is the water?"

"Before us," Kathryn said, grinning and tossing me a pear-shaped pouch covered in fur. A waterskin. I pulled the stringed cork from the top and gulped down the hot liquid inside, both hands wrapped around the unfamiliar bottle and pressing to increase the flow. I was thus distracted by my ministrations with the waterskin when my camel stopped abruptly and snorted, an action that threatened to throw me over the front of him. I felt then Simon's uninjured hand grip me firmly on my shoulder.

I was about halfway through my turn to thank my friend when I noticed from what he had saved me. There was a sudden absence of sand before us. Several hundred feet below, waves were crashing on jagged rocks at the bottom of the cliff face, enormous shards of stone not dissimilar to the ones Butterfly Company's ship had foundered upon just days before. We had made it to the coast.

"Janus!"

I looked over at Kathryn, hair plastered over half her face with the wind from the ocean. It did not diminish the look of pure terror on her face. I followed her gaze out into the distance. Two massive ships with shredded yellow sails were bobbing among a mess of smaller vessels, ones bearing the red, white, and green of the Erifracian emblem: a red desert dog with a green curved sword in its mouth on a white field. A third of our ships was further along - all of its sails seemed intact. I could not see from this distance the signal flag on any of our ships, the one that indicated which belonged to which company.

I prayed that there was a white Dragonfly painted upon the yellow sails of the lone unharried vessel.

We waited in silence for a few moments for the ship that had escaped to turn and rescue the other two vessels. And waited. And waited. Black smoke began to rise from one of the two vessels that were surrounded. I was torn between anger that men of the Yellow Order were shamefully leaving their fellows behind and worry that my brother and father were on one of the unlucky ships.

"If the King is on-"

"Yes, Andrew, I know!" Kathryn spat the words, not breaking her gaze from the scene before us.

We watched for a time. The black smoke from one of the trapped Thrain ships soon became a raging inferno, the flames licking up the side of the mast to the shredded sails, which caught like a wick. I noticed a little grey cloud appear in the sky above the ships, starting with a dot the size of a pea and quickly growing. It seemed draw its substance from the nothingness of the thin blue air that surrounded it until it was as big as one of the ships, hanging just above the horizon line. After it had fully substantiated, a bright flash accompanied a skeletal finger of red lightning that materialized to tap the mast of the assailed ship that was as yet untouched by fire. It simply exploded, sending bits of flaming wood into the surf and down onto the deck of the ship, which soon succumbed to a conflagration.

It had just been a matter of moments for the Yellow Order to be brought to its knees.

"Queegan," Kathryn muttered. "If Janus was on one of those ships-"

"Fuck the King," I snarled. "If my brother or father were killed, I will feast on the coward's guts."

As I said the hateful words, the now-familiar sickly green and yellow invaded the edges of my vision and I heard a growl that seemed to come from far off in the distance. The sound had a quality to it, a lilt that was intended to convey meaning. I concentrated on it for a moment, feeling understanding trickle into my mind, as if I were learning a new language and had grasped a basic grammatical point that unlocked the door to fluent communication. There was a message wrapped up in the growl.

It was approval.

Chapter Twenty-Five
Dichotomy

"Why do you not just fly over to the ship and check to see who survived? I am sure you have the power. You told me you can control the wind? How do you get messages to the Red Tradition and back when you are this far south? You must fly."

Kathryn snorted. "We are not without limit, Andrew. We tire with excessive use of magic. The most a Red Mage can hope for is levitation, a spell that takes incredible concentration and allows one to move at the speed of donkey with a lazy gait. And that power is not granted to every member. We all have our specialties, areas of study where each Mage has preternatural aptitudes. Wind magic is definitely not mine. The Red Tradition uses couriers on trade routes," Kathryn said with a shrug, "same as everyone else."

I looked up again. A sea of stars pierced the black veil above. The three-quarters full gibbous moon was pale yellow, high in the sky, and most certainly waxing. I found my eye drawn frequently upward that night, each time reminded of the buzzing I had heard in the sea cave before I transformed.

I kept that unnerving fact to myself.

Kathryn and I were the only ones still awake. The little fire that we had built up in the sand, a hissing and crackling affair made with wood that Kathryn had conjured out of thin air, over which we had cooked conjured food, had diminished to embers. Well, perhaps 'food' was too strong a word. Grasped out of nothingness by our Mage, they were scraps of tough, stringy meat and thin roots that looked as though they had been extracted from an anemic dirt farm in the poorer fields outside Isha. Conjuring was not her forte, Kathryn had forewarned sheepishly before she closed her eyes and reached into the fabric of reality.

I could not even be impressed that Kathryn had a solution to the issue of food almost literally up her sleeve. I was too distraught by what we had witnessed occur upon the waves.

We had trudged silently for a few hours, each of us quietly nursing our own dark fantasies of what would happen to us if the King had indeed been killed. There were heirs, of course. The King had his wife and his daughters, each no doubt capable of running the Kingdom in his absence. But there would be those in the populace, the majority even, who would have a problem with a woman taking the mantle of regent. It was unlikely to lead to rebellion, but those attitudes would cause issues, issues that the Kingdom sorely did not need at the moment.

The problem in that context was informational. As far as we knew, none of the royal heirs were aware of the imminent threat the Red Tradition posed. Erifracia had declared war by hammering the Yellow Order to pieces on the open water and we had been at never-ending 'war' with Liseria for decades, a generations old internecine conflict that had come to a standstill with no peace treaty. There were more than enough problems without the Mages. Mages that, as far as we knew, none of the heirs knew anything about. A Prophecy-fueled interloper with a penchant for raising the dead, one who could control destructive elements with ease, who may very well have killed the King, who sought immortality itself, was a wildcard that no one currently in Isha could be expected to predict.

Queegan's threat made the fights between Thrairn, Erifracia, and Liseria seem like childish bouts over a dolly.

"What are we going to do, Kathryn?"

"Exactly what we set off to do. Get you to Isha. Find Libélula. He will remove the curse, you shall return to serve the Yellow Order."

"But what if-"

"You can paint your fucking cottage with 'what ifs,' Andrew," Kathryn whispered hoarsely, clearly exasperated with my incessant questions yet trying not to wake the two men snoring nearby. "There is no end to them, and it is a trap to think that they offer a solution. We continue the mission."

✷ ✷ ✷ ✷ ✷

The following morning, Simon, Reed, and I insisted that, rather than more of the foul conjured rations for breakfast, we would eat some of the bread, soft cheese, and figs that Kathryn had packed from the Tunuskan market. She smirked at that, agreeing that she would reserve the magical 'delights' for when we absolutely needed them.

Again we set out towards the mountains in the distance. We moved away from the cliffs, though not so far that we could not hear the waves pounding the rocks below or the periodic squawk of the sea birds circling and diving into the surf.

The heat built up again as the sun approached its midday height. I found myself reaching again and again for the waterskin. After more than a few swigs, I noticed that the leather had deflated to a third of its original size. I looked over at Kathryn, who had her eyes on the horizon. Recalling the terrible victuals from the previous night again, I decided against drinking any more against a backdrop of the imagined threat of boggish conjured water that would be almost certain to emerge from the nether region whence Kathryn plucked the food.

"Caravan."

I looked over at Reed. It must have been the first thing I had heard the man say in twenty-four hours. He had been quietly brooding since our time in the Black Mamba, using terse single-word sentences to communicate. I had thought to say something, but words eluded me. Neither Kathryn nor Simon made any attempt either. So he was left to wallow in his silence.

Following Reed's finger to where it was pointing, I could scarcely make out the moving figures, though the image cleared as we approached one another. There were a dozen camels ahead, walking their loping walk towards us, weighed down by a seemingly unending number of saddlebags. Sitting atop the beasts were men and women in thick beige robes and lengths of white and blue cloth wrapped around their heads, coverings which made it such that only their hands and eyes were exposed to the sun.

"Easy now," Kathryn said without breaking her gaze from the man on the lead camel. "Let me do the talking. Do not forget that we are still in Erifracian territory."

We came to a stop about a dozen feet from each other. I noticed then that the first man was wearing a curved Erifracian blade on his hip. A wave of fear washed over me as the shades of disease threatened to eke into my vision again. A private guttural hiss sounded along with my trepidation from some dim cavern within my mind, an exclamation that welcomed the potential for battle. I fought down the bloodlust, which tried to grab me and pull me off with it into dissolution, like a hook in the mouth of a fish.

The man spoke first. He said something in Erifracian. I thought then that we would be at an impasse, given that these desert people were much less likely to speak Thrain than the metropolitan Tunuskans, before Kathryn responded in what sounded to my untrained ear like perfect Erifracian. The discourse went on for a few minutes, the voices never rising in anger or misunderstanding. At one point Kathryn laughed. I felt the tension that ran along my shoulders dissipate.

"These people are on a pilgrimage," she said. "They are going to a holy site in the lands to the south of Tunuska. They seek the tomb of their prophet. As part of this pilgrimage, they are tasked with giving succor to all those they meet on the way. They ask if we would like to eat of their food. It is getting to be about lunch time, so I said yes."

✳ ✳ ✳ ✳ ✳

We dismounted, leaving the camels off to one side and, after receiving instructions through Kathryn, taking our seats around a small fire seemingly built up from nothing in an instant by one of the men.

The bread that we broke with the desert people was as alien as the people who offered it to us. Unlike the airy country loaves popular in Isha, these discs were thin, flat, dense, and chewy. They were served up with steaming crocks pulled from the fire, vessels filled with yet more curried goat and rice, which Kathryn explained to be a regional specialty. The sauce was different from what we had eaten in the market, spicier even, but no less delicious. I felt a pang of sadness as I was chewing my lunch, realizing that I was unlikely to taste food like this again. The war with Erifracia all but guaranteed it.

After I finished my meal, I found my hands searching for the leather bottle once more, this time less to quench my thirst and more to put out the fire in my mouth that had been lit by the goat meat. Before I could lay a desperate finger on the bottle, a different plump waterskin was thrust into my hands by an Erifracian man seated to my left. Thankfully taking a long draw on the vessel, I watched as the man gently unwound the cloth from around his head.

Long white hair began spilled out as the fabric wrapped neatly around his two hands. Newly revealed olive skin was interspersed with deep lines cut across it at seemingly every angle. The hair on the man's head was as prodigious as his beard, which dangled down past the man's navel. He was wearing a large smile with teeth as straight and as white as any I had ever seen before. Most impressive was the colour of his eyes. They were not painted with the icy shade I had seen in the people from my homeland but rather a deep rich blue, bordering on purple.

"I like your armour," the man said to me, speaking Thrain well but with a thick accent and pointing at the Snake on my chestpiece. "*Cuir d'arbalest*. An Erifracian specialty. But that Snake - it is Atikan, is it not?"

I hoped that my shock at the fact that the unassuming man could speak Thrain and recognize a symbol from a foreign land did not make itself known on my face.

"Uh, thank you," I replied after finishing another cooling draught. "Yes, it is."

"Excellent craftsmanship." The man tore off a piece of his bread and thrust it into a crock sitting next to him, removing a hunk of meat with crust between his thumb and forefinger. He took a bite, slowly chewed it until finally swallowing the lot, then spoke again.

"As your friend told you, we are on a pilgrimage to Yaruz's grave. Yaruz was a great man of God, but he was not always so. In his early years he was a drunkard and a gambler, a wastrel of noble birth who destroyed all that was good around him. In his darkest hour, as he contemplated taking his own life, he heard the call from God. Yaruz spent years shedding his sin, before becoming a wanderer who freely shared his wealth and knowledge with others, without expectation of anything in return. In honour of his charitable spirit, during our journey we are called to give of ourselves to travelers on the road, offering food and fellowship to all those we encounter. We are also called to share whatever Wisdom we have garnered throughout our lives with our guests.

"You have our food before yourselves," he continued with a smile and a gesture to the crock before me. "Now, I will tell you a story." The man paused again, this time to drink from another waterskin that had appeared from the sand next to him. He smoothed his beard, looking down at the sand as he did so, evidently lost in thought. After a moment, he looked up at me and smiled yet again. I decided that I liked this man.

"My name is Lykander," he began. "In another life, I was an Armourcrafter. It was good work, and paid well. I used to make and sell my armour in the Tunuskan market. I learned every language I could so that I would have an advantage over the men in the other stalls. When the neverending throngs of foreigners washed into the harbour and came to see if they could not find a suit of the famous *cuir d'arbalest* for themselves, I was the one to whom they turned. I developed a reputation for quality and service. One year, I was even called to craft ninety suits of armour for the King's personal guard. It did not matter to me then that armourcrafting was a vocation I took up as a means to an end. Money, of course. I wanted to 'make a living,' as you Thrain-folk are fond of saying. I worked long hours, seeing my wife and daughter only a moment during the morning hours before I went to my workshop. My fingers bled and bled, until hard-earned callouses gave me protection from the sewing needle. The dinari flowed. But it was never enough for me."

The man took another bite of his food. I noticed then that the conversation had dried up around me. All eyes were on this man, whose words had cast a spell upon the lot of us.

"One day," he said with a comforting lilt, "like most other days, I returned home well after dark. As I approached our impressive villa in the reaches just past the city, I noticed that all of the lanterns in the many rooms were still lit. A dark anticipation slithered into my heart. By this hour, my wife would normally have extinguished all but one in the front hall, so that I would be able to find my way in the dark. There were simply too many lights. Something was wrong, and I knew it. One of the servants burst from the front door and nearly bowled me over as I approached, having completed his mission to find me before it had even begun."

"It was a Snake," Lykander said with a glance at my chest, "a desert cobra. My daughter, Irina, she had only seen her tenth summer. The creature had gotten into her bedroom during the day, and had taken shelter in her bedclothes. It bit her almost directly on her heart. There was nothing to be done. She died in my arms."

I noticed then that a tear glinted in the corner of the man's eye, before it dripped down his cheek and evaporated in the hot sun. The man took a piece of his head wrapping to wipe the spot that had already dried.

"After I buried her," he continued, his voice cracking. "I could not return to work. I had lost the girl whom I had neglected for years, and all I felt was horror and shame that I had been a terrible father. My wife was a stranger to me and I made no effort to try to remedy that, given how sorry I felt for myself. I sat at home and drank wine and smashed my possessions in drunken rage after drunken rage. My debts went unserviced. Soon gone was the wealth I had coveted to the detriment of my family. My home and all that I had built were taken from me. My wife returned to live with her parents, having blamed me as much as I did myself for Irina's death. Before the year was out, I found myself destitute and living on the streets of Tunuska, begging for meals and trying not to freeze in the cold desert nights."

"I was utterly alone," Lykander continued after a moment, "worthy only of contempt from passersby and scorn and mockery from those of my past who were all too gleeful to witness my fall from grace. From time to time a gentle soul would drop a quarter or sixth dinar into my cup, but it was barely enough to survive. I came to a resolution. I took the coins that I saved over the course of weeks and went to the apothecary. The man gave me a small phial. Just enough poison to make sure that the man who drank its contents would never wake up again. I resolved that I would drink it the following night, as the sun was setting.

"The morning of the day I planned to end my life, I encountered a man who was kind. He gave me roasted meats and sweets, luxuries I had not tasted in half a year. He listened to my story. He told me he was a disciple of Yaruz, much as I did to you just now. And when it came time to share his Wisdom, he said this:

'You are on a path walked by many before you, and will be walked by many yet to come. It is the path to wholeness. Becoming whole means that you have to explore every inch of your being. The exploration of the light is an easy task. It is a free, floating experience that requires nothing of you. It is not exploration, it is simple enjoyment. All men that were children once have enjoyed what the light has to offer.

'What you do now, exploring the darkness, this task is without equal in the lives of men. It is the most important voyage set before a soul at the beginning of its life. The reward for doing this is entrance into Eternity, what the lovers of the Christ-man call Salvation or Heaven, what the followers of the Buddha-man call Nirvana or Non-Attachment, what adherents of the many-faced God call Moksha or Yog. It is what Yaruz called True Freedom. It is a liberation from the chains of the past and dread of the future: a present moment replete with wonders and joy. It is the spring from which creation flows. But the cost to enter the palace is great.

'You must descend into the deepest, darkest caverns of your heart, the place where serpents of greed, wrath, jealousy, and lust find their residence. You must traverse this road of knives, where pain is the toll that all must pay, to the homes of these Demons and let them offer you a meal, as I have you this morning.

'Only then can you light the lantern in your heart and illuminate that which had been darkened. You will find that you are in your own throne room, where you are the King and

223

the serpents are your most loving servants. As the Christ-man said, the Kingdom of God is within you.'"

As Lykander finished his story, the goose flesh that had taken to prickling the small of my back arced up to my neck and the back of my head, forcing each hair to stand out on its own. It was a strange feeling, a new sensation. Bliss the like of which I had only felt a handful of times throughout my years on Clovir. I let myself dissolve into it.

Lykander reached into a satchel that had been placed near the edge of the fire, which had gone untended and was now naught but orange embers in the afternoon sun. His arm emerged with a small package made of leather, wrapped up with a length of twine and secured with a bow. He also retrieved a shallow brown crock with a lid that looked as though it had been cracked and repaired several times over, with veins of glinting silver in the channels where the shards had been joined. He pulled off the lid to reveal several triangle-shaped pastries that smelled strongly of honey and nuts.

These delights were offered to us. We all accepted readily, no one saying a word as we each fished out a sweet and took the first bites. It was one of the most delicious things I had ever put lips upon. Nothing I had eaten in Isha, not even my mother's finest carrot cake, approached the way I had felt about that pastry. I wondered if I was not feeling that way just because of Lykander's moving words.

'You are a fool,' I heard the dark voice deep within me say. As the nauseating shades appeared at the edges of my vision, I recognized with some certainty that the voice that had been haunting me since the time before my fight with Gerard was the voice of the Jaguar. 'This man is a fool,' it continued, 'and you are a fool for believing him. There is no such thing as God, just the world that you can see and touch. The only 'Heaven' is the one that a man plucks for himself from those around him. I will help you. The power I offer can be yours to control. When the moon waxes large, you will see for yourself.'

New sensations electrified my body. A feeling of raw strength, such that I had never felt before, rippled up and down my limbs, screaming to me that I would be without match as a swordsman, even better than I had been in my fight against my brother. My mind operated with pure clarity and my eyes became incredibly sharp. I looked beyond Lykander to see the snow-capped peaks of the mountains far to the north, noticing birds of prey nesting in a small crack on a cliff face. The smell from the pastry exploded into millions of new notes, as if the spectrum of scent had just expanded a hundredfold. I could hear the subtle wheeze of one of the embers as a speck of glowing coal made its escape into a pile of ash below.

And then, just as quickly as the sensations washed over me, they receded, leaving me feeling feeble and spent. I looked over at the mountains and quietly sighed disappointment that all I could make out was their shape and some faint white colouring near the tops.

"What is your name?" Lykander asked me, snapping me out of my reverie.

I told him. The man then plopped the leather-bound package into my lap. I looked over at my companions, wondering why I had been singled out.

"You are the man who deserves this, Andrew. That is why it is yours. If it was for one of your companions, I would have given it to them." Lykander paused and stared intently into my eyes, the deep purple-blue of his eyes unmanning me. "You must understand that I did not become a man of Yaruz immediately after I met that man in the streets of Tunuska those many years ago. I thought him mad, that he was kind but subscribed to a bizarre fiction. It would be years before I ever sought out the Temple of Yaruz of my own accord. But his words did stop me from drinking poison that evening.

"And that, my friend: that was enough."

Chapter Twenty-Six
Vulture

"Are you ever going to open that fucking package?"

It was Reed who had addressed me, the man whom I barely knew, the one who had retreated deep within after the death of his brother. He was seated across the low fire, arms folded as if to punctuate his displeasure with the delay and lassitude that I had displayed towards the mysterious gift I had received at our meeting with the strangers in the desert. I began to respond then halted, considering.

Three days after we left Lykander and the people of his caravan, we now found ourselves in the foothills of the mountains that seemed so far away in days past. We had arrived so quickly that I felt genuine surprise when we were suddenly there. Rock face made of amber stone stretched up before us as we approached, making it impossible to see the peaks. Drawing our camels into a pear-shaped nook several feet deep that seemed as if it had been carved into the mountainside, I noticed little bits of charcoal speckling the sand, faint evidence that fires had been lit in this place some time in the past. We had stopped for our evening meal as the sun was disappearing into the horizon, the fading light casting the first tentative shadows of the night.

In addition to the leather-wrapped item I had received from

the holy man, the people of Yaruz had given us several crocks of the spiced meat and rice, along with some of their saddlebags to carry the victuals. We put on a weak show of refusal, more out of well-ingrained instincts toward politeness than a true desire to turn down such a generous gift. Memories of Kathryn's rank conjurations were still fresh in our minds. The Yaruzians skillfully deflected all of our feeble protestations against accepting the food and we soon found ourselves with a refreshed bulwark against starvation that now accounted for the two men we had picked up on the way out of Tunuska. They had not finished with their abundance: the desert people also insisted that we take two of the camels that they were riding, as well as grain and water for the beasts. They assured us not to worry: the caravan would be in Tunuska soon, where they would be able to purchase more of the necessaries of desert travel.

The food was welcome, but the greatest as yet known treasure we received was found within a cylinder made of ebony wood, encrusted with a brace of blue triangular jewels on each end and a pewter clasp in the middle. Unlatched, it slid apart, revealing a long rectangle of yellowing parchment that had been rolled up inside. It was a map, one that would see us across the desert and into the southern reaches of Thrairn. The cartographer had clearly been less a utilitarian than the Ishan folk whom had drafted the few maps I had seen in my twenty-five summers at home. The level of detail in the Erifracian specimen was truly amazing. Each individual mountain was clearly delineated and there were landmarks painted large in the areas where the path twisted and turned. Sea serpents gliding in and out of the waters of the ocean and wispy little spirits hiding behind dunes in the desert were flourishes that completed the adventuresome look.

Simply put, the map was a work of art. And it gave me much more Faith that we were on the right path than Kathryn's reassurances that we simply trust that she was guiding us correctly, whatever her mastery of magic might be.

I asked Lykander why he was giving us so much and asking nothing in return.

"I could tell you that we give because we want to, that giving is a source of great pleasure, and that would be true," he said with a happy grin and a twinkle in his eye. "I could tell you that I saw that you needed food, transportation, and guidance for the road ahead and wanted to provide for that need. That would be true, too.

"The deeper truth took me many years to see," he said with a mirthful laugh. "The light of creation shines on those who have proved that they understand the joyous game that is living. When I give to you, I give to myself. To you, that may sound like a pretty-sounding aphorism from a self-professed holy man that feels nice but is of no real consequence, especially in a world where the religious are cast aside by the powerful as weak lovers of children's tales. I do understand such skepticism. I myself used to be beholden to that nominally reasonable perspective myself. But I ask you this: would it not simply be... funny, if the keys to unraveling the mystery of life were kept hidden in plain sight for all to discover? Some say that God is laughter."

His eyes had blazed their purple-blue as he smiled enigmatically.

"Faith rarely comes to us all at once. As I told you, I spent many years living a life of despair after my daughter Irina died. Bits of spiritual sustenance keep us on the trail, gently chipping away at doubt the way a sculptor chips away at marble. They are like breadcrumbs on a path that leads you to the home that was right where you were all along."

"Make sure you taste of them, Andrew," Lykander added.

The man's words left me confused, though I was not completely sure why. Lykander had said something that sent chills rippling down my back, but I also thought that he was ignorant and crazy for believing it himself, never mind the gifts. Where Reed had seen in me a man who had gone quiet for three days, I had been rolling Lykander's words around in my head, trying to figure out why his sudden profession of Faith had upset me in this way. In the night time, when the nearly-full moon rose in the sky, my life became a wearying haze of greenish yellow. There was no end to the darkness and vitriol fed to me by the Jaguar, a declamation of the ignorance and weakness in the old man.

I sometimes would like to think that I resisted valiantly against the promises of power and mastery over the world that the the Jaguar oozed indelicately into my consciousness, but the truth is less defensible. I found Lykander's words to be intriguing but without any practical merit: the words of a God-struck fool. The beast's whisperings, though, I took those to heart. After all, the Jaguar had granted me the power to fight my enemies, chief of all the rapist bully William Rice. I was also still certain that my newly masterful swordsmanship was a gift from the Jaguar. I had convinced myself that I would still have been a fat useless slob without the Jaguar's aid.

The beast had commanded me the evening I received it not to open the mysterious gift from Lykander. And so I obeyed.

"Never you mind the package," I eventually responded to Reed, attacking with a spoon the little wooden bowl of steaming goat and rice that Simon had handed me. The meal had started to lose its allure, as do most good things when repeated over and over without break. We had been eating it at every meal for the past three days out of a concern that the cooked food would spoil in the desert heat. Not to mention our collective worry regarding the foul magical victuals that were the alternative.

Reed glared at me over his own bowl. I should have realized then the hatred burning in his eyes. But I was distracted by ruminations over my meeting with Lykander, and so I turned from him.

Kathryn was seated beside me, her head buried in one of

the many books she kept in one of the saddlebags on her camel. They were bound in wood and painted a multitude of colours, the script upon each page an unfamiliar jumble of characters and symbols. When I asked her about them, she told me that they were the last connection she had to magical study, stories written in ancient Heraclytan about old Heroes and cataclysms that had rocked the world of our ancestors, back in the days when sorcery was known to exist by all and magical beasts roamed the land. In an attempt to get Reed to forget about the package, I asked Kathryn to read us one of the stories after I finished my meal.

"Yes," said Simon, perking up from the haze of poor spirits in which he had been mired since we left Tunuska. "I would love to hear one."

Reed looked at me and snorted at the haste with which I changed the subject, shaking his head and turning to look at our female companion.

Kathryn smiled and closed the blue-painted tome she had been reading, her green eyes catching the light of the fire. I took a moment to appreciate her yet again. Something stirred in me then, an all-encompassing sensation I had only ever felt when I looked upon Marissa Rice, one that made me feel clumsy and inept. Kathryn moved lithely over to the rock where we had tied on the camels, pulling open the buckle from the saddlebag on her beast of burden and returning the book. She retrieved a book bound in orange wood with metallic gold alien lettering on the spine, flipped it open, and began reading.

I felt my pulse rise as I truly took stock of the woman before me. Lustful thoughts crept in like soldiers marching in time with some beat in the shadowy depths of my heart. Beautiful, quick-witted, powerful, I felt drawn to her in a way that eclipsed even my youthful attraction to Marissa. Perhaps I could ply her with some wine, to somehow overcome a lifetime of misanthropy to figure out exactly what to say to end up bedding the woman.

I admonished myself my foolishness. She was a Mage of the Red Tradition and I was a defrocked Knight, cursed with Atikan magic that rendered me a liability. There was no way that she would be interested in me. Besides, without the Jaguar, I was nothing. And we were on our way to get rid of the spirit that had taken up residence in my body. So I would be nothing again soon.

In any event, we had much more important concerns, like the survival of the Kingdom!

I looked out through entrance to the nook into the sky to avoid watching Kathryn any further. The Heavens were beginning to reveal all of the sparkling treasures they keep hidden in their breast all day. I pulled up the simple brown riding cloak I had bunched up to sit upon and placed it under my head as I lay back in the sand. I could not see the nearly-full moon rise from my vantage but something told me that it was beginning to make its appearance. Based on the chatter from the two previous nights, that meant that the Jaguar would begin filling my ears with dark promises and threats in earnest at any moment.

That is when I heard it.

The call of a bird, though it was unlike any bird I had heard before. It was a horrific screech that dissolved into a staccato as it finished. It dried the spittle in my mouth and ejected sweat from my palms. My shoulders tensed up. A stabbing sensation burned in my heart. I looked into the sky, barely seeing a tiny shadow moving in the sky as it blotted the stars. Something felt wrong. I prayed to the Jaguar for aid seeing again, and the stars suddenly came into sharp relief.

With vision enhanced by Atikan magic, I saw the bird with intense clarity, though it was only a speck in the air above from where I had observed it moments ago. I stared in silence as the bird flapped an immense pair of wings. It was covered in greasy jet black feathers, with a long fuzzy white neck and a hooked beak. I could see one eye from my vantage, a sphere

231

painted the red of fresh blood, as crimson as the life-giving fluid that I had spilled from my brother's wrist onto the desert sand just days before. As I looked into the burning orb, I sensed an intelligence without equal in all of the people I had known to that day, even my newly-beloved Kathryn. Seemingly in response to my sudden identification of the bird's mental abilities, an intense malevolence fixed itself upon me, a crushing despair that threatened to pull me down into a Hellscape whence I would never return.

And then I had a vision.

In my mind's eye, a staggeringly real hallucination tore me from reality. Starting the next morning, I found myself dragged from the campfire in that nook in magical bonds by Kathryn. I had lost my faculties and become a raving lunatic who had slain Simon and Reed in the night, thinking I was killing blond men in red robes. A narrative of dissolution played out, with Kathryn taking me to the Meadow Hill Sanitarium in Isha, that place where I would be discarded by society for time everlasting. Inside the walls of the prison for lost souls, I was taken down a seemingly endless number of steps to a tiny decrepit cell barely big enough for the bunk pushed up against one side of the cell. Unceremoniously thrown in, Kathryn uttered a few words in the dead language of the Christ-man Priests and I found myself unable to move. Here I was to stay, with faceless men and women bringing me gruel to sustain myself, meals that I could not refuse to eat. Foul-smelling dark black water dripping down the bars of the cell and rats skittering around the floor beneath me were my only company in this pit of eternity.

A low, threatening growl heard only in my own mind pulled me out of the deep waters into which my consciousness had sunk. I thanked the Jaguar over and over again for its mercy in rescuing me from the nightmare, looking away from the sky where the bird had been and keeping my eyes fixed on the side of the mountain until my pulse returned from its breakneck pace to something nearing normal.

I had never felt such utter terror and despair.

"Kathryn," I said, sitting up and staring at her, interrupting the story she had been telling my companions. I was soaked in cold sweat. "Have you ever heard of a shapeshifter magician that numbered among the Red Tradition?"

She looked at me, eyebrow cocked. She must have seen something in my face in the dim firelight, or perhaps it was the moisture glittering on my face. She quickly snapped shut the book that was in her hands, to the grumbling of Simon and Reed.

"Tell me why you ask. Now."

After I related to her my tale about the bird and my descent into madness offered by the bird's gaze, Kathryn's eyes went wide and she cupped her hands around sand to her left, throwing it onto the dying embers of the fire. Not satisfied with how quickly the fire was being smothered, Kathryn muttered a few words under her breath and thrust her open palm over the fire. Droplets of what looked to be her blue fire formed out of the nothingness beneath her hand, sprayed down in an arc towards the campfire, a driving rain that chilled the air around us and sent the sand-covered embers sizzling and smoking.

"What the fuck?" said Reed. "We are going to freeze!"

"Better to risk exposure than take the chance of being discovered by a Servant of Kronos."

Chapter Twenty-Seven
Mountain

"Kronos is an old god, one whose time has long since passed," Kathryn told us as we shivered in the dark. "He emerged from his cradle in the days when fire rained from the sky and molten rock bubbled up from cracks in the earth. Before life itself. He has nothing of civilization in him. The advance of human beings on Clovir, the movement towards Order that we represent: this is the gravest perversion in his eyes. We are a blemish on the perfect Chaos of the place where he once ruled. He refused to acknowledge that his domain was merely a starting place, a crucible whose purpose was to give birth to life. Like any creature that clings forever to its era of ascendancy, he refused to admit that his time was past, so the new Gods of humanity bound him in a place beyond time and space. Kronos would like nothing more than to escape his bonds and see all of humanity return to the earth in a tomb of blood and ashes."

Kathryn did not speak for a while.

"Those are the stories told of him in these books, anyway," Kathryn said, gesturing to the pile in the dim light of the stars. "I have a suspicion that Kronos is simply Chaos personified, that opposite pole to Order. He is an utter lack of control, whereas Order represents the unwavering desire to subjugate according to one's will. The Rift that was closed by the Red Tradition created something of an imbalance on Clovir. There is much Order in the lands that surround this Rift, more than is natural. There are those that would see the Balance between Order and Chaos returned. His Servants seek to free him."

With that, Kathryn ceased again.

Dawn had barely broken and we were on our camels, spurring the beasts on as quickly as possible. Before we packed our frigid and chattering selves onto their backs, Kathryn had placed her hand on the temple of each camel, murmuring something that we could not hear. As we got moving, it became clear that she had bewitched the animals. No longer as slow as ill-tempered donkeys, our camels were now moving along as fast as prize mares. Kathryn told us that the pace would kill the beasts before too long, but we could not risk being caught out by the Servant of Kronos or his agents.

"Who the Hell would want to serve a 'god' like that? And how do you know it's one of them?" Simon asked, tripping over his words as his camel jolted him up the narrow path on the mountainside.

"I know of them only because my teacher taught me lessons about the old Gods and their Priests years ago. He said that such people are in pain, pain that has twisted them into creatures that wish to drag all others into the muck in which they wallow. Unsatisfied with simple suicide, they would see all of humanity burn. If these Priests have made a return, our situation is much more dire than even I had supposed.

"I do know this: the Servants of Kronos can afflict a man with madness with a simple look, to remove the shackles of Order and let Chaos rend from him reason and sanity. It takes a great deal out of the Mage to mire a man in such an abyss, but it is possible. I know of no other magical avocation with such power to ruin a man's mind. Permanently, in many cases."

"It appears that your passenger has his uses, Andrew,"

Kathryn said, turning to face me. "Do not get accustomed to it. As you know, there is no option anymore. We cannot go to the Red Keep to try to learn to control the Jaguar. Queegan would never have attacked Janus' army without the sanction of the Red Tradition. There is no question that it stands opposed to us. At best, we would be *personas non grata* if we suddenly showed up at the ramparts of the Red Keep. At worst, we would be burned up by the Watchers. I know it was to be backup plan, but I am doubly resolved now: Libélula is going to have to draw the curse out of you."

My mind raced. I did not want to give up the power, not after all I had been through. The Jaguar might whisper to me dark thoughts from time to time, but he made me strong! I would learn to control the creature on my own. I decided that when we arrived in Isha, I would somehow lose Kathryn and make my way to the foreigner's cottage. I would tell Libélula that his help as exorcist was unnecessary, ask him for any advice he might have to keep the spirit beholden to my will, then go to meet my brother and father so that we could fight the threats against our homeland together. Assuming my family was still alive. I prayed again that I had not witnessed their end in the coastal waters.

The sun rose and fell, drawing us ever upwards. At one point, the path split in two directions and we consulted the map. A mesa shaped like an owl jutting out from the mountain face above one of the roads was matched to a picture on the parchment. We said our thanks to Lykander and continued.

As night fell, I assumed that Kathryn would stop for rest and food and to let the camels catch their breath. Foam had frothed over their bits onto the leather of the bridles. When the Mage refused, we said our words of protest to the woman, cajoling and threatening to stop regardless of what she said.

Then the hideous squawk of a bird of prey in the darkness above perished all thoughts of retiring for the night from our heads.

Looking up, I noticed that the moon was missing only the smallest hair's breadth of a slice. Tomorrow it would be full. I was surprised then at the absence of noise in my mind. The Jaguar had fallen silent. No dark words, threats, or promises came from within. No greenish-yellow hues nor rainbow visions. There was simply peace. This quiet discomfited me even more than the bile and hatred the Jaguar whispered to me about the weakness of my companions and how I would not need anyone, if only I submitted to it. I hoped against hope that nothing would come to pass, that I would be left with all of my improved skill and Strength and not find myself lost to the beast.

As if reading my mind, Kathryn said: "You will travel with me on my camel tomorrow, Andrew."

✷ ✷ ✷ ✷ ✷

"Do you wonder after Marissa, Andrew?" Simon asked, pulling his camel up alongside me. "I wonder after Kelsa, whether she has heard any of the news about the Yellow Order. She may very well think me dead."

I did not answer the man, thinking better of dwelling on questions with no response.

We were still loping up the mountain as day broke again. I made the mistake of looking over the side of the mountain now that night had fled and we could see where we were. There was a sea of tan below, past the crags and sharp angles of copper-coloured stone that made up the mountainside. It was pure desolation. In the distance to my left I could barely make out the azure waves rippling in the ocean proper. Vertigo threatened to pull me off my mount. I looped my arms around the neck of the camel and hugged the creature tight.

"Yeah, I meant to mention, don't look down," said Simon with a mirthless laugh. "My heart is still racing from when I had a peep a little while ago."

I gave Simon a half-smile, trying not to lose the little bit of

Erifracian food in my belly that had cooled with the night air, a meal that we scooped out with our hands as we bouncily passed the crocks around. I thought that if I responded I would vomit for certain. Taking this as his cue to speak, Simon went on.

"I killed someone, Andrew," Simon said, not looking at me. "It was cold-blooded murder. That man had a name - Aziz. I'm sure he had hopes and dreams, a family. I know he did. Family, anyway. He spoke kindly of his mother in the quiet moments after he finished. People that cared about him. His father had disowned him, calling down the Tunuskan Guard on him and threatening to kill him if he ever showed his face around their home again.

"I guess I did the job for his old man," Simon said with a mirthless laugh. "All because I was worried about people finding out that I took him in my mouth. I still can't believe I did it - the slaying, I mean. But what does my remorse matter a shit? A man is dead and I am escaping Justice.

"My biggest fear is that I am actually a bugger and have put up all kinds of blocks in my mind. Kathryn is talking about some Hell-Priests that want to bring about the end of the world and all I can bring myself to care about is whether I'm queer or not. I mean, I love women. I love Kelsa. I want to fuck Kelsa and she turns me on, but how do I reconcile this with the love of cock-sucking that takes me over when I am deep in my cups?"

"Christ-man, Simon, I have no idea," I responded, still praying my breakfast stayed down and feeling quite uncomfortable with the turn the conversation had taken. "I am no Psychoprobist. I cannot tell you what the workings of your mind mean."

Psychoprobists. They claimed to know the human mind, using something they called 'empirical observation.' I had no personal experience with them. My father had little time for what he called "peddlers of vacuous trash." Only the rich and idle had the need and means to pay the charlatans for their "services" - my father, again. According to him, they stuffed their coffers on the misery of humanity. I had pointed out to him that the same could be said of Priests of the Christ-man, who tithed unwitting fools out of their hard-earned coin with promises of salvation, growing fat and gilded on the ignorance of their flock. My father grunted at that. I was unsure at the time as to whether it was meant to signal assent or disagreement, but I have always suspected the former.

"Perhaps you are simply worrying too much about this," I said after a time. "You are right about the murder – that was a tragic accident, though one that would not have occurred had you not struck the man. But is there a chance that this does not matter as much as you think that it does? I know that the Priests of the Christ-man call men who love other men abominations and we have buggers swing from the gallows in Isha, but is there a chance that there is nothing wrong at all with you, that loving women and loving men is a matter of no import? Men have blond hair, red hair, white hair, grey hair, black hair, brown hair, and there are as many shades to a human being's skin as there are stars in the sky. You would not begrudge a man these traits. Perhaps we have ourselves fooled with hatred. Perhaps there is no one or the other: lover of men or lover of women. Perhaps the contents of one's heart can vary in the same way as the shade of man's eyes."

As I spoke, the rainbows at the edge of my vision returned and ghostly fingers of bliss danced down my spine, raising the hairs as they went.

Simon looked at me, smiled a grey smile, clicked at his camel, and pulled the beast away from my side, leaving me to my thoughts.

✶ ✶ ✶ ✶ ✶

"Halt."

We all looked to Kathryn, who had drawn up her camel to

239

a stop lengthwise across the narrow path in front of us. I leaned and drew back on the reins, as did Simon and Reed. Before we even managed to cease moving, Kathryn had dismounted and was looping a rope around my camel's bridle. The rope was attached to the saddle of her own beast.

The sun, which I could not keep from glancing towards for the preceding few hours, was low in the sky, almost kissing the horizon. This must be how a condemned man on his last day feels, I mused. A single small cloud scudded on the wind towards us and did not seem that far above us. I knew that we were very high up, but I would not look directly over the side again. Owing to the altitude, the desert wind had transformed into an icy lash that carried with it flakes of snow. A white blanket now lay across the dirt of the trail. I noticed as we stopped that I was exhausted as well as cold, having foregone sleep the night before and for the moment having lost the constant jostling of the camel that was keeping me artificially alert. I looked at my companions - dark circles were etched into the skin below their eyes.

"Are we now finally going to stop for a rest?" Simon asked, dismounting.

"We are exposed up here," Kathryn responded, "in more ways than one. The Servant of Kronos is spying upon us. For what reason, I do not know. What I do know is that we cannot make her job easy. We can stop long enough to change into something warmer. Given the snow and what I observed of the mountain-"

"Her?" I asked. "You said 'her' – do you know who this Servant of Kronos is?"

Kathryn looked at me strangely for a moment, furrowing her brow with an inquisitiveness wreathed with surprise. Then it was gone.

"I merely guessed this person to be a 'she,'" she responded. "There are those among my number that say that the draw of Chaos is a feminine thing, that the aspects of Chaos in our ordinary reality are traditionally associated with women. Intuition, for example, is believed to be a woman's lot, whereas reason is a man's. Dogmatic rot, if you ask me. But the imprinting of the culture in the Tradition goes deeper than I have convinced myself, perhaps. That it is a woman is a suspicion on my part, no more. And most likely unwarranted."

"I dare say we will be cresting the peak soon," Kathryn continued quickly. "Maybe on the other side we will cross a place we can hide for a little while. Until then..."

Kathryn muttered a few words into the whistle of the desert wind and an earthenware jug with a cork stopper materialized out of the air into a flourish of her right hand. A twist of her left created a small mug, not unlike the one that Queegan had conjured to carry beer when I met him in the Black Mamba. The memory sent a shiver down my spine. Kathryn pulled the cork out with her teeth and poured a little of the contents of the jug into the receptacle. She dismounted and walked over to pass it to me.

The dark brown fluid smelled like dirt mixed with rotting flowers. I raised an eyebrow at Kathryn.

"Just drink it."

I was too tired to put up a fight. I slugged the vile drink back through chattering teeth and swallowed as quickly as I could. Surprisingly, it was not foul at all. It tasted a bit sweet, like the juice of a delicious fruit I had never tasted before. As soon as the liquid passed my gullet, I felt a bloom of warmth expand out from my chest, down my arms and legs, into my extremities. When the sensation blossomed into my skull, I realized that I no longer felt tired. In fact, I felt good. Really good.

It reminded me a bit of the Cistern Ale I used to guzzle endlessly at the Green Dragon.

"It is not the same as rest," Kathryn said, snatching the mug back and refilling it before walking over to Simon's camel and handing it up to him. "Your body still needs sleep, even if your mind is telling you that you are perfectly content to stay up for days. Eventually your heart will give out if you keep imbibing it."

"And do not be deceived by the euphoria this draught instills in you," Kathryn continued. "It lasts a long time, but eventually the effect will wear off and you will find yourself doubly tired and craving more. Every once in a while a Red Mage tumbles into addiction to Ephestor's Folly. Unless the addict adheres to counsel from a Psychoprobist, madness and death are what await. You will be getting no more from me."

"You have Psychoprobists in the Red Tradition?" Simon asked after he swigged his mug, his interest no doubt spurred by the conversation he and I had had earlier that day. Before Kathryn could say anything, Simon whooped, the euphoria of the potion washing over him.

"Yes," Kathryn replied, in a way that brooked no further questions. She gave a mute Reed his drink before finally taking a slug herself with grim determination on her face. Placing the flask in a saddlebag on the side of her camel, she then remounted on the rear half of the beast and patted the area in front of her, looking at me expectantly. I raised a finger towards the sky and looked at her. She nodded grimly.

Having pulled a few blankets out of the stiff cool leather of the saddlebags and fastened them on my skin into a makeshift swaddle against the biting wind, I walked over to her camel. With confidence born of the potion's magic, I managed to pull myself onto the beast in a single leap and swing of the leg. Kathryn reached past me and tried to grab the reins.

I noticed then how close she was to me, how the faint smell of her days old perfume had mixed with her sweat. It was not the acrid smell of a man's body. It was softer, sweeter, and reminded me faintly of my mother. I felt the heat of her breath on my neck and closed my eyes, dissolving into the moment.

"Andrew, would you please pass me the damn reins?"

I noticed then that she had shoved me, and had been

shoving me, for at least a minute. My lapse must have been obvious to Simon and Reed, because they snickered at me.

"What do you suppose is going to happen, when the moon is up?" I asked, drawing the loop of leather over my head into Kathryn's awaiting palms. I was surprised at how unperturbed I was by the nominally embarassing situation, one that would have made my face turn red and needles attack my chest in normal circumstances. It must be the potion, I decided.

In response to my question, Kathryn murmured a few words in Heraclytan and an unseen force pushed me down onto the upper back and neck of the beast. I felt my arms pulled into place along the side. Kathryn reached over and slid little circles of leather that she had produced from a saddlebag into the space between my hands and feet and the side of our camel. I noticed that they bore the same raised texture as the *cuir d'arbalest* I wore on my body. I questioned the purpose of this strange ritual.

"If this Jaguar curse is anything like the lycanthropy I have encountered in Thrairn," Kathryn said, "you are going to transform into a beast. I will not have you shredding the camel with your claws."

She intoned more Heraclytan and my head was pressed down against the tan scratchy fur of the camel, forcing my cheek to the side closest to the edge and giving me a view of the land below. If I were standing, I might have felt the kiss of vertigo again. Instead, all I sensed was resignation as I struggled for a moment against the invisible bonds. It was as if a cage of iron kept me from moving even a fraction of an inch in any direction. The final insult was a mask of leather that Kathryn slipped over my head and tightened from the back. My mind was involuntarily drawn back to the bondage implements offered up at the Black Mamba.

"A muzzle," I said, my voice partially muffled by the mask. "Is this really necessary?"

"I would prefer if you did not kill our only means of

transportation - or any of us - when the bloodlust takes you."

"Why did you give me the potion, if all you were going to do was lash me to this fucking beast?"

"We are pursued, Andrew," Kathryn said, much more softly, as if she were apologizing. "If we are caught, by whatever creature or army that might be after us, loosing a Jaguar might be the difference between life and death for all of us."

Chapter Twenty-Eight
Luna

Kathryn's precautions were not completely without merit. After a half hour or so of riding, I heard that familiar honeybee buzzing in my ears again, oscillating its path towards me and away. It was accompanied by the equally well-known tendrils of multi-colour light at the edges of my vision. This time the volume and intensity of the sound were much greater than what I had heard in the days leading up to the full moon, more so even than the time when I found myself in the cave, fighting for my life. At that time, there had been the urgency of battle that coursed through me before my transformation. The only thing running through my veins as we crested the mountain's peak was Kathryn's conjured stimulant potion. The iridescence, too, was brighter. And it encroached further into my field of vision than it ever had before.

As the buzzing reached a level that seemed as if it were going to shake me apart in its entirety, I noticed that the snow on the ground beneath the sprinting camel had gone dark. The sun had finally sunk below the horizon.

"How are you doing, Andrew?" It was Kathryn. Where normally her voice was cold, matronly, and impersonal, a warmth now suffused her tone. She had let genuine concern enter her voice. The terror of anticipating the unknown that was approaching abated somewhat when I heard her speak. I felt comforted.

As much as I wished to say something clever and strong, I could not reply with much more than a grunt.

I felt a soft hand on my back, soothing me. It reminded me of the way my mother used to touch me when I was at home at the family cottage, suffering with a head cold or some other sickness borne on the frigid winter winds. The tension abated at this. I tried not to remind myself that Kathryn was completely above me in station and would never be interested in a man like me as a romantic partner.

It was with the peace of her hand's caress upon my back that the buzzing made its final approach and entered my skull once again, plunging me into a rainbow oblivion.

"Andrew," said a voice, heavily accented and as thick and unctuous as cool honey. Masculine, deep, commanding and, to my surprise, not terrifying. Instead, the voice was suffused with what I can only describe as a patience more palpable than anything I had ever heard before.

"Andrew, stand and face me."

I was lying down on my back, in a world of darkness, black as the tar my father used to seal our roof every autumn when I was boy. Like thoughts of my childhood with my father, there was a familiarity to the place, something that seemed to call back a time faded to memory but as indelibly a part of me as any strong feeling of home that made up my soul. I tried vainly for a moment to place where I was, then slowly got myself to my feet.

As I stood, I noticed that there was someone standing far away, though I could not see his body. The only part of him obvious to me was his head - it appeared to float in space. There was no source of brightness to light the visage up, but it was as plainly visible to me as if we were in the oppressive sun of an

Erifracian morning. As quickly as I had laid eyes upon it, the head shot towards me, rapidly growing to a size double that of a normal man's before stopping just feet away. A disembodied giant's head, it had dark skin like Ernesto Libélula's, with large features and dark eyes like that man's as well. But the curves of its face were much more angular and hard, bespeaking hard roads and thin rations. Short grey hair on the top of its head transitioned to white on its temples. Its eyes blazed with unblinking intensity.

I knew with full certainty that I was standing before the Jaguar. Or the spirit of the beast. I was more than a little confused.

"I have chosen a human form to make you more comfortable," it said. "My true form tends to put men out of ease." It grinned then.

I gaped.

"You have come to me," the Jaguar continued, ignoring my discomfort, "though I must say I am a little surprised by the way you look and how you have acted over the past month. I have never seen a man such as you before, white-skinned and speaking in an unfamiliar tongue. And you are not sick. Most men who come before me are dying or laid low by one addiction or another. The only pestilence you are subject to is that you simply believe yourself to be weak-willed."

I noticed then that he was scanning me over. He nodded and smiled at me when he saw the Snake on my armour.

"What?" I said, finally finding my words. "'I have come to you?' What do you mean by that? People actually seek you out?"

"Yes, of course." He paused. "I assume you think me evil. Where did you get that notion?" There was a knowing smirk on his face.

"You attacked me! And the magician, Ernesto Libélula. He told me that you are a curse that he needs to excise." The full oddness of this exchange was beginning to dawn on me. "And

247

you have been whispering evil thoughts into my ear for the past week!"

"Master Libéula. He is a good man. His ways are those of Unity, though he does not view the world in the same way you do. He sees the world as a battleground of spirits, angels and Demons that suffuse the entirety of reality. He intends nothing more than to see the will of the helpful spirits exercised. Which is why he sent me to you."

"Sent you to me? You were after him, sent by one of his enemies from Atika! It was only by luck that he came upon me in time and saved me!"

The Jaguar threw itself back and laughed, the head bobbing up and down in space in an exaggerated manner that was mesmerizing.

"That is what he told you? He is crafty, that one. He recruited me to find you and attack you. If I wanted you dead, we would not be having this conversation. Not that I would have obeyed such a command, even if it were from Master Libélula. I used just enough force that my medicine would transfer into you. And so that you would have a wound that Master Libélula could heal. Then he banished me back to the realm of spirits, where I stayed until your thirst for transformation and my magic began to ease me into your heart.

"What else did he tell you? That you would need to stay by his side for some time and he would remove the curse?"

I nodded.

"Tell me: did he make any great effort to stop you when you told him you could not stay, if you were at such a risk from me?"

My world felt as if it were turning upside down. Ernesto Libélula was a stranger, but he saved my life. I had no reason to believe he was intentionally misleading me. And to what end? 'The will of the spirits'? What was that cart load of donkey manure?

"You killed Captain Rice!" I accused. "That is perfect evidence of your evil."

The Jaguar spirit's face darkened. "That man had given himself over to Separation as surely as Master Libélula is a Servant of Unity. He intended you harm, I could see that in every word he spoke, in every action he took. I saw Demons swirl around his spirit as clearly as you see me now. If I had not killed him, that man would have cut a piece out of your soul, a section of your essence that you would have spent years trying to recover. And we simply do not have time for that. He did it to your friend, Simon. The murder of that prostitute will see him paying for his crime. But pay it and walk the path he will. Please understand that I was protecting you, Andrew. All I have done is protect you."

I felt the hairs along my spine rise in tandem with a pleasant sensation, as if the tendrils of some unseen being were playing my back like an instrument.

"That is a signal from God, did you know that?"

"What?"

"That feeling, on your back. That is a signal from God, that you are on the right path, that you are in the presence of Truth. Truth is a stream that cleaves a road through reality, one that you can follow to your Destiny, if only you have the Courage."

"That seems a little self-serving, does it not?" I replied. I cocked an eyebrow at the Jaguar spirit.

The head moved a little. If the spirit had had a body, I suspect it would have been shrugging.

I thought back to the moments I had felt chills down my spine in the weeks preceding this encounter. My eyes widened as I realized that the spirit might have been on to something. When I had found the Atikan armour, when I had put it on, when I had listened to Lykander's words, when I had mulled over them - all these things were accompanied by the sensation.

When I thought about Marissa. And now Kathryn. A

realization entered my mind like a flash. What I felt for Marissa - it had been juvenile. I thought Marissa sweet, but we had never connected in any real way. Built of the world of senses, a worship of an ideal form, there was nothing of Truth in it, just the grasping lust of a boy not yet a man. But it was a step along the path. My feelings for Kathryn, though, there was something there. The hairs on my back rose again.

The spirit smiled again.

"Use it, Andrew. Let that sensation be your guide. You have many doubts about your abilities. You need to learn that doubt is unnecessary, that it will keep you from fulfilling your Destiny. You are a capable man, as awe-inspiring a warrior as any I have trained before. You simply do not know it yet. Why do you think I drip these evil thoughts, as you call them, into your mind? So that you will listen to me? Have you thought perhaps that maybe they are tests? That perhaps by denying your self-doubt and staying your true path you grow stronger?

"At first you needed encouragement, and so I gave it to you. When you started to believe, I began to test you. You will never believe in your own Strength if you do not first show yourself your own worth. So, I will continue to voice your doubt, and you will continue to feel the fullness of it. The difference now, is that you know the Truth. The voice of self-doubt is the voice of a fool. Do not let your Kingdom be ruled by a fool."

I nearly fell to my knees. The paradigm of life I had created in my mind had seemed so solid just moments before. Certainly, the world had gone crazy: magic was real and the world was on the brink of destruction and war. But I had *known* that the Jaguar was an evil curse, albeit one that I wanted to keep. I was certain before that Libélula had not lied to me, that Lykander was a weak fool, that what I felt for Kathryn was the same as what I felt for Marissa...

"You said you train warriors," I said, trying to take my mind off the immensity of the revelations, "tell me about that."

"One day, many, many, many moons ago," the Jaguar

boomed, "men arrived in Atika. Bizarre creatures, these ones that thought themselves separate from the world around them. They had come to the jungle from strange lands, bearing strange customs, and they did not pay the jungle the respect it is due. They eventually found the great tree, the Heart of the Land. It is from this tree that all life on Clovir is descended. It is said that drinking of the golden sap of the tree will give eternal life. When the men realized this, they tore swathes of bark from the tree and drank greedily, watching their infirmities and age slough off like the old skin of a Snake. In their ignorance, what the men did not understand that they toyed with their very destruction.

"Still, the tree had allies," continued the Jaguar. "The natives of Atika, the noble monkey-men, the Vanara, and the Woodwose, the children of the great tree, are sworn to protect the Heart of the Land from destruction. They banded together and there was war with the humans. I aided in preventing destruction of the world. I sent my children to attack the humans. Jaguars would lie in wait, jumping from trees to put an end to the settlers and their children. In retaliation, the men laid traps for my children. Many died, on both sides. Before long, the men asked their magicians to intervene. These magicians reached out to me, to parlay."

"I wanted an end to the destruction," said the Jaguar. "Having tasted of the Heart of the Land and its promise of immortality, the men were not willing to simply give up without anything in return. So we struck a deal - they would live in a way that respected the jungle, and I would train their warriors to be men of honour and ferocity. Ones that knew the true immortality that beats within the breast of all. Ones that remembered who they were."

"Snake," the Jaguar said, looking down to my chest, "throughout it all she had watched our ceaseless battles with dismay. She knew that nothing could grow from a perpetual war. She wanted peace. And so she was a - how do you say it -

an independent third party who witnessed the pact. And the pact was this – there are now Three Tribes of Atika: Vanara, Woodwose, and human. They live separate lives but each is sworn to protect the Heart of the Land. Snake remains neither friend nor foe to any side, but ensures that the pact is kept and kept sacred. Snake represents Balance, that middle way through which Creation flourishes. Which is why the Atikans put her image on their greatest creations."

The spirit smiled at my chest again.

"I am not going to train you in the ways of the blade, Andrew. You have trained for years. Your body knows the way very well already. You have lacked confidence in your abilities, mostly because of your mother's coddling, and you are shedding that now. But you do need to learn the 'why' of fighting, the creed of the servant of Unity.

"Take your brother, for example - you fought ferociously in your battle with him. I did not help you - your sword arm is as well honed as any other man's. Better than most, even. But you let me deceive you into giving in to wrath. And you maimed your brother, for what? For old wounds, given when you were children? For his receiving of a gift from your mother that you thought you deserved? A small man does this. A warrior knows that ancient injuries are merely lessons already taught, so long as the message has been taken to heart. A warrior does not begrudge a man - his brother - the love of another. Especially not the love of their own mother."

I felt shame burn in my cheeks. I had done such wrong by Gerard. And I had soiled the memory of my mother in the doing. I wondered how I could make it up to him.

"There is nothing to do but apologize to him. Tell him you are sorry. And tell him why you did it. It will be hard for you - you have kept so much inside for so long that letting even a little out will sting like physical pain, at least at first. And he will most likely think you mad, when you speak to him fully of your experience. You must have no expectation of forgiveness.

Your brother may always hate you and feel like you betrayed him, that there is something wrong with you. But you cannot let your fear of that outcome prevent you from doing what is right."

I felt the hairs on my back rise, run up and down in a crescendo until it actually felt like a wave of bliss rolling over me. I understood then the truth of the Jaguar's words.

"It is love, Andrew," the Jaguar said with a smile. "You might think that an effective warrior and love are like the sun and the moon: they cannot be in the same place together, that love will make him weak. But that is a misunderstanding of the word. Love is always the hardest path, the one that requires you to let go of all of the small-minded thoughts you carry. The Atikans, they call these negative thoughts Demons, as do the adherents of the Christ-man and other deities. In your father's world of Psychoprobists and rational beliefs, you know them simply as fearful thoughts - I do not care which term you use. They are the same thing in a different tongue.

"Love is the only thing that matters," the Jaguar continued. "It the essence of the universe, what has created all that you see around you. It is a song that plays through every moment of your life. You can either deny its presence, or you can dance in harmony with the melody. When you serve love all of your troubles become lighter and lighter until they eventually float away. All that do this become free. It is indeed the path of liberation."

The Jaguar fell silent then. I was nearly writhing in ecstasy in reaction to the words of the Jaguar.

"So, why me?" I asked, after the goose flesh subsided. "Why did Ernesto - Master Libélula - why did he choose me?"

"Why does anyone do anything?" the Jaguar asked. "He spoke to the spirits - he listened to the melody and chose to act the harmony. The spirits sang to him that you are one of the three servants of Unity foretold, a member of the trinity that shall return Balance of the world. Your Destiny is to become a member of the Trimurti of Unity. You shall oppose the Trimurti of Separation."

I frowned.

"Destiny-" I began.

"When you believe yourself to be separate and apart from the world," the Jaguar said, cutting me off, "you believe that your thoughts are your own. When you believe yourself to be a part of it, connected to surf and sky and forest and all the men and beasts within as surely as your feet connect to the ground beneath you, who is the one doing the thinking?"

I was not quite sure what to make of what the Jaguar had said. Something dug into my chest, a burning feeling that demanded an answer.

"So it is simply Fate, then? It sounds like you are saying that I was Fated to be chosen by Master Libélula. Do I have no free agency? Am I to be shuttled down a path for the rest of my life, regardless of my own thoughts on the matter? How is that freedom? That sounds like bondage to me! What if I do not want this Destiny?"

The Jaguar spirit frowned, then.

"Is that how you truly feel? I do not think so. Basing questions on dishonesty is a dangerous game. I want you to think on what I said. Think too on what Queegan said to you: you do not understand the difference between Fate and Destiny. You choose your Destiny, but your Fate is immutable." The Jaguar paused. "You have missed the mark, but I am confident that you will grow to understand my words.

"I have used the colour of pestilence to show you when I test you," the Jaguar said after another pause, "but you do not need it. Keep in mind - fear gives you signals, too. That burning in your chest, when you feel unsettled by something? That usually accompanies thoughts which serve only to separate and cloud your mind. These are the tests."

I felt deflated. It was as if I had been hurtling towards some great source of knowledge, something that would blossom over me and grant me further understanding, but I had been unseated just before arrival, sent back down into the darkness whence I had sprung.

"So what now?"

"You need to continue with your training," the Jaguar said. "You cannot become a member of the Trimurti of Unity until you yourself are unified. You must also prepare to bring Balance back to the realm. This Red Tradition - there is rot within. They believe themselves to be the sole keepers of magic, that the excessive Order that they have wrought in sealing the Rift is proper, that no magic exists but that for which they have fought and died and now use as a political wedge. They have peddled lies for so long that they have grown to believe them. You cannot go to them. You will return to Isha with the others, but you must go to see Master Libélula. He will have further instructions.

"You must find your answers in the old ways," the Jaguar said, his tone having become extremely serious. "There is a temple, in Atika. A temple to a goddess that the first men who arrived in Atika brought with them. It is crumbling, on the verge of being swallowed up by the forest. But the magic of the place is still strong. You need to get there, if you wish to have any chance of defeating the coming Separation.

"Make no mistake: it is coming, Andrew. There are three agents of Separation, a fellowship of lost souls that threatens the very existence of the world. This servant of Kronos that your companion seems to think is after you – this is the first. This person has denounced love. She would like to see the whole world burned down to its foundations and beyond. And Queegan is another. He is blinded by his own pride and arrogance. He has convinced himself that he is separate from the world and can break its laws with impunity. There is another, one who has not yet shown himself. He will do so, eventually."

"You have to stand against them," the Jaguar insisted. "But

you will not be alone: two others shall find their way home and will lend you their aid. Do not let yourself get caught up in this war between men. It is a distraction from this, the real conflict. Get to Master Libélula, then get to Atika. You will find your own magic there."

"Take heart, Andrew," the Jaguar said with finality. "In a war between Unity and Separation, there can be only one outcome. For one is the Truth and one is a lie."

Chapter Twenty-Nine
Strength

Eternity.

That is the only way to describe the all-encompassing sensation that swallowed me up after my meeting with the Jaguar. Time, a constant companion throughout my life up to that point, perfect in its rational chronology, lost all meaning. It was as if the fourth dimension had suddenly become a childish fancy sprung from the mind of an ignorant little boy. I did eventually drift back to reality from the dark realm where the Jaguar roamed, but before I got back, it felt like I had always been in that place. Like there was no before.

The loud crack of thunder was the first memory I have after emerging from that black hole of consciousness. I was still facing down, watching a wide path below us, recognizing that something was different from the last time I looked upon the ground, though I could not place it. We were bouncing at a feverish pace, but I could tell from the growing light that reached my eyes, even at this downward vantage, that dawn was breaking. I tried my arms against the magical bonds. I was surprised to find that I was no longer bound.

I sat up.

"Andrew," came a voice from behind me Kathryn's deep feminine tones, a welcome sound after the stillness of the

Jaguar space. A ghost of a ripple wound down my back. I was comforted. After a few moments, I registered the infinitesimally faint thread of panic that wound through Kathryn's utterance. There was something else, too, and it was much clearer. Exhaustion. She sounded on the verge of collapse. I turned to face her.

Behind Kathryn, I saw that sunlight was shining somewhere near the horizon, but only just. The clear skies that had accompanied us since our arrival in Erifracia were gone, replaced with a thick grey fog that reminded me of the pea soup that rolled in from the ocean on a regular basis in Isha. It was then that I noticed that we were being pelted with rain. Heavy rain. Thunder pealed and a finger of lightning jabbed the path behind us.

Floating in space just an inch above the camel's hump and slightly inclined towards Kathryn was Lykander's map. The falling rain that had soaked the thin cotton garments I wore beneath the *cuir d'arbalest* seemed to spread apart a foot above the map, rolling down the sides of an invisible dome that seemed to keep the parchment from getting even the slightest bit wet.

Kathryn's face was set, her green eyes blazing as she looked from the map to the path beyond me. Black soaking hair plastered the sides of her face in a way that did not diminish her beauty, but rather added to it. I noticed for the first time the shape of her ears. They pulled away from the sides of her head just slightly and arced up in an elfin curve. A smile traced Kathryn's lips as her tired eyes met mine. I returned it.

"Glad you could join us!" she shouted over the rain.

I looked around.

To the left and right of us, Reed and Simon were galloping on their own camels. They were soaked, too, their traveling cloaks stuck to their bodies and thickening beards wicking water away from their cheeks, beards which had been merely noticeable stubble when last I had looked upon them. They had a haggard look about them, like harried men who seemed ready to pay for a night's rest at any price. There was something else on their faces, but I was still too fresh from my foray into eternity to discern what it was.

I noticed the backdrop behind them and realized then that we were on the other side of the mountain, past the foothills and racing into red stained flatlands. Red clay! That had been the strange thing I had noticed about the path. Gone was the tan of endless sand, replaced by blood red soil. From the dirt on the side of the path sprung little bushes and grasses, standing at regular intervals as far as the eye could see in the curtain of fog, which was not very far. Vegetation with a much more familiar look about them than the strange spiky things of the desert.

"How long was I out?"

"Three days," replied Kathryn, her response punctuated by another crack of thunder. This time red lightning arced down just feet away from Simon's camel, a display of power that made his beast's eyes pop open even wider. The camel uttered a disconcerting noise and looked as if it was threatening to stop. A ferocious expression appeared on Simon's face as he smashed the beast with a crop that seemed to have materialized from nowhere. The camel fell into line and continued apace.

"Queegan!" yelled Kathryn. "This storm has been upon us for a day and a half. He seeks to slow us down. He and the Servant of Kronos are no doubt in league."

The way Kathryn said these last words seemed strange, as if she had contrived them. There was something she was not telling me about this Servant of Kronos, I was now sure of it.

"What is the plan?" I shouted back to the woman behind me, ignoring my growing doubts. I noticed then that the fourth camel, the one I had been riding, had disappeared. "And where is my camel?"

Kathryn nodded at the map.

"There is a cave up this path and to the east," Kathryn yelled over the driving rain. "It is in the forest. It marks the border between Erifracia and Thrairn. You cannot see it through this fog but it is so close we will be there within the half hour. Within lies our salvation. We just need to get there without leaving a trace."

"Your camel died about an hour ago," she continued. "Its heart gave out, a Fate which will certainly befall these beasts as soon as we stop. We have made extremely good time but we need to..."

Kathryn did not finish her sentence before the camel beneath us made a sickening groan and collapsed, throwing us from our seats. I braced for impact, an impact that did not come. As if we had been caught by a gust of air, Kathryn and I slowed to a soft stop in the red mud. My companion's lips were still moving, reciting the alien Heraclytan words of a spell, but her eyes had closed. A moment later, the words ceased and a loud snore, a rumbling the likes of which would put my father's nighttime sawings to shame, began to emerge from her sleeping body.

The effort of the spell had taken the final snatches of consciousness from her.

I looked back at the heap behind us, a mess of saddlebags and tan fur. The camel's eyes were open in a death stare. Simon and Reed had stopped, their camels making uncomfortably bizarre noises and clear unease blossoming on the men's faces. I assume they were realizing how much they relied on the sleeping woman to ensure their safety.

As if on cue, their camels fell dead themselves. I surmised that the spells Kathryn had cast on the beasts to keep them upright were tied to her conscious mind.

"Christ-man!" shouted Simon. He extricated himself from the wreck of his camel, staggered back to the one that Kathryn had been riding, and began rummaging through her saddlebags. After a moment, he found what he was looking for.

An earthenware jug. He uncorked it and took a swig. A look of pure pleasure blossomed on his face. Ephestor's Folly. He placed the container in a pack he had slung across his body and walked back to where we lay, a spring in his step. I thought about protesting, but I did not wish to admonish my troubled friend and risk his balking at the task ahead.

Reed looked back at the path whence we came.

"We need to get moving," he said simply.

I stood and looked down at Kathryn. 'Leave her,' said a dark voice, the familiar yellowish-green haze accompanying the nasty tones of the Jaguar. 'She is nothing but a burden. Plus, she is lying to you. Queegan will find you and cut you open, to hazard your blood in his sick experiments. He will turn you into a monster. You need to run, and leave these others behind.'

I would be lying if the Jaguar's words did not have a certain charm, a dark draw that made me think twice about making my escape from all of the responsibility that sticking around entailed. After all, I was no hero. I was just a nobleman's lazy son, raised up by nepotism, the product of a wink between my father and the King. An utter failure. After a few moments, the feeling passed.

Shrugging off the Jaguar's words, I squat down next to Kathryn. Remembering with a surprising clarity the first aid training I had received from Terence, I hoisted my friend over my shoulder and stood up with her body draped over mine. Unlike my companions, I had slept for days, and was refreshed and ready for the task that lay ahead.

'You are a fool!' shouted the Jaguar. 'You will die! Leave them all! Run for your life!'

"Reed," I said, "pick up that map." I motioned to the parchment that lay on the ground. Thankfully, the spell somehow endured and the parchment remained dry. "And grab what you can from the saddlebags, both of you.

"Reed," I finished, "we are going to the little cave painted on the outskirts of the forest. You are on navigation."

The first few paces were not terrible, though it became painfully clear before too long that I had not used my legs for days. To add the weight of Kathryn's unconscious body was skirting the limits of possibility. I staggered. Reed, barely upright himself, trudged in silence. Simon, mind flying with Kathryn's potion, moved quickly, urging us on with excited tones.

The rain somehow seemed to gain in intensity and the fog was an ever-present curtain of obscurity. I was not certain how Kathryn could have used the map to navigate without the help of any landmarks at all, and I was not sure how Reed was doing it now. I put my concerns to him. He shrugged and pointed at the muddy path, which was visible enough.

'You are lost,' hissed the Jaguar, 'best to simply stop and wait for Queegan, throw yourself on his mercy. You are a failure. You will not prevail against the sorcerer or his master. You will be less than a footnote in history. You will be the man who could have made a difference and who failed to even walk back to his home.'

Again, I thoughtfully considered going to Queegan. He had not killed me before, perhaps he would not do so this time. After all, it was his master who sought me out, who had told him to make the *cuir d'arbalest* available to me in the roundabout way that he did. Perhaps if I gave up, all would be well...

"Fuck off," I muttered, quietly enough that Simon and Reed did not hear me.

This went on for some time, the Jaguar telling me I was a doomed wretch, that I was lost, that I would drop Kathryn to the path, that the King was dead, that my brother or father fed the worms, that I had failed before I even begun. It told me I would never see Libélula or find my magic in Atika. I thought back to the words of the Jaguar, that the poison he spoke to me were tests. Could that benevolent teacher that I met in the pitch of the place beyond time and space really be the same vile thing that told me I was worthless?

I must admit that I was tempted. There were moments when I thought to give in to the Jaguar, that I would like nothing more than to end it all by simply stopping and waiting for my certain death. But every time I was brought to the brink, the now familiar expression of rebellion, what I had realized to be my conscience, the voice of Truth, insisted that I not give in.

My legs burned with every step, my back felt as if it were going to break, the arm I used to steady Kathryn seemed about to fall off. Where I normally would be thinking several steps ahead of myself during a walking trek, I pulled my mind back to the moment at hand, willing myself to take another step. And another. And another.

After a few minutes, I began to realize that the things the Jaguar was saying to me were similar to the doubts I used to have about myself in the years before any of this began, the internal dialogue that ripped pieces off my self-confidence in chunks before I was called into the Yellow Order. It was as if those thoughts were given an boost in volume, making screams out of whispers.

I stumbled more than once, and nearly dropped Kathryn a few times as well. At one point I actually put her down in order to stop myself from actually letting go of her. When I did, it was as if the Jaguar's voice were a flame and I had blown a massive lungful of air onto it. There was a gleefully hateful cackling and the Jaguar recited to me all of my faults as if he were a military leader rattling off conquered territories to his king after a campaign. I was socially inept and disliked by my peers. I could not tell Marissa when I was younger and now Kathryn that I loved either of them. I was fat and lazy and ugly. My father thought that I was a dishonour to him. My brother was a better man than me, even if I had bested him with a sword.

The final needle that he poked me with was an admonishment that I was responsible for my mother's murder, as I had let her go into Isha alone on the night she was killed.

It was something I had thought to myself during my quiet moments, a secret belief that I could have stopped it, I could have somehow prevented my mother from dying beneath a cutpurse's knife. So much self-hatred had found its genesis there, self-hatred that the Jaguar was using to try to ground me down, to diminish my will.

Where I had felt self-hatred before, I now felt understanding. I did what I had to do when I was younger. I had made a choice, and that choice led me to where I was that morning, giving all of myself to what I believed to be right. All of my past – every single thing that had ever happened, every choice I made, was necessary. When I was a child, I chose to never exercise my will: I allowed the world its way with me or simply did not participate. And it made me miserable. Now I chose to resist.

I gritted my teeth and grabbed Kathryn's body, straining as I lifted her up over my shoulder and walking forward with renewed vigour. Vigour that could not last. Before too long, we had slowed to a near-crawl again.

The Jaguar's energy certainly did not subside the way mine did.

"Where are we?" I asked Reed over the cacophony in my head. He had two sets of saddlebags draped over his own shoulders and was 'holding' the floating map in his palm.

"Still following the path," he said simply, his eyes slitted with exhaustion.

Interminable.

That is the only way to describe the moments at the end of that hike to the cave. The only thing in my mind were the din of foul promises of dissolution communicated to me by the Jaguar and a contrasting barely audible hopeful desire to not let my friends down. To not let Kathryn down. I could not explain it, but I felt certain that to stop would spell the end of us, that if we stopped we would be caught and most likely killed or perverted to some fell use by Queegan. And so I drew on my own Strength, praying that it would be enough.

I could have cried when Reed told us that the boulder that materialized from the mist was the landmark on the map, the place where we needed to leave the path and venture into the woods. I could have fallen to my knees in gratitude when he pointed out a barely noticeable little hole under a stump in a copse of trees in the forest. Trees with big trunks and oval-shaped leaves, leaves that had shifted into the burning reds, oranges, and yellows of advancing autumn.

Trees the like of which I recognized.

With an order barked from me, Simon called upon his own training with Terence to cover up our trail, to make sure that no one following us would be able to track the area where we left the path. There was much less rain under the cover of the trees, making it easier to brush out foot steps with muddy clay. I noted with some dismay that his plaster cast had melted in the downpour to reveal the linen beneath. He did not seem to be favouring his injured arm at all, most likely a side effect of Ephestor's Folly.

I realized then that I no longer trusted Simon. Whether it was because of his readiness to attack the man in Tunuska or because of the alacrity with which he had clearly thrown himself into the maw of addiction, Simon seemed to be a man no longer in control of himself. I watched him work with the eyes of a hawk.

Satisfied that my wayward friend had cleaned up our tracks the proper way, I staggered into the hole beneath the tree after the man himself.

The opening spread into a tunnel several dozen paces long that led into a cavern large enough to stand up in and wide enough for all of us to spread out. Little roots descended from the ceiling to jiggle by my head as I passed through to the end of the space where Reed had lit a little torch and jammed it into the wall of red soil. I knew that these were the last few steps before I would be able to rest my legs, legs that were aflame with a white-hot pain that seemed to reach up into my eyes to blind me. It would have been easy to throw Kathryn down in a heap before dropping myself, and the Jaguar called me to do so. Instead, I squat down on my beleaguered legs and placed her on the ground.

I fell down on the ground next to Kathryn. I looked over in the dim torchlight at Simon and Reed. Both were soaked to the bone, same as myself and Kathryn. Reed was in the twilight space between consciousness and sleep, seated with his back against the wall and head lolling. Simon seemed to still be altered by the potion he had stolen from Kathryn, his eyes flitting around. He smiled at me when our eyes me. I tried to give him a disapproving look, but I was so tired I am not sure what expression found its way from my mind to mash upon my features.

I could still hear the rain slamming into the earth above us. It was a low level roar that was soothing in its unchanging tempo, making it easy to drift off into unconsciousness.

'Now you begin to see what you can endure,' murmured the Jaguar into my dimming ear. 'Casting aside fear and discomfort for what you know to be right: this is what Strength truly means.'

★ ★ ★ ★ ★

My sleep was dreamless. When I woke, it was to a dim light from the ground next to me. I struggled to sit up, shivering with cold wetness that had not dried in the cool air of the cave we found ourselves in. All of my movements were laboured, all of my muscles burning with the after-effects of my efforts. I felt a heaviness, a weariness I knew was born of the abject frigidity that clawed at my body. I looked around.

The light was coming from a little orb of icy blue flame that hovered two inches above the ground. The fire flickered and pulsed but it did not try to reach up into the air the way the flames of a campfire might - it was a ball and it was confined to that shape. I tried to get my hands closer to the flame to warm up.

It was as cold as I was.

"Queegan might be able to trace us if he detects the heat of a fire," came a voice from my right. "I have heard of Red Mages with this power - it is not all that uncommon, actually. With our luck the bastard is sure to know how to do it. So we do not press our fortune."

Kathryn was seated next to me with her back against the wall. She had her hands clasped together in front of her, seemingly comfortable in the dim light. I noticed then that both Reed and Simon's lying forms were motionless on the other side of the blue fireball. I could still hear the rain pounding on the earth above us.

"You would risk our lives to the sure death of cold rather than a mere possibility like that?" I asked her over chattering teeth.

"Of course not, Andrew," Kathryn whispered back with a disarming smile. She picked up a little flask that was sitting next to her.

"What's that, another potion?" I asked testily. "Another draught to addict Simon over there so he can steal it from you when you are unconscious?" I knew that anger was in my voice, but I was not angry with Kathryn. Nor was it anger with Simon himself, who was a man clearly haunted by what he had done. It was anger at the situation. Foolish anger. The Jaguar laughed its approval.

Kathryn's eyes widened and she glanced at Simon. Then she looked back at me, jaw set.

"It is whiskey, Andrew. I do not think that it is cold enough for us to freeze. But you might wish to come sit closer to me if you are really that worried." Kathryn smiled at me. I thought for a moment I saw some coquettishness spark in her smile, then it was gone as quickly as it appeared, replaced by mere friendliness.

I moved closer, though not quite as close as I might have. I did find her appealing, but I still worried that she would think me unworthy, that she was not truly interested in a man like me. Kathryn's eyes, a little droopy with drink, glittered like emeralds in the light of the fire as I approached.

I already felt warmer.

I took a swig of the whiskey after she handed it to me, her hand brushing mine for a moment and sending warm sensations up my arm and into my chest. Whiskey was never my preferred drink - ale held that spot in my heart - but I appreciated the burn for the first time as the spirit made its way down my gullet to settle into my belly.

"Tell me what happened," Kathryn said, more a command than a question.

I complied, rattling off an account of the march from the spot where our camels died to the cave we found ourselves in. Kathryn smiled at me again.

"So, you carried me the whole way, did you?" Kathryn said, her eyes wide. "I think I owe you my thanks."

"It was my pleasure," I said, smiling. "Well, maybe pleasure is the wrong word to describe what it was, but I am certainly happy to have done it."

Kathryn laughed, nudging me with her arm as she did so. It seemed that the drink had affected her – she was much warmer with me than she had ever been before. And I liked it. I liked it very much. I smiled as I put a finger to my lips and pointed at the men sleeping next to us.

"I appreciate what you did for me, Andrew, but that is not what I meant by my question. I want to know what happened. When you were gone."

I looked at Kathryn intently. My interaction with the Jaguar... it felt strange to be asked to speak about it. There was something unfamiliar about how I felt about it. I did not want to disrespect that conversation, that communion. I had always dismissed this kind of thinking as foolish superstition in my younger days, but I felt it was sacred. I considered telling her nothing about it, just that I needed to get to Master Libélula and then on to Atika. That felt wrong, too. When I thought to speak to her of all that I could remember, to be as completely as honest as I could be, I felt hairs rise on my soaked back.

"Let that sensation be your guide." The Jaguar's words echoed in my head.

And so I told Kathryn everything of my experience in that place beyond reality. She listened quietly as I spoke of the Jaguar's lessons. When I told her about the Trimurti of Unity and the Trimurti of Separation, that the Servant of Kronos, Queegan, and one other were destined to rise against me and two more unknowns, Kathryn looked very strangely at me. When I told her about where I was destined to go next, down to Atika to meet with a goddess, the look passed. Finishing my story, I felt as though a great weight had been lifted off me. It seemed right, telling Kathryn these things.

"This magic is different, Andrew," Kathryn said. "Much different than anything I have encountered through the Red Tradition. The Red Tradition is about forms and thoughts that are easy to trace to the physical realm we find ourselves in. I knew that Atikan magic was threaded with divinity, but I never really understand what that meant. I feel like I have a better idea now."

We slipped into a comfortable silence for a stretch of time, watching the little heatless orb of sapphire flame and passing the flask back and forth between us.

"How does it make you feel?"

Kathryn's question caught me off guard. I had not really thought that she cared much about how any of this made me feel. I had assumed that she considered me to be her charge, a package to be delivered up to the strange man from the strange land so that she could get back to her precious 'Janus.' That she actually gave any consideration to how I felt about any of it...

"Kathryn, how does what make me feel?" I said, sensing something burst into my chest like the blow of a bellows on a fire. "A month or so ago I was slipping into a pretty ordinary life, if you can call the life of a Yellow Knight in service to the King ordinary. Since then, I was bitten by a magical beast, learned that magic exists and has been under my nose my whole life, was inducted into the Inner Council, was nearly killed by a dead man before I transformed into the same magical beast that attacked me, met a necromancer who wants to learn the secret of immortality, killed a man, nearly cut off my brother's hand during a spar, was nearly killed escaping from Erifracia, learned that a servant of a dead god threatens our existence and was nearly driven mad in the process, was told by that Jaguar spirit that inhabits my body that I am being trained to become a member of the Trimurti of Unity, whatever that means, and need to go to an alien land to find my own magic, then to finally have been chased into this cave by the very same necromancer... Did I miss anything?"

Kathryn snorted, a snort which flowed into a deep belly laugh. I smiled and motioned for her to keep it down, pointing at our companions again.

"I am still in awe of the whole situation," I said, more seriously this time. "I had always hoped that there was something more to life than being a failure in my older brother's shadow, but we are talking about the impossible suddenly becoming the real. It feels like colour has seeped into a dreary painting that I was thinking about throwing into the midden and in the process it has become the most beautiful image I have ever looked upon. I am worried about the dangers ahead and behind, but it feels as though these fears are being transmuted into acceptance, if that makes any sense at all.

"My mother used to say something to me when I came back from the training grounds," I continued. "*Que sera, sera.* Do you know what that means?"

Kathryn had a huge grin on her face and was nodding vigorously. For a moment, gone was the affect of distance and superiority that was a barrier between her and the rest of us throughout all my knowing of her. She seemed much younger than the thirty or so summers that she appeared to have seen.

"Whatever will be, will be," she said excitedly. "It was the motto of a legion of warriors from the old Heraclyte Empire. The Amaril Company, I believe they were called. Their exploits were recorded on ancient scrolls by gleemen and poets from those days, scrolls that the Red Tradition keep secure against the tide of time. I had the chance to look on them during my younger days. I thought it a strange motto for men who go to war, although perhaps not, knowing what I know now about the acceptance of one's mortality demanded by such a life. They were men of honour. When Emperor Traximus was killed, they took to the wild lands outside of the cities, and fought only in the defence of those weaker than them."

I stared at Kathryn. "I had no idea. I thought it only a phrase my mother used to tell me when I was especially defeated by my time at training. She called it a comfort, but I thought it an insult. I have only recently realized that it was indeed as my mother said. It is the key to Courage, as far as I can see."

Kathryn continued to smile. "Your mother was a wise woman."

"I... she..." A wave of emotion crashed down on me. Tears welled in my eyes. I thought I would choke them back, as I had so many times before. This time, raised hairs on my back accompanied the thought of permitting them to fall from my face.

For the first time since my mother's death, I let go.

I sobbed and sobbed. I did not look up at Kathryn, though I felt her hand on my back, rubbing me in concentric circles in a way that yet again reminded me of the dead woman. I cried harder.

After a little while, the tears stopped flowing. As they did, I noticed that something had changed in concert with the end of the flow. I paused, trying to figure out what it was. I realized after a moment that it was the rain. It had stopped. I looked at Kathryn.

She was gazing at me with concern. There was something else there, too, but I could not precisely say what. Whatever it was, it made me want to confide in her. Again, ripples on my back urged me to say what I felt.

"She died five years ago. I should say, she was killed five years ago. It was in Isha. She had asked me to come with her from our cottage into the city. She wanted to pick up some cheese from Mr. Robinson: the best cheesemaker in Isha, according to Mother. She frequently sang the man's praises. It was my father's birthday the next day and his favourite meal was a dish she made with meat, cheese, and potatoes. She hoped it would be the perfect surprise.

"It was after dark, early in my training," I said in clipped tones. "I had just gotten back from the grounds and had taken a beating from one of the other Squires. I wanted to escape from the world, to retreat into one of my books. I told her I would not accompany her, even after she tried three different ways to cajole me into coming with her. I refused, slamming the door to my chamber." I paused. "A final denial of the woman who gave me life."

I felt tears well in my eyes again.

"When she did not return after a few hours," I continued, "my father told me to come with him to look for her in a way that brooked no argument. We went to Mr. Robinson's residence, a place just on the outskirts of the Purple Run. He told us he had sold her a half wheel of cheese an hour or so before, after which she disappeared into the night. I am not sure why, given the man's obvious innocence of any mischief, but my father was furious with Mr. Robinson. He barged into his house and clomped around, shouting my mother's name. After he was satisfied that my mother was not within, we returned to the streets. We searched the roads and alleys for hours, before returning to the homestead, hoping that she might have returned while we were gone. Dawn was breaking when a white cloak with his helmet removed out of respect showed up at our door with a grim expression on his face. I remember the blood fleeing from my father's skin when he saw the naked-headed man through the window.

I paused for a moment, feeling emotion wash over me in my recollection.

"My father hoards coin and my mother spends it... that was what she used to say. It had been a thief, a desperate creature who must have seen the sizable purse from which she drew the money to pay Mr. Robinson. That is the theory, anyway. In this assumed explanation, my mother foolishly fought back, which is why her life's blood had been relieved of her with a gash across her neck as she lay dying in that alley near the Run. That, or her killer drew his joy from killing as well as stealing."

I knew that the dam in my heart was on the cusp of breaking again, but I had to finish.

"My father has always blamed me for her death, for failing to go and protect her. I hated him for it, for so long. But if I am being honest, I cannot fault him, for I blame myself as well."

Sobs wracked my body. Kathryn pulled me in to her shoulder. Her scent filled my head and calm descended on me in a torrent. I settled into a hug. We held each other for what seemed like an eternity. When we pulled away from each other, it was only with great reluctance. We stared at one another.

"If I can be so bold as to offer advice," Kathryn said, her voice quavering. "*Que sera, sera*, Andrew. If it is Truth, let it apply to all areas of your life, not just your combat training. You must let your mother's death lie in the past. You give it power when you let it affect you. The stone in your heart controls you, not the other way around. Talk to your father. He is a good man. He will forgive you."

"And you must forgive him," Kathryn said. "For

everything."

My back exploded at Kathryn's words.

Chapter Thirty
In Your Blood

We exited the cave under cover of darkness. The usefulness of Lykander's map had run its course once we recognized the little curlicue-laden Dragon of Thrairn painted next to the path that disappeared into the lands beyond the scope of the parchment. The Regent's Way. The road that ran the length of Thrairn, starting in Ecta Province and running up through Tyro, ending before the moat of Castle Isha. Kathryn did not like the fact that we were taking the Regent's Way back to Isha, given the pursuit we seemed to have just evaded, but we did not really have any choice. We had no way of navigating side roads and forests without a map.

The little conjured orb of blue flame led the way through the night.

Though Reed had distributed saddlebags to both myself and Simon before we left, he did not say much more than was absolutely necessary. I tried to engage him in conversation, but he scowled at me as he pulled something from one of the saddlebags and handed me what I recognized to be the wrapped package I had received from Lykander. It was unmolested. I thanked him for his discretion and asked him why he had not opened it, given his obvious curiosity. Reed simply sighed and turned away. I placed the package in a pouch that hung from my belt.

While he was sleeping a fitful sleep that took his drug-addled body against his will, Kathryn took the liberty of relieving Simon of the stolen bottle of Ephestor's Folly. Upon waking, Simon searched around the cave with a look in his eye that made me feel uneasy. He complained about the shredded mix of cloth and plaster on his right forearm and said that the draught made it feel better. I thought again that we needed to get him to Isha, into the care of a Psychoprobist, no matter my father's opinion of "the craniometer-wielding fops."

'He is an addict and a liability,' hissed the Jaguar. 'Drop him at the next village, into the care of the magistrate.'

Magistrates. This far from Isha, those men might as well be Kings themselves. And conducted themselves accordingly. Terence had taught us to take care when and if we found ourselves around the border villages. Aside from the stamp of his head on the coin they exchanged at their markets, tax collectors and patrolling bands of Ishan City Guard with dismal reputations for unnecessary violence were about the only reminder for the village folk that they were the subjects of a King. And these representatives visited rarely.

Besides, despite misgivings about him, I was not about to hand Simon over to strangers. He was still my friend and I felt compelled to see him home safe.

There was still a burn in my legs from carrying Kathryn, but the pain settled from a sharp acute stab into a dull roar soon after we got moving. We traveled in silence for most of the night, aside from the sound of Simon trying to cajole Kathryn into giving him some more of Ephestor's Folly from time to time. After the third ask, Kathryn stopped the march and stared intensely at Simon until he wilted under her glare. Thus ended Simon's asking.

My clothes eventually dried. Suddenly curious, I asked Kathryn how she ensured that I did not soil myself while I was unconscious for three days. She told me that she placed an herb in the side of my mouth, something that was given by herbalists to elderly folk dealing with the embarrassment of incontinence in their older years. It only worked for one of a human's needs, however. With a mischievous smile, she told me I had pissed through my clothes onto the camel a couple of times. If I didn't smell it, that was because the rain must have washed it away.

I am not sure if she was joking.

Kathryn was serious about the constipation medicine, though, for it wore off just about when dawn was breaking and I was forced off into the woods for an extended stop while the others rested in a nook close to the path. My business finished, I made my way back to my friends. I was about twenty paces from where I had left them when I heard a commotion approaching on the road in the opposite direction whence we came.

Crouching next to a tree trunk, I watched as a wagon crested the hillock before us, drawn by two sickly looking horses. It looked to be in serious disrepair. The wood was warped and bent. It was painted with a trio of silver cups crossed at close angles on a purple field, the Aquester family crest. The paint was faded and cracking. It was piloted by an elderly man in appropriately shabby formal wear seated atop the wagon proper. There was something familiar about him but I could not place it. I noticed then the source of the racket: the axles were banging about in their bushings.

It was about to pass us when Reed emerged out of the bushes ahead of me, his weather-stained and torn white cloak hastily repositioned on his back. He flagged the man down and called for him to stop. I gaped, silently cursing Reed for his disobedience to Kathryn's admonishment to stay hidden at all times.

"I h'aint seen a white cloak this far south in quite some time, me b'y."

As soon I heard the wagon driver utter the words, my heart

sank. I would have recognized that voice anywhere, but I assumed the man whose throat bore it had died in the accursed sea cave near Tunuska. Willis Coulter. The duplicitous son of a bitch.

The Jaguar laughed, fanning the flames of my rage as I gripped at a sword hilt that was not there. I had noticed with concern a few times that I had forgotten to take a proper sword with me in my haste to leave Tunuska, after I had nearly severed my brother's hand with the dulled training blade. A sword's absence became as painful as a lost limb when Reed began to converse with the creature. Our white-cloaked companion had travelled on Mosquito Company's ship, and clearly did not know that the traitorous wretch on the wagon was in league with Queegan. He could not know and that this was a trap as plain as the sun that was edging up beyond the horizon and bathing the morning in a gloaming that momentarily made the world indistinguishable from one in the lap of twilight.

I considered running at Willie with my bare hands, a plan of which the Jaguar approved vigorously. The haze of rage seeped in through the corners of my rational mind. I nearly went through with the foolish non-plan, then I caught sight of the wide-eyed stare of a crouching Kathryn to my right as I approached the threshold of the forest. A touch of calm dripped into my mind as I looked upon her, a drop of blue in a pool of red, peace that soon dissolved the wrath as I watched the interaction play out.

"I need to get to Isha," said Reed. I noticed with relief that the palm of his hand rubbed at the hilt of his sword. "A tax collector, are you? You are heading in the wrong direction. There are no villages to the south."

"I h'aint going to tax no villages," said Willie, spitting on the red clay. "I come down this way to see if I cain't find someone. Fer da King an' dat, right?" A shit-eating grin spread on Willie's face as if to punctuate his words.

"Who are you looking for?"

"A young feller named Andrew," said Willie. "Andrew Cardiff. He's a Yeller Knight, and a right dangerous prick at dat. You h'aint seen him, 'ave you?"

"Yeah," said Reed. "I may have. If I tell you where he is, will you give me one of those horses so I can get back to Isha? I'm done with him, done with the King."

Willie nodded vigorously. "If ya gives him to me I'll give ya da works, horses and wagon!

Reed paused for a moment, looking over the dilapidated wreck atop which Willie was perched. "Just a horse'll be fine." Reed straightened out of a deep slouch I had not noticed until it fled his frame.

My mind reeled as it came to grips with Reed's betrayal. His stony silence over the past days was not out of a desire to hide sadness, it was out of a gathering dissatisfaction. He was ready to throw me to the dogs and did so at the first opportunity. What did he owe me? He had met me the day his brother died, gotten swept up in this madness, and now was rejecting all of it, me included. I understood his pain. I felt a wave of compassion for the man wash over me, even though he had just sold me out to my enemy.

Looking at Kathryn, I set my face set and mouthed the word "go" to her. She had a pained look on her face. I glanced at Simon, urging her with my eyes to take him with her. I stepped out from the forest and onto the red clay of the highway. The door on the side of the wagon burst open in unison with the sole of my boot touching the road. A man in a blood-hued robe with golden hair spilling down past his shoulders hopped out, plastic grin bright in the morning sun.

"Andrew! It has been much too long."

"Queegan," I responded with ice on my breath.

"Ah, so you have learned my name," he said, smiling. "That must have been a gift from my beautiful counterpart Kathryn Aquester. She must be around here somewhere!" Queegan shouted out at the trees and waited a moment before continuing. "No matter, she is not whom I seek. And she does not have the stomach to cross me again!" Queegan looked to the forest again as he yelled, then pointed at the open doors leading into the wagon. "Come now, do not make me ask twice."

"What about my horse?" It was Reed. He was gawking at Queegan and Willie. "I was promised a horse! Give it up now." Reed's hand dropped to his hilt.

Without breaking the gaze he had locked on me, Queegan muttered a few words, raised his arm, and opened his left palm. An enormous ball of crackling red lightning materialized from the ether and traveled quickly towards Reed. Before he could draw his blade, the magic orb exploded on his chest and sent him flying towards the woods. It was sickening to watch his limbs contort into a series of impossible angles as his feet left the ground. He came to rest on his back on the edge of the road. I could see bits of his skull poking out of charred skin where his face had been.

I was not as sorry as I might have been to see Reed die, but the display of power cowed me. I recalled burning ships in Erifracian waters as my hand again made a fist a couple of times above an imaginary sword hilt. The mystery of who had been on the Holy Yellow Sailing Ships that this man had destroyed loomed large in my mind. My father? My brother? The King? All of them? The Jaguar tried to egg me on into a bare handed confrontation. It almost claimed me then, sent me into a futile attack that would have seen Queegan easily incapacitate or kill me. Then I recalled something Queegan had said just then: Kathryn Aquester. Aquester, I had heard that name before...

"Kathryn," I said to Queegan. "She is the King's daughter then?"

Queegan laughed. "Queen Sylvia would likely have something to say about that! She's not his daughter, nor his bastard. She's his niece. Come now." Queegan pointed and murmured a few words. I felt a sharp grip cut into my legs, invisible claws that were operating my body like a grim marionette. I was being forced towards the wagon. And it was horrendously painful. I gasped. Willie grinned triumph as I approached the door.

"I told you not to make me ask twice," Queegan said, opening the door for me and following me in.

✶ ✶ ✶ ✶ ✶

"What do you want?"

Myself and Queegan were seated across from each other in the cramped little cabin, which was in as poor shape as the exterior. The patchy velvet was rough against my arse and a faint smell of mothballs was quite apparent. The windows on the doors were streaked with brown grime. Every time we rode across a rut I felt pain shoot up my spine as if someone had banged it with a hammer.

"I already told you what I want, back during our time in King Revanti's care."

"To learn the secrets of the afterlife, of immortality... I remember." How could I have forgotten, I mused to myself. "Are you any closer to realizing your goal?"

"Nearly there, now." Queegan murmured a few words and I felt the vice grip return as I was forced back on the velvet. He produced a little round glass flask and a ruby-pommeled dagger. I felt fear wash over me as he stood hunched over in the cramped cabin and approached.

This is it, then, I thought. I was about to die at the hands of this insane man. Would I remember my old life when I came back as a monstrosity? Queegan muttered something in Heraclytan and I closed my eyes, awaiting the crackling red doom that was sure to claim me. When it did not materialize, I dared to part my lids again. Queegan laughed at me and then gestured. I felt an invisible force wrap around me, coupled with an implacable suggestion in my mind that could not be reasoned with. It told me to extend my arm towards my captor. My body obeyed. The movement sent a searing pain ripping through my arms. I watched in awe as he lowered the dagger and sliced open my palm. The enchantment Queegan had laid on me forced me to squeeze my hand into a fist and blood flowed into the flask. After a little while the flask was filled nearly to the top with my blood and Queegan pulled it away to stopper it up with a cork. A moment or two later, I felt the spell flee and I was released. The gash stung as I held my hand to the leather of my pants.

"What..."

"Was that for?" Queegan finished my question. "Never mind that. Tell me, do you know who your mother was?"

"I... my mother?"

I thought back to the memories that still burned in my skull of the woman who had given me life. Violet Cardiff. In my mind's eye, she still had the black hair of her youth, only recently speckled with the steel grey of encroaching age. Kind brown eyes and a pretty round face, she bore the patience of a saint. She always smelled of lilacs and freshly turned earth. I became aware I missed her terribly, a sensation of loss that was immediately cut off by the mutterings of the red-robed jackal before me.

"She was a descendant of Emperor Traximus," Queegan began, "last ruler of the Heraclytans, the man who tried to open up magic to everyone, to make sure that all were given the same chance in life. He was a great man, and a prodigious magician in his own right. Some of the scrolls from that age speak of his power to pass between the spheres, to reach beyond the fabric of reality and pluck... knowledge, from beyond. It is said that he made a pact with a Dragon, that he traded in a portion of his humanity for his ability to travel between worlds. He drank of the Dragon's blood and became something... other. He was loved by the people, but he had many jealous detractors.

"In his folly," Queegan said, gazing out of the window, "Traximus opened a Rift that permitted Chaos to flow through from beyond and kiss everyone on Clovir. The Old Tradition supported him in this. The Red Tradition, originally a rebellion of the nobility against the classlessness that this rift represented, rose up to fight against him and the wizards of the Old Tradition that supported him. A bloody war followed. Traximus was eventually killed in the climactic battle that brought the conflict to an end, the one that reduced the Heraclytan Empire to ashes, but it was always rumoured that a few remnants of his line survived the purges that heralded the birth of the Red Tradition in its current shape and the rise of the Kingdom of Thrairn.

"You are of his issue, Andrew. His blood is your blood." Queegan gazed upon the bright red contents of the flask in the dim light allowed through the dirty glass of the wagon.

"So what are you saying? That I am a Dragon spawn?"

Queegan laughed. "Your blood has been diluted by centuries of outbreeding. You are merely human. But there is something within here, a magic in your blood that I hope will allow me to peer through to-"

Willie shouted something above and we slowed to a stop.

"Ah, we are here. Time to meet my partner."

Chapter Thirty-One
The Road of Red

Seized again by the needles of Queegan's spell, I was forced out the door of the carriage into the crimson dust of the road. I barely had time to notice that the sun was fully up in the morning sky. Invisible fingers cut me as I was forced to my knees. A felt slice in my chin lifted my head up to look upon the creature that gave Queegan his orders.

Flame red hair spilled down over a tight black suit of *cuir d'arbalest* that left nothing to the imagination. A full bosom that threatened to split the V formed by the few buttons which kept the chestpiece together was rounded out by an equally full arse and long legs that ended in black stilleto boots. The woman was wearing a brace of daggers on her belt and her eyes were a shade of golden yellow that was unlike the hue of any human iris I had seen before, caught in hard angular features that were both severe and heart-meltingly beautiful at the same time. She looked about a decade older than me, still caught in the last clutches of youth. Her appearance screamed sex in such an over the top way that I thought for a moment it was a joke. Her features briefly reminded me of someone I could not place. Then I felt Queegan's spell dig in to force me onto my knees.

"Sir Cardiff," came a voice as sultry as such a caricature

demanded, "pleased to meet you. You gave us quite the chase over the mountains. Kathryn is a slippery Mage, is she not? Glad to see Queegan finally caught up with you. Now, on your feet."

I felt Queegan's spell relax and I pulled myself up to stand. I brushed red dirt off my knees and then returned my gaze to the woman.

She was standing in front of the ornate wrought iron of a gate. They were attached at the sides to grey stones stacked together into a low wall, sealed with mortar, and nearly buried in a tangle of ivy that was encroaching onto the gate proper. Scanning the area around the red dirt of the path beneath us, I noted that we seemed to be deep in the wild of a forest. Beyond the gate, up on a hill above the reach of the trees, I could see a castle, made of the same grey stone of the walls.

"I see you got your armour," the woman said, approaching and placing her palm on my chest and tracing the Snake with the same familiarity one might expect of a lifelong lover. "Rufil's Atikan certainly did an excellent job of it."

"Who..." My voice dissolved into pieces, my mouth suddenly dry, the bizarre nature of the circumstances setting in with a ferocity I was not expecting.

"Am I?" The lady laughed, stepping back. "There will be plenty of time for introductions. Later. For now, we march."

The woman said something in what sounded completely unlike any language I had ever heard and extended her arm. The earth before the gate lashed up at an angle with a thick and wide shard of dark brown stone that impacted and shattered the iron as if it had been a piece of brittle glass. Queegan muttered something in Heraclytan and I felt the razors cut into me as I was forced into a walk.

It was so painful that I kept looking down to see if Queegan's spell was breaking the skin. But the rivulets of blood that I was expecting were absent. There was nothing stilted about my movements, either. The only indication that someone else was controlling my body were the internal signals of Hellish intensity that plagued me with every single step.

"Where are we going?" I managed to gasp the words out between waves of pain.

My question fell upon deaf ears. Queegan and his mistress were several steps ahead of me, speaking quietly to one another. They must have trusted entirely in the spell Queegan had cast upon me, for they did not once check to ensure that I continued to remain their prisoner.

The path soon became less a path and more a narrow corridor where the bright hues of the autumn forest had not completely reclaimed the walkway. It had nearly fallen to the creep of disuse, a problem I was well familiar with. When I was a small boy, my father had identified wandering bits of forest around the family land and admonished me to ensure we never saw the wild retake any part of our homestead. My hands were still rough with the old callouses formed by swinging axe and scythe in those early days, tears streaming down my face as my father yelled at me to keep at it. Eventually my mother had intervened on my behalf and a Serf was given the task. I had happily returned to my books.

Trudging along the ground by dint of horrific pain, I was reminded of my time carrying Kathryn after she had passed out. I had not given up even when every pain receptor in my body and the Jaguar screamed at me to do so, with no mother around to rescue me from the task at hand. Not that I would have even wanted to be rescued, I realized. When it was over, a feeling of blissful relief and accomplishment had washed over me. The value of perseverance could not be denied.

I had been possessed of choice in that test of endurance, though, whereas the experience at the hands of Queegan was completely out of my control. It made the pain worse, somehow. I hissed and grunted as little as I could, not wanting to give the bastard the satisfaction.

The yellows, oranges, and reds of the forest began thinning

after what seemed an eternity of torture. I noticed then that we were approaching the castle proper. Its walls were enormous and rectangular, with little circular windows cut into the stone closer to the top. No doubt created with the local earth, the red clay tiles of the roofs sloped down at sharp angles and a trio of spires extended so far up as to reach nearly into the scudding clouds. I noted with thanks that the brace of garrison towers near the large rounded wooden doors were empty.

The red-haired woman stopped about thirty feet from the portal. She mumbled something into the wind and I began to hear a loud crackling behind me, like the sound of twigs snapping, but several degrees of magnitude more intense. It was the roar of logs breaking. Queegan's spell dug in and forced me to my knees as Queegan and his partner did the same. A monstrously large boulder sailed through the air just barely over our heads and smashed into the hard wood of the castle doors. There was such a terrific bang that my ears screamed out in rebellion. The door exploded into bits.

I noticed then a winded expression on the red-haired woman's face. Ever since the moment I saw the cold blue flame in Kathryn's palm those weeks before in the presence of the King and his Inner Council, I wondered at the cost of magic. When I carried Kathryn's unconscious body, who remained beyond the waking world even after I stumbled and swore so close to her ear, I had inferred that some piece of vitality fled with the casting of spells. But Kathryn had been awake for days and barely conscious when she said the words that saved us from injury as our camel expired. The red-haired woman's clear exhaustion at two violent spells was proof that magic users were not some invulnerable lot who could simply use sorcery with impunity, to cast and cast until all of their enemies were left transformed into charred piles of bones. There was a price. The more spectacular the spell, the more it required of a Mage, it seemed.

A wave of stiffening hairs rode up my back with the

thought.

We rested for a few moments then, so that the red-haired woman could catch her breath. Queegan scanned the forest behind us but remained mute. I asked more questions, but my captors continued to ignore me. The red-haired woman asked something of Queegan that I could not hear. He looked at her with a hard skepticism, then murmured something and flipped a flask out of thin air. She took the bottle, unstoppered it with her teeth, and took a long pull at the contents. Then she straightened up, smiled, and returned the bottle to Queegan. After watching Simon gob the stuff with fiendish glee, I could tell by the drooping eyelids and the unnatural smile exactly what she had drunk. Ephestor's Folly. I kept the knowledge of my discovery to myself.

Resuming the Hellish enchanted walk, we entered into the foyer of the castle. Sunlight was streaming through a few of the windows in the stone above us, as well as the ruined doorway behind. On the floor were a number of upholstered chairs and low tables near a great big fireplace to our left. Several of these pieces of furniture had been knocked over by bits of rock and massive splinters of hard wood. Long moth-eaten purple banners were draped on opposite sides of another door further in. The silver cups of the Aquester crest were barely evident in the tatters.

"Valtha," the drug-addled woman said, turning to me. "The old seat of the Kingdom. Janus's great-grandfather used to rule from this castle, before it was abandoned and everyone moved up north to the coast, to the simple fishing village of Isha. You would not call that place a simple fishing village anymore, would you?"

"No," I said warily. I had heard Valtha mentioned before by Terence. It was in Ecta Province. He had told us that it was too close to the western border with Liseria, which is why King Thusor had simply rebuilt the Thrain capital in Isha, which is about as far east and as far north as you can get in our home country. The Blue Cathedral was only finished being rebuilt a year or two before my birth, by all accounts a great feat of construction of previously unknown alacrity. "No, I would not."

"You must have been told the lie that all children are told about this place," she continued, "that the old King moved the capital out of a desire for security from the scourge of Liseria. Well, to be fair to him, it was not entirely a lie. It was indeed a desire for security that prompted Thusor in his actions. But it was not security from Liseria or anything as mundane as that." She paused. "What do you know about Chaos?"

The woman moved to sit down on one of the ratty couches. She patted the cushion next to her. Queegan looked bored, arms folded and foot tapping slowly as he scanned around the foyer. He absently waved a hand and his spell forced me to sit next to the woman. Her head was cocked and she stared into me with her golden eyes.

"Chaos?" I responded after a time, trying to figure out if this was a trap. "You mean the opposite of Order?"

"You cannot define something by simply referring to its opposite. Chaos itself - how would you describe it?"

"I... It *is* the absence of Order." The woman looked annoyed, so I blustered on. "There are no forms, nothing is dependable. But it is an abstraction. It could be used to describe a rioting crowd. Or a country without a ruler. Or pieces on a chess board knocked over and piled up at odd intervals. My mother used to tell me that my bedroom was pure Chaos."

"Ha!" the woman laughed. "Your mother, yes. I am not surprised. Chaos is, as you say, an absence of Order. But it is not an abstraction. It is woven into the fabric of the universe. Chaos and Order pull at each other with equal force in order to maintain the world as it is. There is darkness to light, creating a world of night and day. Up mirrors down, forwards has its backwards, and left needs right, placing three dimensional limits on that world. Frost is at odds with flame, creating the flow of water. Everything you see around you, it is all the product of a Balance between Chaos and Order in some form or another. Everyone always assumes that Order is preferable to Chaos, but I ask you - why is that?"

"Order is stability," I said, feeling my mouth parrot words that Terence had said to us several times during the early days of my training, explaining to his young Squires why Coloured Knights must ensure that Order is maintained in the Kingdom. "Order promotes a higher good. With Chaos, people are disorganized, looting and murdering each other. Order brings law and predictability. Chaos favours criminality and arbitrary Justice."

"That sounded as rehearsed as a speech in one of the shite plays I have attended in the capital," she said with another laugh. "You are correct. Order does promote something, although whether it is a higher good or not is a matter for debate. It also keeps people in their place, it keeps the world stagnant. Without Chaos, there would be no change, no evolution. It is not the even drumbeat of Order that changes a man's heart: it is the screech of Chaos."

The woman shifted to lean back in the couch and I became intensely aware that the cleavage of her breasts had split a little further.

"I ask you," she continued, "do you think that the forces are currently in Balance? Order ensures that classes remain stratified, that the rich are above the poor in social station, that kings rule with the support of their sycophants. Order ensures that every person of low birth remains a good little servile wretch, instead of masters of their own domains."

I shifted, realizing that Queegan's spell had gone dormant again. Anger flared and the Jaguar laughed in delight. "You are a Servant of Kronos, are you not?" I said. "You wish to render the world back into Chaos? For what? So that humanity is wiped off the face of the planet? Or do you simply wish to turn everyone into raving lunatics?"

"You are referring to that little dip into pure Chaos that I sent you into on the mountain?" The woman smiled a viper's smile. "That was a test, my dear boy. One that you passed admirably."

"A test?"

"I needed to make sure you are who I now know you to be," she responded.

"And had I failed?"

"If you failed you would have remained one of those raving lunatics you just described," she said with a shrug.

The woman shifted again, this time getting so close that I could smell her musky perfume. Arousal nipped at my loins.

"In any event, I do not simply wish to plunge the world into Chaos," she said. "That would be foolish. Order is necessary, otherwise everything would break down. If every single person was completely beholden to Chaos, the world would burn. I do wish to see more Chaos enter into the world, because I think there is one point that you have not yet grasped. The world is out of Balance. When the Red Tradition 'rescued' the world from the excesses of Traximus and the Heraclytan Empire, the Balance shifted. Order is dominant, and the world suffers for it. You do not feel it because you are highborn, the child of a Baron who does not have to worry about the inequality in this world. Order serves you perfectly. But I would see noble houses crumble and every human being on the same social footing. I seek only to bring the world back into Balance."

As the woman spoke, I realized that my body was overcome with risen hairs. There was Truth in what she said, but a sharp feeling of anxiety in my chest told me that something was wrong nonetheless. The Jaguar had warned me that she was to be one of the Trimurti of Separation – I sensed something was amiss in her understanding.

"Chaos is self-determination," she said. "Order is giving one's self over to something else without question. Chaos is magic. Thanks to the ascendance of Order, only a select few, the Red Tradition, have access to magic. And it is a secret. With

Chaos back in Balance, everyone will be able to use it. Everyone might be free."

"That is a high-minded goal," I said, unconvinced. "Does your master Kronos appreciate the subtleties of your position?"

The woman barked a laugh. "I like you. My name is Patricia, by the way."

With that, she rose from the couch and sashayed towards the doors that led further in to the castle. The Jaguar roared with lust at her form, the way her hips shifted from side to side. I consciously pushed those thoughts aside and rose of my own accord, pleased that Queegan had not seen fit to bind me yet again.

"How can you be sure?" I called after her. "How can you be sure that you are only returning Balance? How can you be sure that you will not go too far? To send it into imbalance in Chaos's favour?"

She did not respond. Instead, she murmured a few alien words and an arm of grey stone lashed out from the floor of the castle, rending the doors to smithereens.

"Like the last one," Queegan said, turning to me with a smirk, "we could have just tried the lock.

Chapter Thirty-Two
When Things Changed

We ventured deeper into the castle, through long hallways with ancient rugs, past mouldering paintings and decomposing hung cloth. Armies of rats skittered and scurried out of our way, finding the holes they had dug into the weakening mortar that joined the huge grey stone bricks. There were a number of smaller doors that we marched past, doors whose contents I wondered at between waves of pain from Queegan's spell. I was interested enough in what we were doing that the spell was unnecessary, and I told my captors as much, but Patricia deferred to Queegan on my 'care' and he clearly wanted to see me suffer.

We lost the ambient light as the windows disappeared. Patricia murmured a few words to create a little orb of pure black that shimmered and somehow emitted a bright light that made our surroundings completely visible, wildly different than the sapphire fireball that Kathryn was in the habit of conjuring yet fulfilling the same purpose. I thought on Kathryn briefly, wondering whether she had followed my unspoken request that she take Simon and run. Then I returned my attention to Patricia's black orb.

Each time I looked upon it I was reminded of my time on the mountain, of the nightmare I discovered in the eye of the buzzard. Wondering why she could not have pulled one of the fucking torches from the endless sconces that jutted from the walls, I stopped looking at it. The effort of the spell left Patricia with a slightly perceptible stoop, even through the effects of Ephestor's Folly. The little trick's effect was not nearly as dramatic as the conjured stone battering rams, and I wondered how close to the precipice of exhaustion the woman stood, false energy from potions or not.

"King Thusor had a court magician," said Patricia as we approached a wall with a narrow staircase leading down within. "His name was Kolar and he did not hail from Thrairn. He was a nomad from the Northern Wastes, those Kingless places where men and women pay homage to elders and make their livings by dint of their heartiness and cleverness. The Red Tradition kept records of all of Kolar's exploits. He was a curiosity, a savage who trekked his way to civilized lands and was somehow inducted into the Red Tradition and Thusor's Inner Council."

"After you," Patricia said, pointing at the staircase. Queegan's spell dug in and I found myself leading the charge into the depths of the castle. Mercifully, the black orb floated just a couple of feet from my face and its light kept me and Queegan from losing our footing, though it meant that I had to look at the accursed black ball. The Jaguar laughed at my unease as I clomped my way down.

We arrived at a landing with a closed door. I thought then that we would proceed on out, but Patricia told Queegan to keep going, all the way to the bottom, and I winced as the spell pulled me down the spiral of the stairs again. We passed a trio of doors, two of which were open into an inky unknown, on our way down to our destination. When we finally did arrive, Queegan's spell stopped me long enough for Patricia to tell him to have me open the door and lead on.

I tried the handle several ways before giving up in light of the futility of my efforts. The door was locked. Noticing his mistress's exhaustion as well, Queegan offered to cast a spell of his own to open it up, but Patricia was having none of it. She told Queegan to get me clear of the door and cast another spell which wrenched a column of stone out from the pillar around which the staircase wound, punching through the metal of the lock and sending the door creaking open into the pitch beyond. I could barely see her from my position near the door, but I could actually feel the witch's energy dim as the stone receded back into the pillar.

'Pride,' whispered the Jaguar, its tone different than it had been when it spewed its vitriol to me. 'See now its cost.'

I was sent into the room, which was soon illuminated by the black orb. Thick bars of rust-pitted steel jutted from the ground to the left and right of me, joining with the ceiling and bisected by more lengths of metal running to the walls into more than a dozen cells. The stone of the floor was angled down towards a large grate in the center of the room, clearly a drain. At the opposite end of the room another door stood closed, steel-braced with an eye-level rectangular opening, beyond which was found what I assumed to be guards' quarters or perhaps a torture chamber.

Queegan's spell brought me to a halt a few steps into the room.

"Kolar was a shaman in his village, a man who learned magic simply through communing with nature and learning to read the wind," Patricia said, picking up the thread of her story again, each word laboured. She produced the flask of Ephestor's Folly again and took a swig, straightening a little as the effects took hold. "There was much of Chaos in him, even then.

"Kolar did not know it, but when he used magic, he was dancing to the song of Kronos. By the time he learned the source of his power, he was well-embedded in the Red Tradition. He understood then that the elitist organization he found himself in had created a perversion of nature with its obsession towards Order and the spell it had cast to ensure its primacy. Kolar decided then to reopen the Rift into other worlds that Traximus had created. He spent secret years doing the preparatory work, making sure that he found a suitable site for the Rift and to ensure that all of the necessary rituals were complete. It must have been happily ironic to Kolar that here was the site, in the bowels of Castle Valtha, a stronghold of Order, where Kolar nearly completed his task. But he did not realize the importance of Traximus's blood, that only through the old Emperor's dealings with the Dragon had he received protection from the places between worlds, protection that runs in his blood and the blood of his issue. When Kolar opened the Rift, he was torn apart by the energy within.

"The history that I read at the Red Keep is not totally clear about what happened next, but what is certain is that Kolar had done something wrong," continued Patricia. "Or rather, there was something that he failed to do. He had "failed to realize Eternity's Embrace before delivering the Offering," whatever that means. Regardless of what went wrong, the Rift became unstable and threatened to split Clovir in two. Red Mages were called by the King to intervene and prevent the end of all things. The authors of the text suggest that this was Kronos's intention all along, to use his unwitting disciple as a pawn in a gambit to destroy the entire world.

"I am not convinced," Patricia heaved, "that Kronos is anything beyond a force of nature, and the idea that it has an intention is as unlikely as anything spouted by those rosary-brandishing fools that bind themselves to the Christ-man. Whatever happened back then, we now have a man of Traximus's blood, and thus the protection of the Dragon. Kronos cannot interfere with the magic of the Dragon." Patricia's eyes glinted in the light of her fell orb.

I knew that this woman was insane, but the depths of her madness only became clear to me at that point. For all her chatter about wanting to bring equality back to the people, it had become certain that she cared only for herself and her speculative plans. I did not want to help her in what she intended, for it seemed obvious to me that her god was using her as surely as he had used her predecessor. I decided to stall so that I might figure out a way out.

"Once this is done," Queegan said, beating me to the punch, "you will allow me to slay him and use his body to commune with the dead, as was our deal? I have killed half a dozen nobles and not a single one has told me anything beyond lifeless grunts and moans. Perhaps with his lineage-"

"Yes, yes," said Patricia, waving him away. "First, we need to find the cell where the Rift was opened." She began to study each of the cell doors, pausing for a few moments on each to examine something that I could not see: they all looked the same to me.

"What is the Dragon?" I asked. "Why cannot the Lord of Chaos interfere with his magic?" I willfully ignored Queegan's request for my head, not straying from my plan to distract Patricia. It was a desperate shot, but I thought back to what the Jaguar said. This woman was prideful, she would most likely not be able to resist a demonstration of her intellect or knowledge.

"The Dragon is Ourobouros," Patricia said, still looking around. "She is the Keeper of Eternity, implacable and impossible to reason with. She does not interfere with the affairs of mortals, which is why it is all the stranger that your ancestor not only communed with her, but received her Blessing. A man with Ourobouros' Blessing is a man who is no longer ruled by time. Kronos, for all his power, is still rooted in the dimension of time, same as us all. He cannot affect Eternity, and it is through this protection by which we are going to prevent him from spilling his full power into this realm. We will allow only enough Chaos through to return Balance to the world."

"So, what did Traximus actually do to cause the end of the

Heraclytan Empire?" I asked. "If the blessing made him so powerful, how did he die?"

"Circumstances of his death are unclear," said Patricia, running her fingers over a rust-eaten lock. "Whatever happened, it was not until he died that the Red Tradition was formally created. They were small men of the nobility, fearful of Chaos and desperate to cling to the control that Order offers. After they banished Chaos through their inhuman rituals to shut the Rift, they gave those who were able to continue to use whatever magic was left in our land a choice: join or die." She paused. "Most died."

"Ah," Patricia announced. "Here we are."

Patricia again called on stone to aid her, pulling dank green stone out of the ground to slam against the door of the cell. Its rusted hinges snapped like twigs. She began to pant visibly after the rock receded, waving away Queegan's aid and taking another swig of Ephestor's Folly. She entered the cell, walked past the rotting cot and bucket on the ground, pulled one of the daggers from her belt, and began tapping on the stones with the pommel. A mutter of something to Queegan saw him pass her a familiar object, the flask filled with my blood that Queegan had taken while were in the wagon.

"If you have my blood," I asked, not sure if I wanted to know the answer, "why do you need me?"

"A dangerous question," Patricia said with a laugh. "You are backup, a way to ensure that our protection spell does not fail. We will spill your blood if necessary. If your life needs to flee your body to ensure that we trap the Dragon's magic, so be it."

"You say you wish to create a world of equality, where people are free to self-determine," I replied, feeling sweat beading on my fingers. "Yet you have no qualms with how this comes to pass? You would bring this about through murder? That is an auspicious way to bring about your paradise."

"A sacrifice," snarled Patricia. I had clearly run over a sore spot. "If the zealots of all the religions of the world have one thing right, it is that sacrifice is the way to freedom. It is for the greater good that you would die! But, no matter. Your blood alone should be sufficient sacrifice."

"Yet you would give me to this lunatic when you are done here!" I said, pointing to a smiling Queegan. "You clearly do not mind him killing me, but think of his goal. He wants to become immortal. Does that not give you cause for concern?"

"That is Order speaking through you. Queegan shall have freedom to self-determine, unbounded by anyone else's opinions or judgments, including mine."

"I will just have to die for his freedom," I said with a sarcastic smirk. "Cannot let anything get in the way of freedom. Like someone else's life. Who are you to say who lives or dies?"

Patricia ignored me, turned back to the wall, and threw the flask of my blood against the stone. It had partially coagulated and chunks stuck to the brick, gleaming in the strange light of the black orb. The witch began speaking in her bizarre tongue, raising her hands to the ceiling and looking up. The air changed, then. It reminded me of the feeling before a rain, when the air becomes heavy on one's body. The darkness around us seemed to dim.

Patricia finished speaking after several minutes. She sagged, grabbing at the bars of the cage next to her. Nothing further happened. We waited a moment, and then my red-haired captor shrieked in frustration. She nodded to Queegan and I felt the bastard's spell seize me once more. I was forced to march over towards the end of the wall. I fell to my knees, my head was pulled back such that my neck was exposed and the crown of my head was little more than a hair's breadth away from the stone dripping with my blood.

"I am sorry about this, Andrew," said Patricia, heaving exhaustion. "I truly am. I wish it could be done some other way."

I considered responding, but then a thought struck my mind like a lightning bolt. There was no rational reason for it, just pure intuition. It was accompanied by goose bumps and I cleaved to it as if it were a life raft and I were shipwrecked.

I needed to touch my head off of the stone. And the idea of doing so scared me to death.

I tried pushing back against Queegan's spell, to make my way against the magic. Pain shot through my shoulders, neck, and all across the top of my head. The more I struggled, the harsher the pain. I cried out after several seconds of this futility.

'Wisdom,' I heard the Jaguar say, but it seemed like he were shouting to me from miles away. 'Brute Strength is not the way. You need to use Wisdom.'

I struggled for another moment, looking at Patricia as she raised one of her daggers overhead and muttered something up at it. I felt certain it was a prayer to Kronos.

'This is it,' I thought, not for the first time. 'I am going to die.'

I let my body go. I was not going to struggle, to give these bastards the satisfaction of my pain as well as my death. I noticed then that my arms were not affected by the spell. My legs, torso, neck, and head were all held by the vice grip of Queegan's spell, but my arms were free to roam.

I saw the dagger at Patricia's belt. I just might be able to grab it and plunge it into her belly. Queegan would still have me, but she would not be permitted to finish her work to leave the world in ruins.

'Wisdom...' the Jaguar called to me, its voice growing faint. 'You will never win this war thinking the way that they do...'

Lykander's image came upon me in a flash. I opened the pouch on my belt, where I had hidden the satchel he had given me. Unable to look away, I saw that Patricia had completed her spell and the dagger was descending in shaky hands towards me. She was on the verge of collapse, which would have sent the blade into my flesh with hideous force. I fumbled with the strings, trying to untie the package. The paper came off the package and I pulled apart the box, grasping at the object inside. I felt the kiss of cold steel upon my neck as my fingers closed around the object within.

As soon as I touched what felt to be a chain and a pendant, I was released from Queegan's spell. I fell from my position, on my knees and neck exposed to Patricia, backwards towards the wall. I felt my head touch dripping stone, and then heard a sound, something like the tearing of thick wet paper but nauseating and magnified to a degree beyond imagining. I was thrown from the cell, out against the bars of the one on the other side of the room.

My last memory before I lost consciousness was a bright orb emerging from the darkness, a cold blue ball of flame that flickered dimly in the fading of my mind.

Chapter Thirty-Three
Escape

"Andrew, wake up."

Try as I might, I could not. None of my limbs acknowledged me. An enormous weight seemed to be sitting on my chest, keeping me pinned to the ground. My eyes were open a sliver, just enough for me to see flickering light dance across a vaulted ceiling in a room made of grey stone brick, but there was a strange filter overlaying my vision. It was as if I were looking through a threadbare sheet.

The veil on my eyes stretched out to fit over my ears as well, it seemed. I was dimly aware of a droning sound, the 'tak-tak-tak' of a hammer hitting wood, except that it was anything but regular in its pace. It too was altered as if it were happening on the beach and I were submerged in water, drawing up memories of the Pond of Sacrifice my brother and I swam frequently in when we were very young. Faint scuffling was evident as well, and I vaguely intimated that people were moving around frantically.

"Andrew, you need to wake up."

The voice was familiar. A woman's voice. Mother? No... Marissa? No... Kathryn? Patricia?

"Wake up, now!"

It was trying to be a shout, but it was restricted to a fierce whisper. I struggled against the weight on my chest, but I was caught like a mouse by a cat's paw, there in that strange land between sleep and waking. I sensed a presence in the corner of the room, something out of sight. Something malevolent. I tried to turn to look at it, but the paralysis held my neck as well.

"Come on buddy, you need to get up."

A male voice chimed in. A familiar one. I could feel the evil thing move closer, but it was still out of view. Panic began to creep in. I could not let it find its way upon me. It sought to destroy me, of that I was certain.

The hammering was becoming more insistent.

"Alright, Simon, get away from him."

The woman whispered an unfamiliar garble. The presence had almost bridged the gap. An invisible claw brushed my left shoulder, sending tendrils of cold shooting down my arm, numbing it all the way to the tips of my fingers. Then I felt a frigid spray on the flesh of my face and sleep finally released its hold on me. I sat up to see a tiny puff of cloud at the center of a kneeling Kathryn's outstretched palm, a cloud that was soaking me in a shower of water so cold I thought I would die of frostbite.

"Christ-man, that's enough, I am freezing."

"Sorry," Kathryn said, releasing her hand down and closing the gap between us on her knees, wrapping her arms around my neck and hugging me as I shivered. "I am terrible at water magic. You are lucky it did not become ice."

"I am so happy you are OK," she said after a while, breaking away from me. "I thought you might have been concussed... or something worse. I was wondering if you were going to wake up at all. Quickly now, we do not have much time."

I noticed then that my body ached, as if I had been at the training grounds for a few days straight with little rest. My head pained sharply. Simon came over and placed his hand on my shoulder, the one that had come in contact with the shade. I barely felt his touch.

"You did have us worried, buddy."

I looked around after Kathryn pulled away, her cold flame present and casting its blue light around the room. We were in a big chamber with a vaulted ceiling, but compared to what I had seen out in the atriums and hallways on my way to the dungeon, it seemed to be one of the smaller ones in the castle. There was a large oblong rounded table in the center of the room, a runner rotting along its length and surrounded by tall chairs with decaying upholstery. Two long and ornately carved wooden posts extended up a foot and a half into the air from the two back legs of each seat. On the walls there were a half dozen tapestries in the same repair as the rest of the cloth in the ancient castle, though through the dust and disintegration I could see they did seem to be replete with faded shades of all manner of dyes. They must have depicted colourful vistas at some point. On two walls opposite the long sides of the table were kite shields crossed with swords.

The shields were similar to the yellow Dragon teardrops of my former Order, but instead of a yellow Dragon they depicted a purple owl's head made of simple geometric shapes arranged in a clever way. The swords were long blades with thick cross guards and deep fullers that ran along the blade. The pommels at the end of the leather wrapped hilts were all purple, but one of them grabbed my eye...

"Andrew," said Kathryn, interrupting me by standing up and pointing. "we need to get out of here. They are at the door. Can you move?"

Kathryn pointed down to the large rounded wooden door that was set into the wall furthest from us. A metal bar had been laid across the middle and little bits of dust were being kicked up each time it shook with impact. I realized then that this was the droning I had been hearing, the irregular drumming that was subsumed into the ambient noise soon after I emerged from unconsciousness.

The sound of someone, or someones, trying to break down

the door.

"Patricia? Queegan? Why do they not just cast one of their spells?" I asked, still supine on the floor. Try as I might, I was not quite able to gather myself.

"They aren't human," Simon rasped, his face dropping into a mask of terror. "I don't know what they are, or how they got here, but we barely made it out of the dungeon with you alive."

"What happened?" I asked. "What is out there? How did you find me?"

"There is no time for this!" Kathryn said, her voice booming in her deep contralto. "We have to get out of here, and there is no way out but through. All you need to know, Andrew, is that enemies stand outside that door. Arm yourselves," she said, pointing at the swords and shields, "and we will fight our way out."

"Maybe you could give us some of that flask you have," Simon said, his eyes echoing his plea to Kathryn. "I'm sure it will make us better warriors. Just a taste..."

"Not this rot again! There is a reason that potion is called Ephestor's *Folly*, Simon," Kathryn hissed. "Gods-damn it all, you will get no more of it from me. The fiend of it is upon you."

As I stood up, I tried using my left hand to push myself up, but Strength failed me. It was still numb from my encounter in the half-sleep. I fell back down to my side with a flop.

"Christ-man, you are both of you cripples," said Kathryn, grabbing me under the arm pit to help me up. "Did you smash it when you were thrown? Never mind, it does not matter. Is it just your arm?"

I checked myself and nodded.

"Well, you still have one that works?" She pointed again to the swords on the wall. Simon was at one display, so I made my way over to the other, the one with the pommel that had caught my eye.

I could see as I approached that the steel of the swords was patched with brown and little pits had formed. At first I thought both of the swords had a regular little ball pommel, painted a purple to the yellow metal on the swords of the Yellow Order. When I approached I realized that one had a simple gemstone, cut with sharp angles which caught the flickering light and pleased the eye. An amethyst, perhaps?

But the other one, the one that had drawn my eye, bore a jewel shaped like an owl's head, as if the patterning of the image on the shield had been transposed onto the bottom of the black metal of the grip. Through the flickering light from Kathryn's spell, it became clear to me that it was made of a deeper purple than the bright amethyst of the other pommel in front of me. I reached out to touch the blade with my good arm, realizing at that moment that there was something in the palm of my hand.

It was the item I had received from Lykander. I opened it up my hand, revealing a large rectangular sapphire lodged in a silver setting, threaded onto a long silver chain. It was warm to the touch, warmer than it ought to have been, even though it had been wrapped in my palm for a while. I was certain I could actually feel it pulse with energy, a heartbeat within the blue gemstone. Without a second thought, I fastened it around my neck, putting it down under the shirt below my armour, against the flesh of my sternum. I knew its touch meant protection from Queegan's magic, at the very least.

I looked back at the owl-pommeled blade. Feeling a strong wave of rising hairs down my back, I grabbed the sword with my good arm. There was no scabbard about, but there was no need for one, I thought, looking at the door. Simon had formed up alongside of it, holding the sword he had selected with his uninjured left arm. It was one of the amethyst-pommeled blades. Kathryn was next to him. I crossed to them, standing on the side of the door opposite to them.

"Can you raise that with your magic?" I intoned to Kathryn, pointing at the bar across the door and surprising myself with the authority that accompanied my words. She nodded. I raised my sword arm and motioned to them to come over to my side, away from the hinges. Then I walked several feet back from the door and had my companions follow.

"Ready?"

Two nods followed my question. I returned them. Then I crossed to the door, squat below it, lifted the bar, and heaved it with all my might before retreating back to my ready position. The door gave to the next smash by the unknown invaders behind it.

I barely had time to register the appearance of the creatures, but they were ugly and inhuman and sent knives of dread deep into my heart the very moment I looked upon them. They had hairless skulls, long pointed ears that ran up and out behind them, and eyes that were pure black. Open mouths gleamed full of two-inch long white daggers, as if every single one in their heads were the canine tooth of a wolf. The skin on their hairless bodies was of varying shades of red and orange and they were dressed in armour that looked to be made of onyx leather. In their arms, the half-dozen or so that spilled through the portal had wicked blades and axes made of chipped black stone.

The Jaguar whispered defeat to me, its words accompanied by the dread miasma of greenish yellow that always came with its admonishments of doubt. I was useless, crippled in one arm and facing off with Demons that even the harshest of my nightmares could not have fabricated. They were armed to the teeth, which teeth were liable to take a chunk out of my neck once they closed the gap between us. My success with the blade up to this point had been a fluke: I had gotten lucky. I was nothing but a failure and I always would be.

Needles of anxiety blossomed in my chest in the seconds between when the creatures entered and when the they made it to us. The Jaguar's words had shaken me. I am certain I would have faltered, but then I noticed the warmth of Lykander's sapphire and was reminded of his words about making friends with one's Demons. The monsters before me aside, if I was ever going to be free of it, I was going to have to break bread with my self-doubt.

I was *not* a weakling. No longer was I a scared child who needed the protection of his mother's skirts. Nor was I a failure with the blade. I was strong, a force to be reckoned with. Live or die, I would fight. I would not perish cowering in the corner of this gilded mausoleum.

The Jaguar laughed hastily at my efforts, but release washed over me and the pestilential haze fled the moment my blade connected with the neck of the first monster upon me.

So did a spray of bright green blood.

For all the shock and awe that accompanied the creatures' entrance, they certainly did not know how to fight very well. At least, not well enough to best a couple of crippled men with the weight of Terence's training behind them. They also had no real defence against the balls of freezing blue fire that Kathryn pulled from the ether and sent hurtling towards the chinks in their armour. Before much time had passed at all, a couple of dozen strange bodies lay piled in the room before us. I noticed with dread that the last few swings of my sword felt strange, as if something were about to give.

"Now!" I said, noticing a lull in the stream of foes and settling into my role as impromptu Commander of our little war party. "Out!"

Kathryn's orb of blue flame stayed ahead of us as we filed out past the carnage, lighting up the hallway outside. I looked around so that I might orient our party. High ceilings of grey stone, unlit torches in sconces on the walls, a tattered old red carpet on the floor: there was nothing remarkable, nothing I recognized from my earlier trek through the place with Patricia and Queegan. To our left, the hallway came to an end and a large pair of doors in the center, about twenty feet high and rounded together at the tops. To the right, the light of the flame was not strong enough to cut into the darkness such that we saw any end of the hallway.

"Whence did you come?" I asked Kathryn. "Which way to the dungeon?"

She furrowed her brow for a moment, then pointed toward the right. Into the darkness. I thought it a merciful revelation. We marched towards the doors. It was unbarred, but I did not feel like dropping my sword from its ready position. I tried my left arm again, but it refused to respond to my command to lift it.

'You are a useless cripple,' the Jaguar said, its hues of doubt returning with its words. 'You will break under the wave if another pack of those creatures comes upon you.'

"Kathryn, could you please open the door?" I said, shaking off the effects of the Jaguar.

Without looking at me, my companion began to comply. As soon as she touched the large iron ring set into the wood that formed the handle, the door was thrown open and she went flying into the wall next to us.

An enormous hairless freak stood before Simon and I. Standing nearly the height of the open door, it roared a guttural cry that brought to mind glass grinding on stone. Teeth the length of short swords and as white as whalebone bleached in the sun of the shores of my homeland shone brightly in the light of the orb. The monster was brandishing a massive mace, a many-flanged thing that he dragged noisily along the stone as he loped onto the bricks where we had been standing just moments before. The thing roared once more. With unexpected quickness, the mace was up in the air then slammed down, just missing Simon and I as we dodged again.

The bricks of the floor snapped to pieces on impact.

'Time to die,' said the Jaguar. 'No one will remember you. If they do, it will be as a coward who let the monsters into this world. An agent of doom, not worthy of a salty piss on his gravestone.'

"Split," I said, ignoring the Jaguar. It was becoming easier for me to shrug off the effect of its words. "We will divide its attention!"

I tried not to think about whether any life remained in Kathryn's figure crumpled against the wall.

The monster came at me first, no doubt drawn by the fact I had spoken. It wound up and smashed again. I barely made it out of the way. Then we did it again. I realized that this encounter would brook no mistakes. I would have to be perfect. I raised my sword and intoned the words of a prayer in my head. I did not know where the words came from or to whom I was praying.

"Please guide my blade. Let me be fleet of foot and let me have the Strength to protect my friends. I will take on whatever burden this demands. Whatever sacrifice must be made, I will make it. If I must die, I am ready. But do not let them die. Do not let me fail now."

Goose flesh rose on my back and I flew at the creature, sliding through its legs as it wound up and slicing open its exposed inner right thigh. Green blood sprayed out onto the bricks. As I made it towards the back, Simon drove his sword into its left calf. The creature roared in pain and brought its mace down onto the bricks near us. A chip of stone shot out and struck me in the temple.

I was dazed. Just for a moment, but that was enough. The creature slid its mace along the grounds towards me and knocked me back against the wall. I hit the wall on my left side and pain shot through my deadened left arm. I fell to my knees and looked up.

The monster was closing the distance and I braced myself for the end that I knew was coming. The mace went up into the air. I started to look away from the certain death that approached. The mace began to come down, slowed to a crawl, then ceased moving midway through the swing.

Surprised that nothing had happened, I looked around. The fire of the orb had ceased flickering: the flames were at a standstill. I could see a bit of Simon's unmoving body through the gap between the creature's legs.

"So," said the Jaguar, his voice as it had been during our meeting on the mountaintop. "We come down to it. Ready or not, you need my help. And I believe you ready. Just for my intervention here, that is. My full blessing is only for those that accept responsibility. You are responsible. For that which happens in your life. And that means you are responsible for all. You have begun to do so, but you do not understand the full meaning of that yet, not completely. Nonetheless, it is time for you to get a taste of your Destiny."

It felt like an egg was broken over my head, yet instead of runny yolk, I was suffused with pure energy that dripped down into my extremities. My body suddenly felt renewed. It was somewhat akin to the effect of Ephestor's Folly, yet completely different. That brewed poison had its cost. It took a chunk of the drinker's soul in return for its effect. Not so with blessing of the Jaguar. The Jaguar's magic kiss felt as if my body and soul had received a scrubbing. My head cleared. A pleasant tingling sensation rand down my left arm as feeling returned to it. My vision sharpened. I felt as if I had slept for a week.

"Witness life," said the Jaguar. His cryptic words confused me only for a moment, then I was thrust back into the melee as time returned to us.

I slipped just out of the way of the mace. It crackled the stone before me and I dove towards the Demon, stabbing my sword into the creature's foot. Simon's slash at the back of his other leg came simultaneously and the creature staggered, then stumbled, a massive orange paw with claws instead of fingernails slamming into the ground where I had been standing a split second before.

Feeling as nimble as a rabbit, I leapt up onto the thing's knee and drove my blade into the inside of the elbow of its mace arm. Our enemy roared in pain and dropped its weapon.

Then disaster struck.

As the creature rose, the age-weakened steel of my blade finally gave, snapping off near the hilt and leaving about six inches of cracked steel jutting past the crossguard. I slipped off the creature's knee and landed on my back, rolling out of the way just as its emerald-dripping foot slammed down. Grateful that my left arm was working again, I pushed myself up and danced out of the way as it tried to smash me with a massive palm.

Simon was on the offensive, coming at the rear of the creature and slicing at its heel. Finally sick of the damage my companion was doing, the creature turned on Simon with a massive backhand. He did not see it coming, taking the full brunt of the swipe and flying into the door that had not been opened. The monster, clearly slowed by its wounds, loped towards Simon's crumpled body.

Looking down at the six inches of broken steel in my hand, I realized that if I had any hope of saving my friend, I would have only one chance at this. There was bare orange flesh on the monster's neck, a place where his mail did not reach and his helmet was not long enough to cover. Scabbardless, I hooked the blade onto the inside my pants and ran full speed at the monster, feeling the broken sword bite into my thigh as I jumped on his back and started to climb.

Mercifully, for Simon's sake at least, it turned its attention from him and began to try to shake me off its back. The creature nearly sent me flying, despite the fact that I was gripping onto the plates of his black armour with both hands. My grip tightened as the shakes became more severe. It was so difficult just to hold on with both hands, the realization that I would have to let go with one in order to climb up sent daggers of fear skittering through my heart.

I nearly froze, then, halfway up the monster's back. But stopping meant death. This was a fight for my life, and I could brook absolutely no self-doubt if I was going to survive it.

"Please, do not let me fall," I whispered, and let go with my left arm, the one I did not trust since the presence touched it in my half-slumber. I managed to grip further up the creature's thorax, finding purchase on another plate of its armour. Closing my eyes and gritting my teeth against the pain in my thigh as the monster bucked and the steel dug in, I put my Faith in the arm that the Jaguar's magic had revived. I grabbed at the next plate up.

Rising hairs rippled down my back as I found purchase yet again and pulled myself up to my new level. Two more plates and I would be there. I kept my eyes open this time as I went for the next "rung."

The relief I felt when I made that climb successfully was instantly replaced with a sinking feeling that seeped into my guts when I realized the monster had stopped moving. I felt a lurch as we began moving backwards. I nearly let go when the monster slammed its back against the wall. It had not oriented itself correctly and missed crushing me with the wall, but the pressure of air rushing past me screamed at me that it was a very near miss.

I hauled myself up to the next "rung" when the beast did it again. It was a glancing blow, but it caught the leg against which the steel of my sword had been pressing. I barely felt the pain, such was the battle haze on me, but the gathering wetness in my trousers was an awfully good indication that the damage was done.

Looking at my target, I could see the ridges of the creature's vertebrae. I grabbed at the hilt with my left hand, pulling the broken sword out of my leg. It dripped with red as I lifted it up into the air and brought it down into the exposed flesh, praying that Terence's lessons about anatomy were not in vain and that this Demon's physical structure was even passingly similar to that of a human's. I buried the blade to the hilt.

The giant slumped forward with an anticlimactic grunt,

leaving me to roll off onto the hallway floor.

Springing into action, I knew from Terence's lessons that I was in grave danger. If an artery in my thigh had been nicked by the broken sword, I was finished, unless I could get to a Chirurgeon. And I did not see a medical tent anywhere around Valtha.

Thankfully, Terence's teachings also included what to do to buy more time. I pulled the belt from my pants, dropping my pants to the floor. The white cotton of my undertrousers were crimson with blood. I wrapped the belt above the wound and pulled as hard as I could, using the broken sword blade, now dripping with a mix of red and green, to cut a new notch. I then pulled back on the pants, willing them to stay up even in the absence of a belt.

I held onto the sword, praying that I would not have to use it again.

I first went to check on Kathryn. She was breathing. I shook her and shouted at her. I could not carry one of my companions, let alone both of them. I silently prayed to whatever providence had gotten me through the battle that just ended that she wake up.

Mercifully, she began rousing after a few moments of screams into her ears. While she was waking, I started towards Simon. Before I made it to where he lay, he drew himself up to stand, bending over and coughing.

"Christ-man," he said, "you did it!" He clapped me on the back and I winced as I put pressure on my wounded leg.

"You're injured," he said, his face transforming from delight to concern.

"We need to get out of here, now," I said, pointing beyond the open doors.

* * * * *

Somehow, we made it through the castle without encountering another soul, monster or otherwise. It was the same empty and ghostly place that I had traveled through on the way in, but there was something in the air, a wrongness that simply defied all logic. Unnaturalness seemed to reek out of the dusty corners of the place, spiking my chest with needles of fear. Whatever had happened in the dungeon below was bleeding a miasma of desecration into our world. I knew it was the opened Rift that had seen that force attack me and deaden my arm.

I was limping, able to carry myself, mindful of the muck of blood that was weeping down my leg. When we burst through the front door back into the sunshine, I nearly fell on my knees in gratitude. But I was well aware that danger for me only grew more acute with every passing moment.

When she realized I had been hurt, Kathryn apologized for not knowing any healing spells, her face downcast. She became uncharacteristically mute then, a woman who embodied her nickname in a way that was not ironic. I thought I saw some wetness on her face in the bright of her fireball while we were in the castle, but her face was dry when we emerged into the sunshine. I decided that it must have simply been a trick of the light.

"We need to get back to the road," I heaved, willing myself to go on. "With any luck the horses and wagon are still there – Willie! Willis Coulter, the man driving the wagon! Did you deal with him?"

Kathryn and Simon looked at each other before looking back at me.

"Yes, he is dealt with," Kathryn said quietly. Simon remained mute.

"That is it, 'he's dealt with'?" I asked. "What happened, Simon?"

"I promised her, Andrew," he said. "I promised her that I wouldn't tell."

"And you would choose her over me, your friend?"

"She made me swear it. I do not break my oaths."

315

"I am getting tired of the lies and half-truths, Kathryn," I said. "What are you not telling me?"

"Please, Andrew," said Kathryn. "I will tell you, but not now. We need to get out of here, get you safe."

We were about halfway through the forest between the door of the castle and the front gate when I started to feel woozy. Without having to say a word, Simon noticed and was under my shoulder helping me along.

"I am going to die," I whispered into my friend's ear.

"Like fuck you are," he roared, attracting a momentary quizzical glance from Kathryn, whose face soon returned to the determination with which it had been set.

When we made it to the wagon, after noting with delight that I could not see Willie anywhere and the horses remained hitched, red dots began dancing at the edges of my vision. I willed myself to stay afloat in the river of consciousness as we entered the wagon, but I slipped beneath the surface when I attempted to step up.

Chapter Thirty-Four
Mahadeva

My memory of the time after we escaped from Valtha is patchy, to say the least. I do recall opening my eyes to see the ceiling of the wagon a few times, and I vaguely remember stopping and getting out at some point, but there is nothing concrete.

The dreams, though, I remember the dreams.

One in particular stands out. I found myself in an enormous building, a massive hall with low couches against the walls that were made simply, with swathes brilliant blue fabric stretched between long wooden dowels, wound together at the bottom in a beautiful twist of wicker. It was a bright day, and light was filtering in through massive windows to illuminate my surroundings. Reliefs etched into the dark stone of the walls seemed to depict battles and sex and agriculture and other stories of life with a strange style that seemed to shift and swirl when I tried to look upon them. I strained over the images, vainly willing these pictures to reveal their secrets to me.

After a few moments of this, someone called my name. I could not tell who it was, nor the name they used to call me, but I knew I was being summoned. I walked up the hall, towards the back of the room. I noticed then that a massive throne made of what seemed to be pure gold with a white cushion in the middle stood in the center on a dais raised up three steps. A large rug with intricate rounded arabesques lay in front of the platform. I had stopped to observe this rug and its patterns, which moved and shimmered and reminded me of Erifracian art, when again I was called by the unknown person.

Veering off to the right, I walked through a Cyclopean doorway that led through a short hallway before opening out onto a huge attached platform without railing or device to keep people from falling off. A figure stood before me, near the edge. This person seemed at first barely a dozen footsteps ahead of me, then suddenly appeared to be hundreds of feet away. I started to make my way towards them, gazing off into the sky as I walked.

I noticed as I approached the edge that beyond the platform was an enormous city below, made of buildings with rounded edges and spherical roofs and coloured what seemed to be an equal distribution of very black and very white. We were very high up, and I could not see an end to the city, even though it was a clear day, without a puff of cloud or a tendril of fog to obscure anything below the horizon.

The figure at the end of the platform called my name again, when I was about halfway to them. I noticed then that it was a woman's voice, but I cannot remember what name she called me nor what her voice sounded like. What I do know is that joy blossomed in my heart as I recognized who she was and I quickened my pace, anxious to be with her.

As I neared, I heard the call of a bird. I was unsurprised to see what looked like a goose high in the air, one of those avian creatures from my homeland that are thick in the marshes and which we slaughter during the Feast of the Christ-man every Yule Month to feast upon as the year draws to a close. It dove when I looked upon it, down past my line of sight and into the city.

When I finally drew up near the woman, I tried to gaze upon her face, but she had her head turned away from me.

Black hair hung low on her body, arranged in tresses and secured with ribbon that seemed to shimmer with every colour of creation. I noticed then that she was wearing a bright orange dress, but it was unlike any I had seen before. It seemed to drape over her shoulder. I then saw the bare tan skin of her lower back.

Her figure excited me, but I was more interested in seeing her face. I grabbed her arm and tried to turn her towards me. As I spun her, her torso moved, but nothing changed about the rest of her appearance. I tried again, and again, but still the woman faced away from me in spite of the turns. It was as though I was spinning one of the tops I used to play with when I was very young, but instead of a little cone that spun on the ground, the arms of this woman turned round while her face remained hidden to me.

I became frustrated and shouted my impatience at her. I let go and prepared to walk away. She did not respond, but simply pointed out toward the horizon.

A large black cloud had formed over the city, one so dark it seemed to draw the light from the air that surrounded it. It was like a light itself, except that it shone darkness out from its core, bathing the buildings below in shadow. Within the cloud, flashes of dark red pulsed every few moments. A strong sense of wrongness came over me. That feeling was accompanied by indignity.

Who was this pretender? They have no authority here!

I looked back at the woman next to me. She was facing me now, but I cannot for the life of me recall what her face looked like. I do recall how it made me feel. It was as though I had been trying to solve a puzzle for days and the final arrangement finally made itself known to me. It was accompanied by a rush of love and passion.

This woman held the other half of my heart! And to have finally found her. I was overjoyed!

It was then that I heard the first crack of thunder. I looked back out over the city. The black clouds seemed to have multiplied, spreading out to cover every bit of sky as far as the eye could see. The darkness had obscured even the light of the sun, though I could see it shining even through the murk. Blood-red lightning arced from the clouds down to the land below, incinerating the black and white buildings without preference for which. Fires set by the storms raged in the streets, but the ebony clouds would not sprinkle any healing water to help put them out.

Usurped in my own home! I was furious. I would destroy whomever had done this.

I looked back at the woman next to me. In spite of all that was going on, she was smiling. She looked at me with eyes of pure love and said to me:

"There is no need. Let us dance."

I took her in my arms, arms that were as blue as the deep water of the cold ocean, feeling the sublime warmth of her body against mine, inhaling a scent of incalculable beauty. We danced. The city around us burned, and we danced. I melted into it. I could feel anger then, a red-hot rage, but it was not coming from within me nor my dancing partner. It was coming from somewhere out there, in the world where the fires had been set. Whatever it was, it wanted my attention.

But I was dancing with my beloved, and I would not let her go.

Chapter Thirty-Five
Anima

This is getting old, I thought, waking up in yet another unknown place.

At least this one reminded me of my father's cottage. A soft bed beneath me, I was staring up at a ceiling made of dark brown slats. Gloaming light filtered in through a window above and behind my head. A large fire crackled in the little stone hearth over to my right, with an empty armchair that looked like the one I had in my room at home pulled up next to it. A narrow night side table with a well-worn pewter mug atop it sat to my left, another smaller chair just next to it. Just past my feet was a familiar-looking door. A small bookcase displaying the spines of books I recognized stood tall next to it. I squinted in the dim light. The titles were familiar: they were the same books I had in my library. I noticed then that the portrait propped on top of the bookcase depicted my mother in her younger years, before the actions of Gerard and myself etched deep lines of worry into her face.

I *was* home!

I tried to sit up. Electricity shot through my injured leg, coaxing an involuntary scream from my throat. I lay back, sweating with the effort. My head swam. I thought then that I might lose consciousness again. I stretched and grabbed for the pewter mug, grounded by the taste of cool water as reward for my efforts.

Summoned by my cry, my father was the first to enter the room. He was dressed in his chains and leathers and yellow cloak, his sword swinging from his belt. A large smile split his normally sullen face.

"Andrew!" he exclaimed. "Thank the Christ-man. I thought I had lost you!"

In a becoming-less-rare display of emotion, my father crossed to me, bent over, and gave me a hug. I returned it with force. He was damp and smelled of untold days of sweat, but I was so overjoyed to see him that the stink did not bother me.

"Father," I said, "I thought you were dead! Did the King survive, too? How did I get here? Where is Kathryn? Simon? Are they all right? Why are you still dressed for war? We are home!"

"They are all fine, Andrew," he said, letting go and a serious expression creeping onto his face. "You need to rest. Do not worry about any of that. Just get some sleep."

I realized as he was speaking that the call of sleep was strong, even though I had just awoken. I let it take me.

✷ ✷ ✷ ✷ ✷

When next I came to, I only got as far as the twilight of half-sleep. I sensed the malevolent presence in the room with me again. It was just out of sight once more, out of view of my paralyzed head. Anxiety crept into my bones, but this time it was swiftly replaced by a feeling of peace. I had a strong intuition that, no matter what this thing did to me, I would be able to overcome it.

In response to this thought, it seemed, the entity roared with rage and I was released into full wakefulness.

Eyes closed, I rested for a moment. I listened to the fire crackle in the hearth. Thirsty, I groped for my pewter mug and took another drink. When I opened my eyes, I noticed that the light coming in from the window had gone. And someone was sitting in the big armchair. Simon. Like my father, he was still wearing his full Yellow Knight battle armour. The brightness of the cloth on the tabard, his back, and the visible brown patches of leather led me to believe he had procured a cleaner version of the road-stained stuff he had been wearing the last time I had seen him.

"Andrew," he said, "you're awake!"

He stood to come over to me, as though he were planning on giving me a hug. A troubled look descended on his face at the last moment. Instead of hugging me, he briefly grabbed my forearm, gave it a squeeze, and then returned to his chair.

"Is everything alright?" I asked, a quizzical look on my face.

"Ha! What a question. We barely escaped from the maw of Hell, and you want to know if everything is alright."

I examined Simon for a moment. I knew him well from our time together at the training grounds. The journey from Tunuska had only made us grow further intertwined. When you spend so much time together, you get close to a person. Close enough that you know when they are telling you the truth and when they are hiding something. Thankfully, I had picked up from our time together that Simon had a tendency to crack under the pressure of silence, so I kept my peace for a few interminable moments.

"Christ-man, you can be such a cock," he snapped after he had had enough, his face dropping even further. "No, everything is not alright. I just returned from the Psychoprobist's office."

"Oh," I said. "And how was that?"

"He thinks I am a sissy, Andrew. Full stop. 'Latently homosexual,' he said. I told him about what happened with Captain Rice. About Aziz. That I love sucking cock when I am deep in my cups but I cannot bring myself to kiss a man, that I feel no love for the handful of men that I have done that with. Only a burning lust and a feeling of shame and wrongness

323

when it is over. He told me that it was immaterial! That merely by the act itself I had proven myself to be a homosexual and that I am in denial."

"I told him of my love for Kelsa," Simon continued, staring at the ground, "that I feel attraction for women and I feel no shame associated with that. He told me that it is a lie that I am telling myself. This man, after meeting me for an hour, feels as though he knows the contents of my heart better than I do!"

"So what does he suggest?" I asked, propping myself up on my elbows.

"He has no prescription! Nothing for me to do, just accept the fact that I am a homosexual and that I should not pursue Kelsa, since it is clear that I will not be faithful to her. His theory is that I will harbour these desires and they will strengthen until I bubble over into a fiend that works every brothel in Isha on a daily basis!"

Simon paused.

"That last bit was my interpretation," he admitted. "In any event, he told me I am doomed to this life of unhappiness and that I should break off my betrothal. Christ-man, for all my jokes, I don't have anything against homosexuality, Andrew. I really don't. It would be easier if I simply knew myself to be gay. But something feels wrong here. I don't know what to do."

"Why must it be one or the other?" I said, suddenly upset for my friend. He was as much a victim of circumstance as any man I had ever met. "Why do these men assume that there are sissies and men that are not sissies? You say you love Kelsa, and I believe you. And perhaps there is something about men that excites you. Whatever happened with Captain Rice, perhaps that is simply here to teach you something. About love. About life."

Simon looked up, hopeful.

"Whatever is happening with you," I said, "I cannot believe that it is simply coincidence. When I passed into the Jaguar's space, he told me that I am part of three – a Trimurti of Unity.

I must stand together with another two who are to become unified as well. You are fractured, Simon, but I believe that you are on your way to wholeness. As Lykander told us, we must befriend our Demons on the way to Heaven. And you are definitely breaking bread with yours at the moment."

"You know that I love you no matter what, brother," I finished.

Iridescent light strained at the edge of my vision. Simon smiled and looked at the hearth. He did not respond.

"What about Kathryn, the Demons, Patricia, Queegan? My father was dressed like you are as well - for war. How did you get time to go to the Psychoprobist's office if we are preparing to defend the gates?"

"We aren't at war yet," Simon said. "At least, we aren't bringing the fight to the Erifracians. Your father ordered us to maintain our battle gear as an excess of caution, as far as I can see it. King Revanti's army is on its way here by sea. After your father and King Janus heard the story of our time in Valtha from Kathryn and me, King Janus recalled the other Orders back to Isha from their positions on the borderlands. They will garrison here and hold the city.

"I don't know what happened down in that dungeon, Andrew, but those things..." Simon continued, his voice dropping to a hoarse whisper, "they were like the Demons the Priests of the Christ-man are always telling us to watch out for. Even now, thinking about them..."

I grabbed at my leg, gingerly touching the parts above and below the wound and wanting to change the subject again. "How long has it been? How did I survive?"

"About a week. And by sheer luck, in my estimation. We managed to load you aboard the wagon when you collapsed, and set off for the nearest town. Kalingshire, it was called. A little hamlet on the border between Ecta and Tyro. One that just happened to be hosting a traveling Chirurgeon. We brought you to the inn. Kathryn actually knew the innkeeper, can you imagine that? Friends from way back, apparently.

"Anyway," Simon said, "we placed you on a table, and there the Chirurgeon was, up alongside you with a long tube connecting a pair of big needles. One of us would have to give you our blood, she told us. I was prepared to do it, but Kathryn beat me to it, thrusting her arm out to the woman and sending the red stuff down the tube and into your body.

"The Chirurgeon worked you for about three hours," Simon continued, "after which you were to have bedrest, she said. After some fighting with the good Physiker, Kathryn convinced her to let you convalesce in the wagon while we came back to Isha. Kathryn pleaded with anyone who would listen that they should follow us to the capital, that they were in danger from an invader coming up the Regent's Way from the south for every moment they remained in that village. They just ignored her.

"Why wouldn't they?" Simon said, letting wrath leak into his speech. "Who the fuck is Kathryn? She destroyed her red robe. Not that that would have been any help, given the nutters that preach in this city. Nobody knows magic exists, not officially. And she wasn't prepared to cast a little parlour trick to convince them of the threat. Seeing something like that, they would have been more liable to burn her at the stake than to follow her to Isha."

"Christ-man," I said, "I need to get out, to find Kathryn." I tried to sit up. Fire ascended my body from my leg. I winced and lay back. "I am in no shape. How is your arm?"

"On the mend," Simon said, drawing attention to the sling draped around his neck as he moved it. "Somehow I never hurt it further when we were in Valtha. It is still broken, the Chirurgeon in Kalingshire told me as much when she replastered it. But it is getting there. Another few weeks and I can start trying to use it again. It might never again be its former self, but I will not be forever crippled. Her words."

"Not crippled enough to get me released from the Order, of

course," Simon said with a sigh. "I would have to transform into a jungle cat and kill my Captain to get that kind of special treatment." Simon smiled at me.

"Any sign of Queegan or Patricia?" I asked.

"When we were in the dungeon, rescuing you, that sex pot red-haired woman – must be Patricia – she was unconscious on the floor. Queegan and Kathryn spoke, like they knew each other. Very well, it seemed. Kathryn had the better of him, and threatened Queegan that she would kill him if he tried to stop us – and then the Demons began pouring in through the Rift. It was a great black hole that seemed to draw in all the light of the torches and Kathryn's orb... I picked you up and we made a hasty exit, Kathryn firing her magic at them as we ran. Queegan, busy with the Demons himself, said that he would come for you – come for you and take your mind." Simon shuddered. "Listen, Andrew, I need to get back to the barracks before curfew. I'll try to get word to Kathryn that you are awake, though I'm not sure how I'm going to do it. She's disappeared into the ether again."

When he awkwardly grabbed for my forearm again, I pulled my friend down into a hug. I held him there for a while, until he stopped squirming and relaxed into it.

"All will be well," I said, hoping that I was speaking truth to my tortured friend.

✶ ✶ ✶ ✶ ✶

The next and final time I woke, I knew something was off. It was cold in my room. There was no fire in the hearth. A strange smell wafted on the air, something the crept back at me from memory. It reminded me of the cocktails my mother used to give me when I was bed-ridden with fever as a child, rich and medicinal, but with a hint of smoke and earth, burnt hair and citrus fruit. I had smelled it before.

"Master Libélula," I said, calling out to the darkness as the connection to memory was made. It was night. There was no moon in the sky.

"Andrew," said a voice from across the room. "It has been a while."

I had thought so much over the preceding weeks what I would say to the man when I encountered him again, rolling speeches over in my mind, inspecting them to see if they had a sufficient mix of admiration, indignation, and demand for answers. This was only compounded when the Jaguar told me that he had been sent to attack me by the man hidden in the shadows of my room. Finally in the situation for which I had waited and planned so long, I found myself tongue-tied.

"You have done well, that much is clear to me," the deep accented tones of his voice seeming to fill the room without amplification. "You have cleared some of the doubts in your mind and are releasing the grip of fear. You do have some way to go yet, but your training is drawing to a close."

"That is it? 'Your training is drawing to a close?' You have nothing else for me, no apology?"

"For what would I apologize?" Master Libélula asked, moving in closer and snapping his fingers. A little green ball of flame appeared in the air between us. It was as cold as the orbs conjured by Kathryn and by Patricia. He was dressed in his colourfully-embroidered black vest, white shirt, and purple pants. He smiled widely at me with a face awash in emerald light.

"Lying to me, for one," I said, propping myself up on my elbows. "You told me that the Jaguar had been stalking you because of an evil magic, that your cousin was killed by one of those creatures. Sent to you at the behest of your enemies in Atika. You told me that my soul was tainted by the beast. But you were the one who brought it down on my head!"

"I merely did what I was called to do," he said, without change in the tenor of his speech. "Just as we all do. It was not entirely dishonesty. My cousin Guillermo did meet his end at the claws of the Jaguar, yet he lives still. He is one of the most

328

honourable men I know, now. Your soul is indeed tainted, though not by the Jaguar's curse. Something from your own past haunts you like a spectre. And black magicians do stalk me, just as they stalk you. Such is the lot of those who serve Unity. I told you I help those in need and that was exactly what I was doing.

"But... you are right," he finished. "I lied to you and manipulated you. I am very sorry for that. I may yet have to pay the price for my dishonesty, but I did not see any other way."

"What price? What price have to pay? It cost you nothing to lie to me!"

"Cost? You think lying has no cost? Of course it has a cost. Every act of dishonesty costs. You simply do not have eyes to see, yet. But I am pleased with my sacrifice. I would do it again in a heartbeat." Master Libélula placed his hand on something that was resting on the chair next to my bed and smiled. I noticed then that it was the breastplate of my armour, the steel eyes of the Snake glinting in the conjured light.

"I ask you this," Master Libélula said, crossing to the cold hearth and turning to stare at the blackened logs inside. "Do you regret it? Would you have preferred it if I had not brought the Jaguar to you?"

I considered the man's words. I would not have survived the sea cave, my first trial. Without the Jaguar's Strength I would probably have fallen to the jaws of one of the monsters raised up by Queegan. I might not have gained confidence in my sword arm. I might have found myself on the ship that Queegan sunk in Erifracian waters. Its lessons had been painful, but I was not sorry for its presence. I had to admit that to myself.

"Why me? Why am I so damn special?" I was sitting up now, wincing at the pain in my leg.

"You are not special, not really. You are just another son of a noble, born with a silver spoon in his mouth and a mother

329

who shielded him from the world, to his detriment." Master Libélula turned to face me again. He was not smiling. "And yet you are very special. As special as each and every person and creature on this planet. As the earth beneath your feet and the water from the streams. I do not know how much you have learned from the Jaguar, but time is running out. You will be faced with a choice. A difficult one. A choice we all have to make some day."

"You will have to choose the harder path," Master Libélula continued. "The easier one, the one that is gilded and rife with comfort - it is the Path of Suffering. It will tempt you every step along the way. You know that easy path - you have walked it for years. This path, the harder one – the Path of Liberation - it is harsh and unforgiving. Once you choose to walk it, it will ask you for everything. And then demand more. And you will give it. Or you will perish, and Clovir will perish with you.

"Choose wisely," he finished, "and awaken to who You are."

Silence hung then. I was still confused by the man's words, but I had gathered from my experience since leaving Isha that all would be revealed in time.

I hoped.

"I am going to heal your leg," Master Libélula said. "Consider it a final gift. Except that it is not a gift. In exchange for this favour, you will return one. You will agree to let me transport you to Atika. Your Destiny is there, as the Jaguar has told you.

"None of us can see the future, but we can all read the signs. And trust."

"That is what he said," I responded. "Queegan. He said that magic was about reading the signs and following the will of the universe. Then he said that it stopped speaking to him, but the magic never left him. He said he was growing ever more powerful as a result."

"Hmm," said Master Libélula. "That is a juvenile understanding, immature in its delusions of control. Let me ask you this: imagine you are made up of the same stuff as the trees and the earth and the sky. Where do your thoughts come from? Whose will is whose? At what point does your will become 'your own?' When you are in the womb? As a baby? As a toddler? Where does the Separation begin?"

Silence reigned once more. I had no answer for the man. I had not thought about his question. At least, not in those terms.

"Who are you," I asked. "Who are you really?"

"You have my name. But as for *who* I am: I am the Seer for the Human Tribe of Atika. I am sworn to protect the Heart of the Land. It is the source of all life in this world. And it is under threat. Your appearance has been prophesied, and it has been my duty to make sure that you are prepared for what is to come."

"Meet me at sundown tomorrow," Master Libélula finished. "I will be waiting here, outside your home. You will bring your friend, Simon. His Fate and yours is intertwined – he must face his own trials before he too will be ready. We will go to Atika. There you will complete your training."

"I cannot simply leave!" I shouted. "A great evil has been unleashed. By me. I am responsible.

"Demons, Ernesto," I continued. "It was a Demon that nearly took my leg. Patricia and Queegan, two sorcerers of great power, they are coming, too. And the Erifracians. They all bring war with them! And you want me to simply leave my friends and family in their time of need? I cannot do that! I will stay and fight."

"The choice is yours, Andrew," Master Libélula replied. "As it has always been. I will heal you nonetheless. I just ask that you search your heart before you make your decision."

Master Libélula left me in the green glow of his healing magic.

✶ ✶ ✶ ✶ ✶

My final visitor was my brother. I had assumed I would

next see Kathryn, or maybe the King, but I awoke the next morning to the screeching of late autumn crows outside my window and my brother darkening the door to my bedchamber. Like my father and Simon, he was dressed for war. His forearm and hand were in a Chirurgeon's cast and and he was not smiling.

"Andrew," he said.

"Gerard," I replied. I thought then of saying nothing, of leaving the mountain of words unsaid to fester where they lay. My vision took on its familiar diseased cast. The Jaguar hissed his approval, that my brother was a weakling who deserved nothing but my silence. To speak truth to him was too good for the likes of Gerard Cardiff. I opened my mouth nonetheless, then noticed something poking out of Gerard's good hand. It was my mother's mirror. The one she had left him over me in her Last Will. Perhaps he did deserve my scorn after all. The Jaguar roared its appreciation of that black thought.

Gerard stared at me while I wrangled my emotions, then threw the mirror on the foot of my bed.

"Take it," he said. "I know you feel like it is rightfully yours, that somehow I have wronged you by receiving it. I know that Mother would never want us to end up nearly killing each other over something like that. A fucking trinket."

"That's not..." I said, letting my voice trail off.

"Not what? Not what you want? Perhaps you wish to fight again, this time to take my life. Would that satisfy you, Knight Cardiff?"

I felt shame blossom in my face, hot and uncomfortable. The Jaguar roared and began playing images from my past, slights as ancient as my memories themselves. My brother pushing me over as I sat in the yard. My brother laughing with another highborn boy as they left me behind in the creek near the woods where we grew up. My brother receiving my father's praise for his performance in the training yard. My mother hugging my brother as he headed off on his first campaign to the Liserian border.

Rage boiled in my blood as old wounds opened and seeped hot pus into my bloodstream. The Jaguar laughed and laughed and laughed. I wanted to kill my brother, wanted to end the pain that this man brought into my life, just by his presence. He was victory fucking incarnate. I involuntarily ran my clenched fist up to my face, brushing something on my chest as I did. Lykander's sapphire. I grasped it and remembered his advice: it was time to break bread with another of my Demons. I could feel magic run from the gem into my arm. The dam in my mind weakened, then collapsed, allowing calming water to swell through and put out the fire.

Tired of the hatred, I let go. Let go of it all.

"I am sorry," I said, just as my brother turned to leave, fury of his own evident on his face. "I am sorry about your hand. I am sorry about the things that I said, for everything. I am sorry, Gerard. I have acted intolerably badly. You did not deserve any of it. Please, take back the mirror. It is yours and she wanted you to have it."

I handed it to him and continued.

"I was always jealous of you, jealous of the confident ease with which you took on the world. Jealous of how easily you impressed our father, how little our parents needed to intervene with you. You were 'good.' I always 'needed work.' I do not remember when I started hating you, but it was a long time ago and it has never stopped. I am sorry for that. I love you, brother."

I had never spoken those words to him, at least not since I could remember. They felt odd coming out of my mouth, but as they did, I became awash in gratifying chills down my back. The sickly haze lifted. I was suddenly aware that my face was wet, that tears dripped from my chin to darken the wool of my bedclothes in large drops.

Gerard watched and did not say anything, not for a long time. It might have been a trick of the morning light, but I thought I saw some shimmering in his own eyes. He opened his mouth, as if to say something, then shut it abruptly. His eyes did not meet mine as he grasped the mirror and turned to leave.

"I... I did not expect this," he said, his back to me. "I must get back to my unit."

The door to my room shut quietly. I lay back in my bed for a moment, exulting in the feeling. What surprised me the most about the moment was that my brother barely said a word in response, nothing to reassure me that my words had resulted in some positive effect on him, and yet I felt good. Lighter. I was certain that, in days gone by, having offered the contents of my heart like that and having received nothing in reply, I would have taken away something completely different than what I had today, some black lesson of mistrust of others when speaking my truth. Instead, I was buoyed by my revelation to my brother. I had not said the words in expectation of anything in return. I apologized and unburdened myself of hatred simply because it was the right thing to do.

For me. For him. For both of us.

When I rose, after exclaiming joy to the empty room that my wounded leg had completely healed, I looked to the chair next to the night table, atop which my armour was piled. I pulled it off, starting to dress myself. When I removed the pants, I noticed that on the wood beneath lay the broken sword I had found in that ancient castle, its rusted blade wiped clean of the green and red blood that had stained it. It was clean of much of the rust as well. The morning light was streaming in in shafts, illuminating the hilt and making the intricate patterning on the dull metal gleam. Clutched in a metal claw, the faceted owl's head had a feature that caught my eye. It was as if a third eye lay in the center of its forehead, but this eye was closed, its lid a half semi-circle etched into the deep purple of the gem.

It was then that I noticed the letters written down the

blade, starting just above the crossguard and below the fuller, nearly invisible in the tarnish, etched in a script that I had only seen a handful of times, on the spines of the Heraclytan texts in the Royal Library. Three letters stood atop each other:

S

O

P

The 'P' had cut off where the blade had broken.

Chapter Thirty-Six
Ancestors

I was grateful for the wool undergarments my father had washed and laid out for me the moment I stepped out of the cottage and felt the cold autumn breeze kiss my face. The armour had shifted and spread naturally to accept the thicker layer. Rather than make the same mistake twice, I had searched through the house until I found a big knife my father used for skinning deer after a successful hunt. I removed the knife and slammed the broken sword into the scabbard. It fit perfectly. I slid it onto my belt, admiring the steel eyes of the Snake on my armour in one of the large mirrors near the entrance to the cottage before I left.

I was still technically banished from the Yellow Order, so I did not feel compelled to go to the barracks. I walked aimlessly for a little while, kicking up the familiar dirt of the paths that crisscrossed our land, waving at Serfs and calling out the names of the people I remembered. There were precious few of the latter. I was never kind to them in my younger days beyond a simple wave or a manufactured greeting, rolling noble superiority around in my head as I veiled thinly my disdain.

It was harvest time. I passed a young man and one who looked to be a few decades older. They were next to a wheelbarrow, their feet buried in the shoots and leaves of a pumpkin row, bending over to cut the gourds from their stalks. Both were familiar to me. I knew I had met the older man before, and the Jaguar hissed at me to rely on my station to simply ignore them and continue on the path. I felt an urge to greet them, but I was concerned that they would react poorly to my having forgotten their names.

'Wait,' I thought, and felt a frisson of goose flesh run down my back. 'It will come to you.' Cyril, I decided, after a moment. The man who had sold my father the fishing rods on my twelfth birthday.

"Good day to you, Cyril," I said, "How goes the harvest?"

I listened patiently to the man as he stood tall, inclined his head slightly and addressed me, ignoring the pull of my mind to go elsewhere, staying present as Cyril relayed to me the trials and tribulations he had had with the crop that year. I was pleasantly surprised to learn that I could now parse the man's accent much better than I could as a boy.

The pumpkins had done excellently well, the turnips and cabbage so-so, and the potatoes were struck with a blight that had knocked off about three quarters of the harvest. It would be a hard winter as a result. The younger man, whom I gathered from Cyril's words to be his son Daniel, interjected from time to time, correcting his father and adding his own words for clarity.

"And I 'ears from Tommy down at da Fox and Firkin, who over'eard dis from a high-ranking officer in a yellow cloak, dat da King 'as recalled all three of da Coloured Orders, preparations for war with Erifracia or summat?" Cyril's question was clearly directed at me. I did not take the bait.

"With all respect due da King," Cyril continued, "'e'll no doubt be sniffing around for war rations once da garrison 'as filled ta burstin' wit' coloured cloaks. An 'ard winter, indeed.

"You're with the Yellow Order, ain't ya, Sir Cardiff?" Daniel asked, ignoring his father's gestures telling him to stop speaking. "We 'eard that you was seriously injured? And I 'eard that the Yellow Order lost many men to an attack by the Erifracian navy. T'ree of the four ships that left did not return. Is any o' dat true?"

"It is just Andrew, please, Daniel," I said with a smile. "I am no longer a Knight, at least, not officially. And I am well again, thank you. I will tell you about what happened in Erifracia some day, but for now, I need to get back on the road. I wish you all the luck with the rest of your harvest."

I tore down the path at a walk run, wanting to avoid more questions about my hasty recovery and about the loss of the ships in Erifracia. Master Libélula's words about the cost of lying echoed in my head. If I stuck around, I would have to, at best, massage the truth.

Magic was still a secret.

★ ★ ★ ★ ★

It was mid-morning when I finally made it into Isha proper. I had been daydreaming, thinking about what I would say to my father, my brother, to Simon, and to Kathryn, if I ever saw her again. Master Libélula expected me to accompany him to Atika at sundown. I felt confused. The Jaguar screamed at me that I was acting as a coward would act. To consider Master Libélula's offer to be anything but an escape from my duty to my family and my King was self-delusion. His arguments did find some sway in my heart. I wondered whether it was truly the right thing to do, or whether perhaps this was yet another test.

In my reverie, my legs had brought me before a house. It was on a street filled with houses, residences of questionable construction and most in relatively poor repair. The paint on the house before me had faded. I could tell that the slats of the siding had been painted some deeper shade of blue at one point, instead of the sun-bleached periwinkle peeling off in chunks that I saw now. Formerly black eaves were a bleak iron grey that matched the overcast sky above. A small garden separated the front of the house from the street, the blooms having long since died back in the advancing cold. Rusted chairs and a rickety table sat on stones in the center of the little front yard.

The place was familiar to me, but I could not place it. I knew that I had been there before...

"Master Cardiff!"

I turned to see Mr. Robinson, the cheesemaker, approaching from the road I had taken to arrive at the house.

"Or is it Sir Cardiff, now?" he said, smiling broadly at me. I had not seen the man in years, having consciously made the decision to avoid him and his stall at the market, buying whatever cheese my father and I had call for from his competitor Mr. Glenwood in the days since my mother's death. He had aged in the years since last I laid eyes on him. The dark chestnut hair I remembered was now full of grey. The lines on his face had become more pronounced, as had the paunch beneath his threadbare clothing. But the kindness I recalled in his eyes had not fled. In fact, it looked as though as it had become richer, somehow.

I smiled back at the man, failing to find any words for a reply.

"It is positively excellent to see you, friend," Mr. Robinson said, not letting the quiet become isolating to either one of us. "My, how you have changed! As slim as your father now. Probably because you have not been frequenting my shop for your weekly cheese!"

"Please come in," he said, passing me and walking through the garden up to the door of his house. "I forgot my cloak and could not stand another moment of this bitter wind. I am needed back at the stall, but Brian the fishmonger can attend to my patrons while we have a quick cup of tea, I would think?" Mr. Robinson winked at me as he opened the door.

The interior of the house was a bright and clean

counterpoint to the rundown exterior. It smelled of fresh pine and leather, with gleaming hardwood floors and couches in a living room just off a little porch where we wiped our boots. A brace of brightly coloured oval paintings were hanging above a fireplace in which a single charred log was sitting in the center. Mr. Robinson told me to follow him through to the kitchen. A large wood stove was the focal point of this next room. In a feat of speed that I have not seen reproduced in any man since, the cheesemaker had a fire blazing inside the metal behemoth and a kettle of water boiling in a matter of moments.

"So, what brings you to my house this morning, Andrew?" Mr. Robinson asked, stuffing a little pot with dried leaves from a diminutive crock on the small wooden counter pushed up against the back wall. "It is quite I am certain you have more pressing concerns, especially with the whispers of war that I have been hearing at the market for the past week."

"Mr. Robinson," I began.

"Please, call me Antony. You are not a shy little boy hiding behind his mother's skirts anymore..." Mr. Robinson must have seen something in my face because he immediately took a more somber tone and said, "I know you were close to her. I am sorry to bring her up."

"There is nothing for which to apologize, Mr. Robin-Antony. She is actually why I have come. I have come to understand that she was special in some way. Special enough that she might have been killed for her uniqueness. I am wondering if you can recall anything she said the night she died, anything at all, that might help determine how she was killed. And by whom."

"My, you are the cryptic one, are you not? You certainly did not get that from your mother. I knew Violet Brace - I mean, Violet Cardiff - very well. She spoke plainly and did not try to obfuscate."

Mr. Robinson looked at me, waiting for me to elaborate. I did not.

"You already know everything I know, Andrew," Mr. Robinson said with a sigh. "I wish I could tell you more. But on the night of her death all your mother did was come here, buy her cheese, tell me a little bit about her plans for your father's birthday, and leave. She purchased one of the mild soft cheeses, barely a month out of the cow, because your father prefers those wheels to the sharper and harder stuff. I had to laugh at that, given your father's position as the King's hard man."

I searched Mr. Robinson's face, trying to determine whether he was telling me the truth. I felt deflated when I assessed that he was.

"I have something for you," Mr. Robinson said, staring back hard at me. He poured two cups of tea, told me to drink mine and wait, then left the room. I stood there for several minutes, sipping the bitter liquid and watching a pair of crows through a small window dance around what looked to be a dead rodent, pecking at it intermittently before flying off into the grey mist above.

"I should have said I have two things for you," Mr. Robinson said, handing me a nine-inch-wide wheel of cheese. "A new brie, just the way your old man likes it. Tell him I have a cellar full of them. It's fresh now, but it is going to get sharper the longer he waits. He will have to pay for those, though."

I smiled and thanked the man as I stuffed it into a small sack hanging from my belt.

"That's not what I was anxious to give you, however," Mr. Robinson continued. "Violet and I were... close, in our younger years. We were foolish, too, thinking that we could actually get away with eloping. A noble and a commoner. A merchant's son, but a commoner nonetheless. Her father put an end to it, but quick. The Lord Brace met with your granddfather Cardiff, made an arrangement for a dowry, and arranged for some City Guard to visit my father's cheese shop and put the fear of God into me if I did not desist in my affections for the Lady Brace. I, being seventeen, of course did not. But your mother saw the danger, and bid me stop coming to her. She did not want me killed."

"When she saw that in spite of all the danger I would rather press my luck, she gave me this," he said, opening a rough palm to reveal a ring made of silver with a faceted jewel grasped by a setting. "She told me it was something to remember her by, something that had been in her family for generations. She told me that it was that which was most precious to her, and it would have to suffice in her stead. She also told me that I would be called to give it up one day, and I must not hesitate when that time came.

"The time has come and gone lo these ten years, Andrew, and I am sorry," Antony Robinson said to me, sighing. "I should have given it to you when she died. I told myself that I would wait for you to come to me, rather than simply walk over to your cottage and place the ring in your hand. She would have wanted you to have it sooner than this. You should have heard the way she talked about you."

"About me?" I asked, incredulous. "Are you kidding? My mother was surely as ashamed as my father about the way that I turned out. A coward and a burden on the family. Are you sure she was not talking about my brother, Gerard?"

Mr. Robinson made a sharp noise with his tongue. "You are young, true, but that is no excuse for foolishness. That woman loved you more than you can know. Your brother was in her heart as well, but she saw in you more of herself than she ever did your brother, who was your father's child through and through. She never worried about your brother the way she did you, but she always had Faith that you would find your way."

Mr. Robinson gave me another once over with his eyes and dropped the ring into my hand.

"And so, it would appear, you have."

Putting my cup on the counter, I held the ring up to inspect it. The jewel was green and cut into a rectangle. It shone brightly in spite of the cold greyness of the light streaming in

342

from the dingy window. On the inside of the band, the words "*Que sera, sera*" were written in Heraclytan script.

"I... Thank you, Mr. Rob- Antony. Thank you so much." I pulled off my glove and slid the ring onto the fourth finger of my right hand. It fit perfectly. A feeling of warmth ran through my arm and into my chest.

I hugged the man and thanked him once more.

After I left Mr. Robinson's shop, I wandered blindly some more, eventually ending up down a wide alley with shacks and tents running along the sides of cobblestones that looked to be in very ill-repair, chipped and broken and liable to trip the unsuspecting. People were wandering around, mostly in groups of two or three. An unsmiling mother and daughter ducked into one of the tents as I passed, the door flap closing behind them.

There was a smell to the street, a miasma of strange spices and the strong aroma of urine that also pervaded the busier parts of the city. It reminded me of Tunuska, and I felt strangely comforted by the scent.

As I turned a corner I noticed a crowd had gathered around a little platform just a few paces ahead, a makeshift dais from which a red-robed man was giving a speech. Black-haired and sporting a thick moustache, I did not recognize him. Surely King Janus had ejected all of the Mages of the Red Tradition, even the magic-stripped heretics, after he had been abandoned by them in favour of King Revanti... Unless I was in a part of the city not patrolled by the City Guard.

Unless I was in the Purple Run.

"King Janus is a man without scruples," the defrocked Mage shouted, "a man who has dishonoured himself and the Kingdom of Thrairn. He is keeping secrets from you, secrets of great power, accessible by each and every one of you. He thinks himself God in preventing the people from knowing the truth of the world. He wishes to keep you ignorant and pliant, subject to his family's rule, a despot in finery. Tell me, do you have riches?"

A low grumbling of disagreement bubbled through the crowd.

"King Janus hoards his treasure like a Dragon from fairy tales," the man said, picking up the thread after the murmuring subsided, "taxing each and every one of you more than your due and growing fat on the spoils. Tell me, why do you think that all of my red-robed brethren have suddenly disappeared from Isha? It is because we are telling you the truth. You are slaves to a mad King and we seek to depose him. We seek your emancipation. Tell me, do you have liberty?"

The disagreement grew louder this time. Two men in front of me in the crowd whispered venom to each other at the red-robed man's words.

"King Revanti of Erifracia," the Mage continued, buoyed by the approval shown him by the crowd, "he is a true leader. He comes to free you from Janus's bondage. His ships will arrive here within the next few days. That is why you must be prepared to act. We must help Revanti make landing on the coast. We must hold the coast for long enough that Revanti's ships can make landfall. Tell me, do you have the Courage to bring Justice to the Kingdom of Thrairn?"

This time there was loud speaking among the crowd, agitated and insistent.

"King Janus 'as recalled he's Coloured Knights to defend Isha, me son," said a man ahead of me. He had blond hair and ill-fitting patchwork clothes. "You tinks dat we can fight dem? They would gut us soon as look at us. 'Sides, theys Ishan boys. Theys our people."

The red-robed man looked in our direction.

"'Our people?' Those Knights are all highborn bastards, the King's overseers, and you are their chattel. They think you are all bugs, scurrying beneath their feet. Well, you can show them how much poison an insect from the Purple Run can carry." The Red Mage's eyes caught mine and he paused for a moment, before a wide grin split his face.

"Well, well, well, it looks like we have one of them in our midst. Andrew Cardiff, I am at your service."

The Mage gave me a low mock bow as the crowd turned to face me. Looking upon the sea of angry faces, I listened to the Jaguar pour a jug full of defeat into my ear and call up the hues of decay in my vision. He told me I was going to die here, face down in a pool of piss freshly tossed from one of the miserable tents, disemboweled by a commoner's knife. I realized then that an appeal to station no longer had any effect on me - I did not see the people before me as anything but equal to myself. A sense of calm blossomed into my chest from the place where Lykander's sapphire sat against my chest, spilling into my head, abdomen, and extremities. I took a deep breath, felt a shiver run up my back, and spoke.

"I am not your enemy," I said to the agitated crowd. "This man wants you to believe I am, but it is not the truth. It is true that we live our lives in different social positions, that I was born into wealth just as surely as the opposite occurred with you. But that does not mean I hate you or think that you are less than me. We are all citizens of the world, trying to bring some happiness into our lives. I might not always agree with King Janus, but I do not think that rising up and killing him would solve any of our difficulties."

"Dat's easy for you to say, you noble son-bitch," one of the men next to me seethed. "You gets ta go back home, where you probably has Serfs to pick the shite from betwixt yer toes. Youse a slavemaster yerself."

"Do any of you know King Janus personally?" I asked. "He is not an evil man. He does what he can to protect the realm from threats, both within and without. Erifracia is not the greatest of our threats..."

"Ha!" the red-robed man interjected. "You do not even

know, do you, boy? Why the Red Tradition abandoned him? Your precious Janus?

I stood mutely for a moment, then shook my head.

"He murdered your mother," the Mage said grimly, "against strict instruction not to do so. We thought for the longest time that it had been a freak coincidence. Here we had a Prophecy from the Viziers, that a female of Emperor Traximus's line would cause the Aquester throne to fall. The Viziers also foretold that if this female was killed by an Aquester, the Red Tradition would see its end just as surely as the King. The Inner Council, in no uncertain terms, told King Janus to do nothing about it."

The Red Mage revved up, pacing back and forth on the dais, gesticulating his points with a finger.

"Within weeks a thief had killed the Lady Violet Cardiff, only known female of the Traximus line. He had us fooled for years, until he killed your predecessor on the Council, Lord Reginald Quigley. It turned out that the thief was a mercenary, hired by none other than Janus Aquester, with Lord Quigley acting as intermediary. Lord Quigley was nearing the end of his life and wanted to unburden his conscience. He must have indicated to Janus that he was thinking about revealing the secret, because the poison that ended his life certainly made it seem like he died naturally. Even if it was upon the privy basin at a whorehouse."

"Thankfully," the man said, stopping and smiling a venomous smile at me, "Lord Quigley wrote a note to be delivered to the Tradition, should anything ever happen to him."

I felt numb as the man's words washed over me. The crowd turned back to the Red Mage, clearly distraught and confused by the sudden strange talk of Prophecy and murder.

"You are a bright young man, Andrew," the Mage's words having suddenly become unctuous. "You have been lied to and betrayed by that pretender on the throne. Why do you not join us? You can help us rise up against the serpent on the throne..."

"I... I... I need to think about it."

I began to stumble away, dazed and unthinking of any threat the crowd might still pose. But no one interfered with me as I exited the alley and made my way back through the winding streets. I wandered again, my eyes on the ground before me as I felt the firmament of the paradigm of my world give way again.

Janus, my betrayer? My enemy? How could this be? My mother, murdered for a Prophecy. Did my father know? Did my brother? This was an open secret within the Red Tradition now, clearly, for that Mage to know all of the lurid details. The shock receded and wrath spilled into my consciousness, the Jaguar roaring with delight and setting my vision awash with the death hues.

I would kill the man with my bare hands. I would make him suffer in his final moments, make him fear the end before it actually came. Perhaps I would gut him, let his entrails to spill out so that he could watch his life ebb. Perhaps I would poison a blade, so that he would sweat out his final moments in a stupour of pain. Perhaps I would kill his own family in front of him, to make it even.

It was with such darkness in mind that I suddenly found myself before the great doors of the Blue Cathedral.

Chapter Thirty-Seven
Piety

I was about to push in the door to the Cathedral, a sanctuary from my tortured wandering, when I noticed something that took my breath away. The stained glass windows on the face of the building, the ones that I had looked upon and dismissed so many times in my youth, the ones that held images of Knights fighting Demons, sent a shard of ice down through my spine. The Demons had black eyes, orange and red skin, and mouths full of razor sharp teeth.

Images of the creatures that I had released in Valtha were set into the side of the Cathedral, perhaps as a reminder to the people of Isha of what had forced them out of the old seat of Thrain power. Or were the battles depicted from days even older than that? I closed my hanging jaw, pressed the door, and went in.

There was a strong smell of incense in the Cathedral, and a scattered few torches burning in the sconces on the walls. Fewer than normal, given the bright noonday light streaming in from the outside through more stained glass. I needed somewhere to sit, somewhere to think. I sat in back row of the middle set of pews.

I meditated on rage, righteous anger at King Janus for taking my mother away from me seething even more deeply than it had in the streets outside. The Jaguar roared ecstasy as I gave myself over to thoughts of murder and baths in the man's blood. It encouraged me to seek him out and disembowel him, the presence his bodyguards and the immediate consequences of such action be damned. Morality had vanished. Even the practical notion that the Kingdom of Thrairn might fall to its enemies in the vacuum created by such a loss found no sway in my heart. The deathly colours of the Jaguar's magic began to turn black.

"Andrew?"

I looked up from the place where I was sitting and gripping the pew in front of me with knuckles of white to see Marissa Rice standing in the aisle. She was about four feet away, wearing a flowing blue dress and carrying a wash bucket in one hand. It must have been Odin's Day. She always helped Bishop Mountpence with the cleaning of the Cathedral on Odin's Day.

"Marissa," I said, my dark thoughts fleeting for a few moments.

"You are up and about... Gerard had told me that you were injured. Severely. He expected you would be bedridden for days. What happened?"

"It is a long story, Marissa. How are you?" I asked, standing and shuffling closer to her. She did not respond. I felt needles dig into my chest as I approached and made to hug her. I ignored the fear. A strange look descended on her face for a long moment, then she dropped the bucket and embraced me. She did not break for a long time. After a while, I felt the woman buck against me, moments before the first sharp intake of air and a sob that followed.

"Marissa? Is everything all right?"

"You ask me that, if everything is alright?" she responded, pulling away from me, her beautiful face stained with tears. "I spent weeks looking to the docks, approaching white cloaks in the street, making daily forays to the castle to speak with an answerless Castellan. 'When is my father returning?' I would say. 'No word yet, milady,' he would respond.

"When one ship out of four finally lurched into harbour," Marissa continued, looking deeply into my eyes, "I was waiting on the docks, to see if Captain William Rice was among those that survived. 'He did not,' I was told by a serious-faced man in a yellow cloak. This was a week ago. I returned to my cold lonely home that day, and spent the afternoon crying into a pillow. And the night. And the next day. And the following. I had assumed that he had died to an Erifracian blade. Imagine my surprise when I finally ventured out of my home to go to market and Giselda Foran cornered me near the Baker's stall, unable to contain her gossip, telling me a story that had been relayed to her by her husband Kier, your fellow Yellow Knight. A story that involved you murdering my father with black magic."

Marissa had been whipped into a frenzy. We spent a few moments staring at each other. I felt a pull to look away, to break from her and exit the Cathedral. It would have been easier, much easier to simply have left. The Jaguar roared approval at the idea.

"Is it true?" Marissa asked, her voice a hoarse whisper, her eyes pleading with me.

"It is," I replied. "But I will not pretend that your father did not deserve his Fate. I am not sure if you have heard..."

"Of course I have heard, Andrew!" Marissa screamed. "I have heard that gossip too, the rumours that swirled about my father ever since my mother's death, how he molested the young men underneath him, how he was a black goat wearing the body of a man! But he was my father. I loved him. And you took him from me."

Marissa turned from me then. I thought again of leaving, this time the pull stronger as the needles in my chest became daggers. The Jaguar unctuously whispered to me that it would be better if I left the woman in her grief, that I had done enough to the poor creature. It took every ounce of Courage in my body and mind not to give in, to simply run and leave her in the Hell in which she now found herself.

"I carried this for you," Marissa said, her back to me. She pulled something from her dress and threw it to the floor, where it clattered on the bare stone before coming to rest on one of the red runners between the aisle. I looked down to see a long narrow knife, a stiletto blade. The preferred weapon of assassins. She turned then, exhaustion apparent in her face.

"I told myself that I would use your trust in me to get close enough to plunge it between your ribs and end the 'great Knight' that is Andrew Cardiff. I almost did it. Just now. Before you hugged me."

"What stopped you?" I asked, picking up the weapon and sticking it into the gap between my belt and my pants. Outside of the *cuir d'arbalest*, I ensured, having learned my lesson in Valtha.

Marissa looked up to the alabaster statute of the crucified man hanging from the apse of the Cathedral.

"The Christ-man? Are you serious? We used to make fun of the pious. I thought you did not believe in God."

"I did not," she said, "until I forgave the man who killed my father."

"I am sorry, Marissa." I said, allowing the words to flow as the goose flesh rose. "I would tell you I had no choice, which is true. But at the time it happened, if I did have the choice, I probably would have done it anyway. I hated your father. I lacked understanding. If presented with the choice today, I would not do it. For whatever that is worth to you."

Marissa looked at my face, searching for something. Then she sighed and stooped to pick up her bucket.

"I need to attend to my duties. Will you be here long?"

"No," I said. "I found what I came for." The rage was no longer swirling madly in my head, though a dull roar persisted. The black at the edges of my vision had receded leaving just the yellowish-green of the Jaguar's magic. I could get down to the business of planning my revenge.

"Good," she said. "I may have forgiven you, Andrew, but I am in no hurry to see you again."

Chapter Thirty-Eight
Regency

The Blue Cathedral was not too far from the barracks. I made a beeline directly there after the great doors shut behind me. The dazed wandering of the morning was over. I had purpose now, purpose that would see me to my father and my brother.

And to my King.

The afternoon sun, cold and naked in a rare cloudless Ishan sky, blazed on the cobbles before me. As the Cathedral was in Hightown, I passed familiar noble face after familiar noble face. Some people who hailed me down to speak. I politely refused each of them, not stopping as I informed them I was in a rush.

I thought back to the last time I had made this short journey from the Cathedral to the barracks, the walk with my brother to get a change of clothes the morning of my induction into the Yellow Order. How much had I changed since then? I could barely even remember what life was like at the start of this journey. For all the dangers that presented themselves in my current predicament, I did not miss it. My old life was not life, of that I was sure. It was some kind of half-life, a sad existence where fear was the rule and withdrawal was my ever-chosen path.

I would not withdraw this time. I would involve myself no

matter what occurred, I vowed to myself.

When I made it to the barracks, I looked up to see Iggy Corcoran standing in the guard tower. He was looking even grimmer than he had been when he gave me breakfast on that final morning in Tunuska. He nodded to me as I passed, clearly not interested in stopping to even ask me what I was doing there. Or how I came to be up and about with my injury.

There were a few pairs of Knights practicing in the sparring yard, but the mood had shifted since last I saw them. They were clearly just going through the motions, their cloaks flapping in the Ishan wind as they banged at each other with practice swords. None of them acknowledged me. Fear was on the air, as palpable as the smell of smoke from the hearths of the city that wafted in on the cold breeze.

Just before I passed into the barracks proper, I stopped momentarily on the front step to examine the ash wood that my father had told me could withstand Dragon fire. When last I was here, magic was nothing but a myth held dear by children and the soft-headed. Now, though, with all that had happened... I pulled off a glove and ran a thumb along the grain, trying to feel if there was anything actually different about it.

"Bear ash," said my father, approaching from the hallway inside. "You would sooner burn down stone than that stuff. How are you out of bed? You know what? Never mind. I do not want to know." He paused before speaking again. "Are you fit to fight?"

"Father," I said, looking upon him with eyes weighed heavy with a terrible secret, "I am happy to see you. Where is Gerard? Is he about?"

My father gestured with his head back in the direction whence he came. "You look like you could wield a blade," he said. "As you know, the Yellow Order is a husk of what it used to be... That foul magician. It was only luck that the Dragonfly ship exited port before the other two. It was again luck that I was aboard it, rather than choosing to climb onto one of the other ones. Well, I would not say luck - one of my sons had maimed his brother's hand in the training yard and I wanted to stay near him during his convalescence." My father eyed me severely as he spoke. "We watched helplessly as that sorcerer called down the Heavens on Mosquito and Beetle Companies."

"I am sorry, Father."

"No need to apologize, Andrew," my father said, waving me off. "Besides, I have my wayward son back. We shall fight the Erifracians when they land here in a few days hence. Our revenge shall be taken on the battlefield with blade. I would love to find that Mage and run him through myself..."

"Where is Gerard, Father?" I asked, making conscious effort to prevent my impatience from showing through. "I need to speak to both of you."

My father looked at me, eyes wide, as if it were the first time he had ever truly seen me. Nodding, he turned on his heel and bid me follow.

Gerard was in his quarters, sitting on the yellow blanketed bed, reading a missive with his good arm. The crippled one lay against his chest in a sling. He glanced up at Father, smiled, which faded when he saw that I was with him.

"Healed up already," Gerard said. "No chance I might get the same treatment?" A weak smile returned and he waved his bandaged wrist at me.

"Sorry, Gerard," I replied. "I did not weave this magic. I would if I could."

"Figures," he responded. "What brings you here, Andrew?" Gerard calmly placed the document head had been reading on the bed next to him.

"Mother was murdered," I said.

"Christ-man, Andrew, we know that!" My father growled.

"By the King."

"What?" both men exclaimed in unison.

I relayed the story I had heard from the Red Mage in the

Purple Run to them, omitting no detail, filling in with what I had heard from Queegan and Patricia about Mother's lineage.

"Fucking magic," said my father when I was done, making a distasteful sound and spitting a large glob of mucous onto the floor of Gerard's room. "I am fucking disgusted with the whole Gods-damned notion. I would sooner we kill every magician in the realm than us normal folk turn blade on each other."

Gerard sat mutely on the bed, looking off at nothing on the chamber wall.

"Did neither of you hear what I said?" I shouted. "The King murdered our mother! Your wife!"

"And what would you have me do, Andrew?" asked my father, his voice quiet and even. "She is gone. We are at war. She was killed by our King. Do you think I should return the favour? Now, when survival is completely uncertain? What would that accomplish, aside from our defeat? Violet has been dead for five years. She is gone, that is all that matters."

"You Gods-damned... coward!" I screamed. The Jaguar, who must have been lounging in some corner of my mind, sprang to life, blowing air on the embers of fury and seeping the colours of pestilence into my sight. A lame duck was my father, a weakling who did not have the testicular fortitude to take action against the man who killed his wife.

"Andrew," he said, somberly. "Do not do anything rash. I cannot lose you, too."

I saw then that there were tears in his brown eyes. I had to look away before they overtook me, too. Gerard would still not return my glance.

"I will not fight for you, father," I said, "especially not when you still lick boot for that son of a bitch on the throne. In any event, I am called away." I paused. "Call it 'fucking magic' duty."

With that, I left.

The barracks were not very far from the moat that separated the city from the seat of power, a deep pit with barely a foot of water at the bottom. A man was sure to break a bone or two from a fall into it. Or worse. Up from the banks on the opposite side of the moat stretched the grey stone walls that ensconced the castle proper. There was a thick creep of dark green moss at the bottom of the wall, moss that meandered up in tendril like configurations to heights even above my head. Across the gap on the city side, opposite the wooden underside of a drawbridge kept up flush with the castle walls, stood a little guard post with a brace of visored white cloaks standing at attention.

I walked towards the men slowly, the wind having been knocked from my sails somewhat by the interaction with my father and brother. I had assumed that, as mother's closest kin, as my blood, they would share my rage and come with me to help see Justice served. I glanced down at my belt, at the stiletto blade previously destined for my heart. I could understand why Marissa forgave me: her father was an animal that needed to be put down. My mother, though, she was an angel who had never hurt anyone. She did not deserve her Fate.

"Andrew," said a familiar voice from an alley just behind a shop next to the moat. It was not very far from where the white cloaks stood at attention. It was a woman's voice, and very insistent. "Come here."

I looked with a smile to see Kathryn. She was not wearing her travel clothes or her robes. Instead, she was dressed in a plain brown cotton dress with pink fringes, like one of the common folk of the city. Her black hair lay tousled around her shoulders. Her green eyes glinted in the sun. I was transported from my concerns for a glimmer of a moment. But she was not smiling. A beckoning gesture urged me on.

"Kathryn, how are-"

"Shh, keep your voice down and get over here!" It was a barely audible hiss.

I walked over to the alley and she grabbed me by the arm to pull me into the shadow.

"What is going on? I was just about to go see the King."

"And lose your head in the process! He is looking to hang you, Andrew. There are white cloaks at your cottage right now, with orders to bring you back to face the King's Justice. For killing William Rice in cold blood."

"What? He knows the difference! I was going to-"

"Kill Janus? For what, murdering your mother? Of course you were," Kathryn said, staring deeply into my eyes. "Yes, I heard. Forget about that. He has been lying to us - all of us. He is in league with Patricia and Queegan. Janus wants the Red Tradition gone. Erifracia, too. He saw an opportunity to be rid of them both. He and Queegan have been plotting for ages to double cross the Tradition and Erifracia.

"And Patricia," Kathryn continued, "she controls those Demons, somehow. They intend to smash those monsters against the Red Tradition and Erifracians from the rear when battle lines are drawn between Isha and the Erifracian landing coast. The three of them: they were controlling you the whole time, Andrew. They lied to you about the armour. After they saw you transform into a Jaguar and speak of the Atikan, they hired that Armourcrafter to stick a few bits of steel on a dusty old set of *cuir* d'arbalest, draw a Snake upon it, and make up the story. Then Queegan enchanted your mind and they arranged for those white cloak brothers to escort you to the Armourcrafter's and that whorehouse."

"They cast a spell on the armour," Kathryn said after a pause, "to make you think it had chosen you. They wanted you to believe yourself special. Something to keep you pressing on till you reached Valtha. The real Prophecy, the one about the female of Emperor Traximus' bloodline, they put all their Faith into that. And that has paid off, apparently." Kathryn shuddered.

"You knew? About my mother? And the rest of it... How do

you know all of this?"

"I... I overheard them, in the King's chamber."

I looked more closely at Kathryn. She was a bad liar.

"Tell me the truth," I said calmly.

"There is no time for this, Andrew! We need to get out of here."

"There is time for this," I said, still calm. "Five minutes ago I was prepared to go and slay the ruler of this City, of this very realm, or at least attempt to do so. Now you are telling me some lie about how you heard about this plot cooked up by your precious Janus... Why would she be working with him? I thought Patricia hated nobles?"

"That she does," Kathryn said, "Janus is King, but he wants power – magical power. And under the influence of the Red Tradition, it is not permitted him. Janus has agreed to depose himself once the Erifracians and the Red Tradition are defeated, to open the Kingdom up to rule by Chaos. Let the strongest creature win. It is their dream, a 'fair' world, they think. They have been planning this since the Prophecy about the end of the Red Tradition was uttered: Janus, Patricia, Queegan."

Kathryn paused.

"The strongest creature will most likely be Patricia... she has changed, somehow. I do not know what happened down in that dungeon, but she scares me now."

"Janus... That fucking coward!" I said, then paused as I processed what Kathryn had just said. "You know her, then."

"She is my sister, Andrew."

My mind reeled.

"Were you... were you a part of this?" I whispered. "Did you lead me through the mountains to that meeting with her so that she could trick me into going into Valtha? To let those... things into this world? I..."

I what? I thought to myself. I thought that there was something more between us. Something that I believed I had with Marissa, when I was youthful and ignorant. And now this betrayal. The Jaguar hissed murderous thoughts, a fantasy of jabbing my dagger into Kathryn's chest. It would be so easy, but I would have to act quickly.

"I thought what we were doing was right," Kathryn said. "Nobles were bastards who looked down on the common people with disdain. The Red Tradition, too. To us, they were horribly selfish fucks, the lot of them, and it was about time that they were knocked off their high thoroughbred horses. It was time that the blight on the land be healed. That was the party line, anyway."

"Why the change of heart?" I asked, clenching my fists. "You could have let me walk in there, just now, to die by the blades of a swarm of Knights, and that would be the end of it. Why the Hell did you not?"

Kathryn looked at me, a slight smile on her lips. "You know, I have been asking myself the same question. Before we set sail from Isha, I was prepared to follow this through to the end. But then I met you. I could not explain what I saw in you, but it happened the moment I laid eyes on you. Something completely irrational. Something that told me to protect you. Our trip through the desert, through the mountains - this was an attempt to save your life. I once thought we were the brave ones, that we knew what Courage was. How else to take on the status quo, the King? By any means necessary. Treachery and dishonour were perfectly acceptable ways of bringing it all down.

"Then I saw real Courage."

"Real Courage?" I scoffed. "Do me a favour, Kathryn. You have already tricked me into unleashing Hell on Clovir. Do not insult me further with false flattery."

"Andrew," Kathryn said, quietly. "I am sorry about what has happened between us. For my betrayal. I will spend the rest of my life making it up to you. If you even let me. I know you might never want to do so, and I will have to live with that. But

I need your help now. Patricia has gone mad, Queegan would kill every man, woman, and child in the realm to get what he wants, and Janus... well, Janus is a coward as you say. But cowards are dangerous, and he is the King of Thrairn: that makes him the most dangerous coward in the realm. We need to figure out a way to stop them.

"You *are* brave, Andrew," Kathryn continued, smiling sadly at me, "much braver than you understand. I need you to come with me, we need to plan..."

"Kathryn..." I wanted to kill her, to kill Janus, to kill Queegan, to kill Patricia. To bathe in their blood and scream hatred into the night. Needles burned in my chest and my face. The black haze had overcome the yellowish-green again. The Jaguar roared approval. I absentmindedly put my hand on the hilt of the stiletto blade. The Jaguar's delight turned into a shout of victory.

I felt a squeezing then, something on my right hand. Around the base of my ring finger. I let go of the dagger and pulled my glove off. The jewel on my mother's ring was flashing, pulsing with every beat of my heart. It was mesmerizing, going at a feverish clip. The black colour at the edge of my vision receded. Then the light of the gem accelerated, faster and faster, until the flashes united into a bright static glow. It got so bright that I had to avert my eyes. My mind swam with confusion.

After a few moments, the gem exploded, sending tiny shards out to dig into the back of my hand and bounce off my armour. Kathryn cried out in surprise. The ring squeezed one final time, feeling like it might cut my finger off, then relaxed. I felt a coolness rise up from my finger, through my arm and into my chest.

"WHAT IS THIS?" the Jaguar roared in my mind.

It was as if a bonfire was extinguished with a massive wave of ocean water. All of the black, yellow, and green in my vision became suffused with a blue the colour of a naked sky. My rage

361

slipped away. I thought back to Marissa, what she said to me in the Cathedral, about forgiveness opening her to God. As the swell of cool water in my body flowed through into my head, my eyes began to pour tears. My body was wracked as I sobbed out all of the pain, every feeling of injustice that all of the betrayal and murder had generated in my heart. In my mind's eye, I saw my mother enter my heart through a portal of light, smile, and take hold of my hand. In the physical realm, Kathryn embraced me.

We stood there for a few minutes as I let go of all my hatred for Kathryn. For Queegan. For Patricia. And even for Janus. I understood his cowardice, understood it all too well. He had made his bed, and might yet die so that the realm survived, but it would not be by my hand.

'The path is a razor's edge, Andrew,' said the Jaguar in his peaceful voice, 'the one of non-violence. You can conquer the world with love, but you must never shy away, never give in to fear, no matter how the world seems to threaten you.'

As I gazed into the brightness of the doorway that had opened in my mind, my mother released my hand, blew me a kiss, and exited once more.

"Thank you, Mother," I whispered, breaking from Kathryn's embrace and looking at the ring on my finger. The setting, any evidence that it had once held an emerald, had disappeared. It was just a silver band now.

"Kathryn," I said, looking at the woman. "I forgive you. Of course I forgive you. I care about you. I care about you more than..."

I trailed off.

Kathryn's face lit up and she smiled at me. Her face crinkled deeply and her eyes twinkled brighter than any of the stars I had seen in the night sky. "I care about you, too," she said.

"But I cannot come with you," I said, "At least, not yet. I have to go to Atika. Master Libélula is taking me there tonight."

"But... what about the Kingdom? Patricia, Queegan,

Erifracia, Janus - would you leave your friends to die at their hands?"

Her words danced in my head. The Jaguar told me to listen to her, to abandon my plans to go to Atika. I could always go *after* we had dealt with the threats to Thrairn. Only a coward would flee at a time like this. Perhaps Kathryn was wrong about me, perhaps I was indeed a coward.

I saw the Jaguar then. For the first time, I saw it nakedly for what it had become in the days since my fight with my brother. It was the call of Separation, the fearful urge to stray from the path of my heart, the path of Unity. In denying it I had become strong.

"I am no coward," I said to the woman before me. "If I stay here, we will never be able to fight them. I need to go, Kathryn. I will find my magic there. Look in your heart, you know this to be right."

Hairs rose on my back all at once. The rainbows of my heart began to encroach upon the edges of my vision. Kathryn stared for a while, her face red and her breast heaving.

"Come back safe to me, Andrew," said Kathryn, embracing me and kissing me with a ferocity that I returned. "Promise me that you will."

"I vow it, Kathryn."

✷ ✷ ✷ ✷ ✷

For the first time in my life, I had to sneak around my home city. In the words of the Heraclytan Empire, I was a *persona non grata*. I would be killed if any of the patrols of white cloaks or City Guard recognized me. I danced from alleyway to alleyway. As I approached the center of the city, I recognized Cyril from a hidden vantage next to some crates in an alley. He was unloading some of his pumpkins from the back of his cart and bringing them to a merchant's stall. His son, Daniel, was seated on the front, holding the reins and waiting patiently for his father to unload.

363

I thought about continuing on through the city on my own. 'How could I trust a Serf?' the Jaguar asked me. As soon as I asked Cyril to help me, he would turn me over to the city guards. He probably would think this was his chance to put it to the nobility, just like the rest of the hateful commoners. He would dance on my corpse with glee!

"Cyril," I said, approaching with my head inclined for subterfuge as soon as he was finished with the merchant. "I understand that this is an odd request, but could I please ride in your cart?" I motioned to the burlap covering that he was preparing to throw over the rest of his pumpkins. "I need to get back to the homestead. I would be eternally in your debt." I paused. "Please."

Cyril narrowed his eyes at me for a moment, and nodded somberly. I waited until no one was looking, hopped in, then sighed relief as he pulled the burlap over me. I was overcome with gratitude for the man as we bumped along the cobbles back to the outskirts of the city.

"Da road's clear," said Cyril. "You can get out now, miLord."

We were in front of Cyril's plot of land, the wheels of the cart deep in the ruts of the dirt road. I stood up and expressed all of the thankfulness in my heart, inclining my head towards the man and his son in a nod that approached a bow. They smiled, nodded back to me, turned the cart around, and headed back to the city. I realized then that they had not finished their business. They had made a special trip to bring me here. Humility blossomed more deeply within me.

The sun was nearing the horizon, bathing the countryside in a pink gloaming. I sneaked up the path to the cottage, staying low to the ground and keeping my eyes peeled for white cloaks and the red inverted triangles of the City Guard. When I was a few dozen feet from the door, I felt a hand on my shoulder. Reacting, I twisted, pulling out of the grasp and fishing the stiletto from my belt and grabbing the interloper.

"Andrew," said Simon, "don't gut me, for fuck's sakes, brother."

I barked a laugh as the tension dropped from my shoulders. "Christ-man, Si, you picked the wrong night to startle me. What are you doing here?"

"I heard from Gerard that you were up and about," he said. "I thought I might come and see you. You know, since the world's about to end. Maybe we could figure out a way to stop it."

"Listen, Simon," I said, giving my friend a hard stare and feeling cold ghostly fingers dance on my back. I pulled him into the bushes and told him everything.

"What do you mean, I'm part of this, Andrew?" Simon asked after I had finished. "What is this 'Trimurti of Unity?' Why am I supposed to come with you? To where, Atika? Where the Hell is that place, even?"

"I do not know, Simon," I replied. "All I know is that we are supposed to wait for Master Libélula and go with him to Atika."

"You will not have long to wait," said a strangely-accented voice from behind me.

I spun to see Master Libélula, dressed in his brightly-threaded garments and holding a carved walking staff with little inscriptions in lettering that I did not recognize running up and down the length of it at odd intervals.

"I am ready, Master," I said. "How are we traveling? By horse? Do you want me to find stallions for us? I am certain that one of our Serfs has riding horses in his barn."

"No, Andrew," replied Master Libélula. "Follow me."

"What about me?" Simon asked.

"You will be coming, of course," said Master Libélula. "Andrew will need your help, Simon Tomley. And you need help of your own, it would seem. In Atika, you will find it."

I nodded and followed the magician as he led us down the path to the Verdant Glen. Into the forest where I had been attacked by the Jaguar. As we walked, the sun eventually dipped below the horizon. Not that we noticed, since the foliage and canopy blocked out most of the light. Once it was too dark to see, Master Libélula had conjured his green orb of light and was mutely leading us into the black unknown ahead.

When we passed the area where Master Libélula's hidden cabin stood, I assumed that we would be stopping, perhaps to get some provisions for the road. Instead, he led us on, deeper into the sea of darkness. I thought momentarily about stopping to question the man, but recognized the folly of that idea.

Finally, we emerged into a clearing. After scanning the area for a brief moment, I realized that I knew exactly where we were. The pond where I used to swim with Gerard. The pond to which my father had taken me on my twelfth birthday. The Pond of Sacrifice. The rising moon was reflected in the shimmering water. It was half-full, yellow, and low in the sky. Master Libélula turned to me.

"Ready yourself," he said. "This will not be easy. You are going to the Temple of Athena. It is in Atika, but it is buried deep in the jungle, far away from any people. It is full of danger, and you will be tested, tested in the most extreme way. Spirits willing, you will both find your magic there. Find it and bring yourselves home. I will open the portal again when the moon is full tomorrow night. Twenty-four hours. The portal will be kept open for one hour tomorrow night.

"Guard each other well. And remember: the Heart of the Land cannot fall."

"What is the Heart of the Land?" Simon asked.

"It is a tree – *the* tree. It is that from which all life flows. As members of the Trimurti of Unity, it is prophesied that you will be called upon to defend it. If it is a question of saving the Heart of the Land or saving this Kingdom, I hope you will know which path to take."

With that, Master Libélula swiveled towards the water, whispered something into the cool breeze and raised his staff into the air. A green light pitched out from it and illuminated the surface of the water, growing large and oval-shaped. The light made a whooshing sound and the bottom seemed to fall out of reality within the bounds of the oval. A tunnel materialized, a twisting thing made of multi-coloured lights. When I peered in, it appeared that there were towers and spires in the world beyond, great big things made of rainbow stuff that were reaching up from an infinite depth, buildings erected in an alien dimension by an iridescent God.

He then turned to us. He looked haggard. The effort had taken much out of him.

"It is time that you wen-"

"You slippery fucking eel, Cardiff," shouted a nasally male voice from the forest path. Queegan. My heart sank. "It is time we put an end to this. You have the blood of Traximus in your body. In your head. You will be coming with me. We shall see what secrets you bring back with you from the great beyond.

"But first, you need to die."

"Quickly," said Master Libélula. "Get through. Find your magic, Andrew. You are needed. I will take care of this."

Queegan whispered something and a massive ball of red lightning appeared from the ether and hurtled towards us. Libélula whispered strange words of his own and a mass of green light shot out from the end of the staff, spreading out into a large round disc. The lightning exploded on impact with the shield. Master Libélula whispered something again and an arrow made of green light materialized and returned to Queegan. He stretched a palm up and the arrow careened away from its target as if it were pushed by a massive cross breeze that I could not feel.

The men continued on in this way for a few moments, Queegan calling on the elements of the air and Master Libélula's magic of the forest countering the red lightning.

I looked at the portal, then up at Master Libélula. He was in no shape to fight, that much was clear. Opening the portal had drained him. And this fight was dragging him down towards exhaustion.

"Andrew," Master Libélula heaved. "Go now!"

"But you will be killed!"

As if on cue, Master Libélula did not respond quickly enough to one of Queegan's spells. A finger of lightning connected with his leg, sending it smoking and shaking spastically. He nearly fell then, but managed to keep himself up with the staff. He continued casting his spells against Queegan. He was nearing the brink.

"Do not let me have died in vain, Andrew!"

Screaming out a roar that was as deep and guttural as the first time I had ever heard the Jaguar cry, I grabbed Simon's shoulder and pulled us into the portal.

Chapter Thirty-Nine
Sacrifice

Of all of the strange experiences I had lived through up to that point, the trip through Master Libélula's portal was the oddest yet. As soon as my foot touched the entrance, I felt as though I was being pulled in all directions at once. Simon's hand detached from my grip, but I had not let go. Any sense of my body fled as I looked down and began hurtling towards the bottom of the rainbow spires. I was certain that I was going to smash into the solid multi-colour horizon.

At the last possible moment, the angle of my descent curved sharply and I began flying just above the 'ground,' winding my way through 'streets' that snaked between the massive 'buildings.' I began gaining altitude again, taking sharp turns to avoid colliding with the sides of the closely-packed towers. My speed of travel began increasing as well. After a few more nauseating turns, I was out of the 'city' of the towers, zooming through open space towards one enormous cylinder of light standing on its own. The acceleration reached a fever pitch. I was certain that I was going to be smashed into a rainbow-hued pancake on the side of the tower.

At the final instant, another oval opened up on the side of the column of light, revealing a verdant forest with alien-looking vegetation. I was thrust through, my corporeal form reconstituting as I exited. I landed with a grunt on my bottom, legs thrust forward and the stiletto blade digging into the *cuir d'arbalest*. I gave a silent word of thanks that I had learned my lesson about the danger of tucking the knife into my pants. I grabbed for the broken sword that had been hanging from the scabbard on my other hip. I breathed a sigh of relief when my hand found purchase on it. I was not sure why it mattered so much, but the weapon seethed importance.

A moment later, Simon came flying out on top of me, the portal zipping shut and disappearing behind him as he did. He sent me rolling over. When we came to a stop, our faces were inches away from each other.

I laughed, but a pall of fear descended on my friend's face. He scrambled away, keeping his back to me as he stood up. I noticed then that he was wearing the teardrop shield of the Yellow Order, the great Dragon in profile, staring at me with a yellow eye. I felt compassion for Simon, for the burden he was carrying, thrust upon him by the former Captain Rice.

"What a ride," I said. Without waiting for a response, I scanned our surroundings.

We were in a forest, but it was unlike any forest I had seen before. Trees with thin trunks and leaves the size of the shield on Simon's back stretched high, forming a canopy above our heads. The low shrubs varied in size and the foliage was made up of a seemingly random assortment of sharp angles and round edges. Some of the shrubs had little yellow berries, and most of them were home to flowers that were sprays of purples, blues, reds, and oranges. We were in a narrow clearing, what looked to be a path that had nearly grown over, one that reminded me of the trail I had walked from Willie's wagon in to Valtha proper.

There was warmth on the air, a thick sticky heat of the kind I had only felt a handful of times in Isha, during the hottest days of midsummer, when the water from the ocean seemed to have jumped up from the waves to hang stagnant in the air. It brought to mind Tunuska, though the smell was different. Earthier. Strange noises were sounding intermittently from what seemed to be every direction. When I looked up, I saw a bird with red feathers and a tail that looked as if it was made of the same rainbow vistas we had traveled through to get there.

"Do you hear that?" said Simon, looking down the path in the direction opposite to the way I was looking. I turned and listened.

A noise that sounded like an enormous sheet of parchment tearing in two drifted towards us from the overgrown path. It was growing in intensity, rife with motion and violence. A few moments passed with the two of us frozen in space, straining to ascertain what was approaching. Simon turned to me as the ground beneath us began to shake. I felt my eyes widen.

"Simon," I said, "move!"

I turned in the opposite direction and began to run, looking back to my friend and motioning to him with my arm. An enormous grey beast burst forth into view, with a massive long snout that looked to be more Snake than a muzzle arcing up into the sky and a roar exploding from a gaping mouth flanked with what looked to be curved spears. There were unstained patches that made them seem as if they were naturally white, but the rest of them were covered with crimson. Given the rage in the beast's face, I processed the fearful notion that it was probably blood before I screamed at Simon and ran down the path.

That run through the Atikan jungle still haunts me to this day. There were sticks and rocks strewn through the ancient path by the vagaries of time, threatening to knock us from our feet. Thick brambles and roots sought to trip us just as badly. It required every ounce of body awareness I had to avoid falling. Branches from the trees and shrubs scratched at me. Before long, I began to lose my breath. When I was satisfied that I was not in imminent danger of tripping up, I took a chance to look back at our pursuer.

The beast was screeching as it approached. And approach it did. We were losing ground. I motioned to Simon with an arm to the right, seeing what looked to be a clearing through a little gap in a sea of shrubs. As I squeezed through, I turned back to pull my comrade through. He had almost made it through the opening when I felt resistance against my efforts.

"Andrew!" screamed Simon. "It's got me!"

I pulled on my friend again, then felt my boots slipping on the ground beneath my feet. I grunted and dug my heels into the soft earth.

'He is doomed,' said the Jaguar. 'You have to let him go. He is a cursed bugger anyways, destined to fail his fiancée and descend into a Hell of his own making. Let him go and run.'

Gritting my teeth against the temptation I felt in reaction to the Jaguar's words, I pulled vainly again. I lost more ground for my trouble. Simon screamed at the horrific traction that must have been seeping into his joints like white fire. If I did not figure something out soon, my companion would be dead. I had to stop pulling, if I wanted to accomplish anything. The thought of letting go presented itself to my mind, something to which I reacted violently.

The thought was nonetheless accompanied by a ripple down my back.

I was more likely to kill him if I let go, I thought, searching for a hint or a trace of a clue as to what to do. He would be eaten alive! The thought of letting go returned, this time with hairs that rose thicker on my back. Again, my mind reeled with fear at the idea. The Jaguar had just suggested it! It would no doubt kill Simon. I glanced feverishly at the mass of green leaves and brown branches that surrounded me. There had to be something around here, an unseen weapon or device that would save our necks in our time in need.

Anything aside from letting go.

'Faith, Andrew, you need to demonstrate it now,' said a

voice. It was the Jaguar, its tone having lost all trace of hostility. 'You will learn that Faith is your greatest weapon. The only weapon worth wielding. And letting go is the greatest form of Faith that exists. How much of the world is within 'your' control?

"And besides, if you do not do this,' it said, laughing, 'you will perish.'

Again, the hairs popped up on my back. I thought momentarily about denying the call once more. But by that time I knew which side of my spiritual brioche was slathered with butter.

"Trust me," I said to Simon, though the words were more to myself than reassurance for my friend screeching agony into the jungle air.

I let go.

Simon went flying backwards through the gap. I scrambled in after him, pulling the stiletto from my belt as I did. Maybe I could climb the creature and bury the dagger in its eye, I thought, realizing the folly of attempting something like that as I did. My eyes focused upon what was before me through the gap. I dropped the knife onto the grass next to me in shock.

Nestled in the forest before me was an enormous building, with walls made of weathered charcoal grey stone and suffering the creep of jungle vines on nearly every surface the eye could see. In the foreground, six massive columns rose from a flat bed of polished black marble in a pair of symmetrical rows to join a triangular prism made of what looked to be clear glass or diamond several dozen feet in the air. Behind this awning, a pair of red doors twice the size of a man and wide enough that ten could walk through side by side was directly below a stone statue carved out of bright white stone. The statue depicted the upper half of a woman who seemed to be emerging from the wall itself in a stooped bend. She was wearing a crown and had a rounded jug in her hand, pouring nothing into the jungle air.

The statue had a knowing grin on her face. I had an unshakable feeling that it was directed at me.

Pulling myself back to reality, I noticed that Simon was lying on the ground before me. The beast that had attacked us was nowhere to be seen. I shouted his name and ran to his side.

"What the fuck was that?" he panted. I noticed then that I was heaving as well.

"I think it was an elephant," I said. "I read a description of one in a natural history book when I was a child. They are renowned for their intelligence. The Atikans would sometimes ride them in to war against each other."

"I'm less interested in that than why the fuck the damn thing disappeared. It had my leg, Andrew. I'd pull these down to show you the bruise if it wouldn't take so long to put them back on." Simon motioned at the leather pants he had on. Then he looked at me with wide eyes, as if he had been burned by an unseen flame.

I laughed, pulled my friend to his feet and approached the large red doors. They met in the middle and bore a rounded upper portion. Each was made of several slats that measured about a foot wide each. The slats were covered in glossy red paint that was so fresh-looking that I would not have be surprised to learn that it had been applied that very morning. I looked up at the sky through the glass to see a huge misshapen yellow orb sending its rays down upon us through the light-bending prism. I realized that I was extremely sweaty under my *cuir d'arbalest* and it was not just because of the extended run for our lives in which we had just participated. Or the fact that I was wearing wool undergarments in a hot jungle.

A sun like that would fade a coat of paint to pink in a week or two.

But the painter was nowhere to be found. Nor was there any evidence of his labours. Nor any sentient life at all.

"There is something odd going on here," I said.

"You don't say," Simon said, laughing nervously.

The handle on the right hand door was triple the size of the biggest I had ever seen before, a massive black iron ring that took nearly all my Strength to pull up from the square recess that had been cut into the door. I tugged and sighed. I could not open the damn thing.

"Give me a hand with this," I said, motioning for Simon to grasp the ring with me and pulling off my gloves to get a better grip. When we pulled, our hands slid down to meet near the center. Simon shuddered when the flesh of his hand touched mine, and he looked fearfully at me. Again I felt compassion for the tortured man.

After several pulls, including synchronized attempts where we pulled on the ring in unison, I sat back onto the ground in frustration.

"You know," I said, "even if we find my magic, we are never going to get out of here. With Master Libélula dead, there is no one to reopen the portal."

"Maybe that's not such a bad thing," Simon said glumly. "Maybe it would have been better if that elephant had gored us to death."

"Jesus, Simon, you cannot think that."

"And why not? You know what my survival means."

"I know what that fucking Psychoprobist told you! Is it really that simple? Is there a chance he could be wrong? Or are you so convinced he is right that you are willing to throw your life away? You are a *good* man, Simon, no matter what. You have a sin to atone for, but that sin was killing a man. By accident. I cannot believe that acts of love, no matter what form they take, can be bad things. Nor does love ever bind a man. It sets him free."

Simon did not respond. He simply began rubbing his hand over the stone to the left of the door, obviously feeling with his fingers to see if there was a button or a latch hidden there. I sighed and did the same with the door. Then I moved over to the stone on the right.

'She needs a blood sacrifice,' said the Jaguar. 'Go to the marble and find the drain. You will need to give her your blood to proceed.' Its voice was not hostile, just patient and authoritative. It reminded me of the faint snatches of memory I had remaining of my grandfather's voice.

I moved to the black rectangle of marble below the glass awning. After a few moments of scanning the glossy onyx surface, I noticed a little hole near the middle. The marble around it was slightly concave, ensuring any liquid that ran onto it would drip down the two inch wide drain.

'You cannot pass through to the inner sanctum without bathing in the waters of Athena,' said the Jaguar. "She is the Goddess of War, of Strength, of Courage. Of Wisdom. These are all one and the same – wars fought within lead to Courage, to Strength, to Wisdom. You cannot save your homeland without her blessing. Please understand that this will not be a pleasant experience.'

I called Simon over from his labours, relaying to him the information I had just received from the Jaguar.

"And you believe that thing?" he said. "This thing has been trying to kill you or force you to do evil, and now you want to listen to the damn thing? It's probably a trap, for the love of the Christ-man."

He was not wrong, I thought. This could very well be a trap. Perhaps the 'waters of Athena' were poisonous. Perhaps the sacrifice would call the elephant back. It did have blood on its tusks. Perhaps it would open the floor beneath us and we would drop into a sacrificial pit.

'Search your heart, Andrew,' said the Jaguar peacefully. 'If there is one thing that I will have successfully taught you, please let it be that the organ in your chest is all you need in life.'

Goose flesh on my back erupted as I reached to my belt, then it dissipated when I put my hand on the stiletto hilt. I pulled it from my belt. I felt nothing. Furrowing my brow, I put the knife back. My right hand brushed the hilt of the broken sword as I shifted to stand up straight. Again the hairs rose on my back, and the sensation was much stronger than before. I pulled the broken sword from the makeshift scabbard, watching in awe as the purple owl's head gem pulsed with internal light them moment my hand touched the hilt.

"Christ-man, maybe you're on to something," Simon muttered. I watched as he grasped at his own sword, one of the intact blades with the amethyst pommels. As he removed it from its scabbard, I noticed that the blade was no longer brown and dull. It had the shine of freshly forged steel. The jewel on his sword did not flash when he touched it.

"I had Terence clean it up for me," Simon said, smiling as he ran a thumb along the fuller. "It barely took any time, apparently. All of the rust was superficial and the integrity of the steel had not been compromised."

It was good to see Simon smile. So I returned it.

Turning back to the hole in the ground, I knelt over it, pulled a glove off and put the jagged edge of the broken end against it. Gritting my teeth, I sliced it open and squeezed, making sure to clench my fist so that the droplets of blood ended up falling into the black unknown of the drain.

I noticed then that the flashing on the sword jewel was speeding up, not unlike the emerald on my mother's ring. Something in my blood had caused a reaction. I angled the gem away from me, worried about the potential for another explosive incident like what had happened with my mother's emerald. There was still an oozing wound on the back of my hand, a little cut from a spot where I pulled an emerald shard out. After a moment, the jewel slowed down its flashing again.

'A blood sacrifice, Andrew,' said the Jaguar, laughing. 'Just cutting your hand is not going to do it. After it is done, you are going to need Simon to carry your body to the statue. Water will flow from her jug. He will place you in the healing waters. You need to have Faith that you will be reborn.'

"What?" I blurted out, suddenly having processed the implication of the Jaguar's words. "You want me to kill myself?"

Simon looked at me with wide eyes, total fear blossoming onto his face.

'You are ready for this, Andrew,' the Jaguar said. 'Victory is only assured if you give yourself over to the truth of who you are. Athena will not give her blessing to anyone without Courage. Without Strength. You might think it paradoxical, for she will grant you more Strength and Courage than you are currently capable of understanding. But she needs you to make this leap.'

And what a leap, I thought. What if it does not work? What if Simon fails to carry me into the waters of Athena? What if I die here, in the sweaty stinking jungle and never see my family again? What if-

'What if, indeed,' said the Jaguar. 'You are not the first to walk a path like this. Nor will you be the last. But your path is your own. It belongs to no one else.

'There are many names for what you do," the Jaguar continued, "as many names as there are places. The men of the lands beyond Liseria, of Kashya, they call what you do yoga. It is as good a name as any, as it means blessed union. It is the practice of yoking or lashing your spirit to your physical body. There are many different practices that help to achieve this, from physical postures with mind turned inward to being of service to others to sitting in contemplation of reality.

'Yours is the Yoga of Strength,' the Jaguar continued. 'Work like this needs to start with absence. You thought yourself a coward as a child. There was an absence of Courage. At least, an imagined one. Then I gave you Courage, and you recognized it in your mind for its bright iridescence. But it was Courage that came from without - this is not true Courage. Strength has to be chosen to be of any value. But you began to believe, just a little bit, in yourself. When you believed in yourself enough, I

378

began to test you. To try to throw you from the path with admonishments of weakness. To show you just how strong you are. To choose the quiet Strength of your soul when your mind screams that you are weak: this is the Yoga of Strength.

'You are no coward, Andrew," said the Jaguar. "You are a champion. You will learn this. But you cannot reach the other side without placing your bet. And the wager must be total. You must show Strength, show Courage, show Faith.'

'What I ask you to do, Andrew,' uttered the Jaguar, 'this is the ultimate test of your Faith. All other tests will be simple echoes of this one.'

'You may say no,' the Jaguar continued without judgment in its voice, 'If you do, I will open a portal for you and your friend to return home. You may fight your wars. You may even win a few battles, perhaps the whole thing. But you will wither and die unhappy, a shadow of the man you could have become.'

'Do this,' the Jaguar said finally, 'and you will meet with Athena. At least, the Goddess who the men that came to this land knew as Athena. In this land, she is known as the spirit of Snake. In your land, she is Ourobouros, the Dragon that eats her own tail. You shall receive her blessing. And you will rise to become the man your homeland needs.'

Fear as a concept is ill-suited to describe the emotion that washed over me as the Jaguar finished its speech. I looked down at the broken sword. The pulsing from the gem was slow and anemic now. I thought about accepting the Jaguar's offer to go home. It would be so easy. I was ready to fight, that much was certain from the way I fought my brother in Tunuska, the way I slew the Demons in Valtha. I could simply return, trade in this broken blade for one of the many yellow-pommeled swords that were standing in rows in Terence's workshop. Besides, my father needed me. Kathryn needed me.

The memory of Master Libélula's sacrifice returned to me in a flash. There was a man, one who knew he was going to die, who continued to fight regardless of the odds stacked against him. He did it so that Simon and I might travel here together. What could have been passing through his mind? It must have been terror. It had to be terror.

'Perhaps,' said the Jaguar. 'But perhaps not. Is there a chance that the three dimensions you see around you do not describe the ultimate nature of reality?'

An unexpected calm descended on me as the hairs around my spine rose in perfect unison. I knelt down next to the drain.

"Simon," I said. He was looking at me with abject horror. "I am going to kill myself now. Allow my blood to drain into the hole. The water will flow from the jug. You will have to bring my body over to rest in the stream. Do you understand?"

"Understand? I understand that you've flipped your lid! Pacing back and forth, saying you are going to kill yourself. Listening to a voice in your head. Christ-man take it all, Andrew. Don't do this." There were tears in my friend's eyes.

"I know this is scary,' I said, smiling patiently at Simon, 'but it is necessary. Please do not fail me. Put me in the water."

I placed the blade next to my carotid artery. I took a deep breath and steeled myself. Pain erupted in my neck as I jammed the broken blade in to the hilt. Blood spurted into the hole in the floor, pulsing with every pump of my heart. Red stars exploded into my vision. I became weak. I slumped over onto the ground. Breathing became a laborious process, slowing to a heaving crawl. With a smile on my face, I let my final breath out.

My last conscious thought was a prayer of thanks to Terence for the anatomy lessons.

Chapter Forty
Moksha

I cannot remember much about death. What I do recall is that it was full of loneliness, at least at first. It was so terribly lonely, and then it shifted to become a blissful experience. The total opposite of unpleasant. There was a sensation of release. It reminded me of being let out for the summer break from school when I was a little boy, when I would go home to find my mother waiting at our cottage with freshly baked buns dusted with cinnamon and clotted cream to celebrate my newfound liberty, temporary though it might have been.

My first memory after I came back to life was the sensation of wetness. It spread through the entire body. My body. I was completely unfamiliar with the concept at first, having lost it somehow. It did not feel comfortable, as if it were a shoe that were too small for the foot that was my enormous self. The feeling increased in intensity, up to the point where I felt like my body was going to rebel entirely.

I opened my eyes as I found myself on my hands and knees, vomiting out yellow bile. It felt like it would never stop. It did, though, eventually. I leaned back onto my knees to look at the mess in the water below me. There was none. Simply black marble a foot deep. Had I imagined the expectoration? I then noticed that there was a stream coming down onto me. The jug. I looked up.

The statue of Athena was no longer hunched over as it poured the jug. She was standing tall. I noticed with wonder that she was not jutting out from the wall. Instead, she was standing on an unfamiliar dais that had been cut in two, and I was in a pool where the other half of the platform should have been.

I looked back down. The water was warm and it smelled faintly of lilacs. I opened my mouth to taste it. It tasted as if it were the juice of ripe strawberries, squashed lovingly into the fluid that rained down over me. I felt peace wash over me as I drank.

"Simon?" I said, having finished my lapping and scanning the area for my friend. He was nowhere to be found. Nor was I lying before the enormous doors either.

I was in the center of a large room, with columns like the ones that had I had seen in front of the temple connecting the ceiling to the floor in rows at regular intervals just a few feet from the sides of the room. White marble was the only building material that I could see, from the statue itself to the walls and columns. A few windows cut into the walls just below the ceiling were letting bright shafts of sunlight into the room. The ceiling was vaulted, with large beautiful reliefs of battle scenes cut into the arches that connected the tops of each wall to the other.

I lay staring for a moment, totally transfixed by the detail of the carvings. Men and animals were fighting Demons alongside each other. In one of the central reliefs an enormous Dragon was lying on a rock, the small end of its tail wrapped around one of its massive fangs.

"Welcome," said a female voice, "you have arrived. Finally."

I looked up to see a beautiful woman with black hair standing at the side of the pool. She was wearing what looked to be an enormous white sheet, a flowing garment that snaked around her like a serpent, secured by a clasp in the middle. A crown sat atop her head and she bore a toothy yet elegant smile. Bare legs emerged from the bottom of the robe, down to feet that were strapped into sandals with silver thongs. I looked up to the statue to compare.

Yes, it was indeed Athena.

As I drew myself up to stand, a massive black cat prowled into view next to her, coming to sit on its haunches by the Goddess' feet. Without breaking her stare in my direction, Athena began stroking the head of the beast. A deep rumbling noise that I recognized as the most deafening purr I have ever heard began to sound from the Jaguar.

I exited the pool, feeling woozy as I did. I sat down on the edge of the water rather than risk losing consciousness yet again. I was just feet away from my 'hosts.'

"Was I expected?" I asked, thinking of little else to say.

"Of course you were, Andrew," said Athena. "As a wise man once said, it is written. You were always destined to end up here."

"Well, here I am." I paused and silence reigned for an interminable length of time. "I think you were supposed to give me your blessing?"

Athena laughed. The Jaguar continued to purr.

"Straight to the point, I see. Do you even know what it means, to receive my blessing?"

"I have not known what has been going on, not really, since the moment I walked into the King's chamber on the ship and was told that I was being made a member of his 'Inner Council.' Things deteriorated from there. Ever since magic has threaded into my life, my ignorance has become extremely obvious to me. So I guess you can safely say that I have no idea what it means to receive your blessing."

Athena laughed yet again. The Jaguar made a snorting noise.

"Fair enough, Andrew. Let me ask you, what concerns you right now?"

"Right now?" I said, "Let me count the things." I gestured with a raised fist. "One," I said, sticking my index finger in the air, "I am a wanted man in my homeland, a 'criminal' who is sought after by a corrupt king, a man that killed my mother in cold blood. Two," I said, extending my middle finger, "There are two magic wielding lunatics looking to crush my homeland into some chaotic place where there is no Order and dead walk the streets. One of them is in league with a Lord of Demons, Demons that I unleashed onto the world due to some Prophecy and an ancestor I am completely unfamiliar with. Three," I said, letting go of my ring finger, "there is an army of angry Erifracians who are about to land and also make short work of Thrairn, unless a plot by the King and the two interlopers succeeds and instead their blood runs in the streets. Four," I said, letting my pinky finger rise, "the woman I care for is back in Thrairn trying to fight all of them on her own. I would be back there to help her, but for some odd reason, I find myself here before you. A dead Goddess. Having just slain myself, no less. Five," I said, extending my thumb," I am supposed to become one of three members of the Trimurti of Unity, whatever that means, face off against the Trimurti of Separation, protect the Heart of the Land, and bring Balance back to the realm."

I relaxed back into the stone seat of the pool's edge beneath me.

"That does sound like a few problems," said Athena. "But right now, at this very moment, what concerns you? Are you in danger? Is there anything at all that threatens your peace?"

I took a moment to look hard at the Goddess and the beast. I let my awareness travel down my body, sensing the wet leather against my flesh, the warm breeze on my face. The scent of lilacs from the water. As my awareness ran along my back, I noticed that my neck had tensed up. I consciously let go of the anxiety that had worked its way into the muscles.

"There you go," Athena said. "Nothing to worry about right

now. Or now. Or now. Tell me, how is that different from moment to moment? How is one moment different from the next? When do you think the right time is to start worrying?" Athena began pacing in front of me. The Jaguar remained seated on its haunches, staring at me. "When you are locked in combat, do you feel anything aside from what is currently happening? Do you worry about what you might eat the next day for breakfast? Or even about an unpleasant conversation you might be required to have with a loved one?"

"No," I replied after a moment's consideration. I stood to face the duo. "Just the battle. Life and death."

"Ah, 'life and death.' Those two opposing forces. The divine syzygy. As a man who has, as you say, just slain himself, do you fear death?"

Death. The end of it all. That black passenger who had been riding my thoughts since I could remember. The creature that whispered in my ear, trying to make me falter. The Jaguar's voice could have been death itself, the way it retreated from life, the way it stood in direct opposition to my desire to grow...

"Not anymore," I said. "Well, maybe I am not completely without fear," I added quickly. "When I killed myself just now, I put my trust in a friend. A friend who gave me much reason to doubt him, but trust him I did regardless. I did not expect it to end, not completely. I had Faith and proceeded, wherever life was to take me."

Athena furrowed her brow. "You call me a dead Goddess, but truly, I am the Keeper of Eternity. There is no real form to what I am, and yet I have form. That form depends on the soil in which I grow: the minds of the beings that need me. You know, in your land, I am known as the Dragon that feasts on itself. Ourobouros. Do you know why that is?"

There was a great flash, and smoke erupted from the place where Athena had been standing, enormous plumes of onyx black clouds billowing out towards me. As it ran over my face, I expected to start coughing. Instead, I found it easier to breathe, somehow. Within a few moments the smoke had cleared. Before me stood a great yellow Dragon, with iridescent scales that gleamed rainbows in the shafts of sunlight. It had a thin angular face with great green eyes. Bone white fangs the size of longswords jutted from both the lower and upper jaw against large open nostrils through which more black smoke was seeping. Its tail came up from behind to its left and was woven through the fangs on its lower jaw, just like the one on the relief above. Hooked claws on its feet scraped the marble as it turned from me and walked to the center of the room.

"Andrew," said the Dragon in a voice that sounded like the pleasant tinkling of small shards of glass bouncing off one another, "you need to know who you are. Look up."

The Dragon murmured something low to itself and a shaft of golden light sprang from the middle of its forehead, shooting up high into the air above it. A great yellow globe materialized out of the nothingness, a ball that resembled the sun on a very clear day.

"This is who you are," said the Dragon, a forked tongue darting from its mouth between breaths. "The unified One. Pure consciousness. Love. God. That word, God, is hated by many, denied for its association for those who misuse it in service of their own schemes of Separation. But it is the force that binds reality together. It is everywhere. We are all ourselves it, from the pebble caught in your boot to the sparrows in the spring to every human being on the face of Clovir. And beyond your planet. We are eternal, living outside of the realm of time. There is no beginning nor end to what we are. We are all-powerful, all-knowing, each and every one of us. For we are all each other. Outside of the physical world, in a timeless realm of non-duality, this is where we reside.

"We reside here while we live in the physical world, too, though it can be very difficult to see," the Dragon continued. "What is required for such vision is remembrance. The act of birth is in some ways an act of death, since we all forget who we are. We are tricked by the physical world, tricked into believing that the world of the senses is all that exists. There is a reason for this. The foe you have been fighting, the one that has harried you since you were a child, do you know who that is?"

I thought back. In my early days, the moments of childhood before true worry set in, I did not have many. That gradually changed. When my brother picked on me, when the other children shunned me, when my mother enabled me to be alone, when my father tried to open me up, when I was hated as a fellow Knight, when my mother died, when I visited the bawdy houses for company...

"Loneliness. I have always been fighting loneliness."

"Good, Andrew!" the Dragon said with a pleasant noise that I took to be a laugh. "Very good. That is the only foe that you have ever fought, though it has come to you cloaked in many different forms. Do you know why that is? The question is rhetorical: I will tell you. It is because it was the first foe we ever fought, before we created the world that we live in. When we created the world of poles, of light and dark, of hot and cold, of love and hate, we created Separation. But it was not true Separation, simply the illusion of Separation. How can one separate that which is indivisible? One cannot, that is the truth of the matter. We are all deeply connected.

"And every single thing, big and small, affects the whole. There is nothing insignificant, no creature or object without value. Enormous value. And for that reason, you must love and respect all as yourself. That is what you have been learning, since the moment you were born. That is the only test in life: how much you are willing to surrender your illusion of separateness into the Truth.

"You need to understand that you cannot die, Andrew, not truly," the Dragon said, happiness redolent in its voice. "There is no death, only life eternal. Love eternal. For that is what you are, Andrew, simply love."

"But what of war?" I replied, feeling bliss wash over me. "I must return home and kill those that threaten to destroy the world. The Trimurti of Separation must be stopped. Patricia, she seeks to unleash Chaos on the planet, to upset the Balance. Queegan wishes to discover the secret of immortality by murder. Janus wishes simply to survive in ignominy in the horrendous world they create, wielding false magic and having murdered my mother in cold blood on the Strength of this Prophecy of an end to the Red Tradition."

There was another flash and puff of smoke and the enormous ball of light faded. When the smoke cleared this time, a Snake with a body as thick as a log from an old growth forest lay coiled in where the Dragon had stood. It was a shade between green and blue, and its scales were as iridescent as the ones the Dragon bore. Its face was the same flat and narrow shape as the Dragon's, but its eyes were a fiery red. It slithered briefly towards me, before drawing itself up to face me from my own height.

"This form I have taken, this Snake: there are those that follow the Christ-man that think I caused the fall of humanity, that by directing a woman to bite an apple, I cursed mankind," the Snake said, its words sibilant through forked tongue. "But they have failed one of the simplest tests of understanding: to believe literally that which was meant to be communicated only through poetry. The Truth of the matter is that all is God, including that which you call evil. By eating of the fruit of the tree of good and evil, the illusion of Separation was created, which in turn generated the possibility for man to return home to the garden. Taking birth as a human being is to eat of the apple.

"The Truth is this," the Snake said, slithering closer to me. "We created the circumstances within which man could become great. I gave him the dream of Free Will, so that he could have a battle between Free Will and Fate in his mind until one day he woke up to realize that there is only One will. Man's

Fate is foretold, but when he chooses that Fate, it becomes his Destiny. And a man ruled by Destiny is a man that drinks of the waters of immortality."

"I know your doubts well," the Snake continued. "You remind me of someone, a warrior whom I had to counsel long years ago, in a land far from here. Arjuna was his name. He was a man who balked at the thought of killing his countrymen, even though they were guilty of horrific crimes and wanted to kill him in kind. Your enemies are wrong and misguided, fooled by the illusion in the worst ways. They have given themselves over to Separation utterly.

"But do you not see that love is at the root of all they do? This Patricia, she sees the injustice that the difference in wealth between the nobility and the common folk has created. And she is right: this difference in power and money is wrong and against love. But she tries to change the world with her separated small mind and force born of that petty understanding. It reinforces the illusion, which leads only to further pain and misery. The world is a process and her small mind thinks it knows better than the force of nature. In her vanity, she has released Demons into the world and must be stopped. Not killed, but stopped. And not out of your own spite for her, but out of duty to life.

"Queegan seeks eternal life through force as well, eternal life of the vessel separated from its home, which is a horrific perversion in its own right. An eternity of Separation. What he actually seeks is Hell. His illusory small mind makes a mockery of life with his experiments. But he does so because of an abiding love of life. He wants to live forever yet is scared of the release of death, that transition which confirms eternal life.

"And Janus, he is a coward, it is true, a man who wishes to wield power and free himself from the bondage of the Red Tradition. But you were a coward once, and a slave to Separation. Do you not see yourself in him?"

The Snake slithered yet closer to me, though I did not feel

any fear upon its approach. Its breath smelled faintly of the spring air, as if cherry trees were blossoming deep within its maw.

"Finally, a few words of caution," the Snake hissed at me. "The truth to a human being is as changing as the ripples on a pond, changing daily as required by the universe. The Truth, though, the Truth never changes. You know the Truth of who you are now, Andrew, but you are a human being, not a God. And as a human being you are greater than a God can ever be. For the stories of Gods and Heroes are nothing more than the stories that we tell ourselves to liberate ourselves: illusions to emancipate the illusionist."

"Equality of all beings is the only Queen that sits the throne, Andrew," the Snake continued. "Lesser Gods and Demons, those creatures with all of the caprice and vanity of humans, are only real because people believe in them. They have too much human in them and remain a reflection of Separation. They are not alive. Their value is in parsing the metaphor that they represent, instead of becoming mired in a literal understanding. But you are beyond that now. You have only One belief, One thing to serve - Love. You must go now and love all, to serve Love in all that you do. Including your enemies and the Gods of Separation that they worship.

"You must love all of your enemies, Andrew, for they are not truly your enemies. Love them, serve them, but you must also remember who We are. Love and service sometimes require that the pests in the garden are dealt with so that it can grow. Pests can always be removed without taking life. True life. Demons are figments of Separation, thoughts that have gained corporeal form. Slay Demons, never human beings. Make all of your decisions in the moment. This present moment - that is the Shield of Eternity. It will keep you safe, keep you whole as you return to the dusks and dawns of the Story of You. Remember that it is the light inside that has led you to this place and it is that which will lead you home. Follow it without fear and all will be well."

"All is always well," the Snake said with finality.

The flash came again, as did the smoke. I breathed deeply of the black fog, smiling with the bliss that blossomed into my chest as it passed into me. When it cleared, Athena stood before me again, this time holding a sword and a shield. She was smiling. I felt a momentary shock as the Jaguar slipped into view from somewhere to my left. I had completely forgotten about the creature during my conversations with the Dragon and the Snake. He dropped onto his side next to Athena and began purring again.

"The Jaguar: he was a good teacher, was he not?"

I smiled. I gave a deep bow to the prostrate beast and said a word of thanks. The purring grew louder.

"I believe this is yours. I fixed it up for you," said Athena. She handed me a sword that was sheathed in a black leather scabbard. The purple owl jewel was held in a claw at the hilt. When I touched the scabbard, the gem lit up with a bright flash. I watched in wonder as the third eye in the center of its forehead opened up. I removed the blade from its scabbard. Written in large Heraclytan script on the blade from hilt to tip the word

S
O
P
H
I
A

shone light from some source deep within. I thrust it back inside and hooked it onto the belt of my pants.

"'Sophia,'" said Athena. "In the words of my people, this meant 'Wisdom.' Wisdom to know that the blade should always be turned inward, for only a fool looks outside himself for foes."

"This is yours too, Andrew." She gave me the shield she was holding in her other hand. It was a teardrop kite shield, almost identical to the shield of the Yellow Order, a yellow Dragon on silver steel. Instead of a Dragon in profile, though, this one had a Dragon circling back on itself, its mouth closing on its own tail. I ran my fingers over the metal in awe, before hooking it onto my back.

"I gave a shield similar that one to a warrior some years ago," Athena said, a fondness in her smile, "a man named Perseus who learned that Separation withers at the horror of its own reflection. That is your greatest weapon, Andrew. Be the best mirror that you can be.

"Go now, Knight Cardiff, you are needed," Athena finished. "But I ask you one more time to remember. Your only job is to Love, Serve, and Remember. A Holy Trinity, if there ever was One. And you do all of those three things by doing One thing: by following your heart with all of your being.

"This is it: you are liberated."

Gratitude

First, I would like to thank my immediate family: those who put up with the early mornings and late evenings, the all-the-time obsession, and the moments of mania. Ashley, I would like to thank you especially – you are everything I could hope for in a partner and more. Mom and Dad – you have been my number one fans from day one and I could not have gotten here without your love and support. Matthew, Aimée, and Emilie – you are the best siblings a man could ask for. Iris – you are the treasure at the end of my rainbow.

This book could not have been possible without all of the help from my community. A big thank you to Laura Casey of Lady Lo's Custom Tattoos for the tattoo / cover art, Cynthia Dunphy for digitizing same and the beautiful Dragon, Duncan DeYoung for shooting my pitch video and author photos, Publishizer for making crowdfunded publishing possible, Belle Sante Beauty for keeping my infant daughter's bum nice and healthy, Zach Leary and the It's All Happening podcast for the love, support, and advertising when the book was just an idea, the advance readers who read and gave me feedback, Janet, Shawn, Kerri, David, Peter, and Reid for letting me post my reviews on my website, the musicians who provided the soundtrack to the writing of this novel: Nahko and Medicine for the People, Trevor Hall, Satsang, mc yogi, Xavier Rudd, Laura-Beth Smith, Fortunate Ones, Hirie, Tubby Love, Mumford & Sons, Wookiefoot, The Arcadian Wild, SOJA, Sadhu Sensi, Jason Mraz, and a bunch more I am sure I am forgetting about at this moment, the authors who influenced me most (in no particular order): Paulo Coelho, Homer, J.R.R. Tolkien, Irvine Welsh, Neil Gaiman, Mark Lawrence, R.A. Salvatore, Hermann Hesse, George R.R. Martin, Steven Pressfield, Frank Herbert, Clive Barker, Andrzej Sapkowski, Franz Kafka, Christopher Moore, Stephen King, Philip K. Dick, Salman Rushdie, Orson Scott Card, Jean Craighead George, Gunter Grass, Kurt Vonnegut, Jr. Check out andrewmarcrowe.com/gratitude/ for more gushing.

I would be remiss if I did not give a shout out to all the kind and loving people from my yoga studio, Modo Yoga St. John's, for all their love and support over the years. A special shout out to studio owner Jill Holden for really going above and beyond, including letting me set up a booth at the Sunset Savasana on Signal Hill in August 2018!

I would also like to thank Nick Courtright and Atmosphere Press for believing in me and providing thoughtful editing advice, interior design, and cover design. It was a joy working with Atmosphere and I am so grateful for all of their help birthing this novel into the world.

Last, but not least, I would like to thank my backers on Publishizer. These people believed in me and my idea, enough that they would buy a copy of the book sight unseen. A huge thank you to Aaron Morgan, Adam Hammond, Alex Healey, Adam Churchill, Aimee Rowe, Alex Allison, Ali Pike, Alison Greenoff, Allison O'Mahony, Allison Whelan, Amy Bowring, Andrew Woodland, Angela Hinchey, Angie Barrington, Anna Abbott, Ashley Rowe, Ashley Hiscock, Bas Snippert, Bernadette Reddy, Beverly Anthony, Bill Reddy, Blake Cryderman, Bonita Brocklehurst, Brad Gauci, Brad Wicks, Brian Crance, Caleb Thorne, Cathy Puddister, Cathy Taylor, Chad Horton, Charlotte

Butler, Chris Hynes, Chris Rowe, Christopher Vaughan, Cody Barrett, Colin Hayes, Conor Stack, Corina Hartley, Cory Clark, Curtis Eagan, Daniel Bennett, Daniel O'Brien, Darlene Lucas, Dave O'Mahony, David Fleming, David Hood, David Cooper, David Mason, Dawn Hinchey, Derek Clark, Derrick Shain, Donna Rowe, Doug Sellars, Duncan DeYoung, Ed Vanderkloet, Elaine Coady, Elaine Sullivan, Emil Caris, Emilie Rowe, Erica Robbins, Fern Greenning, Gail Toner, Gary Ball, Genevieve MacEachern, Geoff Winsor, Geoff Boyd, Geoffrey Davis-Abraham, George Horan, Gillian Langor, Glen Noel, Gloria Peterson, Gordon McAndie, Grace Sweeney, Heather Sellars, Hilary Sellars, Jaclyn Whelan, Jacob Prince, Jamie Dominguez, James Strickland, James Stitchman, James Valk, James Farrell, Janey Power, Janine Woodrow, Jarrett Reaume, Jeanette Andrews, Jennifer Galliott, Jess Dellow, Jessica Babb, Jill Holden, Jill Currie, John Crosbie, John Nichols, John Francis, John White, Jonelle Steele, Joshua Martin, Judy Gulliver, Justin Caines, Justine Candow, Karen Langlois, Kari Bishop, Katherine O'Brien, Katie O'Neill, Katie Jackson, Kayla Churchill, Keira Thorne, Keith Snelgrove, Kelsey Foote, Ken Reddy, Kerri Best, Kim Cleary, Kim Hendricken, Kimberley Short, Krista Marshall, Kyla Miettinen, Kyle Taylor, Kyle Mercer, Kyle Rees, Laura Casey, Laurie Crann, Lesley O'Neill, Leslie Redmond, Linda Collins, Linda Goldsack, Linda Ivany, Lisa Smyth, Lisa Haye, Lise Rowe, Louis Legault, Lydia Kean, Maggie Sparling, Marilyn Pike, Marilyn Moore-Prince, Mark Murray, Mark Mills, Mary MacDonal, Mary Hatfield, Matthew Strong, Matthew Rowe, Matthew Craig, Matthew Manning, Matthew Flight, Matthew Walsh, Matthew Cook, Matthew Rowe, Megan Taylor, Melanie McGrath, Melissa Hill, Michael Furlong, Michael Walter, Mike Gillingham, Morgaine Parnham, Nancy Burton, Nicholas Lacour, Nick Crosbie, Omer Nazir, Padraig Mohan, Patrick O'Grady, Paul Blackwood, Paul Carter, Paula Dalton, Peter Shea, Peter Leduc, Peter Blackwood, Rana Fudge, Randy Smith, Raymond MacDonald, Reg Morgan, Reid

Barrington, Richard Dalton, Robyn Chippett, Ron Parsons, Rosemary Neil, Ryan Green, Sandra Halliday, Sandra Bochner, Sarah Learmonth, Scott Allison, Shannon Mackey, Shirlee Lacour, Stephanie Molloy, Stephen Hinchey, Steve Barnes, Steve Scruton, Susan Sellars, Suzanne French-Smith, Suzanne Thain, Suzy Godbolt, Tatyana Telegina, Terri Higdon, Terry Rowe, Thomas Campbell, Thomas Brannagan, Tiffany Henderson, Tim Warren, Tom Crosbie, Tommy Lush, Treva Aberle, Valerie Barrington, Virginia Leduc, Willis Wiseman, Zack Rousseau, and Zona Rogers-Cox.

About Atmosphere Press

Atmosphere Press is an independent full-service publisher for books in genres ranging from non-fiction to fiction to poetry, with a special emphasis on being an author-friendly approach to the challenges of getting a book into the world. Learn more about what we do at atmospherepress.com.

We encourage you to check out some of Atmosphere's latest releases, which are available at Amazon.com and via order from your local bookstore:

Mandated Happiness, a novel by Clayton Tucker

Spots Before Stripes, a novel by Jonathan Kumar

Leaving the Ladder, nonfiction by Lynda Bayada

Let the Little Birds Sing, a novel by Sandra Fox Murphy

They are Almost Invisible, poems by Elizabeth Carmer

Love Your Vibe, nonfiction by Matt Omo

Transcendence, poems and images by Vincent Bahar Towliat

Gone Fishing, children's fiction by Carmen Petro

Letting Nicki Go, nonfiction by Bunny Leach

Time Do Not Stop, poems by William Guest

Adrift, poems by Kristy Peloquin

Dear Old Dogs, a novella by Gwen Head

Owlfred the Owl Learns to Fly, a picture book by Caleb Foster

Bello the Cello, a picture book by Dennis Mathew

Ghost Sentence, poems by Mary Flanagan

Winter Park, a novel by Graham Guest

That Scarlett Bacon, a picture book by Mark Johnson

Makani and the Tiki Mikis, a picture book by Kosta Gregory

What Outlives Us, poems by Larry Levy

How Not to Sell, nonfiction by Rashad Daoudi

That Beautiful Season, a novel by Sandra Fox Murphy

What I Cannot Abandon, poems by William Guest

Surviving Mother, a novella by Gwen Head

All the Dead Are Holy, poems by Larry Levy

Rescripting the Workplace, nonfiction by Pam Boyd

Such a Nice Girl, a novel by Carol St. John

About the Author

Born and raised in St. John's, Newfoundland and Labrador, Canada, Andrew Marc Rowe grew up with a kind introspective lawyer for a father and a warm outgoing sports enthusiast for a mother. He has three siblings, all born within eight years of each other, and the quartet remains close to this day. Despite his mother's best efforts to get him out of the house, he spent most of his free childhood time locked in a basement dungeon with fantasy books, video games and a small tight-knit circle of friends.

When adulthood struck, Andrew gradually began coming out of his shell, traveling to locales as far flung as France, Germany, and South Korea before finally returning home to buckle down and pursue a law degree. All was not well in the realm, however, for upon completion of law school, Andrew found himself in a downward spiral of anxiety and depression.

Andrew's trail upwards began in earnest after a pair of life-changing trips to Peru sent him on a return mission to repair the parts of his life that were broken. His journey culminated in marriage to his soulmate, Ashley, and the birth of his daughter, Iris.

His first three books, the Yoga Trilogy, are Andrew's attempt to marry the thematic threads of the fantasy and mythology he so loved in his youth with the spiritual fiction and yogic philosophy that provided the respite he so sorely needed in his adult years. When he was a child, the former, like the works of Homer and J.R.R. Tolkien, allowed magic and adventure to flow into his world, giving life colour by dint of the strength of his imagination. The latter, like the works of Paulo Coelho, Hermann Hesse, and, well, Patanjali, were balm for his soul during those darker days. His humble intention with his work is to create a colourful chimera of adventure, magic, and spirituality.

Soul medicine for anyone, yogi or not, with a soft spot for Knights, wizards, and Dragons.

...

Master Libélula

Queegan stood from the corpse and shook himself. It had taken much from him, the battle with the foreigner and the spell he had cast after the man had finally fallen. He put his hand to his belt, to the flask of Ephestor's Folly that dangled and tantalized him. It would be easy: to simply do as Patricia foolishly preferred to do, to give himself false Strength until his inevitable collapse. No, he was no weakling. He would not give in. The Mage forced himself to turn his mind from the call of the draught. Instead, he scanned the forest around the Pond of Sacrifice for others. Perhaps it would be Kathryn that tried to come to the dead Atikan's aid, the back-stabbing bitch. Queegan sat down on a log and waited.

Hours passed, and, thankfully for the tired Mage, no one did come to Libélula's aid.

By the time the half-full moon reached its zenith in the night's sky, the first stirrings began. Queegan steadied himself. He had had so many failed experiments, so many dead men that came to life only to spit and hiss nonsense and generally disappoint him. In fact, he had only cast the spell on a whim, a bet with himself to see if there was anything of worthwhile stock in the charred savage. Andrew was still Queegan's goal. At best, he would have simple answers from Libélula, a tale from the lips of the dead man about where his quarry had gone.

When Libélula rose, it was unlike any raising Queegan had seen before. None of the man's movements were stilted. It was as if he were simply shrugging off unconsciousness. It was when Libélula looked at him that he was certain that he had struck gold.

It was the eyes. Gone were the man's whites, pupils, and irises. In their stead, Queegan looked upon a microcosm of the universe, all inky black and interspersed with little dots of light, clouds of yellow galaxies and pink nebulae that seemed to call to the Mage with an inexorable intensity.

"You who seeks," said Libélula, its voice completely absent emotion or humanity: it was as if the void itself were addressing Queegan. "You have long abandoned your own heart. You wish to live, yes?"

"Y-yes," said Queegan, rising to his feet, flustered. "I wish to live – forever."

"Obsession is a game played by many men," said Libélula. "You do not know the price of what you are seeking, not yet. But the debt will be paid."

"You know the secret!" said Queegan. "Tell me!"

"Secrets like this cannot be told," said Libélula's body, staring its cosmic stare. "They must be seen to be believed." Libélula paused. "You are like the alchemist who dreams only of the worth of the gold he will receive from the lead, and not the value of the process itself. It is no matter: we all have our parts to play. All the world is a stage, as a wise man once said."

"Enough of that," said Queegan, becoming frustrated with the thinly-veiled insults. "Tell me how to see the secret, then."

"There is only one place where a man can find immortality in the world around him. It runs golden in the Heart of the Land. Drink of its sap, and you will live forever."

"Where is this Heart of the Land? Tell me!"

"In Atika," said the corpse of Master Libélula. "The Heart of the Land is in Atika."

CPSIA information can be obtained
at www.ICGtesting.com
Printed in the USA
LVHW031057250219
608656LV00001B/1